FROM IAN WATSON, THE INTELLECTUAL GENIUS OF British SF, a bumper collection of rare and cogent gems . . . Here are powerful stories which have never been collected before, such as 'Jingling Geordie's Hole', voted both the best and the worst story of the year by readers of *Interzone* magazine (sometimes by the same readers!), the kernel of Watson's novel *The Fire Worm*. Likewise, the short story which birthed his novel *Deathhunter*. And there's a stand-alone story related to the masterful *Mockymen*, never published before now. The mischievous 'Divine Diseases', which appeared in the science journal *Nature*, brought protests to that august publication; a similar satirical brio informs 'The Real Winston', a clever alternative take on George Orwell's *Nineteen Eighty-Four*.

Besides stories, gathered here are many entertaining and often profound pieces of non-fiction, yielding deep insights into the author's creative works. In 'The Author as Torturer' he asks a question even more urgent today than when first voiced 20 years ago. Here are Watson's inspired impersonations of H. G. Wells (even if the period clothing doesn't show in print). Aptly, the *Times Literary Supplement* commented à propos Watson's fiction: 'A phenomenon, a national resource to be conserved, Ian Watson resembles H. G. Wells in both invention and impatience.' Well, *The Uncollected Ian Watson* is devoted to conserving these and other pieces previously scattered across anthologies and magazines—as well as Watson's views on films ranging from *The Wicker Man* to *The Matrix*, plus his perspectives on artificial intelligence as published in *Intelligent Systems* journal. His relationship with comics is explored, and much much more.

The Uncollected
Ian Watson

The Uncollected
Ian Watson

IAN WATSON

EDITED BY NICK GEVERS

2014

PS PUBLISHING LTD
Grosvenor House
1 New Road
Hornsea, HU18 1PG
England
editor@pspublishing.co.uk / www.pspublishing.co.uk

Contents

The Uncollected
Ian Watson

Para Guapa, también

Three Kinds of Close Encounters
with Comics

I'M LOOKING AT A PHOTO OF MYSELF READING A COPY OF *MARVEL TALES*, which my wife Judy took in 1968 or so in Tokyo. Behind me similar comics spill off the bookshelf next to a Mao doll and pin-ups of the Beatles. I bought some of those comics in a long narrow English language bookshop on the Ginza—where I would break my subway journey to Keio University, for a beer and roast eel and rice. The others I bought in a toyshop near the Imperial Palace, called Kiddieland, largely catering to the American armed forces. While Moms and kids were occupied with the toys, Dads headed for the basement which stocked comics and pornography.

On the pornography shelves I found copies of highly innovative, deconstructive, radical hardcore porn novels with a lot of dystopian science-fictional and fantasy aspects penned by poets such as David Melzer and Michael Perkins, published for a year or so by Essex House. (When the parent company realised what was going on, Essex House promptly ceased.) Reading those Essex House novels had quite an influence on my first novel, *The Woman Factory*, a satiric subversive hardcore female liberation novel, which I wrote after returning to England and while listening to Judy Collins and Traffic's 'In a Chinese Noodle Factory'. This novel, which only appeared in French, entitled *Orgasmachine* (but which is about to be published in Japanese in a much superior version), owed quite a bit to comics too, or rather to *comix*, the underground counterculture sort, which I was to discover just after leaving Japan in 1970—and that was to be the third phase of my relationship with comics.

The first phase, ah . . . For any British chap of my generation, that had to be the *Eagle*, starring Dan Dare, Pilot of the Future, who debuted in April 1950 a year before the Festival of Britain with its futuristic tapering rocket-ship Skylon and its giant-UFO Dome of Discovery which the *Eagle* anticipated visually. I remember the sheer frustration, as a boy just turned 8, of having to wait *several weeks* before I could get embroiled in the mission to Venus because not enough copies of the *Eagle* were available to meet demand at our newsagent, Mather's, on the Coast Road from Newcastle to Billy Mill where I lived (not in the derelict windmill itself, but a few hundred yards away) two miles from Tynemouth where I attended school. Getting off the yellow double-decker Number 11 bus on my return from school on Friday afternoons I would hasten into Mather's to collect my *Eagle* so that it wouldn't get crumpled by being delivered, though I wasn't clutching a threepenny piece in my sweaty palm because the cost went on my parents' newspaper bill. Ah, the rocket ships, the alien cities and vegetation and beasts. The slippery slope to becoming, ultimately, a Science Fiction writer!

I wasn't quite so interested in the other stuff in the *Eagle*, Sergeant Luck of the French Foreign Legion and plucky Corporal Trenet ('Courage, mes braves!') or the portly detective Harris Tweed or Black Bob the shepherd's dog, so as copies of the *Eagle* mounted high in my room eventually I tore off and retained just the front Dan Dare pages. Such vandalism, such a loss of future value! Though perhaps anticipating the Deluxe Collector's Editions of *Dan Dare* which now sit on a bookshelf here.

Copies of the *Saturday Evening Post* (I think!) arrived regularly at my Grandmother's from Canada and I devoured Mandrake the Magician. A respectable lady friend of the family somehow came into possession of a few American Horror comics (titles utterly forgotten), which she handed over to me. Very scary and sinister and interesting—a Lovecraftian monster menacing an island in the Pacific, a creature called The Heap, and so on. The lady promised me more of those but when I went to collect them the supply had dried up. To console me she gave me two shillings to buy some substitutes, and I duly bought some *Superman* and adventures of Billy Batson—but these lacked the same frisson, being distinctly wholesome compared with the eldritch horrors I had glimpsed.

By the time I was a lecturer in English Literature in Japan my take on that fascinating country was not an aesthetic one—Kabuki and No drama and Zen Buddhism—but a science fictional dystopian vision plus a love of the vermilion garishness of Shinto cut with Japanised American pop psychedelic culture. Japanese comic strips appealed to me, and, imported in Kiddieland or down on the Ginza, I discovered *Doctor Strange* whose transdimensionality and swirling psychedelic artwork very much turned me on. Consciousness-expanding, almost. Much more innovative than the Hulk and Spiderman, fun though those were—the mutations into superhumans and alternative beings excited me. This was phase two.

And then I discovered underground comix: wonderful Robert Crumb's strutting Rough-Tough Cream Puff. Or should that be Ruff-Tuff? I'm writing this all from memory. I seem incapable of hanging on to things that I ought to hang on to. I sold the best of my comix collection to a Davenport's Beer-at-Home delivery guy and comix-head some time in the Seventies. I sold my Essex House titles to Maxim Jakubowski to hang in a hammock of books suspended from his ceiling . . .

And Robert Crumb's A Gurl, sinking her teeth into the windowsill as she gets her rocks off, and Victor Moscoso's mechanical Mickey Mouses and bendy geometries, and S. Clay Wilson's orgiastic female pirates and his Sistine Chapel Roof, The International Fuck-In & Riot Orgy. Ah, *Zap Comix* and all those others! By now, the early 70s, my wife Judy was publishing cartoons in *Oz* and *Cyclops*, and had completed a marvellous underground version of Ambridge (doing for the Archers what *Schoolkids Oz* did for Rupert Bear), but *Oz* collapsed and they never returned the artwork, try as we might to retrieve it.

Since *The Woman Factory* hadn't found an English language publisher— Olympia Press wanted it but promptly went bust—I moved on and wrote a straight SF novel, *The Embedding*, featuring psycholinguistics, drugs, mind-expansion, head-hunting alien traders, the eccentric French visionary Raymond Roussel, and the Amazon. Prizes occurred. My course was set.

Yet always at my back I hear, not time's wingèd chariot, but:

He takes no guff when he struts his stuff, didderump didderump dump dump didderump. And: *By the hoary hosts of Hoggoth!* And: *Treen fighters astern!*

How I Was Shot by Adolf Hitler

LAST MONTH I WAS IN FINLAND, AND I MET FATHER CHRISTMAS.
Well, to be strictly accurate I met a Finnish drunk in a bar in the town of Jyväskylä 150 miles north of Helsinki. He could only speak three or four words of English but he quickly developed quite a compulsion to talk to me . . . at great length, in Finnish, with much sentimental emotion. Finally, in frustration, he pointed at himself and announced, 'Nicholas! Saint Nicholas!'

So now I know where Santa Claus spends his summers. He spends them getting very drunk in a bar in Jyväskylä in Finland.

Unfortunately, this information was no use to me—because I had already written a story about Santa Claus, called 'When Jesus Comes Down the Chimney'. In this story I reverse the traditional roles of Jesus and Santa Claus. Jesus possesses a magic sack—but Santa Claus climbs into people's homes so as to take away their most treasured possessions in order to redistribute wealth.

Usually for me, visiting somewhere interesting results later on in a piece of fiction, or at least in part of a piece of fiction. Hence the title of this talk, 'How I Was Shot by Adolf Hitler'.

This incident occurred where else but in Munich. I'd been invited to a Science Fiction festival held in the ultramodern palace of glass and pink concrete, the Gasteig cultural centre; and I discovered that this building stands on the site of—and obliterates the memory of—a one-time beer hall called the Burgerbräukeller. It was here that a Bavarian minister of state was

9

about to address a political meeting when Hitler burst in with his storm troopers. He smashed a beer mug, leapt on a table, and fired a pistol at the ceiling. Anybody who laughed at him was beaten up.

Naturally I realised that the auditorium in which I was addressing an audience must be directly above the place where Adolf had fired his pistol. Passing through the four-dimensional space-time continuum, Hitler's bullet hit me–metaphysically and imaginatively at least. In reality, no doubt, the bullet had lodged in the plaster of the ceiling below long ago . . .

At this point I should confess that the things I discover are not always true. I mean, was that really Santa Claus whom I met in Finland, even if he seemed to say so?

And when I was in Barcelona I became intoxicated with the weirdly surrealist Sagrada Familia cathedral designed by Gaudí, but still unfinished. I felt compelled to write a story about how this might be completed holographically, as part reality and part illusion. Alas, my delightful Catalan hosts told me a number of jokes—which I believed. They didn't realise that, even while we were wandering around bars, the data-processing tapeworm in my brain was digesting everything hungrily.

But no matter! After they read the story in *Asimov's* magazine, they confessed so I was able to revise the story for book publication.

So maybe Hitler didn't actually shoot me in Munich; though as far as I'm concerned, he did. A lot of the time life itself is part reality and part illusion. One of the answers to that daft old question 'Where do you get your ideas from?' is that a writer perceives the spectrum of possible illusions which wrap around reality. The ghosts of other possibilities. The spectres of alternative realities. The writer generates these instinctively as a rebellion against mundanity and conformity which dull our vision. Nietzsche once said, 'Who wishes to be creative, must first destroy and smash accepted values.' Well, you don't actually have to go around destroying, like King Kong let loose in Lilliput. And I seem to recall that Nietzsche died insane.

Schopenhauer said—this is definitely the intellectual part of the talk—he said, 'In order to have original, uncommon, and perhaps even immortal thoughts, it is enough to estrange oneself so fully from the world of things for a few moments, that the most ordinary objects and events appear quite new and unfamiliar. In this way their true nature is disclosed.'

For me, fiction comes from this kind of momentary estrangement, where the world turns upside-down and inside-out. A radio commentator delighted me by discussing a change of government in the West African country, Mali, in these terms: 'Mali, which had been drifting towards the Soviet Union, is now moving in the direction of America.' What if that could be literally true?

I'm quite interested in changing my perceptions of the ordinary, so as to write fiction which will also alter other people's perceptions. The last time I was in America, I discovered the cure for jet-lag by means of a sensory deprivation tank. I'd been invited to a convention in California, and I could only travel over for the weekend. Pondering about the upcoming ten-hour flight from London, I decided to put myself into a trance state—a sort of suspended animation—by taking some cans of Everard's wonderfully strong Old Original Ale on board the plane.

Soon after we took off, a stewardess came along with a trolley to inquire if anyone wanted a drink. So I thought I'd do the decent thing and buy one beer from her. Alas, questioning revealed that at Heathrow they had loaded on board a rather ghastly British brew called *Long Life*. Now, I had taken an oath never to drink this stuff if possible. So I replied, 'I'll just have an empty glass please.'

The stewardess fixed me with a stern gaze. 'You've brought your own liquor on board, Sir,' she said, 'and under Pan-Am regulations I'm supposed to confiscate it.'

Well, I fluttered my eyelashes at her, and she relented. She gave me an empty glass and a napkin and said, 'If you're discreet, Sir, I'll look the other way.'

The plane was fairly empty. I had three seats all to myself. So I stretched my legs out along the seats, clamped the open beer cans between my thighs so that the beer wouldn't spill, and laid the napkin over the cans as concealment.

Unfortunately we soon encountered strong air turbulence—with the result that blob after blob of beer was thrown upwards out of the cans to stain the napkin. Plop plop plop. It began to look as if I was suffering from spasmodic incontinence, and needed a nappy change.

My scheme was fatally flawed.

But then in San Francisco I climbed into a flotation tank, a soundproofed black coffin full of buoyant magnesium sulphate solution. I wasn't in the tank long enough to begin hallucinating, which could have been really interesting. However, I did become extremely relaxed; and on the flight back to Britain I found that I could go into the same beautiful mental state as in the tank. The return journey only lasted subjectively for two hours instead of ten.

It felt like a necessary juxtaposition when, in my novel *The Flies of Memory*, I put a sensory deprivation tank in the very room in Munich where I was shot by Adolf Hitler.

The Gasteig cultural centre had forgotten the existence of Hitler, architecturally—or so it seemed to me. What I was writing about in the novel was in a sense memorising myself—my nature and location—within a void. I was filling that void: the only existence within it. And because a bit of Munich had forgotten a bit of Hitler, in the novel the whole centre of Munich is forgotten—lost. The centre of the city vanishes—and reappears on Mars. And then the ghost of Hitler reappears too.

When writing, I believe in magical juxtapositions. I try to attract magical juxtapositions in order to unpeel the wallpaper of the world, and reveal the fabric beneath.

These happen in life too. Many writers are aware of the Library Demon. You walk into a library, and discover quite at random the very thing you need to know urgently right then—of which you were quite unaware beforehand. And this fills you with wonder and excitement. And with a sense of fertile estrangement from the ordinary.

This state of illuminated estrangement is the creative source not only of stories but also of my own original, innocent involvement, long ago, in a literature such as Science Fiction.

Recently, we had new floors put in our house by Britain's first ostrich farmer.

Hang on a moment. What is an ostrich farmer doing putting new floors in our house in a little village in the British countryside?

Well, the farmer in question is also a builder. But in his role as a somewhat eccentric farmer he recently decided to diversify. Being aware that ostriches have been ranched in Southern Africa for over a century, he decided to aim for a herd of three hundred of the big birds running free in a meadow near where we live, as neighbours for the perhaps puzzled cows and sheep.

The ostriches oughtn't to be too puzzled. Apparently an ostrich's brain is smaller than a chicken's; and with that tiny data processor they need to operate a body the size of a lesser inhabitant of Jurassic Park.

Though actually they seemed quite bright and inquisitive creatures when we visited the first five breeding birds so as to hand over our house keys to Farmer Frank. Their necks, resembling vacuum cleaner hoses, snaked up and down from ankle level to high overhead as they jostled to take a look at us.

And people do manage to organise ostrich races. Could an elf or leprechaun successfully race a chicken?

These ostriches are being raised for gourmet meat and quality leather.

So there has been some local protest at this from animal liberationists. On the other hand, a delightfully daft vicar spoke out in favour on national radio. At 6:25 every morning we have a 'Prayer for the Day' on Radio Four, introduced by a short meditation. 'In these troubled times,' discoursed the guest Vicar, 'it is encouraging to hear of an example of initiative from Northamptonshire, where a local farmer is raising ostriches to provide meat and feathers for his neighbours ...'

Ah yes, I can just see it.

Villager (tramping through snow... By the way, the ostriches enjoyed running around in the snow last winter.) Villager: 'Ar, Farmer Frank, it been hard what with the plague and the building societies repossessing our houses ...'

Farmer: 'Why, take this drumstick for your lads and this bag of feathers for your duvet.'

Villager: 'God bless you.'

When I was young, in the 1950s in the North-East of England, I also encountered an ostrich.

The 1950s was a very boring and austere postwar decade, preceding the joyous, rebellious psychedelic eruption of the 60s, and the North-East of England was a fairly barren, boring, downbeat place. The inhabitants have a fine sense of doom and pessimism, which is nicely captured by the best-selling novelist Catherine Cookson. My father actually went to school with Catherine Cookson in the slums of South Shields. Common remarks about the weather in the North-East of England were, 'Why, it's treacherous today.' Common responses to unusual ideas or ambitions were, 'You're flying too high,' and 'You'll bring about the downfall of nations.'

In a dusty shop window in my home town there was an ostrich.

It was a miniature plastic toy ostrich. This ostrich used to dip its head into a glass of water, then raise its head up, and lower it again—endlessly, all day long. The ostrich seemed interesting by comparison with the neighborhood.

So it wasn't surprising that I was delighted to discover Science Fiction, nor that I stared up at the stars as an imaginative escape route. The 1950s was the real 'Golden Age' of Science Fiction; though I didn't know so at the time. Compared with dull British names such as Smith or Brown or Watson, people with names the like of Isaac Asimov or A.E. Van Vogt seemed to be possessors of alien wisdom. I remember buying one particular copy of *Astounding Science Fiction*. The issue had a story in it by Cyril Kornbluth called 'Our Share of Glory' which was about linguistics. Its hero belonged to a guild of interpreters who spent all their time memorising vocabularies for all planets which Earth's traders might visit. I'm sure this story had something to do with my eventually writing my first published novel *The Embedding*.

Also in the same issue was a story set in mind-warping hyperspace, which really puzzled me and sent a cold shiver down my spine.

Yes, a cold shiver. Back then, I didn't read in quite the same way as nowadays. Science Fiction, Horror, Fantasy: they were all one. Rather as in the early universe before the strong force and the weak force split apart—before gravity and electromagnetism ruptured asunder, generating a universe responsive to several seemingly distinct forces. Thus 'hyperspace' must be a kind of deathly supernatural ghost region—into which one could nevertheless enter inside a flying machine. In that story the starship was adrift in hyperspace, and for some reason the hero had to climb through the airlock on to the hull of the vessel. This exposure could be very harmful to the human mind.

Outside, in hyperspace, the hero perceived 'an infinite plane'.

An infinite plane! I was oblivious to the geometrical meaning of plane. I visualised the hero standing on the hull, seeing the wings of his space-plane stretching infinitely in both directions rather like a narrow grey road through nowhere.

This completely wrong image terrified and thrilled me.

I think I should comment here on the post-structuralist, deconstructive theory that it is the reader—the lecteur—who constructs the text for himself or herself, rather than the author being in the driving seat. I definitely constructed a text of great visionary power for myself when reading this hyperspace story—based upon a complete misunderstanding.

On the subject of unusual ambitions, when I was a schoolboy I used to subscribe to a publication called *Wide World Magazine*, which was all about terrible journeys through the green hell of the Amazon, and being adrift on a raft in the shark-infested Pacific. Myself, I decided to become a cactus collector in the Arizona desert. This might be a distinctly sleazy occupation nowadays, due to collectors raping the environment of rare orchids and parrots. But at the time it seemed a noble quest. I remember writing some doom-laden poems about exotic plants. Cacti, orchids, and such definitely had some connection with literature in my mind.

I contented myself with simply growing cacti and succulents, because they looked to me as though they came from an alien planet. To my chagrin, the only one of my cacti that would ever flower was the peyotl cactus, the source of mescaline. Back then in the 1950s it was actually possible to buy peyotl cacti from specialist cactus growers in Britain. This was well before the psychedelic revolution. I haven't noticed any peyotl on sale at garden centres in the last couple of decades. Perhaps the peyotl was trying to tell me something by alone and uniquely flowering. For I had read Aldous Huxley's *The Doors of Perception*. If Hugo Gernsback was keen to encourage readers to wire up radio sets, when I finally got my Science Fiction act together, one of my main aims was to suggest to readers what it might be like to rewire minds.

Ungratefully, I did eat my faithful peyotl cactus a few years later—with no noticeable effects at all. The immediate consequence of its flowering, though, is that I sold an article to a popular gardening magazine, quoting extracts from Huxley and from Robert de Ropp's *Drugs and the Mind*. I was fifteen at the time. But the idea of becoming an Indiana Jones of the cactus world was waning. Literature beckoned.

I had also thought of becoming a chemist. Alas, I swallowed a large dose of methylated spirits while misperforming a titration experiment during my final Chemistry practical examination. Literature beckoned more vigorously.

And also, the desire to be a writer. Not a writer of Science Fiction, though. A writer of proper literature. Serious fiction. As practised by Aldous Huxley or Graham Greene. (Actually, I'm sure that the structure of Graham Greene's novels rather influenced the tripartite plot patterns of my first few published novels.)

I mention Huxley and Greene because they both went to the same college in Oxford where I was soon reading English Literature. In the college library were leather-bound uniform editions of their work, shelved in a place of honour. Another writer of amazing vision and imagination also went to the same college. Someone by the name of Olaf Stapledon. I do recall the day when I met the Senior English Literature Tutor in the street and mentioned that I had just bought a book by Olaf Stapledon; and he asked me, 'Who is he?' He had never even heard of Stapledon. So I knew that I shouldn't write something as lacking in respectability as Science Fiction. Yet even while I was reading all the proper books, schizophrenically I still clutched Van Vogt's *Voyage of the Space Beagle* behind my back.

British culture marginalises Science Fiction—perhaps even more so nowadays. Back in the 70s the quality cultural magazines and Sunday newspapers used at least to review SF once in a while. Now they hardly ever do so. When Ballard writes a non-Science Fiction novel, even though it is almost the same in texture and technique as the bulk of his SF work, he is nominated for literary prizes, almost as if to reward him for seeing the light at last.

One major reason for this is the British educational and social system whereby those people who run the country and dominate the media have an arts background and are to a large extent scientifically illiterate. At university they discover next to nothing about the universe we are in, and regard the wider horizons of existence with disdain. The fact that Margaret Thatcher (cursed be her name) was originally a flavours chemist in the food industry is quite irrelevant—since she starved Britain's research scientists of funds almost contemptuously.

Charles Babbage, designer of the world's first mechanical computer (which has now been built at last by London's Science Museum), was keenly aware of this a hundred and fifty years ago. He complained how 'a young man passes from our public schools'—which of course in Britain are the very expensive private schools such as Eton—'a young man passes from our public schools to the universities ignorant, almost, of the elements of every branch of useful knowledge.' Babbage campaigned for science education. Smart society laughed at him.

Personally I like the margins of the world rather than the self-satisfied centre. Cacti are plants of the margin. I preferred the decadence of the 1890s to the central Victorian territory. Innovations so often occur at the margins. Great artists and poets—a Van Gogh, a Baudelaire—flourished at the unacceptable margins, even though they might later be sucked into the black hole of solid reputation, of cultural deification. The horizon lies beyond the margins. Horizons are what matter for the renewing of the imagination. Ursula Le Guin might remark, in one of her neat Taoist antitheses, that the margins are the centre. I don't believe she *has* said this—but she might. With writers like John Crowley or Tim Powers, we're seeing an excavation of the secret history of the world. And indeed there are many secret histories. The history of female painters is one such. The anthropology of conquest is another. The Christian Bishop Landa burned the vast majority of the Mayan written texts, yet those texts are now emerging from the stones in the jungles where they were also carved. And we discover whole alternative civilisations and world views, as if hidden aliens have dwelled among us. I was recently reading the book published by Re/Search Publications in San Francisco, called *Modern Primitives*—about tattooing, scarification, and piercing of the body. Beneath some business suits—some; not many—dragons writhe, and nipple rings gleam. For some people have a secret life; and perhaps some of these people are the most alive. The British police recently raided and prosecuted a bookshop in London—which also specialised in Science Fiction—for stocking this *Modern Primitives* book, which contains a fair number of quotations from SF writers. Re/Search Publications also produced a handsome book on Ballard and reissued his *Atrocity Exhibition* in an illustrated edition. So there are profound connections out at the margins. One might almost say 'occult' connections, because they are hidden from general view.

The Police, of course, lead their own secret life—as we discover when a scandal finally erupts, about the fabrication of evidence, for instance.

For a while it worried me that SF and Fantasy writers seem to be strip-mining the alternative cultures and past societies of our world for material, increasingly and promiscuously. The Aztecs, the Mayans, the Australian Aborigines . . . Whoever next? Back in the early 70s James Blish wrote an essay for *Foundation*, which I had just joined as one of the editorial team. Blish was much influenced by Oswald Spengler's *Decline of the West*, and he singled out one of the characteristics of SF as 'syncretism'—the joining together of disparate, contradictory elements borrowed from all over the place, borrowed from contradictory, exotic traditions. This was a symptom, according to Spengler, of decadence and the imminent collapse of a society. As in society, so in SF. Obviously this process has accelerated since Blish wrote his rather pessimistic essay.

Yet might not this process represent something healthy, reinvigorating, and reconstructive—appropriate to our global village, if it is to thrive? On the one hand the global village suggests worldwide homogenisation and uniformity—the same novel by Isaac Asimov on sale in every language, in every country, remorselessly and deadeningly. On the other hand all the secret histories of the global village are now being highlighted, ever more so. This can of course lead onward to a theme-park world where alternative cultures are merely wallpaper, merely decoration in the international cocktail lounge or airport terminal. But maybe the secret histories are more vigorous than that.

I think that it's appropriate that Science Fiction should use all these secret histories of Aztecs or Aborigines or Neoplatonists in a syncretic, mosaic manner. For SF is mutually contradictory and multifold. Thus it helps us think, and feel, flexibly, about the vast range of radically alternative possibilities which lie ahead. And it also illuminates the secret history of our own times, the fears and desires that we feel as regards the futures that rush towards us.

I myself probably wouldn't have started to write Science Fiction if I hadn't lived abroad, away from Britain. Living in East Africa in a socialist republic gave me some insight into the political realities of the Third World, and at least some awareness of alternative traditional world views. Living in Tokyo subsequently slapped me in the face with future shock. Tokyo was the dystopian 'disaster area' of SF: a megalopolis of overcrowding, pollution, new industrial diseases, cherry trees kept alive by bottles of nutrient fastened to their trunks. It also contained all the utopian wizardry and gimmickry and techno-fun of next century. Tokyo compelled me to write Science Fiction as a psychological survival strategy to cope with the environment.

Actually, William Gibson told me that an early piece I wrote about life in Tokyo for *New Worlds* back in 1970 had quite an effect on him. Maybe, if I had been able to foresee the future (which Science Fiction writers notoriously can't) I could have founded Cyberpunk fifteen years ahead of schedule. However, things arrive when they arrive. And I didn't know too much about the cyber aspect; I knew more about structural anthropology...

Ah, these great missed opportunities!

But equally, though I was in the right place, not quite at the right time, I don't think I could have gone into a cyberpunk state of mind. What bothers me about the most vivid cyberpunk is how on Earth the characters are able to function at all as electronic supermen in those mean streets, with their brains zonked out, and their bodies quivering with drugs, and frequently beaten up as well. They ought to be in a hospital bed from page 2. I don't think I'd have the stamina. Flaubert advised, 'Be regular and orderly in your life, so that you may be violent and original in your work.'

Personally I tend to be regular and orderly, which is how I get lots of books and stories written.

Readers don't always quite appreciate this. I received one fan letter from a fellow in Florida who told me how he was in telepathic communication with a sperm whale, had made love to a dolphin, and had written an unpublished book about this which he suspected I had stolen from to produce my own novel about whales, *The Jonah Kit*. He had sent his 1000-page manuscript to Scribner's in New York. Scribner's had published *The Jonah Kit*. Therefore Scribner's had promptly xeroxed his manuscript of love and interspecies communication and rushed the xerox to Britain to someone who could quickly turn it into a sordid pessimistic best-seller for them.

Rashly I reassured my correspondent that if he looked on the copyright page of the Scribner's edition he would find that *The Jonah Kit* had first been published two years earlier in Britain itself. Mollified, by way of apology, this gentleman sent me a photo of a Reichian orgone machine he had built to detect UFOs. And he moved from Florida to Oregon; which is much further away from Britain.

But then his girlfriend—old or new, I don't know which—discovered by intuition a 'power centre' in Wales, which she needed to visit. My dolphin lover wrote saying he needed to come and interview me for *Future Life* magazine so as to pay for his and her trip to that power centre.

Future Life magazine was glossy, upbeat, and quite expensively produced; and I had already experienced a spot of surrealistic trouble with this particular publication. It ran a regular series about 'The Future of . . .' —transportation, medicine, lifestyles, or whatever, written each month by a different Science Fiction writer. The editors of *Future Life* invited me to do one of these, and to suggest the subject. Quite a lot of subjects had already been covered, so I suggested the future of religion.

Fine. Good idea. They commissioned me. I delivered my essay. The editors liked it. They paid me. Publication scheduled for July.

June came, and the June issue advertised my essay as due next month. July came, and *Future Life* published something else entirely.

To my enquiry, there came an anguished response, accompanied by the sound of editors tearing out their hair. The publisher and owner of *Future Life* was an Irish American. I think his name was Kerry O'Quinn. He was also a fervent atheist, and when he saw the very word 'religion' mentioned in the June edition of his magazine, he raced to the printing press. 'Stop Press!' My essay for the July issue, already being printed, was torn out bodily on his orders, and a different one substituted.

So I had somewhat negative feelings about *Future Life*—and I didn't particularly wish my Reichian dolphin lover to turn up as an ambassador of *Future Life* to pay for this trip to his girlfriend's power centre. I put his letter aside.

He must have intuited that I had done so. A mere 3 weeks later, on Christmas Eve when John Brunner was visiting us, an envelope dropped through our door. It contained a 7-page drama in which—to rebuke me for destroying his trip to Wales with his girlfriend—my would-be interviewer fantasised arriving in our village, cutting our telephone wires, and beating my nose bloody. . . because with my books I had 'mind-fucked' him—and if you fuck with your readers' heads, you can expect them to mess with your face.

Flaubert would not have wanted such an interviewer.

A while earlier, I had an enthusiastic postcard from an army base in New York State. 'Hey Ian!' this said. 'I been reading your books, man. Far out! Like, where do you get your dope, man? The Amazon? East Africa? Do you snort it man, raw? You got an old lady? Bet she's a fox. I bet you do that tantric fucking, too. Keep it hard for hours, right? Any kids? Any whole chromosomes? Were they born with their brains sticking out of their heads? You sure know your needles, man, i.e. "Thy Blood Like Milk" [this was a story by me]. But I liked it!! I like all your shit, man. Does this make me nuts too??'

Now, that's the kind of message that a cyberpunk character ought to receive.

As Schopenhauer said, 'It is enough to estrange oneself fully from the world of things for a few moments.'

Not quite all the time. In my case, anyway. I suppose other writers might operate differently. Rimbaud, for instance. (The French poet—not Sylvester Stallone.) But Rimbaud wasn't writing novels. Novels take a certain amount of long-term concentration.

On the other hand, after you have estranged yourself fully objects and events can appear new and unfamiliar at any time, and reveal their true nature.

Or at least an imaginative truth.

Then you can be shot by Adolf Hitler—and a bullet can become part of a book.

Jingling Geordie's Hole

O N THE CINEMA SCREEN: A GREY ATOLL IN GREY SOUTH SEAS. A bulb of light expanded suddenly; boiling cloud rushed skywards. Within moments the screen rocked at the impact of an implacable, blasting hurricane.

'This is the first moment of the thermonuclear age!' said the newsreel announcer, proud and cheerful as ever.

Ted Appleby felt such a thrill rush through his whole body at the power unleashed. The eleven-year-old paid scant attention to the rest of the newsreel: the Queen touring her Commonwealth, the French Foreign Legion losing a battle in some country called Indo-China, British troops successfully rounding up Mau Mau suspects in Kenya, a woman athlete running round a cinder track. The therm-o-nuclear explosion continued to boil through Ted, seeking outlet, expression.

Curtains slid across the front of the proscenium, luxuriously hung in tiers of pleats, spotlit in pink and orange and green. The main Art Deco lights came on, illuminating Egyptian-style papyrus columns and friezes. A recording of Mantovani's string orchestra playing *Charmaine* began. Ted tagged on to the crowd of children stampeding from their seats, squeezing through the foyer to erupt down mock-marble steps into the bright breezy salty June daylight.

He'd come to the cartoon matinée on his own. As half-expected, Gavin was waiting some way down the street pretending to look in a newsagent's window. Gavin wouldn't wish other boys, who might be from the same school, to see them meet; so Ted loitered, to let the mob clear away.

It was thus with all the older boy's interceptions of Ted; Gavin wanted the two of them to talk alone, to walk alone. Gavin Percy was sixteen. A fortnight earlier a couple of other sixteen-year-olds had surprised Gavin chatting to Ted at a time when Gavin thought they were safe. The older boys had started kidding on. 'Got a big sister, then, titch?' Ted had, as it happened: Helen. He nodded. So far as he knew, Gavin had never even set eyes on her. 'Percy's after her—watch out!' Gavin had flushed with embarrassment. 'He must be, mustn't he?' Ted had agreed with the tormentors. Gavin had looked relieved at Ted's comprehension, at this evidence of his young friend's complicity.

A lot of smut was talked about girls at that school, a day school for boys only. Lately Ted had been growing ignorantly interested in girls; obviously his own sister didn't count as an example, though the mysteries of her life would be regarded as fair game by any other boys. Bill Gibbon related that his older brother Brian and chums would go to a chum's house when the parents were out at the cinema and would undress a sister and pour ink over her then bath her clean *thoroughly*. They would stick a carrot up her then make white stuff into the dirty bathwater where she lay. Later, after they'd dried her down thoroughly, Gibbon said that they tied a lump of carrot to a string, put this up her to stop her having a baby then stuck their cocks inside her. When Ted told Gavin about this game, Gavin had looked offended—resentful at his friend having such things in his mind.

In Ted's classroom ball-fights were the rage among half a dozen of the boys, chiefly Gibbon who once exposed his cock in class under cover of his desk. Ted steered well clear of ball-fights which seemed excruciating. Two fighters would square off, each with one hand cupping trouser-clad balls, then they would dart at each other to claw the other's defences aside and squeeze his knackers. Howls of pain went up from the loser.

'Hullo,' Ted said to Gavin.

The newsagent's window display consisted of a row of sun-faded paperback westerns and war stories, a line of pens and pencils, and a box covered with red crêpe paper. On that box stood a glass of water and a yellow plastic ostrich a few inches high. The ostrich slowly dipped its beak into the water, raised its head, dipped it, raised it.

'I wonder how that works?' mused Gavin. 'Perpetual motion is scientifically impossible. Something to do with water and sunshine, I suppose.'

Ted stared in trembling fascination. The novelty ostrich reminded him . . . of the crane on the pier!

From where they stood he couldn't quite see the pier. The clock tower at the bottom of the street was in the way, as was part of the miniature Rock of Gibraltar which housed the castle, a small army base, and the ruins of the priory. Turn right at the clock tower and descend the steep road alongside the grass slopes of the castle moat, and into view would come: the great north pier of granite blocks, high whitewashed lighthouse at its seaward end.

The massive wheeled crane rested on several sets of rust-bobbled rails running along the mid-section of the pier, high and low. Anyone walking out to the lighthouse had to pass underneath its looming, girdered bridge then along beneath its hundred foot jib arm. These days the crane never rolled to and fro nor swung its jib out over the sea. Why had it ever done so in the past? To unload boats tying up formerly at the lower stone quayside, safely clear of the Black Midden rocks?

Many steel hawsers as thick as a boy's arm tethered the crane to iron rings in the pier walls; at these points the granite was streaked orange with salt-water rust. The crane had to be chained like some mechanical Samson or winter storms could smash it into the bay. Wild waves sometimes broke clear over the top of the crane, even over the top of the lighthouse. But perhaps the machine couldn't move, ever again; perhaps it was rusted in place. Ted sincerely hoped that this was so, but scarcely dared believe it. Whenever his parents had taken him and Helen for a walk along to the lighthouse of a sunny Sunday afternoon, the passage under crane and jib was fraught with terror. He was sure that the crane's many wheels might creak into life, and start rolling, that the jib would duck down, dangling chains like octopus arms, to snatch him, crush him. He'd endured several nightmares about that iron giant which brooded over the pathway out to sea.

He imagined a therm-o-nuclear explosion hurling that metal monster into the bay where river met sea-tide, drowning it safely, though bits might still protrude.

Ted's Dad had told him that a tunnel ran all the way along inside the pier; that's why there were those opaque green glass slabs set periodically in the concrete path. But how, even in a dream, did you get inside the tunnel which would protect you from the crane?

The ostrich ducked its head into the glass of water, rose erect, ducked, arose, hypnotically.

'I just saw the H-bomb test,' Ted told Gavin and imitated the rush of a hurricane, as he imagined it.

'Oh,' said Gavin. 'Are you walking home or catching the bus?'

Buses departed from beside the clock tower. A crowd from the matinée horsed around the bus stop; a melée. Ted knew that Gavin wouldn't want to mingle with that.

'May as well walk and save the fare,' said Ted.

So they strolled away together from the hidden sea, past a closed fish and chip shop with amber Tizer bottles lining the window, past a barber's dustily advertising Durex sheaths, a gaunt Congregational church, a small shrubby park with floral clock. Then came a dingy pub, The Dolphin, smelling of stale beer with a blue star mounted outside on a bracket; next to a grocer's and a greengrocer's. The plate glass reflected Ted and Gavin both dressed in dark blue blazers with crimson badges framing three black anchors, both wearing grey flannel trousers, in Ted's case short ones—but he'd been promised long ones when his next birthday came around. Both with close-cropped haircuts: Ted's hair chestnut, Gavin's gingery. Gavin was slightly plump; Ted was slim. Gavin's face was freckled; Ted had the complexion of an angel, so his mother said embarrassingly. She used to say: cherub, which was worse.

They entered the wrought-iron and dirty glass cavern of the small railway station and climbed the wooden bridge over the rails, pausing at the summit to watch an electric train pull in below. Gavin produced a red-bound school book from his blazer pocket and showed it: *Edward the Second* by Marlowe.

'We've started reading this for the exams.'

'A play.' Ted regarded the volume with mild disgust.

'It's exciting. It's the best play I've ever read. Part of it happens right here—down by the castle. Edward's best friend sailed from France and landed here to meet the king.'

France seemed a great distance from this northern port. Such a voyage—in an ancient sailing tub—made very little sense. If the king's friend had been coming from Norway, that would have been a different kettle of fish. But then, old plays often didn't make sense either.

'All sorts of things happen. Do you want to know how the king gets killed? He's in a dungeon up to his ankles in filthy water. They bring in a table, hold him down with a mattress—then they jab a red-hot cooking rod up his bottom.'

'That must hurt.' Ted felt sick. Another image had arrived to join the crane in nightmare land, one which he knew his mind would dwell on.

'Maybe we could read a bit of it together, another week? Act it out? It's terribly good.'

'Yes,' said Ted.

They descended the far flight of steps and headed through streets of houses, each with a tiny walled front flower garden, most with stained-glass panes above the doors. From a number of chimneys identical aerials rose in the form of a large capital 'H'. Those homes, unlike Ted's or Gavin's, boasted television sets. The 'H' reminded Ted of H-bomb.

'Pow!' he exclaimed, and made a noise like rolling thunder.

Beyond those streets was a large, tree-dark park with bowling green and pet cemetery as prelude, and a soot-blackened institution set within iron railings as finale. The old workhouse, from Victorian times, was still tenanted by aged paupers, mostly ailing. Some of the residents were sitting on park benches, passively. A few stood watching the bowling, over a low hedge. The players—more prosperous pensioners in white Panama hats and club blazers—ignored their derelict audience of shabby overcoats.

Ted wondered whether any work was performed in the grim building known as the workhouse. He imagined old women knitting sweaters for sale to Norwegian sailors, old men whittling wooden boats, or maybe sewing mailbags. He'd heard that husbands and wives were kept separate inside, spent the nights in separate phlegm-racked dormitories. Only when they were let out could a married couple meet.

Presently Ted and Gavin came abreast of a hunched figure in greatcoat and cloth cap shuffling slowly along. This Methuselah with rheumy red eyes held a huge vile handkerchief at chest level to catch a constant string of grey gluey drool proceeding from lips or nostrils; Ted couldn't bear to look more closely. He had passed this fellow on other occasions and presumed that he and his like were the reason why this park, which dropped away steeply to the south down a leafy ravine with cascading stream in the direction of the fish quay, was known as Spittal Dene. On account of the sputum.

Soon they were in sight, over treetops, of the roofs along the river bank: those of ships' chandlers which supplied the trawlers, of wholesale fish merchants, the smelly guano works which manufactured fertiliser from tons of imported bird droppings, the Jungle Arms public house ill-famed for

Saturday night fights, and Hood Haggie's rope factory, staffed mostly by notorious women.

Gavin also was staring at the roof of the rope factory. He licked his lips.

'Do you know what Brian Gibbon in my class heard happened at Hood Haggie's last month? There was a new supervisor on the job—a young chap. The women pulled his trousers down and fitted an empty milk bottle over his cock. Then they pulled their skirts up over their waists to excite him.' Gavin was sweating, nauseated and excited. 'His cock swelled up stiff inside the milk bottle, and wouldn't go down again. He had to go to hospital in a van to get the bottle off. You know about cocks swelling up, do you?'

Ted nodded.

'Does yours, sometimes?' Gavin asked.

At this very moment it was trying to, and Ted walked on awkwardly. Just the other evening, in his room, he had drawn a naked woman on a sheet of paper torn from an exercise book. A woman with breasts and a smooth sweep of flesh between her legs, like a flap glued down. Soon he had ripped the drawing into tiny pieces and flushed them down the lavatory in case his mother discovered. Some scraps had floated; he had to flush the pan again and again.

'I haven't told my Mam, but I've got hairs growing on me down here,' he said to Gavin.

'Have you? That's natural.' Somehow Gavin looked as though he deplored this development. 'So have I,' the older boy added after a while. 'They're called the short and curlies.'

The sky had been clouding over. A hooter sounded from the river, just as an air-raid siren might sound.

A thought occurred to Ted. 'Do women have short and curlies too?'

'Yes!' snapped Gavin, a peevish note in his voice. 'Gibbon brought a picture magazine to school last term. I glanced at it.'

Ted brooded about his drawing. It had been copied, to the best of his memory, from a photo of the statue of a goddess in an encyclopedia. And it had been wrong. No wonder he had felt so odd about it, and baffled as to what a husband and wife were supposed to do, as regards that seamless flap of skin down there.

'I'd like to see a magazine like that.'

'What for?' asked Gavin.

'You'll not laugh?'

'I promise I won't.'

Ted explained about the drawing. Gavin smiled.

Rain started to spit in their faces. A Vespa putted along the nearby road, the rider perched upon the scooter's ample casing as though upon two creamy metal buttocks.

Dreams could trap and trick you. Ted was hastening through the giant crane's shadow. He could hear noises up there: rattling, clanking. He had to look up! Scrambling out along the jib above him was . . . Bill Gibbon, bare body bristling all over with hairs. A 'Gibbon' was the name for some kind of ape, Ted knew. Therefore Gibbon was a hairy beast. The person overhead looked massive as a gorilla. Could that be Gibbon's elder brother? Or both of them fused together?

Now that Ted had spotted him, Gibbon began gibbering and capering. One huge paw grabbed his groin in preparation for a ball-fight. Catching hold of a loose hawser, Tarzan-style, Gibbon swung down.

Ted fled towards the tall white lighthouse which seemed far away. Gibbon easily overhauled him.

A paw clutched at Ted's cock and balls, to squeeze. Pressure mounted, painfully—but also thrillingly. Squirming to turn, Ted found himself pressed against not Gibbon, but the naked goddess of his drawing. Her breasts squashed against his face; the hair at the base of her stomach prickled him. A bright light, bright as the sun, crescendoed somewhere. He felt wet, and woke. Down inside the bed his fingers touched his groin which was soaked with hot sticky liquid. He smelt a salty-sweet tang.

Gavin didn't coincide with him, the next school day; but the day after he was hanging about near the park gate. Ted hadn't wanted to tell his mother what happened in bed, but now he told Gavin.

Gavin nodded. 'That's natural. It's called a wet dream. Was I in the dream?'

'You?' asked Ted, puzzled.

'If Gibbon was, I thought I might have been.'

'The woman I drew was in it. I told you.'

Gavin shook his head dismissively.

Above the school playing field was a small wild grassy plateau with precipitous sides. The boys called it 'the Lost World' and occasionally agile disobedient pupils such as Bill Gibbon would climb up there to lie hidden on top. The headmaster had put the plateau out of bounds, as a boy once fell off and broke his leg. Cricketers who weren't yet in to bat were supposed to stay near the greenpainted pavilion, with its scoreboard and changing room. Those who had already batted could watch play from anywhere around the fringes of the field, on the flat.

As Ted, in white shorts, shirt, and sandshoes, was sprawling on the grass eyeing bowlers and batsmen in total boredom and watching a ladybird climb a green blade, Gibbon and his chum Malcolm Davies loomed over him.

'You're sucking up to that Gavin Percy,' Gibbon said. Even Gibbon Junior was much burlier than Ted. 'You're his pet, hoping he'll help you with your homework.'

'No,' Ted said feebly. 'That isn't true.'

'I'll tell my big brother about you and him if you don't come up the Lost World with us after the game. We're going to tie you up with strong grass and leave you. You'll miss your tea, and get five hundred lines and the slipper for being up there.'

The two boys ambled off, leaving Ted hollow and scared.

Strong grass braided together would cut wounds in his wrists and ankles if he tried to free himself. Gibbon might debag him too, steal his shorts. If he didn't do as they said, Brian Gibbon would be told. Ted worried desperately.

After the game, however, he ran off home. In bed that night he fretted for ages because he hadn't gone up the Lost World and wished morning would never arrive, when he must go to school to face Gibbon and Davies.

He turned up as late as possible, nearly missing the school bell. Though he was full of jitters all day long, oddly neither of the bullies paid any attention to him. Could they have entirely forgotten something which preoccupied Ted so desperately? Although he still worried a bit the next day too, nothing at all happened. That evening, walking home, he realised that if the headmaster had discovered about Ted being tied up on the plateau, then he would have demanded to know *who else* went up there with him and tied him up. Davies and Gibbon would have been punished too; tanned with the slipper, kept in for an hour or two to write lines.

Following the cartoon and news matinée the next Saturday, Ted met Gavin in the usual place, beside the ostrich which Ted tried not to notice. An early bus had cleared everyone away from the clock tower so Ted and Gavin went to perch on the edge of the stone horse trough dated 1841 below the tower. The trough was bone dry, empty apart from a screwed-up fish and chip paper; buses didn't drink from horse troughs.

From that vantage point they could see a stone man standing in mid-air: statue of a commander in Nelson's navy, a victor of Trafalgar now surveying the river protectively from a high column. The column rose from an imitation castle, and Ted could make out one of the cannons from a man-of-war which poked riverwards over mock battlements.

Gavin took out a red book; his play.

'You don't have to go home yet, do you? We could climb up to the monument and act a bit. It's super. Would you like that?'

'All right. I can only stop for half an hour.'

As they climbed the wide, crumbling steps to the battlements, the sun shone bright. Up top, a fresh wind blew, to discourage other visitors. Over the river herring gulls and kittiwakes milled and screamed. The kittiwakes nested on all available upper storey window ledges along the river front, distempering walls with their droppings.

More sheltered spots might be basking in warmth, and the beaches to the north of the real castle, though rather exposed, would no doubt be spotted with flyspecks of plodgers and sun-bathers. Not the haven nestling below by the pier, however. The haven's sand was a mess of washed-up cork, sea coal, black weed, driftwood, nubs of polished glass, on which hulls of beached yachts rested. Several yachts were tacking out in the bay, with tiny crew. Otherwise, the scene seemed deserted of people.

They sat by a cannon, its wheel sunk in concrete and muzzle plugged likewise—as though someone might otherwise vandalistically fire a stone ball at a trawler.

Tilting the open play towards Ted, Gavin read aloud:
'Like sylvan nymphs my pages shall be clad;
'My men, like satyrs grazing on the lawns,
'Shall with their goat-feet dance an antic hay.'
Ted felt confused. Was there straw spread to dance on, to stop the satires from spoiling the lawn with stiletto heels?
'Sometimes a lovely boy in Dian's shape,
'With hair that gilds the water as it glides,

'Crownlets of pearl about his naked arms,
'And in his sportful hands an olive tree,
'To hide those parts which men delight to see—' Gavin broke off. 'Those parts. Do you understand that, Ted?'

'Sort of. He's talking about . . . down here. Is the boy hiding behind the tree?'

'No, tree just means a bit of a tree. A bunch of leaves, to hide his parts. It has to rhyme.'

Ted grinned. 'Maybe the boy has a lot to hide.'

'I shouldn't think so. The men want to see . . . and touch his parts. Shall we explore the tunnel down below?'

The false castle was hollow. An empty space the size of a train tunnel circuited the square core of the column. The entrance side was dingy, the other three sides pitch black. Ted had only once stepped through that entrance and taken a few paces into the thickening gloom. The floor was of dry soil, and just inside the entrance he remembered clumps of dogs' dirt, some of it white because the dog had distemper. He'd heard Bill Gibbon say that youths took girls into the tunnel under the monument for a feel.

'I brought a torch,' Gavin said. 'To show those parts, down below.' From his blazer pocket he produced a small flashlight.

Ted shook his head. 'Dogs do their business in there. You could catch distemper from touching it. Look, I'll have to go. I said I could only stay half an hour.'

'With the torch, we can keep clean. Let's just explore quickly.'

'I can't! Next week, maybe. I have to run for the bus.'

Ted dashed down the flaking stone steps away from the looming cannons.

That night Ted dreamed he was tied up, on the Lost World. It was twilight; Venus shone. He could see the stone man looking in the wrong direction, atop his column, unable to turn round just as Ted was unable. The rope of grass bit into his wrists which were fastened behind his back, so that he couldn't touch those parts. Those parts itched and swelled painfully. Touch would change the pain to pleasure, relief.

He woke, to find that he'd been sleeping with his palms squashed under his buttocks. His hands were paralysed, two dead animals fastened to his wrists. Soon they prickled and stabbed with pins and needles.

It rained a lot during the next week, so that he didn't meet Gavin at all, only spying him once or twice in the distance down school corridors. However, the following Saturday was a scorcher. When Ted arrived for the matinée, Gavin was already waiting near the cinema.

'I've got one of those photo magazines to show you,' said Gavin. 'You know? It's in my pocket. I can't take it out where anyone might see. Why not skip the cartoons? That'll give us longer to look at it.'

'How did you get it?'

'From a newsagent's down on the fish quay. I went specially. Sailors must buy these.' From the strain in Gavin's voice Ted could guess how hard it must have been for his friend to sneak into that shop, down in rough territory, where at least he wasn't likely to be known. No doubt Gibbon Senior never had such qualms. Had Gavin worn his school blazer?

'Did the newsagent make it hard for you?'

'Not much.'

'Are there lots of pictures?'

'Quite a few. Some show everything.'

'Where shall we go? The monument?'

Gavin shook his head. 'How about the rocks below the priory? It's more natural there. More beautiful. We could climb up into Jingling Geordie's Hole. We'd be private; it would be light and airy and clean.'

Jingling Geordie's Hole was a small cave a little way up the cliff face, which high tides lapped into. Legend had it that the cave drove deep into the headland on which castle and priory stood; it had supposedly been used by smugglers, and was haunted by a ghost who jingled chains. According to an old book called *North Country Lore and Legend* in the Percy household, a young knight had once fought his way past demons into the pitchy depths to drink from 'the chalice of truth'. An engraving showed him wielding a sword which shone as bright as the sun, against beasts resembling pterodactyls and prehistoric crocodiles. In reality, the cave was only shallow.

'All right,' agreed Ted.

Ten minutes later they were crunching over shingle littered with torn-up bladder wrack, broad black whips with explosive air-pods. They skirted pools inhabited by button anemones, limpets, whelks, and small crabs, then clambered over tumbled white boulders to the towering cliff. Gentle waves slopped and hissed. The tide was barely on the turn, so they couldn't be cut off for another two or three hours. Further along the shore a couple of blokes were sea-angling from a spit of black rock, but a deep inlet of water carved its way in between. No one else was exploring their area; most kids would be at the matinée.

Past storms had tossed weed into the cave but no recent wind-whipped waves had reached as high, thus crisp black heaps matted the stones thickly. Hot morning sun had been warming the weed mattress. Gavin shucked off his blazer, encouraged Ted to remove his, and laid both down as rugs. From his inside pocket Gavin slipped a small folded magazine and creased it the opposite way to straighten the pages. On the colour cover: the upper half of a smiling naked suntanned woman with raven hair and big bouncy breasts.

'*Health and Efficiency*. It's for nudists.'

'Oh boy,' said Ted.

Inside were black and white photos. A dark-maned young woman splashed naked in the sea, her bottom turned to the camera; Ted thought he saw a hint of hair between her buttocks. He felt those parts tingle and swell. A blonde woman lay supine on a towel, her nearer leg raised to conceal her groin. Gavin turned the page. The same blonde was leaping in the air, but between her legs was only a blurred grey smear. However, on the right hand page a flaxen-haired girl with little pointy breasts showed faint delicate curls on the mound where her legs met.

Gavin propped the magazine open on a hump of weed. 'You'll hurt yourself, keeping your parts squashed up like that. So will I. It's dangerous.' He opened his belt and unbuttoned his trousers; opened Ted's gently too, his hands brushing Ted's aertex-clad parts. 'Better let it right out. In fact, we ought to take our trousers and pants right off. We don't want to stain them.'

Remembering the hot wet gush in bed, Ted agreed. Soon their flannel trousers and aertex pants lay discarded. Gavin looked at Ted's now urgent parts; Ted looked at Gavin's hairs and swollen cock, then at the photo. Ted wanted to hold himself but Gavin pushed his hand aside. From his pocket he took a blue and white glass jar, unscrewed the lid, scooped a mass of Nivea skin cream on to his fingers.

'Watch the photo, Ted. Pretend I'm her.' Gavin massaged him teasingly with cream-smeared fingers. Presently he whispered, 'Lie over. Let's pretend you're a woman too.' Briefly he took his hand away to smear cream on himself, emptying the jar. Now Gavin gripped Ted's cock wonderfully; and a creamy cock butted up Ted's backside. 'This might feel strange. It's worth it.'

Ted stared at the photo in front of his face, moving his own parts up and down now in Gavin's fist. His bottom felt as if he was straining on the toilet with a huge turd stuck half way out, but this discomfort was secondary to the pleasure in his front part. He shut his eyes. From deep inside him something was rising, a snake of hot jelly that lived in his belly. Hotter, more urgently it rose. The therm-o-nuclear explosion was coming—the blinding light; that was why he had his eyes shut. For timeless moments boiling milk burst through the squeezing fist; he saw whiteness everywhere. Simultaneously the burning rod which killed the king entered Ted's bowels. Gavin gasped, 'Sweet Prince, I come!' Fiery stars exploded throughout the blank smooth whiteness, and Ted cried out. The world boomed as though the cave was a bass drum which the sea beat upon. Ted felt that some door had been torn open in him—a door which was also in the backside of Jingling Geordie's cave. A dim tunnel stretched away. Far off, a transparent ghost gibbered and writhed. Ted's limbs were the ghost's, his gibberings and writhings, its. At the heart of the ghost floated an albino tadpole. Somehow that tadpole swam within Ted too.

Then the wild wave which had burst its bounds hissed back to its source. Gavin let go of him, turned him over, kissed him on the lips.

Ted drew away, and saw vivid blood streaks on Gavin's foamy cock like strawberry syrup on an ice cream cornet. As he drew on his underpants hastily Ted felt cream and blood ooze out to stain the cotton.

Feeling sore and awkward, Ted walked home alone, worrying about his underpants. There'd hardly been any need for Gavin to say so strenuously that he shouldn't tell anyone; he had no intention of telling. But his soiled pants! Maybe he'd stained the inside of his trousers too.

He detoured through the huge cemetery near his home. Around the back of the chapel and crematorium was a shabby public lavatory; he could examine himself.

He generally admired the marble chips within the boundaries of graves: little lakes of emerald crystals, ruby crystals, ice, and amethyst. He usually enjoyed seeing the glass bells covering bowls of china flowers faded to pastel. Today he hardly noticed. Rooks cawed from their black stick-nests in the green heights of elms. Decaying wreaths lay heaped along one new grave; nobody had cleared the rotting flowers away yet. He hardly heard, or saw.

The men's lavatory was a short dark concrete tunnel with pee-stained wall and yellowed gutter sloping to a drain-hole. The stone floor was slicked with damp. Cocks had been pencilled on the wall as if to remind users—in vain—which way to aim. At the end: a door battered with bootmarks, carved with initials, a stout brass mechanism bolted to it. Ted fed it a penny.

Behind the door he found a china bowl with no seat, a string dangling from the overhead cistern, a piece of metal where a toilet roll would fit, had there been any. He forced the bolt shut with difficulty, fearing that he might lock himself in. He undid his trousers, which to his relief were reasonably unblemished. But a big dark brown patch disfigured his underpants.

He recalled how much soaking and bleaching his hanky had needed, when he had a nose-bleed. He couldn't possibly clean this mess in secrecy. It mustn't be known that he had bled between the legs. His sister presumably bled—Gibbon told dirty jokes about tomato sauce—but that was different, and private. He wasn't meant to.

So he eased his trousers off, keeping them clear of the wet floor, removed his underpants and put his trousers back on. The underpants he stuffed behind the chipped bowl. Maybe his mother mightn't notice for weeks that he only now owned three pairs of underpants instead of four. If she did find out he would say that he messed his pants at school one day, took them off in the school bog and got rid of them. Because there was dirt in them. But he'd been ashamed to tell her.

A week later the summer term ended. In the hall the assembled school sang:
Lord dismiss us with thy blessings,
Thanks for mercies past received . . .
Ted had avoided Gavin during that final week, and on the last day once again he caught a crowded bus home in company with a gang of boys rather than walking. For the first two mornings after the events in Jingling Geordie's Hole he had found smears of blood on the toilet paper, but then no more.

During the first ten days of the summer holiday Ted mainly stayed at home, re-reading old copies of *Hotspur* and *Wizard*, sorting out his cigarette card collection, drawing pictures of therm-o-nuclear explosions. Though he was no nuisance his mother chased him out occasionally for a breath of fresh air. He stayed close to home, wandering round the wooded back lanes of the cemetery.

On the eleventh day the Appleby family set off by train to spend a week in Edinburgh. Ted's Dad, an electrician with the Council, was now on holiday;

also sister Helen who had left school the year before and now worked as a dental receptionist.

The family stayed in a boarding house off Hanover Street, ate porridge and kippers for breakfast, explored the city. The Botanic Gardens of Corstorphine seemed to Ted a paradisiacal version of the cemetery back home. The tiny room Ted stayed in was directly behind the red neon sign, *Princes Guest House*, which stayed lit all night long, tubes humming and buzzing, bathing the room even through the curtains in a blood-stained light. Though it wasn't obvious from the street below the sign was thick with spiders' webs and hundreds of insect corpses.

On the fifth morning of the holiday Ted was sick before breakfast. He vomited clear bitter liquid into the tiny wash-handbasin and couldn't face kippers or porridge. Likewise the next morning.

'You must be off colour,' his Mam observed. Ted wondered if this could be some reference to the neon sign outside his window.

On the train home he felt nauseated, then better once they had returned. He carried on reading, drawing, walking in the cemetery, day-dreaming about the botanic gardens of which he'd bought picture postcards. He wished he could live there forever, camping in the orchid or fern house, after a therm-o-nuclear war which had killed everyone else. Since that would include his Mam and Dad, he cried a little. Soon it was September, and the new school term began.

'Have a good holiday?' Gavin asked, meeting him in the corridor near the physics lab.

'We went to Edinburgh. I was sick a few times.' This stuck in Ted's mind since he had hardly ever been sick before, and never on just getting out of bed.

Gavin looked hurt, as though Ted said this to reproach him.

'We went to the Lake District,' said Gavin. 'I thought about sending you a card but I decided not. Your parents might have asked. I bought you a present.'

A tin of butterscotch with a picture of a hill called Helvellyn.

'I climbed that mountain. Early on, I found a sheep lying on its back in the bracken. I rolled it over but it couldn't stand up. I thought about you at the cairn on the top and added a stone for you. Are you going to the matinée this Saturday?'

'I don't know.'

Noisy boys were clattering in their direction. Gavin slipped away into the lab.

On Saturday Ted set off for the cinema, since his Mam expected this; but he went to the cemetery instead. Parking himself on a bench, he read most of the stories in a new copy of *Hotspur* and ate all of the butterscotch. Careful that no one saw, he chucked the empty tin under a laurel bush before returning home. For several hours afterwards he had indigestion.

Playing rugby that winter, Ted soon got puffed out and could only trot around after the ball. The crush of the scrum bruised and scared him. Bill Gibbon often shouldered into him, tried to trip him.

Ted was very hungry these days, sometimes gobbling four slices of bread and marg with his Mam's meals. He sneaked biscuits from the pantry. He always bought chocolate bars with the money he saved by missing the cartoon matinée; these gave him the energy to endure the cold of the cemetery.

Towards Christmas his Mam said, 'You're putting on weight,' and it was true. His trousers—long ones, since his October birthday—pressed cruelly into his waist. He hadn't seen much of Gavin at school; Gavin seemed offended by Ted's long trousers instead of admiring them. Ted found that the trousers tried to cling together at the turn-ups when he walked; he waddled, legs apart. The turn-ups filled with fluff which wadded into felt, but he couldn't bend to clean them out with his finger. If only his elastic belt, with the silver snake-clasp, would open out still further.

In January as the new term started his Mam said, 'You're becoming a fatty. You shouldn't eat so much. But maybe that isn't it, maybe it's glandular. It can be, with boys of your age. Maybe we should take you to see the doctor.'

'No,' said Ted, 'I feel fine.'

He didn't. Rugby games were a nightmare, made slightly less so only by the general indifference of the sports master. On sports days Ted longed for rain, then the class would stay in the school doing prep. As often as not, it did rain; or sleet. Worse, now there were marks on his belly like thin red worms as though his skin was slowly tearing. His Dad had a feeble, brief word with him about the facts of life, embarrassing them both.

The radio news announced how British troops were leaving the Suez Canal Zone, and how France was sending thousands of troops to Algeria.

Ted felt proud for the French. Their Prime Minister, who was also called France, was making everyone drink milk because it was healthy. Ted used this as an excuse to persuade his Mam to order an extra pint bottle a day all for him. But the British hadn't done so badly after all; tommies had crushed the Mau Mau who butchered settlers with long knives. In Algeria the natives threw bombs into cinemas. In America President Eisenhower was guarding Formosa against the Red Chinese. By the autumn of that year there would be television with adverts, just as at the cinema. Ted wished there was a TV set in their house, and a big 'H' on the roof, so that he could see all the news-reels he was missing; but his Mam said they wouldn't get one while he was still at school with homework to do. Helen didn't seem to care whether they had a set or not; she was a dull, boring sister who read *Woman* and *Ideal Home*.

Ted always locked the door when he had his weekly bath; he never let anyone glimpse the red worms on his tummy. He didn't dare go to the surgery because he already knew what Dr Robson would discover. Nocturnal visions of a tunnel and of a white tadpole—coupled with furtive reference to a big maroon volume titled *The Home Family Doctor* which was kept on a high shelf—had made it plain; and if Dr Robson found out he would find out what Ted and Gavin had done.

Ted was having a baby.

One day he met Gavin after school. The older boy no longer seemed to like Ted much, not only on account of those long trousers but because Ted looked swollen and blotchy as well as being a bit taller. They walked the streets together as of old; unlike as of old.

'Gav, I have to tell you something.'

'Yes?'

'I'm having a baby. I think it'll come in March.'

Gavin grabbed Ted by the shoulder. 'You can't! You aren't a woman. What do you mean?'

Ted began to blubber.

'What's wrong with you?' Gavin had gone white.

'Scared.'

'Why?'

'I told you. It's because of what we did in Jingling Geordie's Hole.'

Now Gavin seemed furious—though scared, too.

'You're making this up. That's scientifically impossible. You don't have a womb inside you. You're saying this to make trouble!'

'I must have something that's imitating a womb. I've got so fat. I told you how I was sick in the mornings during the summer hols—that's morning sickness. I looked in a medical book. There are all these red marks on my tummy, because it's stretching. Can I show you them?'

'I don't want to see.'

'Won't you help me, Gav? My Mam wants me to go to the doctor.'

A cunning look crossed Gavin's face. 'You haven't told your Mam?'

'No.'

'Women drink stuff to get rid of a baby. I'll find out. But you mustn't tell anybody else.'

Ted winced. 'Ouch, I felt it move.'

'What?'

'In my tummy. Feel it, Gav!'

'Here in the street?'

'Feel while it's moving, or you aren't helping me!'

Gavin glanced up and down the deserted street, scanned the nearby net-curtained windows. Hastily he stepped close to Ted, let his hand be guided clammily.

'Do you feel it?'

'Something's shoving, kicking,' the older boy mumbled, bewildered and terrified now.

Two days later, by the deserted chilly bowling green, Gavin said, 'I've asked Brian Gibbon.'

'He'll tell his brother.' Ted felt betrayed.

'No, he won't. I gave him my new fountain pen. I'll do homework for him, and I promised him some of the money I got for Christmas if he helps. Gibbon knows about girls and babies. It has to be him, Ted. Anyway, I didn't mention *you!*'

'So what did you say?'

Gavin sniggered bitterly. 'That I got a girl into trouble. She's threatening to tell her Dad. Gibbon respects me now, because of that. He wanted to know all the details. He would!'

'And?'

'I pretended she's a friend of my cousin's. I said I took her to one of those concrete pill-boxes from the war, along the dunes among the spiky grass, and we did it there. Last term. I thought she might only let me have a feel but she took her knickers off and let me do it all. That's what I said.' Gavin looked disgusted by his story. 'Gibbon'll find a way.'

Ted thought about carrots tied to string, and milk bottles. His tummy curdled. Gavin too looked haunted with anxiety. Let him be haunted!

He whispered to Gavin, 'If I have a baby and people find out you're the father, the police'll take you off to a reformatory.'

Gavin bit his lip.

'Gibbon says it's done with a bottle of gin and a bent wire coathanger,' Gavin told Ted. They were on the railway bridge. 'The woman drinks the gin to upset her stomach then someone pushes the coathanger up inside her and scrapes the pregnancy loose. The thing comes out.'

This news filled Ted with alarm. 'You'd shove a coathanger up my bottom?'

'Gibbon says that only works properly in the early months, and the woman sometimes bleeds a lot. He said if the baby's bigger it's best to stick to the gin, to try to cause a miscarriage—'

'Hey! I thought you told him that girl and you did it last term.'

'Yes, but I asked him *what if?* and he told me. The baby would get born prematurely, and die. It could be buried or chucked in the sea. Gibbon'll get the gin for me from an off-licence if I pay him.'

'I'd be drunk. My Mam and Dad would know.'

'It takes three or four hours for a miscarriage. You'd probably have got over being drunk. We can do it this Saturday if you can find a good excuse for being out all day.'

'I'll say I've been invited to a birthday treat. Matinée in the morning, fish and chip lunch in a café, and the skating rink in the afternoon. Where shall we do it?'

'We'd need to be alone. What about the cave? My Grandad mentioned the tide won't be very high this weekend—I'll find out what time it's rising. The sea would cover the rocks but it wouldn't reach the cave.'

'Are you sure?' Ted imagined coastguards, soldiers, police climbing down the cliffs on ropes to rescue them. Even the lifeboat being launched and a breeches-buoy hauling them from drowning.

'Unless there's a storm.'

But there was no storm. When they climbed into Jingling Geordie's Hole that Saturday at ten o'clock the sea was already sluicing across the boulders.

White foals—only junior horses—capered along rock-broken, breeze-flicked waves. In deeper water, swells and gulfs of dark green glass undulated frigidly. The sky was a dismal uniform grey.

The cave was damp though not too chilly. Ted had on his thickest jumper as well as blazer and mac; Gavin likewise, with the addition of a woollen scarf. From his deep mac pocket Gavin pulled a bundle wrapped in the *Shipping Gazette*, unwound a bottle of Gordon's Gin almost as darkly green as the sea; then he produced a small First Aid tin with some bandages and gauze in it. Finally, a chocolate bar and mince pie for himself.

Ted disgorged a crumpled envelope with birthday card inside and something in gift wrapping.

'It's a Dinky tank. Fires matchsticks. Cost my Mam four and sixpence.' Ted tossed the wrapped present aside.

Health and Efficiency and the empty Nivea jar were still where they had left them, though the magazine was now a damp wad, the pages sticking together. Ted thought of other places where they might be doing this. In a pill-box along the dunes? With its machine-gun slits facing the beach where concrete blocks still lay slumped, waiting to repel the Nazi tanks brought on landing craft from Norway...a pillbox with no door, where courting couples went for a feel. There was nowhere else.

Gavin uncapped the bottle. 'Don't swig it like lemonade or you'll cough it up again. Gibbon said so. Get as much down as you can, slowly, and keep on getting it down.'

Ted started swallowing gin.

Though Ted was lying flat he felt desperately ill and dizzy. The cave roof rocked from side to side. The walls rotated. The largest of the slapping waves just below tossed their icy spittle inside, which gave some momentary relief. He sweated, he shivered. His tummy burned and churned. He longed for it to spew out everything, including that living creature that lurked there. But it would have to come out of his bottom, like the biggest turd ever.

Suddenly he did vomit. A stinking flood pumped out over Ted's mac and over weed, as convulsively as though his guts were unreeling through his mouth. Gavin squirmed aside, swearing, 'Bloody *fuck!*' Even after nothing more would come, Ted was still racked by gasping spasms, deep down in him now, doubling him up on his side.

Gavin began to press Ted's midriff excruciatingly.

'You can do it, you filthy little tyke!' he screamed. Ted hardly heard. Waves of pain were squeezing downward rhythmically.

Gavin hadn't *entirely* believed till now. Even though he had felt those spasms in Ted's tummy. The younger boy was loopy because of what he and Gavin had done together. Gavin knew that people could make themselves ill by imagination. If only he could purge Ted, 'catharcize' him—just as Mr Brennan the English teacher said that a tragedy like Marlowe's was supposed to do to the audience. Drive the nonsense out of Ted which had cost Gavin a fountain pen, money, extra hours of homework, worst of all: obligation to Gibbon. Make Ted utterly sick of it! This had been in Gavin's mind as a safety valve of sanity alongside the mad steam-boiler of Ted's impossible pregnancy. A safety valve, till now.

Now Gavin unbuttoned Ted's spew-smeared mac and his blazer and hauled his flannels and underpants off over the shoes. If Ted was to give birth—to believe he was giving birth—he must be naked from the waist down. The sight of Ted's parts gave Gavin no joy now. Swollen, red-streaked tummy. Shrunken knob, wrinkled nuts, hairs. Ted seemed to have passed out, but his midriff convulsed; with each flux the boy's legs slid further apart—and his bottom gaped. Now there could be no doubt in Gavin's mind: the boy *was* giving birth. Having a baby, in a cave cut off by the sea. Gavin backed away up against the cave wall, chilled with dread and disgust.

He forced himself to look.

Ted's anus had split open amidst reeking shit, blood, and yellow juices. Something rather smaller than the boy's head had forced its way out and lay between the spread of his legs, writhing, wriggling.

Was that a miscarriage? A premature baby? Premature meant feeble, weak, unable to survive. Let the thing stop moving, let it die! But it wouldn't; or not immediately. He should snatch it up and toss it in the sea; he'd have to touch it, though. Or bash it with a stone.

Ted looked dead. *I've seen my Teddy bare and now he's dead; the stuffing has come out of him. I didn't kill him!*

Roll Ted's body into the sea? The corpse might float, pointing at the cave where Gavin sat imprisoned.

The thing between Ted's legs thrashed about as if to right itself; as if growing stronger. Gavin crept closer, then jerked back. The baby looked more like an octopus with bulbous body, suckery arms. Or legs. How many?

Where the coat of blood and shit had rubbed off, it was white as cow-tripe, white as cooked cod. Made of strong white rubber. A glossy patch might be an eye; a puckered ridge: a mouth. It was a monster, a terrible deformity. Gavin scrambled to the back of the cave where a hill of stones was piled, rubbed smooth by years and years of sea-grind at highest tide. He cast about for a suitable instrument with which to destroy it. The stones were jammed into a lumpy jigsaw. When he tugged loose an ostrich-egg of speckled, salt-whitened granite another stone shifted of its own accord; then its neighbour, and the next. As if that particular granite egg had been a keystone the whole top of the pile started to slide, scraping and grinding. As Gavin jumped clear, dropping his bludgeon, it almost seemed that the stones were being shoved from behind. High up, an opening appeared—big enough to crawl through.

The creature slithered up over Ted's body. Floppily, fast, it squirmed up the tumbled hill—Gavin shrieked and dodged—and disappeared through the gap.

When his heart stopped thumping Gavin re-armed himself. Cautiously he climbed the slope, having to duck as he came to the gap between stones and roof. The opening appeared to give on to a rough tunnel—faintly visible, extending away upward into almost darkness. If only he had brought his torch today.

Maybe he was just seeing a rear section of the cave, one which the stones had blocked off? Surely there couldn't be a tunnel—not an actual Jingling Geordie one! Why, it would have been discovered years ago, explored, and barricaded with a padlocked iron gate not with a heap of stones. Its existence would be common knowledge, not some legend printed in a Nineteenth Century tome. Yet he perceived a tunnel. Yet a faint foetid breath wafted against his face.

The creature's breath? If such creatures breathed.

He couldn't see it anywhere, though he could see little enough. As his vision adjusted, however, a blob of grey appeared to flee uphill.

Gavin descended to where the half-naked boy lay sprawled with filth and blood between his legs. Discarding the stone, he shook Ted, slapped his cheeks, tried to find a pulse, tried to find a heartbeat. Ted's flesh felt unnaturally cool; bleeding had apparently stopped.

No one knew they were here. Gavin dragged the boy towards the rear of the cave, humped him up the slope. Using all his strength, he eased the body through the opening until Ted's weight finally pulled him down out of sight.

Quickly Gavin collected Ted's trousers and pants, the wrapped present, the card, and stuffed those through the gap, too. After he had crammed the opening tight with fallen stones, he sat to await the sinking of the tide, trying not to think of what was behind him.

An hour later, having looked to see that no one was visible on the pier, he climbed from the cave and worked his way over high slippery boulders, still sloshed by the waves, back to safety; to the stone steps with their rust-bobbled rail that led up from shingle to where the granite pier rooted into the land.

In the early hours Gavin sat up in bed in a sweat of fear. With blankets dragged up to his throat, he pressed his spine against the wallpaper. The bedside lamp, which he'd switched on with a panic hand, illuminated the same familiar bedroom: blue imitation-velvet curtains, untidy work-table, chair with flat orange cushion, full bookcase, calendar of Canadian scenes sent by an aunt that Christmas, ticktocking Swiss chalet clock with chain weighted by a metal fir cone, a long framed school photograph: four ranks of tiny faces all topped by caps, one of them Ted.

Gavin had just dreamt the worst dream of his life, and knew that Ted was linked to him by an invisible cord which could stretch for miles, miles which had no meaning.

Gavin had been within Ted in that dream much more deeply than he'd been within him the previous summer. This time, he'd been wholly inside his skin.

He woke, half-naked on cold rough stone. His tummy, and beneath, was a cavern of dull pain. His head ached.

Light. More in the distance than close by, as though light needed to gain depth before it could show him his surroundings: a tunnel in rock, stretching one way and the other way to the limit of the light, the limit of his eyes.

Ted knelt on bare knees. He noticed clothes nearby. Staggering to his feet he reclaimed his underpants and trousers and managed to draw them on, over a kind of emptiness as though something was missing from him. His mac stank of stale spew; he dragged the raincoat off and dropped it.

Some way along the tunnel he noticed movement. Something small, complicated, and white was climbing along the floor towards him. Pulling, sucking itself along.

He mustn't let it reach him! He began to limp away—but now ahead of him he saw another white thing, twin to the first, an afterbirth, only the second creature was retreating from him as if filled with loathing. As he moved, the thing behind advanced, the thing in front fled. He was a kind of mirror between the two. The one ahead wanted nothing to do with him. The one behind—they were both like swollen white balls dangling long soft cocks—was doing its best to reach him, touch him, cling to him. He feared it would join itself to him suckingly, and though he sensed a hole in himself he didn't want that inside him ever again.

Therefore he must trudge along the tunnel, to escape from one white thing while tormenting the other white thing by pursuing it. He hadn't the strength to overtake the creature ahead, unless it stopped to welcome him; and he hoped it wouldn't. If he himself stopped, the creature behind would catch up. The tunnel seemed to extend from forever to forever, perhaps because space and time had changed.

Night after night Gavin dreamt the same dream, as if Ted was calling to be let out from behind the wall of stones.

Police visited the school to question Ted's classmates. In assembly the headmaster said a prayer for the missing boy and his family, and warned of the dangers of not confiding in one's own parents. Word went around the school that Ted Appleby had killed himself—probably by jumping in the river—since he was depressed at putting on weight and being useless at games. No finger pointed at Gavin. Bill Gibbon may have felt scared and guilty at having persecuted Ted a bit. So if he knew any other explanation, he wasn't saying—even to his big brother.

Brian Gibbon asked Gavin furtively whether the gin had worked.

'Like a bomb,' said Gavin. 'But maybe she wasn't really knocked up in the first place! I think she was having me on.'

'They do. Slags! Did you use a coathanger?'

'She refused. She just drank.'

'She just wanted the gin.'

'She got pissed as a newt and sick as a dog. Serves her right, I say.'

Gibbon nodded, approving Gavin's new worldly wisdom.

The next Saturday Gavin went back to the dreadful cave, to try to purge his dreams. Scrambling to the top of the stone pile at the rear he began pulling the salty granite eggs loose one by one, tumbling them down behind him. Within five minutes he had cleared the upper reaches. He shone his torch.

On blank rock.

No opening, no tunnel, no body, no octopus-baby, nothing! Just the solid back wall of the cave.

For a moment, in spite of his clear recall that there was one cave and one cave only in the cliff, he wondered wildly whether there might be another, very similar, a few yards away. Then his gaze lighted on the empty Nivea jar. Frantically he began unloading all the loosened stones, tossing them out of the cave mouth to crash and bounce down the boulders. Then he attacked the bulk of the pile.

He worked hard. Half an hour later the cave was bare. He had even torn up the weed matting from the floor. He stood gasping for breath in an empty hollow, a barren stone womb. The only way out or in was the way he had come already.

Gavin sat on the stone floor and wept.

That night in the dream for the first time Gavin's perspective altered. Now he himself was the terrified, nauseated creature which groped and sucked its way along that dim tunnel—to escape from the zombi figure of Ted which lumbered helplessly after him.

Images began to form in Gavin's mind. He saw that something ancient existed behind that hollow pocket in the headland known as Jingling Geordie's Hole. It could open up its own spaces when it wished. The previous summer the creature had opened a door from its stone depths, to enter Ted; to put part of itself into him, to grow there for a while. Two weeks ago it had opened the door again, to reclaim itself. And to claim Ted, its spent host.

Why? Its thoughts weren't human thoughts. Maybe it wished to escape, but didn't know how. Maybe it wanted to taste the outside world, like an octopus poking an arm from its lair then pulling it back in again, a phantom, ectoplasmic arm emerging out of stone.

Now it was claiming Gavin too, sucking him through the cord which joined him to the dead boy; who wasn't exactly dead. Just as the creature, though cased in stone, wasn't dead.

Gavin glimpsed a fossil: of a primeval, mutated octopus-thing which possessed strange and terrible persistence, a suction upon existence; which had somehow stayed alive in stone. Imprisoned under prehistoric mud, its flesh had changed to rock during a million years but its whole pattern persisted, the pattern not just of body but of *will.*

Yes, he saw this image clearly now!—as a distant, mute beckoning, from the far end of the tunnel though really the tunnel had no end. Its earlier stretch and its later stretch were the same, eternal stretch.

It must get lonely inside that rock. But the everlasting creature didn't seem to be imaginative. Or insane, or sane. It merely exerted power over the space around it and, over time, power which caused it to survive.

People in the past had sensed its presence: the 'knight'—a naïve medieval youth on a quest for some holy grail?—and the old time smuggler, Geordie, with his trinkets clinking about him, whom it swallowed into the rock as he was stowing kegs of rum or whatever. Possessing them both.

As it had possessed Ted, and was now beginning, from a distance, to possess Gavin . . . until one night soon he would find himself out of bed, dragging coat and shoes on, tiptoeing from the house, hurrying helplessly through the darkness down to the sea, to climb into the cave for one final, everlasting time. The door to the tunnel-which-wasn't-a-tunnel would open and close behind him, and he too would be encased in stone, a fossil continuing to think clinging thoughts, and dream, and sense existence. In the grip of the octopus-wraith, near the ghost-fossils of Ted and the knight and the smuggler who must be insane long since, buried alive in their solid, perpetual, cold hell.

'Only a therm-o-nuclear explosion right above the pier could melt us out of our rock! Turn us to gas and dust, and end us. Could kill the white stone octopus. Bomb the priory, Gav! Get in the crane and rip the cliff open!'

Ted's thoughts were reaching Gavin! Gavin was thinking the boy's thoughts now. Their minds were mingling. Or was the octopus-creature transmitting Ted-like thoughts—which it hardly comprehended? Whichever, Ted and he would have ages together to think such thoughts, ages haunted by a foul noise of monotonous, circulating reverie, degenerating yet never fading. Unless a thermonuclear war broke out.

As if the fear was parent to the deed, the next night Gavin woke to find himself standing in near-darkness. He was out of bed. Something soft clutched at his arms.

Gasping with panic he blundered towards the hidden light switch. Iron fir-cone and Swiss chalet clock flew askew. With his brow he butted the switch. Light blossomed. The thing that was gripping him was his own raincoat, half donned. His sockless feet were stuck into unlaced shoes.

Tearing off the mac and kicking the shoes away, he plunged back under the blankets where he shivered with dread.

That night, or the next night. That week, or the next . . .

Deep within mad Jingling Geordie's Hole, there in the young knight's hell-bound corridor, next to the cracking fossil of Ted: forever the stone ghost waited. Ghost out of ancient Carboniferous seas, prehuman, perpetual. Potent—and imbecilic.

Forever its petrified prisoners whispered their crazed memories of the greed or fierce desire or yearning which had led them into that cave, and which had spurred the living fossil to open its stone door.

Beware the pedicating Tribads!
An erudite erotic essay.

'I cannot speak more plainly without offending decency.'

IN THE HEART OF THE BEAUTEOUS COTSWOLDS, IN CHARMING AND salubrious Stow-in-the-Wold, where shop windows compete with displays of imported Italian nougats the size of wedding cakes, I discovered in a second-hand bookshop the abominable text *De Figuris Veneris* (On the Forms of Sex), *Manual of Classical Erotology* by Fred. Chas. Forberg, published in 1964 by the Medical Press of New York, a limited edition facsimile 'sold by subscription only to doctors, historians, adult students of the classics and psychologists'.

Soon my vocabulary was being swollen by pedicators, irrumators, exoletes, cinedes and drawks, categories of persons who might have strayed from Gene Wolfe's *Book of the New Sun*, yet who are much more ancient and abominable. At the cost of sounding like an erotic H.P. Lovecraft, it's essential to emphasise the abominability of the practices described in Fred. Chas. Forberg's erudite manual of, hmm, love craft, which must needs be concealed from the understanding of less educated members. Of society, I mean.

An unusual feature which helps in this concealment is that the Medical Press of New York's printer apparently possessed no Greek alphabet font, so that when any Greek word occurs this is represented by asterisks, as for example in the footnote from Julius Caesar Scaliger's *Poetica*, book I, p.64: 'One of these infamous dances was the * *** **—involving wiggling haunches and thighs. Do not miss, reader, the motive of this dance, with their buttocks wriggling the girls finally sunk [*sic*] to the ground, reclining on their backs, ready for the amorous contest. Different from this was the Lacedaemonian dance * ** * ** when the girls in their leaps touched their buttocks with their heels.'

Either gentle readers might be too severely assaulted by the actual Greek names, or else the publishers forgot that the book needed the host of asterisks replaced by alphas, betas, gammas and so on before printing the thing. Or maybe medical handwriting is to blame.

How could Fred. Chas. Forberg have been so sloppy, and who was he anyway?

Diligent research (otherwise known these days as googling Wikipedia) uncovers the German philosopher and classical scholar Friedrich Karl Forberg (1770-1849) who gave to the world in 1824 this commentary, *De Figuris Veneris*, upon his edition of an erotic poetry sequence written in Renaissance Latin entitled *Hermaphroditus* authored by Sicilian lawyer, diplomat and chronicler Antonio Beccadelli (1394-1471). By 1887 the poems themselves had been discarded and the commentary alone was printed for Private Circulation Only.

Yet hark, what are those pedicating tribads of whom we must beware? Well now, pedicators are anal penetrators, so far so simple, but tribads (aka frictionists) are women whose clitorises are so well endowed that 'the monstrous organ of love feigns the absent male'; 'The tribad can get it in erection, enter a vulva or anus . . .' Indeed one tribad's organ was as long as the neck of a goose, such prominent women being quite unable to admit a man 'normally'. Now it's quite true that an endocrine disorder can cause clitomegaly in perhaps 5% of the female population (the size of a middle toe being mentioned on some non-porn internet sites), yet there must have been quite a tribe of tribads in antiquity to merit a whole chapter. Or maybe they stood out more back then.

Consider Philaenis, 'tribad of tribads' in the words of the poet Martial, who 'pedicates boys, and stiffer than a man in one day works eleven girls.' A learned footnote comments: 'Instead of "pedicating boys", Martial might have said, if the metre had allowed it, "entering boys". Seneca's expression (Letter XCV), *viros ineunt*, which was a source of great trouble to the great Justus Lipsius, signifies nothing else: "The women will contest for the crown of lubricity with the men. May the gods confound them! One of their refined lubricities reverses the laws of Nature: they have connection with men!" There you have in plain words the turpitude which Justus Lipsius considered worthy of the infernal regions; tribads pedicating.'

Incidentally, this is 'a man's book, written for men', whose virile member should rightly be referred to as a *mentula* (which sounds a bit like a diminutive mind); although as regards personal experience the author declares that 'books are our only authorities. We [the authorial We, I presume, like the royal We] are solely and entirely bookmen, and scarce frequent our fellow creatures at all.' (Which was when Lovecraft came to mind, though not to mentula.)

It's wonderful what a range of depravities one can encounter in a library. 'The pleasure felt by the patient by the introduction of the member in his entrails is more difficult to make out,—at least for my feeble intelligence, for such practises are quite strange to me.' Why, then, do you catalogue those remorselessly, Mein Herr? Have you not at least *siphnianized* once or twice experimentally? Footnote: 'In order to appease the ardours of the anus, the Siphnians (Siphnos, one of the Cyclades) were in the habit of introducing a finger up the anus.' To such an extent, apparently, that this practice left a permanent mark on the island.

Yet maybe the author felt too inhibited. After all, Jean-Jacques Rousseau confesses that he passed through life coveting, yet not daring to tell the persons he most loved, that he would enjoy a good thrashing.

Alas, as with the asterisks, frequent references to numbered illustrative plates in *Monuments de la vie privée des douze Césars* elude one, unless one happens to have a copy of that tome in one's gentleman's private library, many of the unnumbered and unexplained batch of pictures at the end of the Medical Press of New York edition being taken through a glass rather darkly.

What else can we learn that is useful?

It was the Cretans who pioneered pederasty, which the English abominate, allegedly. Outstanding among the 'scrupulous ancients' is Diogenes who masturbated in the market place, remarking, 'I would to heaven I could in the same way satisfy my stomach by rubbing when it barks for food'; which drew the praise of stoical Chrysippus.

Beware of inviting a disgraceful recipient of irrumation to supper, since (doubtless due to the absence of good toothpaste), the foul breath of the mouth used by fellators betrays that this fellow is fond of sucking mentulas, rather than mints. Either deny him a cup of wine, or make sure that you smash the cup afterwards. Confusingly, to *lesbianize* is to use a man's mouth abominably. (Resulting of course in bad breath.) An oiled leather dildo may benefit from pepper and crushed nettle seeds.

Do suck in your breath to increase the size of your member; then people will cheer appreciatively when you enter the public baths. If taking an important message, for instance to the Emperor Galba, first shave your anus using dropax or psilothrum unguent, rosin melted in oil, or a plaster of hot pitch, since Galba joyfully buggered the chap who carried the news of Nero's death to him in Spain; it's only polite to be properly prepared—boiled bottom polished by pumice. Not for nothing did Spartianus describe Hadrian (he of the Roman Wall, the Library of Athens, and other notable edifices) as a great depilator who corrupted the freedmen of Trajan (he of the Column) by bum-shaving.

Whereas, young ladies, rejoice that a beauteous posterior is a dowry in itself (or its twin selves)—unless you happen to marry a pedicating neglecter of vulvas and are obliged to cry aggrievedly: I also have *buttocks*! This book lends a whole new meaning to passages from the Ancients, although might it occasionally be that scholarly commentators are hallucinating?

Assuredly 'nothing is more common in Egypt at the present day [presumably the 1820s] than for young women to have intercourse with the he-goats'—but does this passage from Plutarch's treatise *On the Sagacity of Animals*—'Quite lately our excellent Philinus, on returning from a long voyage to Egypt, told me that he had seen at Antaeopolis an old woman sleeping with a crocodile stretched comfortably beside her on her pallet'—really mean in subtle code that the old lady had first submitted to the lust of the crocodile? Regarding such shameless wantons, 'Observe the subtlety of the expression adopted by the poet: "offers her buttocks to an ass to get on them." Juvenal knows, wise chap, that a woman has no chance to have an ass's mentula in her except by turning her back to the beast' ('offers her ass to an ass' might be a better contemporary translation). Oddly, Plutarch in that same treatise, reports—dear me, concerning Egypt again—that the he-goat 'shut up with a great number of women, all of them beautiful, refused to have anything to do with them, and prefers goats by far.' No accounting for bestial tastes!

A passage from Ovid's Metamorphoses, III, 308-12, reads thus: '. . . Mortal woman could not survive the celestial fire; she was consumed by her spouse's favours. The infant but half formed is torn from the mother's womb, and, if we may believe the tale, is sown still immature in the father's thigh, and there completes the period of gestation.' Upon which our learned guide comments: 'This scarcely needs an explanation. You can picture the *cunnilingue*, with his mouth glued between the thighs, at work.' Silly me, this interpretation had simply not occurred, even though my novel *Converts* is a version of Ovid's *Metamorphoses*. Nor had I known that babes wail inside their mother's womb at a tongue in the vulva. In my defence, and for clarity, I can only call upon page 168: 'Homer taught you to call voice ****; but who taught you to have the tongue **** (in a slit)?' 'The unknown poet plays upon the ambiguity of the word ****, which is used with respect to the tongue in an honest sense, when derived from ****, I speak, but as a vile usage when derived from ***, a slit.' Is that perfectly clear?

Any problems encountered are caused by us not being educated enough. Occasionally the anonymous translator (who often sounds quite like Lovecraft) intervenes: 'To understand this, the sentence must be complete; the worthy Forberg takes his readers far too learned ...' Later, confusingly, in the main text we find (p 202): 'Lucian's witty and licentious pen has made famous another tribad, Megilla ... the virginal modesty of our Wieland has not dared to translate it into German.' Why on Earth the good Forberg is equated with Wieland/Wayland the Smith, the Vulcan of northerly legend eludes me, except that Wieland's sword was so sharp that it cut a rival down to his thigh (so that he fell apart as soon as he moved) rather as Forberg dissects ancient passages concerned with thighs, and that Wieland was a bit hamstrung (though also a rapist, in one version).

We must be assured that the doctors and psychologists of 1964 who subscribed to the Medical Press of New York edition were more educated than we are today in these degenerate times when sex is spoken of openly anywhere, except perhaps in North Korea.

As to how a rare copy of the erudite text ended up in a bookshop in Stow-on-the-Wold (along with two complete bookcases of similar material) I can only assume that it came from the private library of an educated local gentleman, deceased.

Yet I remain haunted by the vision of pedicating tribads roaming the rolling local sheep pastures and woodlands, snacking for energy on giant wodges of nougat embedded with pistachios and strawberries.

King Weasel

DIANE COBBETT WAS DRIVING ALONG THE NARROW, TWISTY ROAD from Upton to Woodburn of a Saturday afternoon. Beside her, pile of exercise books balanced on his knee, Saul Cobbett was grading maps of imaginary nature reserves drawn by his class of twelve-year-olds. In the back of the ageing Renault young Tim turned the pages of a comic while his younger brother Josh steered a model harvester around the seat as though it was a racing car.

Tim had already begun school; Josh would follow in another year. Diane would go back to teaching then. Craft and Design; preferably in the same school as Saul, or else they would need two ageing cars. The family income would rise; lean times would be over.

No doubt several years of belt-tightening had fully justified themselves—in the production of Tim and Josh. In some other respects . . . Saul stared at the bare, October-sodden, misty fields and hummed a low dirge-like noise, of unvoiced, displaced complaint which the car engine mostly drowned.

Stuck on her own in a small village with two young kids, energetic Diane had become—what was the diplomatic word?—obsessive.

It wasn't that Saul jibbed at their totally vegetarian diet. That made financial as well as moral sense. It even made gastronomic sense, since Di worked wonders with spinach quiches, vegetable curries, spiced rice, pea soup. The last time Saul had tasted meat, by necessity—a greasy lamb cutlet which was all that the school canteen had remaining on offer that day—he'd felt disgusted and contemptuous.

It wasn't that nowadays Diane would shake her fist and shout abuse at passing fox-hunters, any of whom might easily be local school governors who might interview her in future and would remember her bouncy chestnut hair, her Rubens milkmaid looks. He totally agreed with Di's hatred of the hunt and all its costumed, bullying, thundering arrogance.

It wasn't that the boys had certain toys taken away from them, others denied to them. Obviously kids oughtn't to play with imitation weapons. And Josh had hardly brooded over the fact that his model farm was culled of its four plastic pigs and two plastic turkeys by Di—since pigs and turkeys were reared for one purpose only: slaughter.

Nor was it the recollection of Tim's tears when they finally released his pet rabbit into the wild that April. Tim had agreed bravely, or seemed to. Diane had prepared the boys well for the great event, so that it seemed a triumph both practical and sentimental. Di couldn't bear to see Teddy-bun captive behind chicken-wire any longer. He should bound free, find a mate, build a burrow with a rooty doorway on the edge of the copse by the safe-looking pasture they chose. Better one summer of liberty and a natural death than life imprisonment. Teddybun had run off quickly enough, tail bobbing as if in agreement. They had waited a whole hour, picnicking on salad sandwiches, in case he came back; but he hadn't—and they were saved the labour of feeding and watering the rabbit and shovelling up its latrine-full of droppings once a fortnight which had earned Saul one nasty bite on the knuckle from the robbed animal. He fully agreed with the *evil* of captive animals. Their own efforts for Teddybun's welfare, prior to liberation, had shown how wretchedly most pet rabbits must fare with cramped hutches, monotonous diets, insufficient water, a dozen other thoughtless cruelties. The notion that rabbits *liked* eating dry hay and their own droppings!

It wasn't just . . .

The Renault rounded a bend. Ahead on the crown of the road a creature thrashed about in broken agony.

Despite the boys loose in the back, Diane instantly stamped on the brake. 'Something's been run over! The bastards didn't stop!'

With the rubbery resilience of kids, Josh and Tim had survived the abrupt stop, though Josh was now bleating, 'Me howitzer! Me howitzer's lost!'

'Harvester,' Saul corrected automatically.

Tim was more interested in the spectacle ahead and in the word 'bastard' which he repeated as though that was the name of the afflicted animal.

Once Diane opened her door and leapt out, the writhing creature promptly disentangled. A sleek russet-furred worm on legs raced for sanctuary in the grass verge; a gray rabbit lurched, staggered, and fell over.

No road victim, this. A weasel had been clinging to the frantic rabbit's neck, about to kill it. Thrusting school books on to Diane's seat, Saul climbed out; Tim also came.

The assaulted rabbit lay panting in shock, making no effort to escape from the approaching giants.

'I don't see any blood,' Saul said.

'Mum!' Tim pointed at the verge. Amid the long grass a lithe little body stood upright. Up on its hind legs the weasel was staring at them with fixed, beady malevolence, with outright hatred.

Saul clapped his hands. 'Shoo! Buzz off!'

The weasel seemed to quiver with intensity—its only concession to movement.

Saul gathered the rabbit carefully into his arms since it couldn't stay in the centre of the road. A scrappy, skinny beast, it only weighed a fraction of what Teddybun had massed; though maybe now, six months later, Teddybun too was as light as this wretched starveling. Mud immediately smeared any part of Saul's anorak which the rabbit touched; it was damp and filthy. But it kicked powerful hind legs a couple of times.

'There, there, poor little thing,' crooned Saul, to quiet it. 'Seems in working order. At least the weasel didn't have time to snap its spine.'

He walked to the nearer verge and deposited the rabbit, which scrambled a very short way before flopping. The weasel watched all this alertly.

'We can't leave it here,' protested Diane. 'The moment we're gone, the weasel will nip across. It's just waiting.'

Saul gathered the rabbit up again. 'I'll carry it a hundred yards down the road. You drive after me. It's half-paralysed with shock. Maybe it can't survive.'

'Can't? Do you suggest putting it out of its misery? With a stone, or a punch?'

'I'd probably bungle it.' Accompanied by Tim, Saul walked on; soon the Renault purred slowly after.

When Saul next laid the rabbit on the grass, it was no more energetic. Across the way, the thin russet body reared again, glaring inflexibly. Refusing to quit, the weasel had kept pace. Its mouth opened. It seemed to hiss at them through tiny sharp teeth, though the sound was inaudible.

'What bloody cheek! I suppose this was its supper. Look at my coat. All filthy from it.'

'Why don't we take the rabbit home, Dad? Nurse it, then bring it back when it's better? We still have Teddybun's run and rabbit pellets.'

'No. We just got rid of one captive animal.'

'It's unfair! It'll die.'

'We're responsible,' Diane called intensely, from the car.

'For everything in the world?'

'For this little bit of everything, where we interfered.'

Saul sighed. Shucking off the soiled anorak, he wrapped the rabbit securely, head and ears protruding. Then he climbed back into the car, where the school books were lying on the floor.

As Diane engaged gear and pulled away, Saul noticed the weasel darting along the verge, rearing to gaze vindictively. A rainbow sticker on the rear window announced: ECOLOGY IS OUR ONLY HOPE. Another stated: BAN CRUEL SPORTS. The Renault very quickly outdistanced the brown smudge.

Saul stroked the rabbit's head, then desisted. Maybe he was terrifying, not comforting the limp animal. Instead he stroked his own beard—that of a younger Solzhenitsyn, said Di—without which his face might have looked at once morose and undistinguished. Those whiskers gave to a puddingy countenance and gimlet eyes a certain messianic nobility.

Terrifying the animal.

He remembered . . .

When Saul and Diane first got married they had lived in a small town flat. They had acquired a pair of chipmunks, plus a large cage with an exercise wheel. That was because they loved animals. However, they were out all day so it would be cruel to keep a dog or cat.

Every time they returned home one of the chipmunks would instantly leap into the wheel and rotate it vigorously *(be-dum, be-dum)* as if in glad greeting. The other would scrabble up one side of the cage, over the roof, and down the other *(be-doom be-doom)*. Up, and over, and down.

Only after some months did it occur to Saul that the chipmunks ran because they were terrified, but there was hardly anywhere to run to. One day he and Diane decided to let Ben and Babs out for an exploration of the living room. Lifting the cage down from its table and opening the wire door, they sat back with quiet pleasure to watch adventures.

Ben's and Babs' twitching noses explored the open gap many times before they dared venture further. Ten minutes went by before the chipmunks at last tumbled out and began to move around the floor. They didn't exactly run, or walk. Instead they plucked themselves along at considerable speed like absurd clockwork toys with wheels in their bellies. They seemed to have no idea how to use their legs normally. After a lifetime spent in cages they had the wrong muscles. Their mode of locomotion was disgusting, as though Ben and Babs weren't furry little pets after all but bags of hairy entrails equipped with claws. Saul rose to pick them up and put them back.

Both chipmunks evaded him. Running flat on their bellies, however ungracefully, they escaped him time and again. At last he'd snatched at a passing chipmunk. His hand closed not on its body but on its tail . . . and that tail came off in his fingers. He clutched, in horror, a twitching bottle-brush; dropped it immediately in disgust. Ben—or Babs—ran on, a long thin spike sticking out from the animal's rump, flicking a drop of blood from the end, then another, the inner core of the tail.

He'd finally trapped each chipmunk separately under a cane wastepaper basket and restored each to the cage. Ben—or Babs—sat beady-eyed, side heaving, seemingly impervious to the loss of its bushy brush.

Over the next few days the raw spike had dried up, withered, fallen off. A week later Saul and Diane took the cage down into the shared, wild garden to set the furry pets free. Though so much like squirrels in appearance, Ben and Babs didn't flee to the nearest leafy tree. They scrambled into an open drain and vanished down it like two sewer rats.

That, in retrospect, had been the beginning of the eventual liberation of Teddybun, of the purging of pork from Josh's toy farm, of fists brandished at riders, of Diane's protestations that all pet shops should be banned. And sideshows at fairs which dangled prizes of goldfish in asphyxiating bags. And. And.

The Ben-and-Babs episode had elements of farce, didn't it? Farce for the humans; horror for the animals. Or was the horror largely in the minds of sensitive people? And had that horror now burrowed so deep into Di— much as he agreed with her, a hundred percent—that it was like a tumour in her brain: deranging her behaviour?

She too had been shut up in a cage, of sorts, for the past few years together with two monkeys, namely Josh and Tim.

Saul wondered as he tugged at his Russian beard. No, of course she was right.

'Can't we keep him, Dad?'

'Of course not, Tim.'

It was the following Saturday morning and they were due to make another trip, to buy toilet rolls and such; and to return the rabbit to its native hedgerow.

Behind chicken-wire the rabbit was cleaning its coat, burrowing and biting at fur. Matted bunches of hair sprouted like tatty tusks alongside its whiskers. It had gorged on pellets and muesli and sultanas, lettuce and cabbage leaves and carrots cut into sticks. Not *too* many green leaves; must avoid bloat. It had failed to learn to use Teddybun's drinking bottle, and had spilled many saucers of water by standing in them. And it had made free with the huge, ever-open, several-chambered, hay-carpeted rabbit house which Diane had adapted and extended from the original hutch. Yet the animal still seemed feeble.

'If we take him back to the fields he'll die.'

'Why should he?'

'Winter's coming.'

'So?'

'He's been hurt, worried. If he was a person he'd stay in a hospital.'

Saul saw the logic of this. Besides, what was the point of a spacious rabbit house and run without any rabbit in it? Diane had once spoken of turning the entire garden into a rabbit habitat, a rabbitorium. That was when they were still wrestling with the ethical problem of Teddybun. Even so, the rabbitorium residents wouldn't really have been free to race and leap as the whim took them. Also, they would have devoured all the vegetables, undermining the Cobbett family economy.

The run, with grass and a few paving slabs underfoot, was built along the back of the modernised stone cottage so that a kitchen window looked into it. The quarter-acre beyond was entirely devoted to vegetable plots, fruit under netting, a herb garden and an area for compost bins and bonfires. A rotary washing line acted as a good bird-scarer when the wind blew and shirt sleeves flapped. Before the Cobbetts moved in, there had been a zone of delphiniums and roses, but they had rooted those out for greater economy. The view was arguably ugly but the immediate neighbours weren't compelled to look at it, and the Cobbetts rarely invited anyone in. They preferred to live a self-sufficient life. The boys were encouraged to play on the green out front. The Sandersons next door had actually had the nerve to complain about the washing Diane so often hung out, and about the frequent bonfires; Saul had told them to mind their own business. There had also been a quarrel about ownership of the boundary fence—the Sandersons were very territorial—which Saul resolved by rearing an inner barrier of tall poles and chicken-wire to grow beans.

Just then, Diane came outdoors holding a cardboard box.

'Tim doesn't want the new Teddybun to go,' Saul said.

'It's not fair, Mum. He's still ill.'

The rabbit hopped over to the latrine which it had by now assembled and let loose a dozen more gray marbles. It nosed and nibbled a couple, exposing green sludge. The real Teddybun had never eaten his own excrement; the Teddybun Hilton was permanently well-stocked with meals, however the guest rabbit had the habits of the wild. Half-digested food shouldn't go to waste without reprocessing. Dung was always good for another trip through the stomach.

Of course, the latrine was also designed to attract passing females. Their guest was a buck, with genitals like flabby red strips of smoked cod-roe pasted under his bob-tail. He wasn't in season right now, but rabbits were generally preoccupied with a cocktail of droppings, territory, food, and sex.

'He's weak as water, Mum. He couldn't run away from a farmer with a rifle! Or a hound.'

With childhood cunning Tim had pressed the right buttons. His mother chewed at her lip, dubiously.

'Yes, we're responsible,' she said. 'We've committed *crimes* against animals. He can stay another week.'

As soon as the Renault had turned on to the by-road to Upton, Diane called to the boys in the back, 'Which of my animals shall I summon?'

'Fox!' cried Josh.

'Muntjak Deer,' suggested Tim.

'They're too shy,' said Saul. 'Only come out from dusk to dawn.' The Cobbetts had only ever seen one diminutive Muntjak, crossing the road in their headlights late one evening.

'Badger, then!'

And the only badger they'd ever seen was a bear-like corpse by the road-side, swiped by some careless driver. Elsewhere in the county illegal badger-baiting still occurred. Sets were dug up; a badger was dragged out and forced to fight dogs to the death, to the terrible damage of dogs too. It made one's blood boil.

'A fox,' said Diane. 'Let's hope there isn't a hunt today.' She wound her window down and called at the countryside, 'Come, fox!'

The idea of 'calling her animals' was recent, and amused the kids, whatever the outcome. Saul recalled the school sixth-formers acting Shakespeare's *Henry the Fourth* in the gym the previous Christmas. 'I can call spirits from the vasty deep,' blustered Glendower, the loud-mouthed Welshman. And Hotspur replied, 'Why, so can I, or so can any man. But will they come when you do call for them?' This was a game, yet there was true passion in Diane's voice.

'Come to me, fox!'

Saul spied quick movement in the verge ahead. A little russet head on a furry snake-like body shot up to stare at the approaching car.

'Weasel!'

Diane braked. The Cobbetts stared at the animal; it glared back viciously. 'That's the same one!' cried Tim. 'Good job we didn't bring Rabbit.'

Saul snorted. 'This is nowhere near. Another couple of miles on.'

'Same weasel, Dad.'

'Nonsense.'

Diane was gazing mesmerised. Leaning over, Saul snapped his fingers in front of her eyes.

'Don't! Look what you've done!' The weasel had dropped low, masked by grass.

For a while Diane drove on in silence, then she said over her shoulder, 'Yes, Tim, we'll keep the rabbit over winter. We'll let him go free in the spring.'

'Keep him captive?' asked Saul. 'Is that consistent with our principles?'

'I'll feed him and clean him—you needn't worry. He's my responsibility. In fact, don't you dare go inside his run at all! You just make empty noises about principles.'

'What do you mean by that?'

'Last month you said, "What'll happen to pigs and turkeys when everybody's a vegetarian? They'll probably go extinct." As though eating them was a kindness!'

'I didn't exactly—'

'It's better if pigs *do* go extinct, than live in concrete Belsens then be trucked screaming to the slaughter. We should join the Animal Liberation Front if we had any contacts.'

'I think,' Saul said carefully, 'that most A.L.F. people live in towns. We'd stick out like a sore thumb, living in a little village. The police would hear about us immediately.' Though of course he agreed one hundred per cent.

'And the Hunt Saboteurs! If only we knew someone.'

He realised that they were verging on a quarrel yet he still felt perversely moved to mutter, 'Funny sort of fox, that was. Same habits, though.'

Diane darted him a look as furious as the weasel's.

A couple of hours later, on the return journey, the Renault had already reached the main road down into Woodburn when Tim squealed, 'There it is again! Over in that field!'

Though Saul swung round, he saw nothing except ploughed earth. Amidst the sea of clods he hardly expected to make out one little slinky brown body. Tim couldn't reasonably have seen one, either.

'Be quiet.' The boy was pressing buttons again trying to stir up trouble.

'It's heading for Woodburn, Mum.'

'Drivel,' said Saul angrily. 'There'll be fifty different weasels between here and where we found the rabbit.'

A pheasant in almost tartan plumage erupted from the near verge, winged low across the road, narrowly missing being struck down.

'My God, we nearly *hit* it,' cried Diane. 'That's your fault, Saul, distracting me. We ought to drive more slowly.' She proceeded to do so, down on into the village.

And perhaps somebody from Woodburn would hit the same pheasant the very next day, with a blast from a shotgun; and eat the bird, after shaking out the lead pellets.

Tim said, 'Mum.'

'What?'

'Kevin Bantock's hamster died. Blood came out of it.'

'*How?*'

'They've got him an albino guinea pig.'

'To live in the *same size* cage?'

'The cage and toys cost a lot.'

'Oh God. People shouldn't be allowed!'

Tim was making absolutely certain that they kept the rabbit and lavished care on it. By way of apology and recompense.

Sunday afternoon. From the kitchen, Tim shrilled, 'Mum! Dad! Mum!'

Saul and Diane arrived simultaneously, to witness outside the window a weasel sneaking into the rabbit run through the chicken-wire. Saul rapped on the glass so hard that he punched a hole in the pane.

'Bugger!' His hand bled.

Diane had run outside and was tearing at the hooks on the wire gate of the run, while the weasel hesitated, half way to the open hutch. As she dragged the gate open, the invader snaked through the wire and away.

Licking his wound and spitting, Saul rushed outside too. He wrestled a handkerchief from his jeans pocket to wrap his fingers.

Diane checked the rabbit. 'He's all right. Chicken-wire's no protection! We'll have to bring him indoors. Fetch a cardboard box for him. We'll shift the hutch, and the wire. I'll reconstruct it all in the kitchen.'

'What? I'll flatten the bloody weasel with a spade first.'

'You'll never catch it. Tim, fetch a box!'

'That was the same weasel, Dad.'

'Impossible.'

Several hours later the rabbit's relocated quarters occupied a full third of the kitchen. The hutch complex stood within a fence of chicken-wire nailed to frames stabilised by a wall of old bricks piled two deep. The rabbit was laying down a new latrine of vegetable ball bearings on the linoleum; unfortunately its droppings rolled all over. Saul had pinned cardboard, cut from the box, over the broken pane to exclude the draught. A replacement pane would have to wait till the following Saturday.

He looked out into the dusk. In the light cast from the window a slim shape slunk from behind a cabbage, then reared on its hind legs to return his stare, eyes gleaming bright.

'It's there again! It won't give up. Tim's right: that's the same animal, miles from where it started out. It's . . . like a Fury! Pursuing us.' Diane had joined him. 'Ah, it ducked.'

'Do you suppose it has rabies?' she asked. 'I mean, such mad persistence.'

'You're persistent too. That doesn't mean—' He didn't complete the sentence. 'It wants its meal. We stole its meal. Maybe we condemned it to starve.'

'If it's starving, it made a damn long journey. Like us walking all the way to London.'

'This isn't natural, Di. Weasels don't act that way. A *cat* might walk for miles, and even hold a grudge. Or a dog. Maybe,' he hesitated, 'we should put the rabbit out for it.'

'What a mad, sick thing to say.'

'If not, we'll have to catch it and kill it.'

'But there's no reason to kill it,' she said indignantly. 'It'll go away.'

'What, after following scent for miles?'

'The scent *of a car?*'

'If we got ourselves a pussy cat,' said Tim, 'it would stop the weasel.'

No one replied. They could never adopt a cat. Canned cat-food was made out of the offal from slaughterhouses.

A noise woke Saul that night. Loud thumpings. Switching on lights, he hurried downstairs; slammed on the kitchen light. In its hutch the rabbit was going crazy. The weasel stalked the run.

With a howl of rage which froze the rabbit Saul hoisted one of the bricks and hurled it at the intruder. Wallpaper burst down by the floor, spewing dusty plaster. The weasel had dodged up and through the chicken-wire, to vanish from sight.

Saul jumped to the window, tore the curtain aside. His cardboard draught-stopper hung loose.

'Saul! What is it?'

'Guard the stairs, Di! Weasel's in the house. The rabbit's still okay.'

He heard her descending.

'Guard them!'

'I don't see any weasel,' she said from the kitchen door.

He gestured. 'Got in the window. It pushed the cardboard loose.'

'You mean you didn't pin it properly. Weasels don't climb into houses.'

'I saw it right there!'

'God, the wallpaper's smashed to pieces. What a filthy mess.'

'I missed it, Di.'

'And maybe you were aiming at the rabbit. Wake up! I'm living with a loony sleepwalker.' She crossed to the window, flicked at his cardboard makeshift, then stabbed a triumphant finger. 'See?'

He saw: six feet away, a weasel standing up on its hind legs, looking at the lighted window.

'So it's still hanging about,' she said, 'but it certainly wasn't inside.'

'Damn thing must have shot through the hole . . . but I'm sure it didn't. I'd have seen.'

'I hate broken sleep. Fix that stupid cardboard back. I'll nail some hardboard on tomorrow. And close the curtain.' She went back upstairs.

As he turned to restore the cardboard, three weasels watched him from outside; his heart chilled.

He snatched the powerful, rubber-sheathed torch from its hook, killed the kitchen light, and pressed the torch to the neighbouring pane. The yellow beam lanced out across sprouts and cabbages, across movement. A rippling of the earth. A wave of small creatures.

'Di!' he screamed. 'Come back down!'

She returned shortly, swearing. A single weasel stood sentinel in the torch beam. 'I . . . I saw more than one.'

'Oh, did you?'

'I swear.'

'How many?'

'Three together. Behind, a carpet of them. Hundreds. It was as if . . . "Come, my animals!"—and they all came.'

'So that's it. Because I criticised you, justifiably, in the car. You're being hateful.'

'Di! Please believe me. There's one loose in the house already—with us and the boys; and the rabbit.'

'I wouldn't be likely to forget the rabbit, would I?'

'Why should we deserve this? Is it because . . . if we have our way, and piggeries and pet-shops disappear, and no one eats meat or keeps animals, the weasels of the world will go hungry?'

'Do you think weasels eat steak and pork? They eat wild mice, wild rats, wild birds! You're the weasel. Look at your nasty little vicious watery eyes. Find somewhere else to sleep tonight. Don't come in my bedroom.'

She dashed upstairs, tossed his pillow down a moment later, slammed the bedroom door. He heard the bolt click home. So he perched a brick on the windowsill to wedge the repinned cardboard—there were no weasels visible at all—then closed the curtain and took his pillow through to the lounge, pulling the door softly shut behind him.

He lay coldly and rigidly on the sofa. He couldn't sleep. After maybe fifteen minutes he rose and went through to the kitchen to eat some chocolate.

Behind its chicken-wire the rabbit lay dead like a bunch of ghastly rag. Blood, guts mixed with half-digested green mush, spilled out of it over the yellow lino. Saul staggered, sick at heart.

He visualised: himself running upstairs, pounding on the bedroom door, even smashing the bolt off in his urgency to make Di understand that the rabbit was dead, torn open, but that *he* hadn't gutted it—a weasel had, a weasel which was loose in the house, hiding, waiting to emerge again.

He also imagined: Di refusing to believe that he was innocent, herself becoming a Fury, tearing at his beard and cheeks in rage and mortal fear as she drove him from the house—'Sleep in the car!'—and locked him out, there where the weasels awaited, a thick carpet of sharp-toothed fur. But he might reach the unlocked Renault, and sanctuary while Di and the boys were left to invasion by the weasels. That single brick wouldn't keep them out.

Why was he imagining this violent scene? He and Di were pacifists as well as vegetarians! Was this some form of rebellion by the beast locked up deep within him? Something malign was tampering with his mind. Blood-lusts were imprinting themselves, or surfacing: the frenzy of a fox in a hen-house, of a weasel on a rabbit's neck. He felt appalled.

The weasel had effectively given them the evil eye—for there was a fury in the home too. That was Di's rage, the rage of a tiger, at everyone who oppressed animals, exploited them, made them suffer.

No one but Saul had seen that pack of weasels outside. Only he had witnessed the invader in the kitchen. Could he have imagined those others? Could he have killed the rabbit himself? Dragged it from its hutch, snapped its neck, and disembowelled it—without knowing his own actions? He examined his hands. Clean. His pyjamas. No blood stains. No yellow streaks of rabbit piss which was like pus. No green slime.

He crossed to the window, shifted the curtain cautiously, wary of being bitten.

The brick had moved. The cardboard hung loose again. Window ledge, tiles, even the steel draining board were patterned as though dozens of tiny feet, muddy from damp soil, had scampered across.

How many of the beasts had already got in and hidden? How many were waiting to slip through any door that opened? Or reach other rooms by way of fireplaces and chimneys? Sooty, oblique chimney-bricks should offer plenty of footholds for claws. He suddenly felt as scared of remaining in the house as of being forced to leave to race to the Renault to shut himself in its tin shell. As quietly as could be he restored the brick to its former position, then added two more from among those buttressing the chicken-wire.

He needed a weapon. A hammer to smash weasel skulls. No, something handier. A poker. Tiptoeing to the illuminated lounge, he hefted the fire-iron. Sneaking to the foot of the dark stairs, he switched on the upper light.

From half way up, to as high as the landing, the stair carpet was hidden by a mass of weasels. On the landing itself, dominating them, one particular weasel stood upright as though making a speech to its troops. Unmistakable: the eyes, the gaze, the poise. A few subaltern heads shifted to register Saul's presence, but otherwise the weasels made no move.

A terrible understanding dawned on Saul, as a thin piping voice pierced his head:

'*You stole from the Weasel of Weasels! From the Archweasel.*'

He couldn't actually be hearing the creature speak! A weasel couldn't use words. Its brain couldn't know them. Somehow Saul's mind was translating what the weasel felt: the message coded by its beady eyes.

'*All species of animals possess a king, a master beast. One which incarnates weaseldom, amongst weasels. Frogdom, amongst frogs. Rabbitdom, amongst rabbits. I raised such a furore in my tribe, across many days' journey of land. They converged here, rallied to their king.*'

A psychic furore . . . because the weasel they had robbed had *understood* that it was archweasel. Perhaps not many archanimals ever knew. When one archanimal died, another beast of its kind was born to be archanimal, and had a chance to know itself.

Saul reeled at this strange knowledge.

'*Two* archanimals of any species, surely?' he whispered.

Archmale—and archfemale. Just as had walked into the Ark in the legend. Preserve the archweasels, male and female, and the whole of weaseldom could be reborn, could spill out from their loins in all its variety.

Likewise with every other species. Just as the whole human race had spilled out from Adam and Eve—which was the true meaning of *that* legend. Primitive, primitive, these myths of the Ark and of Adam! Deeply, primevally engraved.

Early man, closer to nature, must have known that archanimals existed. Hence the concept of the totem animal. That knowledge persisted, deeply buried. It rose in Saul this night.

How could that be? Unless...

'*I* am the archhuman! Out of all the human males alive on the planet today, I—Saul Cobbett—am it!'

Someone had to be. A definite individual with a name, and a home, and a life.

Watching the archweasel watch him, Saul felt hot, glowing, illuminated. Conscious as never before.

Maybe Jesus Christ had been an archhuman too. When Jesus was thirty years old he realised this, and interpreted his new-found knowledge according to his milieu—as Messiah.

Adolf Hitler had almost made himself into a war-god, inexplicably...

Some archhumans might never awaken to the fact. Others might be born in a remote jungle where even their neighbours were strange foreigners; they would still be the archhumans of their time, until they died.

'Who's the archhuman female today?'

Diane? Hardly. She would have seen the horde of weasels massing in the garden; been impelled to see them. She would be seeing them on the stairs right now. The archfemale could well be Chinese or Indonesian or a Russian citizen. She might be seventy years old, or newly born.

'How did you realise who you are, Archweasel? Unless... my own scent awoke you, last week! My aura, as archhuman. Just as your aura has awakened me.'

The archweasel glanced away, sank down as if in compliance. Then it raised its head, and spat-hissed defiantly—for why should it submit? It made no move to lead its band against Saul, to attack. He felt that an uneasy truce prevailed.

'Shouldn't my face be more full of character? More startling, more defined—with mesmeric eyes, or signs of grace?'

Why so, if he was Everyman? Maybe the sheer volume of people alive today diluted, rather than enhanced?

Saul thought momentarily of the Pied Piper, who had charmed the horde of rats led by the Rat King. Another legend of an archhuman? One who had led away all the sons and daughters of Hamelin. As Saul gazed at the weasel army hugging the stairs he chuckled, then laughed aloud.

He needn't try to smash these weasels with the poker. Why should he be aiming to kill the archweasel—instead of acknowledging a fellow archbeing of a different species?

Pied Piper.

Saul started to whistle loudly, then to sing:

'Oh I'll take the high road

And ye'll take the low road—!'

'Shut up!' Diana shouted from inside the bedroom. So she wasn't asleep. However, she didn't open the door to see.

Whistling again, still keeping his eye on the archweasel, Saul withdrew towards the kitchen. The weasel army turned about, flowed downstairs. He leaned over the chicken-wire, spitted the rabbit on the poker through a loop of intestines, hoisted it, detached it. Tossing the fire-iron clatteringly on to the draining board, he carried the corpse to the back door. Weasels poured steadily after him.

Striding out into the night, now less coaly thanks to a risen gibbous moon, and still whistling, he threw the dead rabbit away from him. The weasel flood parted around him, to claim and devour their prize. One weasel alone stood aloof, watching the fray.

Disturbed, and perhaps also scenting blood, the Sandersons' Doberman— which was kept outside *every night,* even in the winter—began to bark frenziedly. The archweasel took to its heels, away through the cabbages. Its whole army followed, a wave quitting a shore and not returning. Saul was left alone with himself, and the moon, and his knowledge. He stopped whistling.

A light had gone on upstairs in the Sandersons', and he thought that someone was staring from a darker window. However, the guard dog calmed and presently the light went out.

'So,' said Diane as she scanned the vacant run. Saul had cleaned most of the mess off the lino before she came down.

Josh was still abed but Tim had to be breakfasted and readied to catch the primary school bus. Within half an hour Saul was due to drive off to the comprehensive school. He swallowed black chicory coffee which was still too hot.

'Where's the body? In the dustbin?'

'Garden. The weasels ate it. That got rid of them.'

'You do seem proud of yourself.' She poured muesli for Tim, added milk. 'Bastard.'

The boy wandered into the kitchen and clutched at the chicken-wire. 'Where is he, Mum? I can't see him.'

Just then the front doorbell rang. Relieved, Saul hurried to answer. Too early for the post.

Brian Sanderson was a chunky, balding man with a tightly trimmed dark brown moustache. Area manager of a meat processing firm. Pies, sausages, faggots. He had on an expensive grey suit and a flat tweed cap with a long, aggressive brim.

'Right,' Sanderson said without preamble, 'you were out in that so-called garden of yours at three a.m., whistling your head off, making our dog go wild. What was the big idea?'

An incensed Diane shoved Saul aside. 'Is there a law against being in our own garden? Your raving hound woke *me* up. No wonder, when it's shut out in any sort of weather. Next thing, it'll be turning vicious. Supposedly! You'll be having it killed so you can buy another to maltreat.'

'Don't you come that line with me, Missus. I'm warning you not to taunt our dog.'

'Oh, shall we whisper and wear cotton wool on our feet? If that animal disturbs our sleep, we'll dance around our garden playing trumpets if we feel like it.'

Sanderson looked at Saul, not her. 'I'm warning you. Watch out.'

Saul felt surprise. Obviously Sanderson failed to realise that he was in the presence of the king of his species; of the only man alive who incarnated humanity, who could whistle the weasels.

Saul exerted himself mentally, trying to awe their neighbour, to impose himself upon the man by power of will or grace. As Hitler, as Jesus had done. He made his eyeballs bulge. He began whistling the same tune which had led the army away the night before.

He imagined Sanderson suddenly overcome with an ecstasy of amazed communion with the archperson fleetingly revealed to him. Sanderson kicking up his feet and dancing a jig, capering over the road on to the green. Alternatively, Sanderson shrinking back trembling, drool on his lips.

Brian Sanderson merely stood his ground.

'The damned offensive impertinence of you two nutters! So-called teacher, covered in hair like a caveman. You're trash, that's what you are. A visual insult—like your garden. Your Missus daring to criticise how we look after our dog; spreading slander to the few people she *does* know in the village. Oh I've heard—!'

Saul gaped as the man ranted.

'What's more, I've heard how your nipper had all his toy piggies taken by Mummy in case he grows up fancying a bite of bacon. Shaking your fist at anyone on a horse; you really know how to be popular. All the other lunacies. Pair of loonies, that's what you are. If you ever had a mongrel, which God forbid, I bet you'd feed it on boiled cabbage. I'll tell you what real cruelty is. It's raising kids on a diet of roots and leaves. Toss a pound of raw veg in the blender, and scream, "Dinner time!" Give them brain damage, like their parents. From malnutrition! You should be reported. Those kids should be taken into proper care. My brother-in-law's a magistrate. Any more bother from the both of you, and I'll take steps.'

Sanderson did take steps: back towards his own large renovated thatched cottage, where a Toyota estate car poked from the garage.

'Bother, did you say?' Diane cried after him furiously. 'We hardly *see* you—and certainly don't wish to.'

Their neighbour paused. 'I saw *him* all right, last night. Bloody three a.m. Out there yodeling at the moon, or whatever ecologists do. Drove the dog bananas.' Sanderson entered his Toyota and drove off.

'*Archhuman, you?*' a thin, inner voice taunted Saul. '*You're nothing of the sort.*'

With numb horror Saul understood that he had simply met, and met by chance—though with all the compelling strangeness of a mystical experience—an actual archbeing, the weasel king. An archbeing had revealed itself to Saul, knowing—in whatever way a weasel knew things—that Saul recognised its true nature. Would honour it. Or else would be torn to pieces.

He'd been illuminated and forsaken; to make of his experience what he cared. Or could.

The knowledge was totally alienating. There was no way to share it—by adopting a weasel as his family or tribal totem. Nowadays there were so many harvesters and crop sprays and hard roads and battery chicken houses and pig units. In another forty years there might be no animals visible in the countryside. In the prehistoric past, it wouldn't have been so.

What had happened, was for him alone, and the knowledge would cripple his heart and life forever—as though he were a rabbit maimed by a gin-trap, a fox by a wire snare, which it could only escape by gnawing through its own limb, amputating part of itself as a sacrifice.

Diane had slammed the door upon their already departed visitor. Saul slunk through to the kitchen, where Tim—ears agog—pretended to be hungrily spooning up muesli from his china bowl which Diane had decorated with painted bluebells. Naturally he had heard the whole exchange at the front door. The boy darted diplomatically blank glances from the empty run to his father, and back.

Glancing down into Tim's bowl, Saul found himself seeing not toasted wheat, rolled oats, bran, hazelnuts, sunflower seeds, and dried apple—but chewed bones and broken teeth, and flakes of dried flesh, swimming in blood. He felt a terrible, unappeasable hunger. If somehow he could satisfy that hunger, he feared that he would vomit.

The comprehensive school where Saul taught geography was set in the sprawling village of Kingsbury, nine miles along the main road which passed their house. After Saul drove out of Woodburn, though, he cut on to the by-road towards Upton.

Di had had precious little to say to him before he rushed off; while for his part he had done little more than indicate to her the many tiny vague footprints on window ledge and tiles and sink unit—at which she had snorted contemptuously. Saul could have made that mess himself by stippling with muddy fingers, scratching with his fingernails.

Why wasn't he driving directly to the school? That was because he had decided to kill himself. Or rather, he was luxuriating in the idea as a form of emotional balm, consoling himself by toying with the notion of suicide. He would reject the sardonic, gnawing gift of the weasel king. He would toss in the weasel's face the gift of life, and of knowledge. Besides, he would erase the mess at home by vanishing from the scene.

Exactly how would he kill himself? By hanging himself from a tree bough with the tow rope? Perhaps; but slow strangulation did not appeal. By crashing the car? The by-road had too many bends to pick up any adequate speed; the main road would have been far more suitable. He would simply end up in a ditch, saddled with a large garage bill for recovery and repairs. Or by routing the exhaust gases into the car through a hose-pipe? He'd neglected to bring one.

'Self-pity, self-indulgence, selfishness!' he growled at himself; and this was true. The night before, for a few minutes he had been an extended self, an exalted self; then he had deflated like a balloon.

He had been driving automatically, unaware. Abruptly he realised that he had reached the bend near where they had rescued the rabbit. He braked, nosed the Renault part way on to the verge, and stepped out.

Could the archweasel's short legs have carried it as far as this in the past five or so hours, if it ran flat out? Unlikely.

The hedge, recently trimmed by machine, was a leafless line of splintered sticks like broken chicken bones. Fields were empty, foggy, with an isolated skeleton oak tree and a few skeleton elms nearby. The air was grey. A crow flapped by. No other hint of life.

Saul climbed a gate and walked out across the field, tacky soil engulfing his shoes, glueing itself to the soles in fat balls. It was a huge field—several ancient fields combined in one for more efficient harvesting—and he walked a long way till fog erased the view in all directions. He felt that he was erasing himself too, murdering the last vestiges of that preposterous arch-self which he had conceived the night before.

In the fog ahead, a figure tottered. A farm worker? Someone out to take a pot-shot at pheasants? A gun-shot in the wrong direction might solve all Saul's problems honourably and meaninglessly.

The figure capered as though treading on coals, not soggy clods; maybe it was trying to keep its shoes clean. It looked weirdly ragged, hairy, and at first the head seemed bound around with a mass of woollen scarves. A tramp—who had slept in some derelict barn overnight?

Noticing Saul, the figure jolted in his direction and suddenly was clearer. A coat of russet fur, with a long band of white fur from the throat all down the underbelly. Jutting whiskered snout, beady black eyes, crumpled crinkly ears. Forepaws flailing the air, not human hands.

The weasel king!—but not the slim little archweasel of the previous night. No, this creature was nearly as tall as Saul and as bulky as a man. He froze in fear as the shape lumbered towards him.

But then he saw the beast differently.

It did wear a coat: of stitched brown fur and white fur. The head was a mask: a fur-covered framework with ears of leather, whiskers of horse hairs, eyes of dark glass. The forepaws were gloves, gauntlets; the hindpaws were tight boots. The tail, a fox's brush. This was a man dressed like a medieval mummer or something more ancient.

'What on earth are you?' cried Saul.

The mummer dropped to all fours and ran clumsily around Saul in a circle, spit-hissing, then rose and raked the air and spoke: in a thick accent, part guttural, part twangy. Saul couldn't understand a single word. What language was it? Anglo-Saxon? Celtic? Norse?

'I don't understand.'

A weasel-glove reached and flipped Saul's tie out, then jerked, tightening the knot throttlingly. The other glove pawed at his jacket. Saul tried to step back but the glove had seized his lapel and wouldn't let go. Both gloves gripped him now, forcing his jacket back over his shoulders, imprisoning his arms as he choked. The weasel king's arms had a wiry strength.

The mummer spun Saul around. Partly to escape and partly because he couldn't prevent it, Saul let his jacket be stripped from him. Hastily he tore the tie loose from his neck, to breathe. The mummer grunted approvingly and peeled off first one animal gauntlet then the other. These were thrust at Saul so commandingly that he accepted charge of them. The mummer's bare hands were gnarled, almost tattooed with ingrained dirt. A finger poked at Saul's white shirt, hooked suggestively at the waist band of his trousers. Backing off a pace, the mummer unhooked and shed his coat of skins from off a dirt-caked torso . . .

Saul stood unsteadily, his feet pinched by the tight beast-boots. The gauntlets compressed his hands into claws. The coat of many furs rasped areas of bare flesh. He peered through the dark glass eyes of the head-mask—faintly misted by his own exhaled breath—at a parody double of himself. For the strange dirty man was now fitted out in Saul's own shirt and trousers, jacket and shoes. The tie was knotted around the man's waist as a belt; the shoelaces were left undone. The idea had been to exchange costumes. Roles. And Saul had had little say in the matter.

But the features of the ex-mummer bore no resemblance. Thin, beak-nosed, rat-like, days unshaven. Dark eyes gleamed at Saul. The man grinned impishly, showing foul black stumpy teeth. He patted his new garments, raised a hand in rude salute, then sang aloud with a kind of crazy joy and ran off across the soil into the fog, shoes slapping.

Should Saul remove the giant weasel-head and carry it under his arm like some deep-sea diver? Or like a knight carrying his visored helmet? Time enough to take it off when he got back to the Renault, he decided.

So he set off in that direction on numbed, constricted feet, wondering whether he had just been assaulted and had his clothes stolen by a tramp in exchange for that tramp's own crazy costume. Maybe the tramp had somehow mesmerised him, or Saul had done so to himself, and in actual fact he was walking across this field dressed in a filthy old fur coat found in a dustbin, with a bag over his head, two plastic insets for eyes.

Exertion fogged the eye-pieces further. It took Saul a minute or two to wonder at how many more oaks seemed to be looming in the dense mist. When he did wonder he felt scared to take the head-mask off, as if to do so would be to lock those intruding trees in place.

When he came to the road, the road was a muddy track hemmed on the far side by dense woodland. He fled along the track, stumbling and sliding, flapping his forepaw-gauntlets for balance, hoping somewhere to find tarmacadam and a Renault.

Presently the forest withdrew behind thick mist and there seemed to be rough pasture to his left. Ahead loomed a cottage: a hovel of stone and timber almost buried under a bonnet of black, rotting straw. Then another. A raggy scrap of a child saw him and ran screaming. A dog began to yelp. A fat woman in a hooded gown made a sign and shouted incomprehensibly. He spied a pond with geese afloat. As mist thinned fitfully other vague hovels swam into view, around a green. A reedy whistle blew penetratingly; voices called out.

Several men in homespun tunics trotted up. They wore little jingling bells on wire around their ankles and clutched wooden staves; these, they clashed together in the air rhythmically. Women arrived, some barefoot, their braided hair held tight in linen cauls—and a motley of children too. The boldest kid darted at Saul, to touch and flee. Wood thwacked on wood, beating out a greeting, yet the adults appeared to regard Saul's presence—the Weasel King's presence there—with a shade of puzzlement. He oughtn't to be here yet; or perhaps not of his own accord.

Before long a good many other smock-clad men armed with staves arrived, out of breath, ankle-bells tinkling. A large circle formed, each man clashing wood with his neighbour on one side then the next, advancing one pace, retreating one pace.

Should Saul remove his head-mask and reveal himself as a stranger? That might infuriate villagers. What would be the outcome of this ritual? Did they mean to beat him to death with the staves? Surely not. The costume he was wearing must be valuable to them; they wouldn't risk wrecking it. Yet why had the mummer forced, or fooled, Saul into exchanging garments? Ordinarily the villagers would have hunted the Weasel King through the woods and fields before herding him into the village—to do what, eventually?

Perhaps the mummer had simply been possessed with greed for Saul's fine clothes and shoes.

Saul thought of corn dollies and of Morris Dancers, but somehow the present situation seemed quite different, and its nature eluded him. He knew of peasants in the distant olden days wearing antlers, imitating stags; and he'd heard of the Fisher King, which he thought must be a heron. But a *weasel* king?

Maybe he was meant to be a bear. He bowed his head to inspect his costume more closely—and it was just as he had thought at first: a multitude of white strips and russet strips cut from hundred of skins and sewed so as to resemble a giant weasel. He felt hoodwinked, threatened, degraded—yet oddly exhilarated too, for he hadn't after all lost touch with the archbeing he had met.

When he raised his head he recognised the chunky, balding, moustached man who stood opposite, scowling and weighing his stave.

'Sanderson . . . ?'

But how . . . ? And *Diane* was one of the women who waited outside the circle, anticipatively. He saw his wife clearly but he didn't call her name too. It came to him then that he hadn't merely been shifted into a country-side of the past—though that would have been disconcerting enough on its own. No, he had been shunted into a different species of past reality, one where a weasel king dominated this assembly and could summon human beings at its whim; one dreamed by weasels, rather than remembered by men.

As though this realisation was a signal, a trigger, his coat writhed. No longer was he wearing a garment of many furs. The costume had changed. He was covered in live weasels, clinging all over him, hot bodies clawing for purchase, nipping his skin with fierce strong jaws. They crawled, they climbed, they hung. All the weasels of which the coat was made had come back to life.

He screamed. He danced. This was the part of the rite which the mummer had been keen to avoid! The reincarnation of all the slaughtered weasels. That, and also—

Clashing their staves one final time, the men rushed in and started beating him. To save him—or break every bone in his body?

He fell amid a squirming, biting furry mass. Blows rained down. The villagers were obtaining materials for next year's weasel coat: that was his last thought as he lost consciousness.

He woke torn and battered, in mud. As his eyes blinked open he saw clods of ploughed earth stretching away at nose level. His body was half paralysed with bruises and with cold. When he turned his head painfully, a five-bar gate loomed high, set in a hedge of splintered chicken bones. A few feet beyond that, the back bumper of the Renault!

Cold knives cut at flesh and muscles as he struggled to stand; he was only dressed in the muddy string vest and underpants which the mummer had let him keep. Somehow he scaled the gate, knowing that—thank God—he'd left the keys in the ignition. Soon he was inside the car, hugging his shivering self. He switched engine and heater on. As the air warmed, his brain unjammed.

He could hardly continue onward to school in this state. If he returned to Woodburn, though, would Di ever believe him? Maybe he had been trying to expiate his supposed crime—of rabbit murder—by lunatic self-flagella-tion: by tossing away his shoes and outer clothes and rolling in mud and on stones, then diving through a hawthorn hedge a few times, on the principle that enough self-punishment inflicted dramatically enough should surely merit forgiveness for the uncommitted slaughter . . . of one bloody stupid mangy rabbit.

'Maybe,' he mumbled aloud, 'I *did* do this to myself. But the Weasel King made me! To show me his importance, his charisma.'

Entering Woodburn, he hunched in the driving seat to hide his undress. Once parked outside their cottage he peered carefully to check that the coast was clear before sprinting round to the back door. And in.

'Daddy's got his clothes off!' piped Josh. Hurrying into the kitchen, Diane gathered the boy to her.

Saul held his hands out in appeal. 'I had an accident.'

'You smashed up the car!'

'No.'

She eyed him warily, hugging Josh. 'What sort of accident?'

'I was mugged. A tramp waved me down on the way to school. He looked distressed. But he jumped on me, and knocked me out. When I came round, in a field . . .' He indicated his wounds and bruises.

'And this happened on the main road?'

'Yes,' he lied. 'There was no other traffic at the time.'

'You must phone the police.'

'I'd rather not.'

'If it's the truth, you'll phone the police! Or I shall.'

'We don't like the police, do we? Why cause trouble for some poor wretch? It's only a few clothes.'

'I suppose it was only a rabbit, too! Where's your watch?'

He remembered that the mummer had taken his watch as a fancy bracelet.

'Let's talk first. I must put some clothes on. I'm cold.'

'You're lying. It was *Sanderson* who stopped you, wasn't it? And humiliated you! How can we live here when we've been made fools of? That's his idea. But he's committed assault—and theft!'

Praying that Diane wouldn't touch the phone, Saul fled upstairs to change his underwear, to shower and dress. He was shocked to discover the time: nearly eleven.

When he came down again clad in jeans, sweater, and trainers, Diane had made hot chocolate drinks for herself and for Josh but not for him.

'Phone the police!' she ordered.

'Look, it wasn't Sanderson.' Saul still ached all over. 'I'll phone the school, though.'

'Coward. Fool. You'll let Sanderson get away with . . . rubbishing us.'

Josh took his daisy-painted mug, and himself, away from this argument. Moments later the boy was shrilling, 'That man has Daddy's coat on!' Hot chocolate spilled from the mug in one hand while Josh pointed through the front window with the other. Diane was beside the boy in seconds; Saul, less speedily.

A thin, ratty, unshaven man was hiking across the green, carrying a roped plastic bag of possessions. He wore a white shirt and familiar jacket and trousers, the waist tied round. The man stepped on to the road, to proceed along it.

'Stay here!' Diane ordered Josh. She wrenched open the front door and dashed out with a 'Hey!' Saul trotted after her.

'You stole those clothes from my husband!'

The man's teeth were badly decayed. His jacket pockets bulged. 'Stole, is it? Why, hullo squire,' he greeted Saul. 'Were you trying to play a trick? He gave 'em to me as a free gift, lady. Like Jesus Christ himself. Don't you go saying I stole. I threw me old things away.'

'Is this true?' Diane turned on Saul. 'You gave him your clothes?'

Just then the side pocket of that jacket, which had been Saul's a while before, squirmed. Out poked a small russet furry head. Glossy-eyed, bewhiskered, crumple-eared, with a white muzzle. Up stretched a white neck like a miniature giraffe's, as the animal sniffed the air.

'A weasel!' Diane gasped.

Blanketing his own—almost electric—shock, Saul experienced a deep, miraculous feeling of relief.

'Oh yes, lady. Why, on the road they call me the Weasel King. I always catches and tames a weasel. So he'll keep the rats off me when I sleep out; and other things. Once, I even had two weasels, but that's risky. Weasels don't much care for their own kind, not *generally*. Boy an' girl only gets together one day a year to mate. Generally.'

Sliding from the pocket the weasel climbed lithely up to the fellow's shoulder, where it reared to survey the neighbourhood.

'Weasel?' Diane repeated helplessly.

'I knew one chap keep a ferret in his trousers. Flush out his supper for 'im, it would. My boy goes one better—brings me a fine rabbit back with 'im. Then I'll skin it, an' feed him the liver and stuff, an' cook the coney over a fire on a stick, I will. A'm known for it, on the road; and no one's ever called me thief.'

Saul hoped to take him by the arm, but the weasel jerked out like a snake, spit-hissing.

'You don't touch me nice new clothes! Mine, now. Me little friend wouldn't like that. Oh no indeedy.'

'Weasel King,' said Saul, 'will you help me? Will you come into the house and talk to me? Please.'

'Saul!'

'Hush, Diane. Will you, Mr King?'

'Mister, is it?' The man grinned, foul-toothed. 'I could take a cup of something hot and a bite to eat. You're like Christ Jesus himself. I won't filthy your fine chairs and carpets, lady. Not today.'

Wouldn't he? His hands were dark with dirt. Was this person genuine? Or was he weaseldom itself in a human disguise? After all that had occurred surely it was an impossible coincidence that a human weasel king of the byways should happen along. Saul didn't exactly feel afraid to invite the tramp inside; the fellow seemed benevolently disposed. He did wish he could recall the actual events of their encounter earlier that same morning. What if the events which Saul remembered had been the real events?

Josh's face was pressed to the window.

'That'll be yer little boy, eh? Needn't fear me fur friend. Won't nip yer lad so long as yon don't annoy 'im. Won't nip no one but an enemy; or a juicy rabbit.'

If this *was* a man, why then, he must be a sort of latter-day enchanter, a down-at-heel, outcast *witch* with a familiar. A week ago the 'magician' had sent his weasel accomplice to catch him a meal . . . and he'd had that meal stolen by the intervention of the Cobbetts.

Once they were all inside—Diane leaving the door wide open despite the chill in the air—the weasel rushed from shoulder to floor. As though familiar with the lay-out and well aware there were no cats nor dogs, it scuttled to disappear upstairs. Josh squealed with a mix of excitement and disappointment.

Soon the tramp was drinking hot chocolate and scoffing cheese, boiled free-range eggs, and bread provided by Saul.

'Wouldn't happen to have a scrap of flesh for me friend, eh? Don't matter if it's cooked flesh.' 'King' scrutinised Saul and Diane. 'No, s'pose not. You wouldn't.'

'And how do you know that we wouldn't have?' Diane demanded.

"Cos me little pal never went for the kitchen. He can smell meat a mile off. Whiff o' blood.'

Mention of blood reminded Diane, who shifted closer to the phone. 'My husband says that you attacked him violently. Why else would he give all his clothes?'

'Look at these, lady, all neat and clean. Do these come off a fellow as was beaten up?'

'The tie isn't too neat.' There was sarcasm in her voice.

'Never could abide a tie. Better as a belt.'

'That watch does look nice on your wrist, Mr King.'

'Is the glass smashed? Are the hands bent? Is the strap broke?'

'I lied about him attacking me,' admitted Saul.

'Then who did attack him, Mr King? My husband's covered in cuts and bruises. Hundreds! How did he get them? Did he inflict them on himself? Or was it done by a balding person who drives a Toyota?'

'King' leered at Diane. 'I didn't say *where* he give me his clothes. Sometimes I meets people in funny places which aren't quite neither here nor there. In-between places; that's me own business.' The tramp's voice hardened. 'Me, I don't belong in your type o' world, of houses an' cars an' employment, lady. I'm outside, an' most folks don't care much for that! Need to know how to duck out, I do. Dodge round the back o' the world a bit.'

The weasel had reappeared. It chattered squeakily as if delivering a report, then ascended its master and snuggled into his pocket.

'It was you we stole the rabbit from, wasn't it?' Saul asked quietly. 'It was you who sent all the weasels. I think you're the archhuman, aren't you? Otherwise you'd never have mentioned Jesus. He was one too.'

Bewildered, Diane hoisted Josh to her hip and retreated to the kitchen. 'You come here a minute!' she called to Saul.

He obeyed. She nodded him urgently away from where the tramp could watch, could hear her whispering.

'What do you mean, we stole the rabbit from him? And what was that name you called him: archhuman? What's going on?'

'Will you leave it till later, Di!' He attempted to return, but setting Josh down smartly she blocked him. Briefly they waltzed like two cars at a fun fair before he thrust free.

'He's gone, Di!'

Saul ran to the door. Outside, the road was deserted; likewise the green. Nobody could have vanished from sight so quickly, even at a sprint.

'He must be upstairs, Saul! Filling his pockets! Go and see.'

Saul leapt upstairs, and checked bathroom, bedrooms, wardrobes. He even threw himself down to squint under the beds. On his return he skidded on the stair carpet, almost taking an ankle-wrenching tumble.

'He isn't in the house.' Saul checked the unlocked car outside. Empty. He darted to the side path which led round the rear, colliding with the dustbin in his haste. Here was the only place where King could have hidden— lurking until they ran to the front door, before escaping by way of the back garden. King wouldn't be finding the bottom fence easy to scale. As Saul pursued, shouting, 'Come back, Mr King!' the Doberman hurled itself at the Sandersons' side of the other fence, barking furiously, shaking the panels. Saul couldn't see King anywhere.

He trampled carelessly through cabbages and sprouts, past the netted fruitery, then stumbled over compost and bonfire remains. Gripping the far fence, he hauled himself up. It had dawned on him that the Doberman only began to bark *after* he arrived on the scene.

Straining, he spied on to a lawn islanded with ornamental conifers. A middle-aged woman, whose name they had never troubled to discover, glared at him indignantly from her kitchen window, a plate suspended in her hand. Supposing that a tramp had just leapt into her garden, she wouldn't still have been washing dishes; that was for sure. Saul was also sure that King hadn't come nearly as far as this. Grimacing at Mrs Somebody, he let himself slide back on to weeds.

Diane had followed part of the way. He rejoined her.

'King didn't scram down the road. He isn't under our beds or crouching in the car. He certainly didn't escape over any fence of ours.'

'Where is he, then?' she whispered.

'Dodged round the back, and ducked out. Almost told us as much, didn't he?' He reached to touch her hand. 'Let's go inside, Di. I have a tale to tell you.' He hesitated till her hand clasped his. 'A tale of weasels and a mummer— and a king of men with rotten teeth.'

They held hands as they returned indoors, into the kitchen.

'Di.' He held her.

'Saul.'

'You'll have to believe me.'

'I think I will.'

'I'd better begin with what really happened last night—'

'Wait. We left the front door open.' Gently, she disengaged.

Moments later, she cried out; Saul came swiftly.

Josh was holding to brown-stained lips what appeared to be a half-con- sumed aubergine . . . except that the inside of the egg-plant was as black as the skin itself, save for a few white lumps.

'What is it you're eating, Josh? Where did you get it?'

'Man dropped it on the chair. It tastes lovely.'

'But it's—'

'A black pudding,' said Saul. 'It's a *blood sausage*. He's eating cooked pigs' blood and fat . . . Give that to me!'

The boy took another large bite and bolted it down. 'Me like it!' Evading Saul, Josh ran to the open front door, and paused defiantly.

'Mum,' the boy pleaded, 'why can't *we* have a pet weasel? Can you catch a baby one—and tame it? We could feed it on stuff like this. *He* must have done, for when it couldn't hunt enough.' Josh crammed more black pudding into his mouth.

'But you and Tim *promised* me,' Diane begged her son. 'Tim swore he would never eat any meat at school—only salads and vegetables.'

Cunningly Josh said, 'I'll promise if we can have a weasel.' He seemed a different child—a changeling—as though the cooked blood had entered not only his belly but his heart.

'No,' snapped Saul.

The boy put two taboo words together. 'Bloody bastard,' he said.

Diane began to scream.

Shell Shock

Weston Willow is a very private village, which guards its secrets jealously. A mile away on the far side of the valley the manor house of Oxwell Canons had recently opened its gates to the public. Oxwell Canons promptly attracted car-loads and coach parties of sightseers. Given the fund of ill will between Weston Willowers and the tiny community across the valley, this was a severe provocation.

'Canons, indeed!' exclaimed Cedric Craig in the Wheatsheaf one evening after downing a pint of mild. 'I'd like to give them cannons! Cannons to the right of them, cannons to the left of them.'

Cedric was quoting from Tennyson's *Charge of the Light Brigade* which had been drilled into him at primary school decades ago by tyrannical Miss Trotter, now retired. Red-faced and burly, Cedric was usually jolly, though not on this occasion. He might own the village garage, but he was most unimpressed by the prospect of selling extra petrol to day-trippers passing through.

The 'canons' actually referred to the priory which once stood on the site of the manor house, until Henry VIII dissolved the monasteries. In the 1950s the owners, the Carthew family, 'buggered off to the colonies', as Cedric phrased it, leaving their family seat to the whims of weather, decay, and a succession of caretaker tenants who paid a token peppercorn rent and hadn't the cash to take much care.

The last lot of caretakers decided to keep some cattle as a sideline in the patch of open woodland adjoining the house. With a hard winter coming, they neglected to order any fodder; and the herd began to starve. Overgrown with moss and ivy and creepers, the spinney came to resemble some tract of Southern American Gothic inhabited by bovine Belsen victims. Weston Willowers did not appreciate this grim spectacle.

Nor did Weston Willow admire the arrangement by which the Carthews returned to their native seat, once Blacks came to power in their adopted bit of Africa. Several million pounds of public money were lavished on the historic house to prevent it from collapsing, in exchange for it being deeded to the nation (with a fine apartment reserved for the Carthews). Weston Willow did not wish us to be on any tourist itinerary.

Only one family in our village tried to cash in by offering farmhouse cream teas on the front lawn of their council house. Within a couple of weeks the Murtons' place was gutted by an electrical fire.

'*Cannons!*' repeated Cedric—while June, the hyperthyroidal landlady who always slopped about in carpet slippers, set up another pint of mild on the bar.

The usual regulars crowded the Wheatsheaf. Deaf John of the crumpled ear was playing dominoes with moon-faced Dumb Fred and Bill Donovan. Young Timmy Cook was courting Sophy Platt whose skin was peaches and cream. Farmers were gossiping noisily about the European Community's plan to monitor all the fields of Europe by spy satellite in the infra-red. This was to catch anyone who was accepting a grant to leave land idle but who was still naughtily using the same land.

'The Froggies are bound to be cheating!' I heard. 'Why should *we* be snooped on? Us buggers never get away with anything.'

Someone claimed to have spotted a wolf a few miles from the village, loping along in their headlights. Light grey and gaunt, with its ears pricked up; unmistakable.

'Seen any gypsies lately? *They* keep wolves.'

'No, Jack, it'll be one of those wolf-dog hybrids like the one as killed that baby—'

The incident had recently been reported on TV. A timber wolf hybrid kept as a friendly family pet by some idiots had savaged their new baby to death. Some similar idiots must have got scared and dumped their own animal out in the vacancy of the countryside, heedless of lambs and sheep.

'Nowt wrong with the tap water,' old Ned was insisting to our landlady. Ned worked for the water company, checking on customer complaints. He was due for retirement; then he could spend all his time beside our little local lake, dangling his fishing rod, just as the willow trees dangled their fronds. Ned accepted a glass of water from June, and simply sniffed it, with the nose of a connoisseur.

'She be fine,' he assured June; and began to rhapsodise. 'Do you know her story? She rises near Bedford. She wends her way west, then to the north . . .' To hear Ned talk, you'd suppose that water was his mistress. With a twig in his hands, Ned could douse the exact site of a leak in a mains pipe under a road, fractured by the vibration of heavy lorries. Gizmos with microchips were rendering his talents obsolete.

'She rests a while at Grendon Reservoir, June, then she makes her way here. She's fine, just fine.'

'In that case why don't you *taste* it?'

'No need to, dear. I can smell her.'

Timmy was trying to persuade Peaches-and-Cream to take a stroll in the woods with him, since it was a mild evening, and by now discreetly dusky.

'Last time,' she hissed, 'I got pine needles in my pants—'

'Aw, come on, Soph. We might see a badger—'

'Watch out you don't meet a *wolf*,' butted in a young farmer, to Timmy's chagrin.

Table skittles went crashing over. Decorative brass shell cases gleamed on a windowsill—Cedric was eyeing those wistfully.

Soon two themes converged. One was the matter of the annual fête due as usual at the end of August, to raise funds for our village hall. The other was all those bloody tourists. You might have thought that a fête and tourists were ideally suited to one another; but you'd have been wrong.

To be perfectly frank, Weston Willow's Grand Fête, Grand Auction, and Novelty Dog Show was increasingly scruffy compared to the carnivals and galas staged by other surrounding villages. The stalls and games set out in the crumbling car park alongside the village hall looked like an appeal staged by refugees or paupers. Donations for the auction had declined over the years from sub-antiques to sheer junk. Attendance was dropping from year to year.

Nevertheless, our fête still had its loyal adherents. Some families travelled miles to queue up then mob the home-made cake stall and the racks of nearly new clothes. The novelty dog show, with rosettes for the Most Obedient pooch and the one with the Waggiest Tail, remained a popular item.

'We need to revamp the fête,' declared Jeff Robinson, who was in micro-electronics. 'How about a tethered hot air balloon?'

Bill Donovan slapped down a domino noisily like someone issuing a challenge to a duel.

'You'd better watch out your balloon doesn't foul no power cables. More to the point, Jeff, do we want strangers spying into our back gardens and kitchen windows from up in the air? Ours is a *traditional* fête, not a circus like all those others are all turning into. That's why people come here.'

'That's why they don't come here,' muttered Jeff.

Here was the eternal argument. Everything must remain exactly as always, otherwise the native villagers would revolt. By remaining as always, profits declined steadily.

Outsiders who already patronised our fête were honorary Willowers—for one day a year, at least—drawn to the village as if mesmerised (or daft). No such dispensation applied to idle tourists whose main goal was Oxwell Canons. Those were interlopers. They would spoil the ambience of the fête. As for tarting ourselves up to appeal to such people—much better to remain shoddy.

The conflict resolved itself ominously with the arrival in the pub of Iron Man, tall and muscular and crew-cut.

Everybody referred to Dave Springer as Iron Man. This wasn't because he ran a lucrative scrap metal business in Wendelbury but because of his hobby. Springer's half-acre of garden was crowded with an assortment of ex-military vehicles which he bought in rusty state and lovingly restored. He owned several army trucks and a couple of armoured cars. This made his garden one of the less picturesque sights of the village, but no one objected much. It was as though, in the person of Iron Man, the village possessed a protector, a bodyguard—its own defence force in the event of some holocaust.

With the collapse of the Soviet Union, the most likely source of holocaust had disappeared. That same demise was why Iron Man was now so cock-a-hoop a new acquisition. Through a contact in Poland, Dave Springer had laid hands on a T-72 main battle tank for less than the cost of a top-of-the-range BMW...

Heaps of Russian hardware were on sale these days at knock-down prices to finance the new capitalist economy. Battle tanks in particular were a bargain, should you wish to own a battle tank. Many governments indeed wished to do so, from Yemen to Malaysia, from Chile to China. So did Iron Man. The

T-72 would soon be on its way to Weston Willow by heavy transporter, the gun barrel and turret temporarily separated from the hull.

As Dave Springer waxed lyrical about his new toy, Cedric also became enthused. Normally Cedric wasn't too fond of Iron Man. This was due to some bygone Parish Council fracas; but now the hatchet was about to be buried because of Cedric's fury at Oxwell Canons and his own passion for vehicles.

'The suspension's six large road wheels, with the drive sprocket at the rear, is it then, Dave?'

'So the idler's up at the front, and there are three return rollers. The really neat thing is how the forward part of the track has four spring-loaded skirt plates on each side.'

'What are those for, then?'

'Ah: in combat they spring forward at an angle of about sixty degrees to give the track some protection against anti-tank missiles.'

'Oh, I *see*.'

'The armour's toughened rather like our own Chobham armour. There's a dozer blade under the hull—'

'That could come in handy.'

'And a snorkel for deep wading—'

'Not in our lake,' chipped in old Ned.

'The beast fires fin-stabilised shells. Smooth bore. Laser rangefinder. Muzzle velocity just over a mile a second. Range, mile and a half or so.' Wistfully: 'I didn't get the machine gun that fits on the turret. I'd have had to do too much dodgy footwork to get that into the country.'

Cedric rubbed his hands together. 'You got the big gun, that's the main thing! Drink up, Dave. June, this one's on me.' He guffawed. 'What if there was a shell still in the breech . . . What wouldn't I give to put a shell into Oxwell Canons, eh? By accident, like.'

A hush descended. People eyed one another. This was one of those collective moments, of complicity. I could sense the spirit of the village stirring.

'A genuine Russian tank,' said Jeff Robinson, 'is just what we need on the playing field to pep up the fête.'

'Absolutely—'

'A true pièce de resistance—'

Did people really mean this? Did they realise what they were saying?

'At present, of course,' said Iron Man, 'the barrel's gimmicked so that it can't fire.'

Nobody would say it aloud, we all knew that between them Iron Man and Cedric would be able to restore the gun barrel to pristine order. And just as surely, a live shell would find its way into the village. The collective mind of Weston Willow was at work now. Where there's a will—or a Willow—there's a way.

'Er, what about casualties? I mean, among visitors to Canons—?'

'They ought to be here at our fête, not there—!'

'No, they bloody shouldn't be!'

'It'll be Daft Henry who finds a shell hidden away inside the tank, won't it? It'll be Henry as loads it. The fête over-excites him. When it's Henry's turn to sit inside the tank, the silly bugger pushes the firing button. Different barrel must have got delivered by mistake.'

Daft Henry, a lanky youth with awful acne and a generally vacant expression, possessed a real aptitude for machinery. Our local idiot savant in that regard, Henry hung around Cedric's garage a lot.

'Can't blame a simpleton for pushing a button. It'll all be a chain of mischance—'

'He'll realise what to do all right, but he'll never be able to explain—'

'There'll only be damage to the building—'

Thus Weston Willow convinced itself.

As the dull green T-72 manoeuvred into position behind the marquee on the sunny evening before the fête, its tracks crushed and tore up grass.

The site commanded a fine vista of Canons across the valley in its parkland. Bisecting the intervening dip like a boundary line was the old railway (minus rails) closed these thirty years. Recently there'd been talk of reopening the line for freight trains to shuttle between the Channel tunnel and the Midlands. At present the embankments and cuts were used to store black bales of rotting straw and clapped-out tractors and stacks of surplus wooden palettes.

Everyone present in the playing field maintained an air of total innocence regarding the actual purpose of the T-72. It was only with a determined struggle that I myself recalled the truth. I even found myself wondering whether I could have imagined that evening in the pub earlier in the year. I suspected that a similar fog hazed everyone's minds. In the presence of the tank all of us were Daft Henries.

'Bit of a writer, aren't you, Iain? Make things up, eh, Mr Campbell? Mysteries!'

That's what people used to say to me in the village, though the terrible truth is that ever since moving to Weston Willow with Jill I'd been suffering from total writer's block. The village seemed determined that my fictional 18th Century sleuth, Montague Hamilton, would never investigate any vintage local enigmas. I must rely on my salary as a history teacher over in Wendlebury and abandon hopes of a best-seller and TV series until such time as Jill and I could make our getaway from this confounded place.

This wasn't proving to be easy. I would apply for teaching jobs in other parts of the country and then at interview be turned down on the grounds that my two previous detective novels had been published to some acclaim—therefore I was bound to produce more novels and quit teaching. This would have been true if living in Weston Willow—so promising a source of inspiration—did not at the same time rob me of the ability to perpetrate, or consummate, more than a few impotent pages. So Jill and I were stuck here. Thus did the village manipulate its inhabitants, interfering with memory and rationality and will power.

In fact, I don't believe that I'd mentioned the Russian tank scheme to Jill at all in recent months. The matter had actually slipped my mind! Only the daunting spectacle of the actual T-72 alerted me—and I couldn't bring myself, or rather couldn't *force* myself, to speak to any of my fellow spectators about its true role.

As I watched that tank trundle into position, puffing exhaust fumes, it seemed to me chillingly that I was succumbing to madness rather than that I was perhaps the sole custodian of the facts. It was the first time I had felt such a fear so strongly. My revival of memory seemed similar to the ending of an eclipse.

Jeff Robinson stood with arms folded, nodding approvingly.

'Jeff!' I called out to him in alarm.

'Got it all ready for the bottle stall tomorrow?' was his reply.

Such was the task assigned to Jill and myself. We would lay out playing cards upon a table, beneath clear plastic to protect against gusts or showers. Little bottles of cherryade and limeade would stand upon a quarter of the cards like lurid day-glo chess pieces. A bottle of wine would occupy the Queen of Diamonds. Cut the duplicate pack, match the card, win the wine.

It couldn't be—could it?—that my mind had embroidered wildly upon the banter and bluster I'd heard in the pub? My writing was repressed, therefore I fantasised, imagining things? Within my inhibited imagination pressure had been mounting. Suddenly a sluice-gate opened, flooding my consciousness with fabrications?

Surely it was myself who was sane, while my fellow villagers were functioning—at least in regard to the tank—as marionettes.

Jeff had lost interest in me. He was admiring the star attraction: the T-72. I needed to flee home to Jill—for reassurance, or for the contrary. Home drew me in yearning and in dread.

How powerful that tank was. It also represented the collapse of a mighty though mouldy empire. The fall of that empire had sent history right off the rails—on to a new and wholly unpredictable track. A few years ago, if I'd devoted a history class to predicting the collapse of Communism I might have seemed potty. Yet here we were in an alternative world. In this world, why should Willowers not fire a shell at a manor house across the valley? The equivalent had happened in Bosnia and was happening in far-flung parts of Russia itself. Would the rational logic of my fictional sleuth—a man of the Enlightenment—be able to cope with the unreason of today? All seemed ordinary and commonplace, yet unreason was loose. Why should the tank not fire its gun?

An acned face loomed before me. Daft Henry's.

Henry pointed to the rear of the tank where the cleated track rose up around a toothed wheel.

'Drive sprocket!' he exclaimed.

It was that sprocket—and its twin on the other side—which pulled the tracks around in a loop to propel the tank.

He gestured towards the front. 'Skirt plates!' Then towards the barrel. 'Hundred-twenty-five-mill smooth bore gun!'

Was Daft Henry the voice of the village, proving to me that what I supposed was perfectly true?

'Henry—' Yet there seemed to be no point in asking him ordinary questions.

Back at our cottage, Jill was cooking bolognese sauce to go with noodles. No child of ours hung around, pestering her happily. Jill could no more conceive than could I. Helping out at the art gallery in Wendlebury filled some of her days and took her out of this cloying village.

'Do you remember me telling you about Iron Man's Russian tank?' I asked.

'Is the ghastly thing on show yet?'

'Do you remember me saying how Daft Henry is going to fire a live shell at Canons tomorrow afternoon?'

'*What?*' She gaped at me.

'Forgot that part, didn't you? So did I. As soon as I saw the tank, the memory surfaced.'

'Iain,' she said crossly, 'who was it who lost their watch last month, so that you had to waste twenty quid buying another?'

The watch must have fallen off at school. I still couldn't understand how the strap had come undone.

'You put it down somewhere,' Jill said, 'and you forgot where. *You're* the one who forgets things, Iain. Losing things is a sign of losing your mind.' She was sure of her interpretation. 'A watch tells the time. Time that is passing us by. Therefore you lost it.'

'Maybe it's a symbol of history,' I said bitterly. 'Look, we're talking about that Russian tank. It's as if the whole village has forgotten about it until now—except for Iron Man and Cedric and Daft Henry who've been working on it like puppets or people in a dream! Please, Jill: can't you remember what I said when I came back from the pub that night?'

Irked, she recollected.

'You were tiddly. Somebody was taking the piss out of you and you were too naive to realise.'

This was really unfair. Jill *knew* about a number of the quirks of Weston Willow—those, at least, that I'd been able to tell her about, or that she'd found out on her own. Some, of course, I wasn't able to divulge.

I'd been cautioned by blind Lucy Prestidge about consequences and retribution. That was after she regaled me with the tale of how John became deaf and Fred dumb and herself blind because they'd drawn attention to the village—they'd tried to win a county-wide quiz by cheating, and the village didn't wish to be in any spotlight.

If I were ever to escape from this rural miasma and become free to write again, I'd better watch out for 'consequences'. So really it might be better that I couldn't leave, even though Jill and I dearly needed the money and distractions which success could bring. For financial reasons, we hadn't tried to have a child until after we arrived here, buying our cottage on the coat-tails of my *Rape of the Rock*, in which Montague Hamilton solved an eighteenth century jewel theft. Infertility had followed, for both of us. Mine, in the writerly sense. Jill's, in the procreative department.

Conceivably (ha!) mine was the fault in both respects. We hadn't resorted to any clinic to find out. Jill and I agreed it was crazy that childless couples should resort to fertility drugs with the world population soaring, and so many abandoned children needing homes. If I struck it rich with another Montague Hamilton book, maybe we might adopt a Third World child; although right now teaching kids every day of the week prejudiced me somewhat against being a parent.

Maybe my writer's block, and physical impotence, reflected one another. No, I don't mean impotence. Of course not. I mean infertility. A writer should choose his words with more care. But was I a writer any longer, prisoner of this village that I'd become? Pressure-keg of imagination, continually thwarted.

The next morning Jill and I duly went up to the playing field to set out our table of cards and arrange the bottles. The day was overcast but calm and mild, promising a dry afternoon.

All was bustle and last-minute fuss. Where's this, where's that? Don't we have *anything* more for the raffle? Potted plants were turning up, and trays of tomatoes and chocolate cakes and bric-à-brac. In the hall half a dozen women were making sandwiches. They're overpriced! No they aren't. The PA equipment won't work! As soon as the plug was back in its socket, a brass band rendition of *The Floral Dance* blared forth briefly. Bunting had come loose and needed tacking up again. The small bouncy castle arrived, to be inflated.

Jill refused to spare the T-72 a second glance, parked there with its barrel elevated towards Canons. I was suffering panic attacks. I dared risk neither proof nor disproof of what I knew. I pictured a shell flash thunderously away through the air.

The turret and hull would lurch as the segmented barrel absorbed the recoil. Almost at once: a far flash of detonation. Part of the distant manor house would disintegrate. If the shell fell short, sightseers' cars would explode in flames. I saw these events superimposed.

As helpers headed home for lunch and the area began to empty, in spite of the bunting and the marquee and the bright bouncy castle and the tank the relative starkness of the fête became apparent. Yet a few cars had already parked on the green. Early devotees were arriving, intending a leisurely boozy lunch in the Wheatsheaf.

'You go on ahead,' I told Jill. 'Jeff Robinson wanted a word with me.'

I hung around till Jill was out of sight. Five minutes later I followed. Half way down the village, I slipped into the phone box. I dialled the emergency number and asked for the police. I spoke through my handkerchief in a slurred voice. No, I wouldn't identify myself. I warned of a live shell in the Russian tank at Weston Willow fête. Quickly I put the phone down.

Our stall attracted a succession of lucky customers. The last of our small stock of wine bottles stood exposed upon the Queen of Diamonds. It was a cheap sparkling Asti Spumante imitation dolled up champagne-style with silver foil over its wired bulbous cork.

Half a dozen girls pranced in the inflatable castle. A couple of boys tried to knock each other off the plastic-sheathed horizontal pole, using pillows. Most male youngsters swarmed upon the tank. The PA system blasted out brass band marches, drowning the yapping of dogs being put through their paces. Visitors hauled plastic bags of second-hand clothes and books and knick-knacks. Sandwiches were being munched, ice creams being licked.

Had I expected a police patrol car with flashing lights? Or a bomb disposal squad? Constable Tate, our community policeman, was talking to Iron Man beside the T-72. Tate wasn't in uniform. A rotund and florid fellow—quite like Cedric—he was a Willower born and bred. His patch embraced a dozen villages in the neighbourhood. He was part of the conspiracy not to draw attention to our own village. The whisper was that if a native son did go in for a spot of burglary or joy-riding he and his parents would get a right rollicking from Tate, and they would need to make amends, but a court appearance would be the very last resort. If Tate's superiors suspected his protective attitude, maybe they approved in private. Less paperwork, less pressure on the magistrates.

Obviously word had come from the police headquarters fifteen miles away for Tate to check this matter out himself. Anonymous tip-off. Bizarre allegation. Presumed malice towards the fête or towards Iron Man.

Sensing my scrutiny from a distance of fifty paces, Tate glanced my way.

'Win a bottle of wine for twenty pence!' I cried immediately. 'Win a bottle of wine—!'

Shooing kids away, Tate and Dave Springer climbed up on to the T-72. Springer lowered himself through the open hatch, followed more cumbersomely by Tate.

A while later both men emerged from the belly of the machine. Tate seemed stern. Iron Man was taciturn. Daft Henry was lurking near the tank. Tate seized Henry by the arm and led him . . . directly towards our bottle stall.

'Henry's thirsty,' Tate told me. 'Needs to win himself a cherryade or something.' He tossed a pound coin upon the table. 'Six tries for a pound, isn't it? Do you know what to do, Henry?'

Henry's acned face gleamed with excitement. His focus was upon the wine bottle. It was just like an upright *shell*, of the size and shape that the tank might fire. And although this shell was of glass, the imitation Asti certainly had explosive potential.

Henry cut the cards five times with no success.

The sixth card was a Queen of Diamonds. Henry chortled, but immediately Sam Tate intercepted the bottle.

'Strong stuff for you, lad. You'd end up being sick in a hedge after getting up to goodness knows what mischief. There's something far better you can do with this champagne than drink it. Ever seen a racing driver on TV, who's just won the grand prix, eh? The big prize, that's what grand prix means. That's what you've won.'

Henry nodded enthusiastically.

Tate stripped off the silver foil. He loosened the wire from around the cork shaped like a horse-mushroom, then he shook the bottle vigorously again and again. Quickly he positioned the bottle in Henry's hands.

'Get your thumbs just under the cork, lad. How far can you fire it? Can you hit Canons, eh? Squeeze that cork, squeeze it . . .'

Henry gazed through the gap between marquee and T-72 at the distant target. Sweating, he squeezed.

The cork erupted with such a bang. A foaming fountain arced for ten feet, almost emptying the bottle, I'd have guessed.

'Where's the cork gone to?' cried Henry.

Tate shaded his eyes.

'All the way to Canons, lad! All the way.' The policeman regarded me steadily. 'Wouldn't you say so, Mr Campbell?'

I nodded numbly.

While the auction was in progress, I noticed Tate roaming the grass behind the big tent. He scooped up something and slipped it into his pocket. Had to be the cork.

That night, a distant loud bang awoke Jill and me. Far louder than any bird-scarer. Had a car crashed? No, no, that was the noise of Bosnia and bits of Russia. Jill insisted there'd been a car accident so I had to go to the window to check the empty street.

After breakfast, on the pretext of buying some free-range eggs, I drove Jill's tin-can Citroen up to the top of the village.

The battle tank still remained in the field, although the barrel looked lower as if it had drooped overnight.

I proceeded onwards, past Home Farm, down into the valley towards the humpy bridge across the railway line. A couple of hundred yards beyond, upslope towards Canons, two Range Rovers were parked in a gateway. In the field a couple of men in checked shirts and jeans were scrutinising a dead sheep.

The bulk of the flock were some way off, alternately gazing and grazing. Not far from the woolly corpse, a crater breached the soil. I pulled in behind the Range Rovers and climbed the gate.

One of the men was Brendan Baxter, a Willower. The other man was some young farmer from just beyond Canons. They seemed like truce nego-tiators, meeting in no-man's land.

'What happened?' I asked.

'Nothing you need bother about, Iain,' said Baxter. 'Whopping big chunk of ice must have fallen off a plane. Or maybe—' he leered at me '—it was a *meteorite.*'

Naturally I looked around for fragments of shell casing.

'Ice would all have melted by now,' said the other farmer. He glanced up at the clear sky.

As if to prove his words, a white contrail was extending across the zenith, proceeding from a glittering metal tip. A passenger jet was flying serenely high above Weston Willow, heading away, away. Away to elsewhere.

In the course of his investigation of the missing jewel Montague Hamilton visited a madman locked up in Bedlam; and now in that open field I felt sure that I was in Bedlam too.

How the Elephant Escaped Extinction

With apologies to Rudyard Kipling

IN THE HIGH AND FAR-OFF TIMES, O BEST BELOVED, A VERY CLEVER apeman lost almost all of the hair from his body.

How could he be so clever, if he lost his hair? Oh why do you ask such things? Because the clever apeman lost his hair he felt very cold and he shivered and he quivered—and he includes she, although this isn't always mentioned. Actually, his apewoman felt even chillier than he did, so maybe it was because of her complaints that the clever apeman invented fire (or rather, tamed fire, since you can't invent fire) and after a while he invented lots of other things too. Such lots and lots of things! Ploughs and arrows and shoes and clothes and money, to name but five. He also tamed the dog and the horse and the cow and the sheep and the goat and the chicken, to serve him, often for supper.

Snuggling so warmly with Mrs Apeman tended to lead to the birth of offspring, and although for a long time many offspring were carried off while still young by dis-ease, or dat-ease, in the long run more and more sons and daughters and grandsons and granddaughters all needed feeding. Before you could say Fiddle-dee-dee, many offspring needed to run a long way away from home in order to satisfy their appetites for food and things.

Mr and Mrs Apeman began to call themselves Mr and Mrs Human. That was because they and their extremely extended family *hew*ed and *hew*ed away at forests for firewood and furniture and to clear enough living space, and they hewed at hillsides to get at coal and iron and copper and gold and jewels until the other animals simply didn't know which way to jump to get out of the way. For many animals it was soon the Time of The End.

A story shouldn't start with the End, do you say? Oh but this one does!

Soon animals were going extinct at an amazing rate. Here today and gone tomorrow. Ex-tinct, to be succinct. Before that, they must have been *tinct*, which means that they added a splash of colour to the scene.

Just who went extinct, who previously was tinct? Why, animals such as the Buff-nosed Rat-kangaroo, and the Blue Pike. (Yes, a fish *is* an animal.)

Also there was the Kansas Bog Lemming. You think you know how Lemmings behave, throwing themselves off Scandinavian cliffs all the time to their doom? In fact they don't. Besides, this was the *bog* Lemming of Kansas, and *was* is the operative word.

Listen and attend! The Laughing Owl had nothing to laugh about—he also went ex-tinct. So did the Confused Moth; of course he was confused, going ex-tinct. The Burrowing Bettong's burrowing didn't help him one bit. As for the Rodrigues Solitaire—only one of him was left after a while, and then none. And goodbye to the Brawny Great Moa, more brawn than brain perhaps.

Also, there was the Slender-billed Grackle and the Spectacled Corm-orant—he couldn't see how to survive. Then there was the Ascension Flightless Crake—how could he possibly ascend anywhere when he couldn't even fly? There was—or were—the Bavarian Pine Vole and the Okinawa Flying Fox and the Dusky Seaside Sparrow and the Sea Mink; say those quickly and you'll hear how fast creatures were going ex-tinct. Don't forget the Crescent Nailtail Wallaby and Goff's Southeastern Pocket Gopher—did Goff offer him refuge in his pocket? Not likely.

Not forgetting the Big Thicket Hog-nosed Skunk. No big thickets remained to hide in; he was quickly forgotten. Also extinct went the Rabbit-eared Tree-rat and the Harelip Sucker who may have looked a trifle unattractive, as likewise the Cape Warthog. The Tennessee Riffleshell was all eaten up. The Oahu O'o was oh so surprised to become ex-tinct. Please do remember the Panay Giant Fruit Bat and the Dodo and the Tasmanian Wolf and the Egyptian Barbary Sheep and the Passenger Pigeon—just along for the ride, was the pigeon? No free rides for those beasts! Soon a whole lot of animals were as out of place as an ice-cream on a violin. They died and they died and they died.

Soon the Time of the End for always and always was coming for the Elephant, not the African one with the big flappy ears but the *other* one with the itsy-bitsy ears that lived in Asia. Terrible table manners he had—he pushed down trees to get at his dinner. Even with *his* itsy-bitsy ears, he heard what was coming. Tick-tock: five minutes to Doomsday midnight, for him!

Among the multitude of things that Mr and Mrs Human had made was what they called an atomic clock—silly them, when everything is made of atoms! They said that this atomic clock told the time with purrfect accuracy to one second in ten million years, and also that it showed how long was left till Doomsday. If a mere five minutes remained until Doomsday, what was the point of such purrfect accuracy as a second in ten thousand thousand years? And who was around ten thousand thousand years ago to say if this clock timed true?

Anyway, right about now the Earth became disobedient. Seas stormed and floods flooded and tornados whirled and cyclones cycled and ice melted where ice ought to be hard, and snow fell upon orchids, all very confusingly. Volcanoes belched and vomited.

Despite all these upsets, Mr and Mrs Human did not go ex-tinct, although you might say they did their best, or their worst, to follow the Kansas Bog Lemming and the Confused Moth into oblivion, what with a First World War and a Second World War and a Cold War and plenty of other wars in between—the One and Three-Eighths War, the Two and Three-Quarters War, goodness knows, and slaughters and genocides and oodles of atomic weapons. More people just kept on coming and coming until there were eight thousand million people. That's a lot of people. How long would it take you to count to eight thousand million on your fingers and toes? Mr and Mrs Human couldn't keep count. You might as well say there were *countless* people.

My Best Beloved, by now there remained about five hundred of the elephants with the itsy-bitsy ears, consisting of grandmothers and grandfathers and aunts and uncles and maternal and paternal aunts, and mothers and fathers and a few cute little babies.

At long last, the elephants raised their trunks high and they made a big trumpeting and a bugling and a clarioning and a crumhorning (if such an instrument exists, although I think it does, or did), and they made a bombardoning and a tubaaaing and a tromboning—until the great God Ganesh Himself, who looks like an elephant, descended to discover what the noise and clamour was all about.

Now, Ganesh was not originally intended to be a God for Mr and Mrs Human.

Nor was the dog Anubis meant to be for humans. Nor were the Winged Serpent nor the Ram Amon nor the Scarab Kephri nor the Owl Minerva nor the Sacred Cow. Humans had *stolen* the Gods of the animals, just as they stole the forests and the wet wild woods and the rivers and the water-meadows and the lowlands and uplands and inlands and outlands, and islands too, and the fields. (Until agriculture, of course, there were no fields at all.)

Once upon a time, O Best Beloved, all creatures great and small each had their own God. (You may boggle at the idea of a God of the Confused Moth or a God of the Cape Warthog, but Nature is wonderful and prodigal.)

Anyway, Ganesh listened to the plea of the Elephants with the itsy-bitsy ears.

He thought for a long time.

And then he made a Magic.

You must understand that when any creature dies, its spirit is born again after a while into a creature of the same species. Sometimes populations explode and sometimes they implode, yet on the whole numbers are reasonably balanced, at least until ex-tinction looms. Where could spirits go then? Where could the spirit of the Confused Moth or the Big Thicket Hog-nosed Skunk find a home? It must do so in any species where available space remains. Unfortunately for such spirits the majority of life on Earth consists of nematodes, namely marine worms. (Plus marine viruses and bacteria, although bacteria don't really count spiritually—they're sort of in between being dead and alive, one neuron short of having a life.)

The myriads and quintillions of worms in the mud at the dark dingy bottom of the ocean, dank and donk, are the final abode of the spirits of animals that become ex-tinct. Animals such as the big dinosaurs—now you know what became of those. How are the mighty fallen! Tyrannosaurus Worm!

Humans are so brainy and wild and warlike that after they die their spirits need a period of *Calmer* (sometimes spelled Karma), a cooling-off time. Consequently, a human spirit may need to spend time in a Sloth or a Tortoise until it can become a human once more. Yes, the humans even stole reincarnation, occupying with their spirits the bodies of rats and bats and cats! Humans are just so prolific.

So long as the human race continued to expand its numbers, like a toxic bloom of diatoms or like mildew on a damp wall, there was spare capacity in its own species for human spirits to take up residence after their time of

Calmer. But, O Best Beloved, at long last Mr and Mrs Human were getting around to using Birth Control by attaching balloons to their excitable parts or taking special pills. Numbers of births would fall.

The Magic that Ganesh made was that many spirits of animals who were still tinct but who might soon become ex-tinct, would now pass into the bodies of human babies. This might lead to many special needs requirements in schools, but never mind. At the same time, many human spirits would pass into the offspring of animals who faced ex-tinction—into Elephants with the itsy-bitsy ears and into other such species. And when those animals ex-tincted, well, human spirits would be forced to live as worms!

Mr and Mrs Human needed to know for sure what was happening, beyond being merely puzzled about the presence in nurseries and schools of jumboboys and jaguargirls. Consequently a baby Elephant was born in a zoo who could speak words through his long trumpet, somewhat nasally as if he had a cold. He cried out to a crowd of visitors, 'Listen and attend! I am a human person! Help me! If I die, I'll become a worm!'

The urgent need for more and more living Elephant bodies, and jaguar bodies, and other endangered bodies, soon became *very* obvious.

And that, O Best Beloved, is how the Elephant with itsy-bitsy ears, and many other endangered species, escaped ex-tinction.

The Drained World

S UN BEAT DOWN ON THE PRIVATE BEACH NEAR MARBELLA, ESPAÑA.
'Today tide seems to have stopped short,' said the plutocrat Vasili
Romanovitch, consulting his very waterproof Rolex. 'Yesterday sea reached
top of that little green rock. Now, only the bottom.'

A popular fallacy is that the Mediterranean has no tides, being the wrong
size to resonate to the attractions of the Moon and Sun. On the other hand:
what's *wet*, and *moves up and down a beach significantly twice a day?* As
opposed to so-called 'meteorological' tides due to shifting distributions of
atmospheric pressure, which have a period of several days; and of course the
longer term slosh of water from east to west and back again . . .

'Only the bottom,' Vasili repeated, eyeing shapely Jacqueline Johnson
who fastened her bikini top and arose to peer. 'And maybe,' she responded,
blue eyes gleaming, 'this is only the *beginning*.'

Jacqueline's speciality was defying conventional thinking, so she endorsed
the opinion of the Spanish and Greeks and other circum-Med nationalities
that their shared sea has tides. *What's wet, and regularly moves up and down
a beach?*

'You mean the beginning of global warming evaporation?' asked one of
Vasili's bodyguard colleagues, Andrei, whose hairy gut hung out over his
baggy trunks.

This idiocy didn't really deserve an answer, but she replied calmly, 'Of the
emptying I predicted as a possibility.'

To be fair, Andrei probably mentioned evaporation because more water evaporated from the Med every day than was replaced by all the rivers flowing into it. Hence, constant replacement from the Atlantic Ocean.

Bending, Jacqueline fished in her Gucci bag for her multifone and swiftly searched the web. 'Hmm, of course oceanic tide levels vary greatly from place to place, but in general it seems the Atlantic is half a metre lower than yesterday. This means,' and she calculated before announcing a very large cubic kilometrage of sea water . . .'has been lost. Vasili, we should return to the yacht.'

'Before it cannot float?' asked Andrei.

'That will be quite a while yet,' snapped Vasili, who understood science, hence his patronage of Jacqueline and her theory which, if true, would require much readjustment worldwide as regards survival and opportunities.

'Where can so much seawater go to?' persisted Andrei. 'Round the bottom of South America into the Pacific? Would not the planet lean over?'

'Into,' said Vasili, 'caverns measureless to man,' since his plutocrat father had sent him to an English public school to be polished, consequently he could quote Coleridge. 'Porous regions deep beneath the ocean floor, which we may well call voids. And which we shall now *seriously* begin to measure, using submarines or bathyspheres and rock-penetrating radar. I shall establish the Romanovitch Foundation, to be headed by Jacqueline. We must try to discover how much ocean will disappear. How the map of the world will be redrawn. I shall need to liquidate assets.'

Andrei, who had been in the FSB, probably mainly still thought of assets as informants, and of liquidation as assassination, since his hand now formed a pistol shape, but Vasili shook his head.

'Our incomplete business with our contacts on this costa is at an end now. Forgive my referring to business matters,' he added to Jacqueline, since he wished to keep their scientific relationship unsullied. 'We shall set sail. We have other fish to fry.'

Jacqueline, and her suspect alliance with the Russian plutocrat, had been vindicated. Even as they cruised out through the Strait of Gibraltar, she was studying the latest news and getting ready to address a plenary session of the Intergovernmental Panel on Climate Change by video link. Colder Atlantic surface water constantly flowed into the Med to replenish evaporation minus river input; and warmer Med water flowed out beneath the density boundary at 100 metres. Since the greatest depth of the Strait of Gibraltar was 900 metres, the diminished Med would become landlocked in a mere 5 years. Yet according to Jacqueline's calculations the rate of oceanic drainage might soon increase to a metre per day, or more. Better to be safe by a long margin than marooned in the Med, even though Vasili and those closest to him could escape in the yacht's helicopter, his yacht being very large.

'As an analogy,' Jacqueline was soon telling the video camera, and the IPCC, 'imagine enormous two-way trapdoors of stone in the depths of the Atlantic, and doubtless the Pacific too, as well as the Indian Ocean. The extra weight of seawater due to greenhouse melting has opened these gates— they reached the tipping point. Formerly some maverick scientists thought there might be giant oceans beneath the sea floor which pressure of magma might push upward, drowning even Mount Everest. But no, currently there are enormous unsaturated porous regions. The question is: *how enormous?*'

'Our bathysphere is stuck,' brave Jean-Luc radioed to the surface eighteen months later. 'The downward suction is too great. Thank God you didn't come along this time, Jacqueline. At least we'll have time until our air runs out to determine the size of the void below us.'

Three hours later Jacqueline finished calculating how much more of the Atlantic would fill the Jean-Luc Void, as the two-man bathysphere team breathed their last. This volume, plus those of other voids already plumbed, indicated a future worldwide sea level one kilometre below the 2010 mean datum.

'Very acceptable,' said Vasili. 'So we won't have a desert world with no rainfall, nor any drop to drink except for a few hundred thousand high-tech survivors pumping water from the underground oceans for desalination to sustain them and their vegetables and chickens and pet cats. This calls for Champagne. Andrei, you may splice the main-brace and cancel the Arks of Water project. We shall drink to Jean-Luc and Marc-Antoine.' Vasili mused. 'Hmm, the Med will be reduced to an Ionian Lake. With no North Sea, Britain becomes part of Europe again. Scandinavia joins the Baltic States. There mightn't be much Caribbean apart from a Cayman Trench Lake. I expect many geopolitical changes.'

Two years later the mass migration from Africa into Europe began. Enough fish trapped in pools sustained the advancing masses until relatively clean nuclear weapons detonated along the bed of the Med as a warning.

—with apologies to Stephen Baxter's splendidly disconcerting *Flood*.

Vile Dry Claws of the Toucan

B Y NOW IT'S BEYOND DISPUTE THAT THE ZETA TUCANAE DISC IS the only surviving in-depth record of a whole alien civilisation.

Found on the little moon of Zeta Tucanae 3 beside the mangled wreckage of a space vehicle, this disc is all we have to go on. Our cyberdrones discovered nothing but frozen radioactive ash down on the destroyed homeworld.

True, we do have the wreckage, plus the suit-shell of the pilot, which the pilot so wantonly and suicidally took off. We also have the interrupted interstellar radio message which has allowed us to read the disc, provisionally. Unfortunately, that message broke off at the 'John and Jane' stage. For our entire knowledge of culture we have to rely on that single disc. History, psychology, philosophy, sociology—the whole shebang.

It is my contention that the text on that disc represents what might best be described, in human terms, as a piece of 'horror fiction'.

Oh yes! Not some dreadful warning about the Ultimate Enemy which devastated life on Zeta Tucanae 3 (and was incinerated by it in turn?), but a dark fantasy etched on the disc purely for entertainment; a horror story.

So how do we track back from the distortions and concoctions of an alien horror narrative to some certainties about the civilisation which produced it?

Already I hear cries of disapproval. But please consider. Pain and pleasure have to be universal to all intelligent beings. Fear must be universal. Complex creatures simply couldn't evolve in the absence of pleasure and pain and fear. As soon as technology permits enough excess leisure, 'Pleasure through Fear' becomes predictable.

Let's survey the facts.

Zeta Tucanae, sixth star in the far southerly constellation of the Toucan, is very similar to our own sun in size and type. Its third planet isn't much smaller than Earth. Atmosphere: oxygen and nitrogen—plus radioactive dust, smoke particles, and suchlike products of a recent massive nuclear war. Shallow seas, low continents, swamps. Lots of craters, of course, and deserts of windblown ash of recent vintage. No remaining traces of life.

Here evolved a race of intelligent gastropods. Snails.

Huge brainy snails with tough shells secreted on their backs, single slimy adhesive feet for crawling and climbing, no bones whatever, pseudopod eyes and flexible tentacles. Valiant, inquisitive, civilised snails.

Ultimately they invented radio telescopes (as witness the 'John and Jane' message), spacecraft, plastics, and nuclear weapons. With homes already on their backs, their architecture would only be industrial.

They were undoubtedly hermaphroditic; otherwise some events on the disc make no sense, even in a horror context.

They stored data upon plastic discs, by squatting on these and laying down a spiral acid trail. They 'read' these discs by crawling on them and decoding the vibrational patterns of rough and smooth. Hence Professor Woodford's fanciful comparison of our alien snails to old-fashioned gramophones. (With horns, yet!)

Conventional scientific wisdom—based on a literal reading of the 'moon disc'—has it that another race, of vicious nocturnal predators, also inhabited ZT3. These implacably evil creatures had invaded from 'elsewhere' (from another star system? from, dare I say it, another dimension? a parallel universe?). The radio message was the start of an interstellar cry for help; and a warning to all amiable life forms. The terminal nuclear war spelled Armageddon for the snails and their dire enemies.

These enemies preyed on the snails not only physically but psychically too. Their minds could possess those of the snails; they could infiltrate snail bodies. A snail thus afflicted might show strange talents: the ability to dry out a fellow snail by staring at it, or glue it to the ground, or cause its organs to boil and bubble out. Eventually the possessed snail would rot away, leaving a haunted empty shell. Intercourse with a possessed snail—these were often luridly attractive—would result in cursed offspring, evolutionary throwbacks or freaks: black shell-less slugs, immovable limpets, tiny winkles, clams.

Let us translate a passage from the moon-disc text:

'The Possessed fired a love-dart point-blank into the [Queen's] hind mantle as she turned to flee . . .'

(I should point out that terrestrial snails elect which sex they wish to be at any particular time. Copulation takes place by coiling slimily around one another. Foreplay consists in the male shooting—or spitting—hormone-primed 'darts' into the flesh of the female to excite her.)

'She felt a dreadful dryness and could not crawl. She smelled the rot of his slime. Knew that he would soon decay inside—but not before he had impregnated her, befouled her, and destroyed [a dynasty].

'"No!" she vibrated at him as he oozed over her locked foot. "This isn't you! This is the Beast inside you!"

'For a moment a tremble of remembrance made the Possessed shudder. Then the Possession tightened its grip.

'"No, you shall not give birth to a mere slug! You'll conceive the child of the Beast itself! With its scrawny claws, its dry tearing claws!"

'She wished that nuclear fire would boil the world dry before that happened. That the atomic hate-darts could fly from hemisphere to hemisphere, cooking all snailkind—as well as the Dry-Leg-Beasts-That-Lurked-In-Caves, the Beasts-That-Hunted-By-Night-With-Scaley-Claws, the Vile-Intruders-From-That-Other-Realm—if that is what it took to purge the evil.

'As the Possessor overwhelmed her she smelt the stench of his inner rot—he who had been the slickest, sweetest, and juiciest of her suitors. Foul ichors ran from within his shell, and she realised that he was already dead, a zombie-snail operated by the cruel mental claw from elsewhere.

'If only she could transform into a he, and save her ovaries from his assault; but his dart had also locked her into the female form! She gagged as the Possessed made love to her, and he ate her vomit for strength to nourish his dribbling seed.'

Isn't it obvious what this is? (Professor Woodford might dispute some elements of this translation, but I've mostly omitted brackets from around 'ambiguous' words for the sake of clarity.)

Here's another passage:

'He was only six orbits old, and the shell-yard fascinated him: the slimy mud paths, the stately row upon row of empty shells which had once housed living snails, a hundred or a thousand orbits ago. To his junior stalk-eyes that shell-yard seemed to stretch out to infinity. The oldest shells of all were furthest from the entrance.

'Often he slid through the mouth of a shell, which easily accommodated his own smaller shell, so as to read the death-song of achievements, boasts, autobiography, passions, apologies, or simply poetry which the aging snail had etched on to the inside of its shell when it sensed its natural death creeping closer.

'That day he slid deeper into the shell-yard than ever before—to a zone where shells were so old that many were cracking and crumbling.

'And so he came in all innocence to the ancient ghost shell.

'Its glittering curves, its apparent lack of fragility, its open mouth attracted him. He ignored the faded taste-warnings dissolved in the mud around it; not understanding them, excited. He slid inside and tongued the walls for the death-song.

'Terrible dry pressure immobilised him. He thought that his own shell would be crushed. He thought that a claw was being driven through it. A claw which scratched at his soft mind, and hid itself inside him . . .'

Likewise, the subsequent passage concerning 'The Power'; and those monsters which I playfully dub 'weretoucans', snails which assumed the form of clawed, beaked beasts by night.

Who in their right mind, you may well ask, would take a horror novel along to read on a black and airless, lonely moon? Surely that would tend to unbalance a mind already under stress? With the result that each shadow would conceal a lurking Evil. Its claws would scratch at the side of the space-ship, seeking admittance. A pilot might well believe himself possessed, inside his suit!

Surely the moon-disc was a literal, true, and inspirational work, intended to keep our lone snail-astronaut's mind devoutly and bravely on his mission—whatever this was—by cataloguing the wiles and vile actions of the enemy? Thus argues Professor Woodford, translating the text somewhat differently from me.

Not so! And therefore all of Woodford's extrapolations from this text, about the history, psychosociology, and every other ology of the snails of ZT3, is so much eyewash. The text is a horror story.

For me, that essential fact 'humanises' the alien snail-people and amply justifies the cost of the expedition.

The Tragedy of Solveig

SOMEBODY HAD BEEN STALKING THE TRAVELLING PLAYERS ALL afternoon. Somebody, or something. Perhaps *two* somethings.

By evening each of the players had caught a few glimpses of the shadower, or shadowers. Or at least they supposed so.

Trees were already taking on the colours of Autumn. Rust and copper and bronze tinged the forest. Those russet glimpses way behind might simply have been foliage stirred by breeze.

Maybe the shadower might indeed be a kind of shadow, in a literal if marvellous sense. Peter Vaara's special talent was the conjuring of visions. He imparted this talent to his troupe. Whenever Peter and Tancred and Stanislav and Natalya and Solveig pulled on their matt black leotards and their coaly skullcaps and performed, they could sway audiences to see pageants.

'Perhaps,' said Tan, 'we're leaving a sort of trail behind us, just as a boat leaves a phosphorescent wake?'

Tan was pushing the cart loaded with their backdrop screens and tents and possessions. The two big lightweight wheels easily rolled along the dirt road. The troupe could easily have afforded to buy a shaggy sturdy pony to harness between the shafts. But then they would have needed to care for the pony. They could almost afford five such ponies. They could have ridden. But Peter's troupe would have begun to resemble a minor circus. Luggage would have multiplied. This would have compromised the purity of their performances. Next thing, they would be needing a servant, a groom, a fetcher and carrier, a tent erector. A servant would have his own needs, and he wouldn't share the affinity which linked the five of them.

Natti glanced back.

'You're denying the obvious, Tan. What's following us is a Juttie. Possibly a pair of them. Keeping in the woods. Keeping pace.'

Juttahats. Unmen . . . Alien servants of the alien serpents.

'Brazen Jutties,' said Peter. He sounded almost pleased. Strangeness was delightful.

'Brazen,' agreed Natti.

The lustrous coppery livery of a Brazen Juttahat would indeed seem like Autumn leaves.

Solli said, 'We haven't heard any reports of attacks or abductions lately.' There was anxiety in her tone, yet at the same time her mind seemed to be dwelling on something else entirely.

'Very likely they're just curious,' was Stan's opinion. 'They sense an aura about us.'

'Maybe it's our sweat they're sniffing!' said Tan. It had been a warm afternoon. Above the bendy boughs of curver trees (their chartreuse quiffs now turning orange with the season) and above the rusting spade-leafed larkery trees, woolly cumulus clouds sailed slowly through a sky which was draining of colour, sapphire becoming opal. A haze of sizzleflies accompanied the players, who could all use a dip in a lake.

Solli shivered, and Natti patted her.

'We have our crossbow and our knives. Peter has his pistol.' Ah, the light-pistol. Would it be wise to brandish the gun? Even when bent on mayhem, Juttahats rarely employed force out of proportion to what they encountered. To fire hotlight would be to invite hotlight in reply.

Solli quickened her pace, outdistancing the cart.

'They're only snooping,' said Natti. 'Only keeping an eye on human beings. We're used to spectators, aren't we?'

Another ten minutes' tramping brought the players to the shore of a small lake. There, they pitched their pair of tents. Stan sat watching the woods, crossbow laid casually across his lap, while the others kicked off boots (or in Solli's case bark shoes), and stripped off leather breeches or long woollen skirts, linen shirts or cambric blouses. As they waded into the water, arcs of ripples progressed through the gathering dusk. Soarfowl took refuge amongst reeds. By now the blue chevrons of the birds were grey.

If a Juttahat came to spy on the bathers, what would it see?

Tan was the burliest. He was sandy-haired and fresh-faced. Masks of laughter and of grief were tattooed upon his upper arms. When he was dressed, the insignia were invisible.

Natti's black hair was cropped short, the better to accommodate a skullcap. She had the lithe muscularity of a dancer, a delicate figure reconfigured with sinew. The little globes of her breasts seemed mischievously to flout the regime of the rest of her body—sallow apples each studded with a tiny cherry. On her right breast, was a tattoo of a winking eye.

Solly was taller than Natti, and fuller in build. Her hair was ghost-blonde, as the idiom put it, and curly like some cherubic child's. Her grandma, when a lass, had worked at a certain *establishment* in the port of Tumio which catered for black sailors from southerly Pootara. The lass had accidentally conceived but had refused offers of *special juice*. A daughter was born, who made a half-way decent marriage later on. Solli was sensitive about this matter. Her skin was the cream of coffee with much milk in it. Solli's breasts were jaunty little gourds. Brown nipples angled upward from umber areolas larger than golden Or coins. A broad gold ring pierced one of her nipples.

Peter himself was so nondescript that right after speaking to him strangers would be hard put to remember his whey-face. This anonymity was of no account (or perhaps it was essential!) when he exerted his charisma, causing an audience to see him and his black-camouflaged troupe transfigured into heroes and heroines or villains.

Presently Stan took his turn in the water. His legs and bum were tight. However, he sported a bit of a belly. The slack excess of his hairy chest suggested a female ape about to give suck. Stan's hair was red, though by now in the dusk all colour had expired. Across the lake a fat harnie bird honked mournfully.

From the larder-box on the cart, Natti brought cheese-bread, cold cabbage rolls, and rye pasties. Last to bathe, Stan had filled a flagon with water to pass around.

Peter and Tan and Solli loved pigs-in-blankets, the baked cabbage leaves wrapped around spiced beef and barley. Natti and Stan preferred slices of sweetfin and pork baked inside rye-dough. All five chewed cheese-bread. The bread squeaked in their mouths as if a playful ventriloquist were nearby.

Presently the stars were glittering. Clouds had mostly departed. The constellations of the harp, the cuckoo, and the cow were all on view. Gassy Otso had risen as high as it ever would, though its moon-cubs couldn't be distinguished. A slim silver bridge arced brightly across the southern sky: the sky-sickle, debris of a long-disintegrated moon.

Even in the gleam from the sickle, lake and shore were only modestly illuminated. The interior of the forest was black as pitch. Ideal conditions for a rehearsal. No need to set up the purple screens or to don leotards and skull-caps.

There was never any rigid text. To write down words (were any of the players able to do so, which they were not) would be to imprison and geld the stallion of inspiration, bridling and bitting it.

'How about The Maiden and the Serpent-Mage?' proposed Peter. 'A new variant on the tale of Saint Georgi . . .'

'*Georgi orgy*,' suggested Stan. 'This time Georgi kills the serpent who captured the maiden. But Georgi only rescues the maiden in order to ravish her. The violated lass sneaks back to the corpse of the alien snake. She flays the snake and dresses herself in its skin of scales like golden armour. Determined to avenge herself, she sets out for Georgi's keep. But as she travels, the skin clings to her so tightly that she can't peel it off. The dead mage's voice invades her mind. She's the first human being who has ever heard an Isi voice in her head—the way the Jutties hear their masters' voices directing them. That serpent had truly loved her—'

'That's far-fetched,' said Natti.

'What does our spy in the forest think about this?' Tan asked loudly. There was no answer—not as yet.

'Why should the serpent always be a male?' demanded Solli. 'Why not a *female* mage? She captures the maiden in order to lure Georgi. When Georgi comes, the serpent tries to seduce and enslave him with her overpowering fragrance.'

'Her yeasty odours,' mused Peter. 'Her menstrual scents. If we evoke those—'

'Will Georgi yield to me?' In the sickle-light Solli's gaze lingered on Tan.

None of the five were lovers. They knew each other too well, or so they thought. Their relationship was too familiar, as if they were five siblings. *Lust* is spawned mainly by the imagination. What hidden mysteries were there for these five to imagine? *Love* represents an abnormal degree of attention paid to the object of desire. In their dramatic roles each of the players became the focus of heightened attention on the part of the audience. Each became an idol—autonomous and self-contained (even if it was Peter who empowered them to project illusions). Idol did not fall in love with idol.

How different from the humanoid Juttahats! Jutties were entirely subordinate to the Isi snakes. Juttahats carried their Isi masters like proud golden tubas when the snakes left their great underground nests (a rare occurrence). Jutties ran enigmatic errands of mischief for the Isi. The snakes controlled their servants through voices in the head.

Did Solli wish to mimic an Isi mage as a way of influencing those lurkers in the woods to behave themselves? Or was she trying to steer Tan into a new role, of servant to her wishes?

Surely they all knew each other far too well. Though, since the recent visit to Kip'an'keep and their private performance for the Forest Lord's daughter Tilly, Solli had been acting a bit oddly. Had something happened in Kip'an'-keep—to Solly but not to the others? Something which now spooked her? People could succumb to obsessions. To bees buzzing in their bonnets.

Peter's scrutiny of Solli by sickle-light failed to enlighten him.

Solli pestered. 'Why shouldn't I act the Isi mage to Tan's Georgi? Why should I be the maiden in distress again? Why should I be the ravished one?'

'We *could* rehearse something entirely different,' said Natti.

'No, no,' said Peter. 'Seems to me there's an impulse to do Georgi and Serpent and Maiden.' *Get to the root of this.* 'Let's improvise.'

Like some conductor of a tango orchestra, he waved his hands, harmonising his troupe, invoking his gift.

'*Let the sway*
'*Steer the play*,' he called softly.
'*Let's find*
'*What's in our mind:*
'*The panorama*
'*Of the drama.*'

Then the five of them began to weave an outline, in a mounting rapture of mutual inspiration. Tan was Georgi, of course. Natti was the captured maiden, the bait for bold Georgi. Stan was the maiden's distressed father. Peter was the Juttahat body-servant of the female snake and enchantress. Solli was that mage.

No audience was present (except perhaps an alien snooper or two, behind trees), but the enchantment became almost as powerful as if many spectators were there. Soon Peter seemed indeed to be a Juttahat—who had sneaked from the fringe of the forest to replace the maestro. Solli glistened in the sickle-light, a silvery version of a serpent, rearing upward upon her coils. Tan wore phantom armour. Presently he must discard his armour, reluctantly, piece by piece. Solli lisped and hissed insinuatingly. Her words seemed to arise inside the heads of the others rather than being spoken aloud.

Thus the proto-play wove itself—a drama of dominance and desire, of fears and gallantry and alien mystery, of father-love and fortune-hunting, of abduction, of indecent molestation by a body-servant, of attempted seduction and enslavement by a giant fragrant snake.

Not only the shoreline but the whole lake seemed to have become an arena of sombre sand where serpents might bask and glide. The constellations were lights in the roof of a subterranean dome.

Afterwards, Peter brought a bottle of blueberry liqueur from the cart. As the dark bottle circulated, each player seemed to be drinking essence of night.

A branch snapped under a foot. The sharp crack must be deliberate—unless the snooper was clumsy and stupid. Juttahats were nimble, except when exhausted. Maybe the play had mesmerised this one. Tan cocked the crossbow in warning.

'Being truce,' called a voice from the trees. 'Being tranquil. Being peace, being placid.' Was the Juttahat trying to sway them? How absurd. No Juttahat could ever cast a sway. Jutties were under the sway of the snakes. Still, the Juttie was doing its best to lull them.

Was a colleague covering it at this moment with a crossbow which fired explosive bullets, a little bonus of firepower to match the superior number of human beings present? Tan's bow only fired ordinary quarrels.

'May as well see what it wants,' drawled Peter.

'Odd choice of timing,' Stan said. 'Waiting till night.'

'It's trying to minimise its alienness.' Solli stated this for a fact. 'In the dark it'll look almost normal.'

'But not sound normal!' Tan imitated: '—ing,—ing,—ing.' He chuckled. 'No sense of timing, or of time. Perpetual present. How can creatures have any sense of history when they don't have any independence?'

'It's time,' said Peter, 'for actors to speak in tongues.' He called out towards the forest: 'Be coming forth in safety, Servant of Snakes.'

A figure approached slowly. Its livery glinted in the sickle-light as if phosphorescing. On one shoulder was a black glyph like a roosting vesperbird. You could hardly distinguish the oddities: the thin nostrils that opened and closed as if this person were aquatic in origin, the prim mouth, the gland-slits on its chin from which liquid beads leaked—of apprehension or appeasement or inducement?—and the nictitating membranes which slid often across the golden eyes.

The Juttahat might almost have been a man. How it must rile the snakes that men and women failed to heed their mental sendings and obey them similarly.

'Admiring your performance,' announced the intruder. 'Much admiring!' Underlying its words were hisses and clicks, as if in ironic commentary. 'Admiring so deeply,' continued the Juttahat, 'that my masters are inviting you all to be performing the selfsame drama in their nest.'

'*What?*' cried Peter in astonishment. '*Saying what?*'

The Juttahat repeated the invitation, and then added, 'Payment being fifty golden Ors, plus yourselves being in the presence of an appreciative Isi mage.'

Fifty Ors. Quite a sum. Not a fortune. Certainly an inducement. Aliens had little use for human money. They acquired it, by trade, by robbery. Contingency funds . . . Here, so it seemed, was an imperative contingency.

Solli caught her breath. Natti exclaimed, 'It's a lure for dupes!'

'Hang on, Natti,' said Peter. 'Now just hang on.'

This business must have been simmering for a while. The Isi must have been gleaning news about Peter Vaara and his troupe. Most likely, cuckoo-birds had been telling tales and reciting passages from plays. No one knew the motives of cuckoos, though people relied on their gossip. The birds could easily be swayed to carry a message—'*Coo-coo, coo-coo, sing the story, tell the tale!*'—although they could never be made to cackle about themselves. Some people thought that the big scrawny green birds with their cat-like ears were really spies of the Isi, more pervasive spies than the Jutties. But no one ever harmed a cuckoo. That would be bad luck. The worst of luck.

'This is a remarkable opportunity,' Peter said.

For a dramatist to see inside an Isi nest, and to come close to serpents! Such a stimulation to the imagination! Their plays would gain such authenticity.

'It's a trap,' insisted Natti.

'I *want* to mimic a mage,' said Solli. 'Wasn't that the whole idea? Now I shall do so perfectly.'

'Refusal being impossible,' said the Juttahat. 'Already a sky-boat coming here to be carrying yourselves and your cart peacefully to the Brazen Isi nest.'

'*Indeed!*'—from Peter.

'Indeed,' replied the alien. 'Much admiring your performance.'

The alternative would be to take to their heels through the inky woods, abandoning their cart—risking bashing their brains out on low branches. These Juttahats might be equipped with night-eye goggles.

'We need to sleep on this, Snake-Servant,' growled Stan. 'Mainly, we need to *sleep.*'

Hard to be sure in the gloom, but did the alien's chin-glands leak, did its dimples pucker? Was that the equivalent of a smile?

'Sky-boat landing, sky-boat waiting, leaving at dawn. Myself sleeping in woods.'

Oh yes, to keep watch—so that they did not sneak out of their tents, except for a pee.

Engines boomed. Jets of air buffeted the lake. A glaring searchlight illuminated sand and tents. Five heads looked out, blinking, to gain the impression of a long fuselage with dark round portholes and swept-back delta wings. Fluted pipes and vanes adorned the vessel. Slowly it settled upon the shore, the focus of its searchlight shrinking and brightening as if to burn a disc of sand to glass before winking out . . .

While the players were in Kip'an'keep, they had given several performances in town, and then a final nocturnal show in the tree-garden on the hill to the east. In fact, they had pitched their tents inside the leafy park itself (with the permission of a granny at the gate, and for a silver half-mark), rather than using a more expensive hostelry.

This arboretum was Lord Kippan's pride, but it was freely open to the public. Kippan himself was a recluse, who never roamed his own park. In Summer lovers would go to the park of an evening. Sometimes they would spend the whole night. Sweethearts wouldn't dream of carving hearts or tokens in any trunk. The penalty for defacing a tree in the park was that the culprit's own face would be deformed. Clamped in a mask of charmed mootapu wood, the miscreant's features would mutate to match the grotesquery of the mask. Nobody wanted this to happen to themselves, although a few freakish faces seen on the streets of Kip'an'keep suggested that a besotted lover took the risk occasionally. Later, maybe his girl took offence, or became furious at finding herself pregnant or spurned, and peached on him.

Several bizarre species of tree grew only in Kippan's domain. The carny tree, for instance. With its sticky resin, a carny could trap and digest birds. Unlike the more widespread leper tree, which would lean away from contact, a carny would jerk its boughs towards a victim. This posed no problem to people who could easily pull themselves loose! Unless, of course, they were roped to a carny, which was another penalty for misconduct down Kippan way...

Even odder, was the mootapu tree. The fermented sap of the mootapu could give you a two-day hangover, but the *raw* sap (along with a powerful sway by a shaman) could alter a person radically. As everyone knew, this sap was responsible for the transmutation of some volunteers from amongst Lord Kippan's troops literally into woodmen, wooden soldiers. Those warriors would live as long as any tree. They would dream blissfully while dormant. They would arouse, and be flexible, mobile, and supremely resilient, impervious to cold, resistant to injury. Mootapu sap remodelled people.

The arboretum boasted two examples of every tree and bush, though never as neighbours. There were two fireproof purple tammies, two inflammable minties (within little moats), two hoary hard sylvesters, two ivorywoods, two musktrees, two larixes with henna scales, two veras with green needles . . . oh, the list was as long as a woodman's life.

Solli had asked the crone at the gate where a mootapu tree could be seen.

Third path on yer left, second path on yer right. Mind you don't go scooping any resin for a pretty bead to hang off yer ear, or yer ear might turn into a goat's, hee-hee—

Peter had bought fish pasties from Granny. Their camp site was close to the gate. No one need fear pilferers in *this* park. The troupe enjoyed a fine vista westward across the town, and a sidelong view of the keep and timber forts to the south.

Kip'an'keep town was laid out in a grid of houses between a cool lake and a smaller hot one from which a geyser erupted regularly every two hours. Carved gables and porches were vividly painted. Elevated boardwalks lined plank-paved streets. Trees sprouted from behind every home. Above a grove of stout stilt-trees bulged the onion dome of the Kirk-in-the-Trees.

The Lord's tammywood keep, with its tiers of verandahs, resembled a purple chest of drawers, all partly open, with a dome on top. Bridges led to lodges and minor manors. One of the surrounding prefabricated forts was being dismantled and reconstructed. Tapper Kippan was paranoid about his security.

The evening was fair. Clouds were breaking up. The red flush of imminent sunset only extended a modest way across the sky, promising blithe
weather. Foliage in the park was also beginning to acquire a sunset palette.

After eating their pasties, the players had set out to visit the mootapu tree.
Solli linked arms with Tan as though they were amorous promenaders. For
the sake of symmetry, Natti linked with Stan.

Peter brought up the rear. Idly he studied the two couples, who weren't
actually couples. His troupe, his family. The channels for his gift. How innocent everything seemed.

Not that magic-drama was exactly an innocent activity! Magic-drama
deeply affected the minds of spectators. It induced illusions. It aroused
passions. The players themselves were hardly immune, but control was part
of Peter's gift. Guidance and direction.

Of beige vellum bark, the mootapu tree sprawled in all directions as if it
hadn't the backbone to stand upright. Stout lower branches leaned knuckles
and elbows upon the soil. The lower limbs were quite vast, and hosted
sulphurous bracket fungi. Orange resin leaked through the vellum,
congealing into ambery pendants. Springy slim shoots of feathery foliage, of
a fading pea-green, surged upward—as though saplings of a different species
were grafted on to the great base.

A freckled red-headed girl was balancing on one of the great slumping
boughs. She was about seven years old, and wore a simple linen shift. Her
twin brother, dressed in shirt and shorts, was prodding at the girl's ankles
with a long twig, trying to trip her. Beware those pools of resin! The girl
shifted from foot to foot. Her expression was halfway between excitement
and panic. Which way would she tip? Into taunting triumph, or into shrieks
and tears?

Their mother came hurrying through the nearby shrubs. The woman
wore a frayed green gown trimmed with orange and purple felt. Her auburn
hair, tied in a bun, seemed dull compared with that of her offspring.

'Oh here you both are! Minkie, don't you go poking her like that!
Be careful, Tammy! Stand still and I'll pick you down. How dare you,
Tammy—!'

'Minkie dared me, Mum—'

The woman scowled at the players.

'Couldn't you lot have stopped her?'

'We only just arrived here,' said Peter, reasonably.

Tammy's mother reached up her arms. 'Jump now, jump well clear.'

As Tammy did so, her white shift rode up her thin bare legs and thighs. Hastily her mother set the girl down. She berated the players.

'Five grown people, who couldn't put a stop to kids' jinks!'

Peter was irked. 'Madam, I notice that you named your girl after the fire-proof tree!'

'What of it? She were born with fiery hair.'

'And you wouldn't want her to be hot-headed, would you? But Minkie, your boy . . . that's very like the name of the Minty tree that bursts into flames.'

'*What of it?* Are you some fortune-teller?'

Peter shrugged, but Natalya piped up.

'You give your lad licence to be naughty, lady. Yet your girl must behave herself. What do you expect will happen? Why did you tell him not to *poke* her? Why use that word?'

The mother flushed. She covered the girl's ears with her hands. 'That's disgusting!'

'You're storing up trouble,' said Natti.

Incensed, the woman seized her children and hauled them away.

'You know what's going on,' Natti called after her.

When mother and children had gone, Stan said, 'Phew, that was a bit stiff.'

'So was the lad's little twig,' said Natti. 'I could see. It isn't funny. The girl wasn't even wearing knickers. If she stains her shift on some moss, oh dear, I can imagine the fuss! Woman like that infuriates me. Causing problems, and willfully blind to them.'

Solli spoke up. 'It'll be the girl who survives. The tammy tree endures fires. One day her brother will flare up and people will quench him. The girl will cope. She'll be the winner.'

'Frankly,' said Natti, 'I doubt that.' She eyed Solli curiously.

The next morning, they toured Kip'an'Keep, found a suitable hall which wasn't already booked for some tango band, and hired a crier to roam through the plank streets and along the boardwalks announcing, *'Kaleva's greatest dramaturge Peter Vaara is in town with his troupe. Come witness the tale of Tycho the Tyrant, Tycho the Tormenter . . .'*

Cuckoos had cackled aplenty about Tycho Cammon's cruelties and ravishings. Still, it was daring—even rash—of Peter to present a show featuring that very unsavoury lord. Admittedly Tycho's domain was hundreds of keys north-eastwards—way beyond Yulistalax. But Yulistalax happened to be where Gala took place every Autumn. A troupe of players worth their salt ought to be performing at Yulistalax. Tycho Cammon would also be putting in an appearance at Speakers' Valley, to exert his will over any challengers. Cammon could will a contestant's head to burst apart.

What if he heard a cuckoo cackle that strolling players had been taking his name in vain? He might ignore the truce which prevailed during Gala (so long as you weren't standing upon the central hillock of Speakers' Stage). He might indulge in some ghastly revenge.

'Alternatively he might be pleased at how well-known his infamy is.' Peter had said this a fortnight earlier when he first suggested staging such a crowd-pulling show. 'Tyrants are usually exhibitionists.'

Solli had taken a dim view. Was Peter right in the head? The troupe wouldn't dare go near Gala this year! Natti, however, felt that Cammon's crimes oughtn't to be swept under a carpet because of cowardice—even if audiences might merely enjoy the thrills rather than be moved to indignation. Eventually Solli was talked around.

'Somebody will trounce Cammon,' Peter had affirmed, as if their little magic-drama might in some way contribute to the tyrant's eventual downfall. 'Perhaps even at this year's Gala!' Which, now, they could not risk attending . . .

Nor, in fact, had they attended Gala the previous year either. They had been over in the far west. Back then, the troupe had been together for less than a year. Earlier than that, Peter had performed solo—and then suddenly his gift had burgeoned.

In town, they gave three performances of *Tycho the Tyrant* to much acclaim, sending shivers down spines. The motive for the final evening performance up at the park was that someone important from the keep might attend. Not the recluse himself! Maybe one of his three bailiffs. A patron was always useful.

And someone important *did* turn up, chaperoned by a taciturn wooden soldier with a lightrifle slung over one shoulder. Tilly Kippan, the Forest Lord's youngest daughter, came to the show . . .

Amongst bushes which were losing their definition in the dying light, illusions were particularly persuasive. The audience ooh-ed and aah-ed as Tan, in the role of Tycho, strutted and menaced and leered, and became for them utterly the brutal lustful bully.

'That's *him* and no mistaking! He's here—!'

'Ooh, cuddle me, Carl, hold me tight—!'

Some of those present may have travelled to Gala and seen Tycho in the flesh. Most of the audience would have heard descriptions. In their collective enchantment they all beheld the heavy jowls and fat self-indulgent lips of the brute.

Gallant Stan stood in Cammon's way. Cammon lusted for Stan's sister—portrayed by Solli, who now was a gorgeous beauty. Tycho tormented Stan. He made him a puppet of his will—until his sister begged mercy and promised herself to the bully. Natti, who was Solli's mother, summoned a witch to help her family. Here was a whole sub-theme. Natti became the witch—and Tycho withered her. Solli's mother summoned an enchanter—Peter—pledging all the family wealth. Here was another sub-theme.

Tycho paralysed Peter and made his head explode. How the blood and brains sprayed into the air. Spectators threw up their arms to shelter themselves. The tyrant locked the frantic mother inside a cage. Everyone saw the cage rise up from the ground and swing to and fro. In various discrete guises the spectators saw Cammon have his way with Solli, who was obliged to protest her delight at his indecencies.

When Tycho was sated, he transformed her brave brother into wood (which Kip'an'keepers could appreciate). Next, he softened the ground to quicksand. Stan sank down into the sand, where he would remain alive though paralysed. This was Tycho's fulfillment of his promise to spare Solli's brother. This was his guarantee of her slavish submissiveness.

Meanwhile, from her dangling cage, old Natti, now crazy, cried fitful curses. Actually, Natti sounded and seemed not unlike a cuckoo. Attracted by the magic and the furore, one of those kettle-sized birds had indeed settled in a nearby tree to scrutinise the spectacle and hark with cocked ears.

By starlight and sicklelight the show ended, with bows. Tan was no longer a monster. Nor was Solli so totally ravishing. Nor was Natti hanging in mid-air. Nor was Stan buried alive, to the relief of all present.

That wooden soldier, who was dressed in a uniform of brown bark, lit a fish-oil lantern and escorted a young lady forward.

How impassive the soldier, how immobile the grainy texture of his hard ruddy face illuminated by the lantern. How animated the young woman by comparison, and how soft-featured. She could only be sixteen or seventeen. Loose golden tresses. A broad face, and a generous brow. A gown of innumerable leaf patterns, as if woven from foliage. A necklace of wine-dark gems. Fine garnets, by the look of those.

'That was awful,' she began. 'The oppression . . .'

'I hope we didn't offend innocent ears—' Peter began hastily.

'No, on the contrary: *congratulations!*'

She was Tilly Kippan, and she had a request. She hoped that the troupe might visit her privately the next day. No, not at the keep itself. Her father might take alarm. But in Maids' Manor, adjoining the keep. That was where Tilly resided. A guard would come in the morning to guide them.

The five of them were shown into a chamber which was bare of furniture except for a tall pink-tiled stove. Several layers of muslin veiled a window. A large rug occupied most of the floor. On the far side of the rug, Tilly knelt upon a velvet cushion, green as moss. On the hither side, a line of five such cushions awaited her guests.

'Would you mind kneeling down? Just like me!'

The rug was woven with little silhouettes of trees, and a maze of pathways. Here and there stood tiny wooden dolls, as well as a scattering of pebbles of lapis and onyx and agate. *Dolls!* Had they been brought to this room to play at dolls with the Forest Lord's daughter? Was the lass retarded? A frown creased Natti's face, but Solli beamed.

'I'll bet those dolls are *so* much more than they seem!'

And they were indeed.

To say that the dolls were Tilly's true friends might convey an impression of alienated inadequacy which wouldn't begin to do justice to the richness of her imaginative life, as she soon revealed it, in confidence.

It was over two years since Tilly first began telling herself a complicated tale of friendships and quarrels and of love and betrayal, using those miniature dolls as her players. She would move the dolls around in a complex choreography. She would imitate their voices. Those chips of agate and onyx gave her characters the power to cast a magical sway or to be rescued from a sway. The game was ingenious and intricate. Tilly herself was so fresh, so exuberant—and also nonchalant, with hardly any trace of obsessiveness.

She wished for Peter to cast a sway so that for an hour or two she might enter directly into this melodrama of hers upon the big mat. The players would adopt the personae of her dolls. She also would become one. She wanted the elaborate woodland with all its pathways to become as real as life to her.

Instead of magnifying themselves, Peter and his players must miniaturise themselves. Instead of projecting themselves outwardly, they must internalise themselves, as it were.

Solli clapped her hands delightedly. 'Oh yes, oh yes . . . !'

Well, Peter could always *try* . . .

Scurrying through the forest of mysteries, seeking a gleaming boulder of power . . .

Enchanted by love for the lass he'd lost, wrestling with a shape-changing rival by a riverbank . . .

The abducted maiden escaping by swimming a lake . . .

On a fine white steed, blowing the horn of summons . . .

Cocking that crossbow, while the gale tore leaves from the trees . . .

It was a tale in which one might become trapped, if Tilly Kippan had been deluded. More problematic, was that Peter and his players relied on exaggeration. There were so many sensitive subtleties and implications. Tilly had outlined themes and characters, but the outcome could only be caricature and travesty. To improvise on such scanty acquaintance with the tangled tale—or rather, such lack of acquaintance—was hopeless.

Nevertheless, when the sway subsided, Tilly seemed joyful. She gazed at Peter, then at Solli. Solli's eyes were moist with mutuality, as if she had experienced a profound emotional communion.

'It was so inadequate,' apologised Peter. Oh, he was self-critical now— even though judgement had deserted him in the matter of Tycho Cammon. Perhaps he feared a fit of petulance from this daughter of a Lord.

Tilly nodded. 'I *knew* it would be. I did at least experience the landscape of my little friends! For that, I thank you from the bottom of my heart.'

'Ah, well,' said Peter.

How warmly Solli smiled at Tilly.

'I don't need to do this again,' Tilly said. 'But please, do stay a day longer at the arboretum. Let me visit you. I want—'

Did she want to run away with players? Did she think of putting all her dolls and lucky stones in a bag and rolling up her rug to sling over her shoulder?

She laughed lightly.

'I want to sense how your gift—' She couldn't explain in words. Evidently she wanted to know how to enter even more intensely into her game. Tilly shrugged. 'I couldn't leave Kip'an'keep. I couldn't leave my father.' She seemed to know exactly what they might have been thinking. With irony rather than irritation, she added, 'Go away? Wed a husband? Why should I wed when my friends are here, forever falling in love and out of love?'

The troupe could hardly refuse her request when the arboretum where they were camping belonged to the Forest Lord himself. As for the story-game, they would not see *that* again. The game had become private once more.

Tilly visited the troupe for several hours, without any guard to accompany her. She strolled for a long while with Peter in the park; and then with Natti; and finally with Solli—though with neither Tan nor Stan.

In retrospect, it seemed to be Solli in whom Tilly had confided the most—not about her game but about her parents. Tilly's dad had gained longlife, but subsequently he had locked himself away like a miser. Her mother became increasingly embittered. Tapper Kippan doted on Tilly, but no longer showed any affection to his wife. Perhaps this was because Edith Kippan was manifestly growing older, unlike Tapper. Tapper's neglect of Edith would hardly sweeten her countenance or her temperament.

Stan had a question for Solli. 'They don't call him Tapper because his longlife happened in the same way as with those wooden soldiers, by him tapping the sap of the mootapu tree?'

Solli seemed startled. She exclaimed, 'Don't you know anything, Stan! Tapper's a longlife because he married one of the Queen's daughters! Those all give longlife to the first man who beds them. Unless,' she whispered theatrically, 'the bridegroom becomes a *zombie*.'

'Oh, I *know* that, Solli. I just thought that in Tapper's case maybe the mootapu sap had *something* to do with it—'

'Well, it doesn't!' How brusque Solli was. To soften this, she said, 'Forget about trees! Tilly told me a secret. She fears her Dad's becoming addicted to a drug from a *fungus*. The drug's euphoric. It changes his sense of time. Don't tell anyone.'

'I don't think we'll be dramatising Tapper Kippan's life,' said Peter. 'It seems a bit static.'

Solli couldn't help exclaiming, 'Unlike Tycho's!'

After a briefer visit on the morning after—during which Tilly went off for a while with Solli—they were all free to leave.

Tilly rewarded the troupe with a purse of silver Marks. She wasn't munificent, just moderately generous. She also gave Solli and Natti each a pair of laced bark shoes which were at once elegant and practical. Unfortunately, Natti's pair were a little too large for her, so she changed back into her boots as soon as Tilly had left. Solli wore her own new shoes happily on the hike away from Kip'an'keep.

Thick morning-mist hung over lake and shore, confusing perception. It was as if the troupe had awoken from troubled dreams into another dream. Vague figures in golden livery were moving around a craft of vanes and propellers and antennae and fluted side-pipes. Unreal, unreal. The five might have been sucked into someone else's illusion, an alien illusion.

A Juttahat stood watching while the players breakfasted on cheese and smoked sausages.

Then the tents were packed. Two Juttahats wheeled the cart to the rear of the sky-boat. They pushed it up a cargo ramp between the tail propellers.

It was time to enter the boat. To inhale alien odours. To perch upon padded seats which weren't quite shaped for human bums. To wear straps.

Engines roared. Air intakes shrieked. The fuselage throbbed as though it might shake apart. Then the vessel rose upward, out of the woolly mist into sunlight—and into sudden sight through portholes of a reversed and diminished world where for a while all the trees seemed upside-down until one got used to being above them instead of below them.

They arrived over a sizeable gap in the forest: a vacancy filled by flat mist. A lake might almost be present beneath that white veil. An impossible, perfectly circular lake.

Two tiny islands (which couldn't be islands) protruded above the mist, bronze and glistening. Domes. Hoods for heavy guns.

Juddering and hissing, the sky-boat descended into the mist. The vessel continued sinking. Sinking into the earth itself.

Suddenly, yellow light flooded forth, illuminating a cavern. A roof was flowing back into position overhead. Another sky-boat stood nearby—and several smaller flying-pods.

'We're inside a serpents' nest,' hissed Solli. The shivering thrill which affected audiences was theirs to experience now.

En route to their temporary quarters, down curves of descending tunnels, they gaped at grottoes and crypts and underground gardens, at a chamber floored with golden sand where a serpent lay basking, at a workshop where liveried Jutties laboured over throbbing machines. Such chimes and twangs! The nest might have been a vast clock. Soft yellow light diffused from panels in ceilings and walls. Juttahats chirped and hissed at one another. Junior Jutties in golden lamé elastic suits scampered, curious about the visitors and the cart which followed them. Their curiosity never became intrusive. It seemed controlled. How fruity the warm dry air smelled.

The quarters were a large chamber. Orange and yellow tiles covered half of the floor. The rest of the space was devoted to a garden. Tiled paths snaked amongst bushes with gaudily patterned leaves such as they had never seen before. A cubicle in one wall would shower hot water, then jet hot air. Another cubicle was a crouch-toilet. Shoe-slots flanked a hole in the floor, which hummed when you stood on the slots. Some kind of moist fabric for wiping oneself poked from a dispenser. A cabinet dispensed chilled flasks of sweetened water; another cabinet, warm cakes of food. Half a dozen padded chairs could be elongated into couches to sleep upon.

They were to perform in this chamber late that afternoon. Then they would all enjoy a night's rest (if they could sleep) before their return to the lake.

Peter was loath to mount another rehearsal in case a serpent might be spying through some lens. The subsequent impact of the show could be lessened.

'I *wonder*,' he said, 'whether we oughtn't to put on the tale of Tycho Cammon instead of Saint Georgi?'

'Why?' Solli demanded.

'It's just that imitating an Isi mage in front of one—'

'—might be unconvincing?' she interrupted. 'I say we ought to have the courage to try it!'

'It's you who'll be in that role—'

'And *you'll* be a Juttie, whom I'll be *seeming* to control.' She smiled sweetly. 'You aren't worried about that, maestro?'

'What I was going to say, Solli, is that in such unusual circumstances some sort of echo might arise . . . The audience might influence *you* instead of vice versa!'

'I'm not worried. Your gift will enfold me, Peter.'

Natti said, 'The Isi are obviously interested in how Peter's gift works. They may imagine he controls us like puppets on a string. Can they learn the secret? Can they copy the trick? If *you* identify closely with a serpent, the serpent might identify a bit too closely with you . . .'

'I said I'm not scared!'

'It was you who didn't want us to stage the Tycho show.'

'I was wrong, wasn't I! We need to assert ourselves here. How better than by swaying a snake to believe that I *am* a serpent?'

Very soon after, a Juttahat entered the chamber and announced: 'Your performance tonight being the same as you were practising beside the lake.' It wasn't a question, but a statement. Having spoken, the Juttahat left. The announcement *might* merely have been a reminder rather than proof of surveillance.

So instead of rehearsing they played cards.

'—ten o' diamonds!'

'—Queen of Ice!'

'—Ace in the hole—!'

Solli strolled slowly around the shrubbery with Tan. She lingered often, showing intense interest in the big lurid leaves. She would catch hold of Tan to direct his attention to this pattern or that. Now and then he laughed. She was pretending that the leaves from an alien world were maps of that alien world. She might almost be courting him.

Peter lay, eyeing the two. *What was she up to?*

Now and then, members of the troupe might enjoy a casual fling with some stranger. A sauna liaison, so to speak. Almost an aspect of personal hygiene. None of the troupe had shown any such inclination towards one another. Their professional relationship worked so much better without that kind of intimacy.

Stan was a stocky tub on stilty legs. Sometimes he looked like a plump bird, when he flapped his arms and strutted and puffed out his chest so that his flab seemed to consist of powerful pectoral muscles. No doubt Tan was more physically appealing. When Tan's shirt was off—to chop firewood or whatever—those wonderful tattoos of smiling and frowning faces would seem about to speak aloud as sinew rippled under the pigmented skin.

Was Solli appointing Tan her special protector in this alien nest? Or had she made up her mind to seduce him?

Peter was puzzled.

Natti was watching, too. She frowned at Peter, but they could hardly exchange confidences.

Stan was snoozing.

The troupe donned their matt black leotards and skullcaps. Presently, thirty-odd liveried Juttahats filed into the chamber. The Jutties sat down in two rows along the edge of the shrubbery, opposite the pair of purple screens.

Now here came the serpent, borne by its body-servant.

The servant's hands formed a cradle for a stout scaly tail. A glittering body, ochre and ruddy, looped twice around its bearer like some hefty brass-band instrument. The serpent was fanfare incarnate. Its horned head rested upon its porter's fuzzy cranium. A thin tongue flicked in and out, tasting the air. Eyes of jet gazed, clever and commanding.

The bearer stationed himself with his master behind the seated Juttahats, just inside the shrubbery. An odour of caramel drifted from the serpent. A scent of anticipation? Who could say?

'This precious enlightened one being *Imbricate,*' announced the porter-and-Voice. Presumably the serpent itself was performing this immodest introduction by mental ventriloquism.

Imbricate meant *overlap.* The serpent's scales weren't particularly like shingles on a roof. The name might refer to an intricate, crafty frame of mind.

Peter replied, 'Being honoured. We are presenting for your pleasure the spectacle of Saint Georgi, the captive maiden, and the serpent. Commencing shortly.'

Again, a reek of caramel. Peter breathed in, to marshal his gift.

'Wait a moment!' So saying, Solli hurried behind the screens.

After a moment's hesitation, Natti darted to peer.

Solli had yanked a little green bottle from her knapsack in the cart. She pulled out a stopper. She gulped.

Must be some fine liqueur from Kip'an'keep. A gift from Tilly Kippan—in addition to the shoes, which had fitted Solli but not Natti. Solli *had* ingratiated herself.

Tiptoeing swiftly, Natti hissed, 'Give us a swig. I can use some spirit too—'

Panic possessed Solli. She upended the bottle, glug-glug. Then she smirked at Natti.

Solli was back on stage again, serene and detached. Very soon Natti would be the captive maiden. The audience weren't restless.

'Peter, Peter,' whispered Natti, 'Solli just drank some mootapu sap—'

'*What?*'

'I'm sure of it.'

Yes, that must have been sap in the bottle.

Solli may only have meant to sip a few drops, to enhance her performance. Not so that she should change her body, but that she might embellish the illusion enormously.

Tapper Kippan's daughter would have been able to ignore the rules of the Arboretum and tap a tree for sap . . . Oh the naivety!

'It must be because of the Pootaran blood in her, Peter. She must fear that she doesn't possess enough glitter. That she might be losing her flair—'

The black inhabitants of Pootara were an unmagical lot. They resisted enchantments, recoiled from sways. Solli must always have feared that in her blood there lurked a foreign current of unmagic.

There'd been no sign of her losing her flair! Quite the contrary. Ah, people could so easily nurse bees in the bonnet, absurd obsessions . . .

'Silly child!' exclaimed Peter. 'Whatever will happen to her? How can I minimise—'

Peter's gift wasn't to minimise. It was to maximise.

'How can I steer her safely?' Oh why had she insisted on the role of an Isi mage, who would be exerting control over its body-servant, played by Peter himself?

Peter stared at Solli. She smiled back triumphantly. It was utterly out of the question to cancel, or even to delay the show.

133

Faint bubbles of pastel light, pink and blue, puffed from the mage's horns. The serpent was exerting its own gift—to savour Peter's sway, or to interfere with it? Golden droplets oozed from its fangs. Its servant's chin-glands dribbled liquid pearls. Alien nostrils valved open and shut. Odours of cinnamon and kasta nuts were intoxicating. The two ranks of seated Juttahats swayed slowly forward, slowly back. They might have been rowers on the benches of a boat, with the mage as the helmsman. They might have been victims of constipation yearning for release.

Stan, as the kidnapped maiden's dad, seemed to be far away. An illusion of distance dwarfed him. He was a tiny shrunken figure alternating between hope and despair.

Peter was clad in golden livery—the very image of any of the Juttahats in the audience. Gripping Natti, he offered her to Tan-Georgi. Then he snatched her away. By this means he lured the would-be hero onward deeper into a labyrinth. Natti attracted Tan with her cries. At the command of his serpent-master Peter was molesting Natti.

'Ravishing, ravishing,' Peter chanted. He fondled and coerced the maiden. Odours of yeast and vanilla wafted from the serpent at the edge of the shrubbery. Solli seemed to rear upright upon a base of coils, spangled and glistening. She swayed to and fro. Her own black-clad body wasn't visible. Illusion prevailed. Such a seductive illusion, here in the presence of the Isi prototype! Solli was a living mirror of the mage.

Her voice was lilting and sing-song, almost a telepathic alien voice, as one must imagine it.

She warbled at Peter, 'Slave, be serving this exalted one!'

Peter staggered. How compelling his master's voice was! Abnormally so. He hardly knew his own identity.

'Be serving!'

Peter clung to Natti as a man in a sudden gale might hug a tree. The Isi mage was trying to manipulate Peter with its mind while he was in an exalted state, detached from himself. But *which* serpent was trying to overwhelm him and steal away his will power? Was it the actual serpent or the imitation one? Or was it both at once?

'Georgi,' the false serpent lilted, 'be coming! Becoming my lover! Spurning the weak and tender maiden!'

Natti struggled against a sway which was enfeebling her. Tan stumbled slowly onward, mesmerised by the mock-mage.

'Submitting, submitting!' sang the Solli-serpent.

Was the Isi mage using Solli as a channel of control? Or was it Solli's own desire which was prevailing?

Wild power swirled around Peter, plucking at his soul. Fragrances dazed him. He was no longer the master of his gift. Soon, a voice might speak within his head—an imperative, undeniable voice.

But then the Solli-serpent began to shake convulsively.

She cried out, 'Holding me!'

Hold her? How? In what way? Hold her as a Juttahat-porter held its serpent master?

Of a sudden, the Solli-serpent fell. She writhed upon the tiles, seeming even more snake-like in her flexings.

Natti shed angry tears over Solli's distorted body. The legs and arms of Solli's leotard had meshed with her flesh. Her flesh had begun to flow through the fabric. Her legs had started to blend together, her arms to fuse with her torso. Her face was no longer human. She was some mutant freak in a sideshow—a snake-woman. The sway had evaporated, but the sap had altered her—half-way altered her!

Kneeling, Stan draped an arm around Natti's shoulder.

'She's dead—'

'Bastard!' Natti cried. At Stan, for his bluntness? At the mage in the audience? At Solli herself?

No longer puffing out bubbles of light or fragrances, the serpent craned its head above its porter's cranium. Then it lowered its scaly chin to rest once more upon that fuzzy red pad. Was it fatigued? Despondent?

The Juttahat-Voice blared: 'Regrets! Deep regrets.' After a moment it added: 'Reciprocity and compensation!'

Compensation? A hundred golden Ors instead of the promised fifty?

Some Juttahats had produced light-pistols. If Tan or Stan or Peter or Natti or all of them together flew into a homicidal rage, weapons would protect the precious one even if massed muscle-power failed.

Two Juttahats hurried from the chamber.

'Be waiting, be waiting,' coaxed the Voice.

The wait wasn't long.

When the Jutties returned they were hustling a young woman between them. Her eyes were blue. Her cheeks were like little buns. Her cropped hair was honey-blonde. She wasn't very tall. Such a pert nose. She was dressed in gold lamé elastic just like a Juttie kid. And she was talking to herself. Even as her eyes widened at the sight of four fellow human beings, she continued to chatter.

'So Sophie was in her cell, busily telling herself the tale of how the sun went missing behind a moon. All the land was dark and dreary—'

At this point, she noticed the corpse. Hard to identify of whom, or of what! Her narration hardly faltered.

'After many adventures, which she'll skip, Sophie succeeded in catching a spear of lightning. She threw this at the moon. The moon shattered into millions of pieces. That's the origin of the sickle in the sky. The sun shone forth again upon the world and upon Sophie, altering her hair from black to blonde, as of course it would . . .'

Words continued to spill forth. 'So while Sophie was telling the tale, two of her captors came to her underground cell, where the sun never shone. Did they interrupt her flow? Oh no—they were just slaves, after all. They did seize hold of her. Off they marched her, still talking . . .'

Was this young woman insane? Was *this* what the serpent meant by reciprocity? That the aliens were offering a demented prisoner as a substitute for Solli? Somebody driven daft by confinement in the serpents' nest and by whatever meddling they had attempted?

However, the players' presence began to figure in the weave of her obsessive narrative.

'When Sophie's captors brought her into the big room where bushes were growing, what should Sophie see there but three men and a woman? And a thing upon the floor, a sort of serpent abortion . . . The four people looked pretty disturbed. They couldn't have spent a year in captivity, chattering to themselves to keep the snakes confused . . .'

She was explaining the reason for all this babble.

A tale could trap you if stories began to nest within stories, generating more and more strands till you lost all sense of beginning or ending. Trapped within this nest of aliens, Sophie had evidently ensnared her own mind within this story of hers to protect her individuality from sways and manipulation. The Isi had failed to enslave her—just as Imbricate had failed to sway the troupe, though *that* had been a close shave. Now the Isi wanted rid of Sophie.

Sophie must possess quite a bit of storytelling energy and dramatic flair . . .

'Reciprocity,' said Peter. 'Accepting compensation.'

Grief would have to wait. And anger too.

On the noisy journey by sky-boat, Sophie kept up her prattle like some deranged cuckoo-bird. If she fell silent, might the vessel veer back towards the nest? Soon they all knew a great deal about plucky Sophie—more than you might wish to know all at once!

The return to the lake was occurring right away. A corpse was involved. No question of spending a night in the nest!

Wrapped in sacking, the body of what had been Solli was in the cargo hold with the cart. Peter had insisted that the promise to return *all* of the troupe should be fulfilled, even if the troupe did now include an additional member. Imbricate had seemed reluctant. The aliens might have liked to dissect Solli to try to explain her alteration. But no, no, no, a promise was a promise. The mage must be mortified by the failure of its attempt to manipulate human minds. The serpent had lost prestige. Accordingly it yielded.

As to the matter of the fee, why, the performance had been abandoned! The only payment turned out to be custody of a corpse, a typical alien swindle.

Contrariwise, the Isi would never now know about the mootapu sap which Solli had drunk. The snakes would remain mystified. In this regard the aliens had been conned.

A wind had risen. Clouds scudded, revealing and eclipsing stars and parts of the sky-sickle. The ruffled lake was inky. The woods were solid darkness. So far as one could tell, no Jutties from the sky-boat had sneaked into the forest to continue spying. The vessel had departed. The tents had been pitched as much by feel and memory as by sight.

Sophie stopped being a rampant chatterbox. She wasn't irrevocably afflicted. Stan shared out cheese and hard black bread from the cart, to be washed down with water from the lake.

'Shall we bury Solli in the woods in the morning?' he asked. Under the humus and the leaf-litter, for insects to eat.

'No,' Peter said. He was still the maestro of the troupe. 'Jutties might come back here to find her, dig her up. We'd better wheel her well away from here before we make a grave.'

'Damn her!' exclaimed Natti. 'It wasn't fear about her talent that caused this. She wanted to be the *boss*. She wanted to sweep you aside, Peter. She thought that by aping a mage she could ape its powers—and not need you.'

'I know...' he said gently. 'Still, if she hadn't done as she did, and confused things so much, the mage might have succeeded—though frankly I doubt it.'

'You're saying that we should be charitable?'

'I feel bitter too, Natti! Yet part of the bitterness is from the loss of someone so close to us.'

'And also so estranged from us,' murmured Tan.

Maybe, thought Peter, most intelligences were estranged from one another at heart. Tilly Kippan, immersed in her pretence game. Aliens, alienated from humans. How about players, forever donning different identities? Maybe the root of alienation was that each individual knew that ultimately they would die, as Solli had died—so suddenly. Longlifers such as Tapper Kippan might be the most estranged of all, fearfully protective of their longevity which must surely one day fail. As for wooden soldiers, those might well live as long as a tree, though only by forsaking mortal flesh ...

'We should rejoice,' Peter said bleakly. 'We have a new player. I'm sure we do.' To Sophie, in the darkness: 'You're so quiet now, my dear.'

'It's lovely to hold my tongue at last.'

'You don't want to go back to your family?'

'I'd like to send them a message that I'm safe. When we come across a cuckoo, I'll tell the bird.'

After a week or maybe a month, the gossip-bird or one of its kin would babble the news to her folks.

'You're magic-drama actors, aren't you?' she said.

Why, as yet they had hardly even introduced themselves! And she certainly hadn't seen them perform.

'Indeed,' replied Peter. 'The very best!'

Sophie sniffed the air. 'Autumn, isn't it? Are you heading for Gala? Have you already been there?'

'We shan't be performing at Gala this year,' said Natti. 'You see, we've been putting on a show about Tycho the Tyrant—and he'll be there for sure. Oh dear, now I sound like Solli—!'

'I really do need to be an actor,' said Sophie. 'It's what I need most.'

Reciprocity indeed...! Had the serpent foreseen this? Had precious Imbricate felt obliged to compensate the troupe perfectly, even though originally it had been intent on enslaving them? Who could understand the motives of the snakes?

'You're adjusting rather well,' Stan said to Sophie.

'This is a continuation, isn't it?' she said brightly. 'Telling myself a story was how I stayed free.'

She was certainly plucky. Sophie's enthusiasm would fill the void left by Solli's deceitfulness, and death.

'It's rather a pity,' said Peter, 'that we can't ever present the Tale of Solli. *The Tragedy of Solveig*: that's what we'd call it . . . How she imagined that the Pootaran part of her was a jinx-in-waiting. How she hated her whore of a grandmother. How she conned Tapper Kippan's daughter. How she tried to become maestro—to control people, just like some female Tycho. How she mutated monstrously and died in fits.'

'Hang on,' growled Stan. 'Not while her body's still lying just beside us.'

'You said that we can't ever do such a show,' protested Natti, 'yet you're already busy concocting it!'

'How do you know she hated her granny?' asked Tan.

'Because it's *appropriate*! Dramatically! She must have hated the woman. Ach, maybe she didn't—but she *pretended to Tilly* that she did! What ambitions Solli nursed. No, we can't ever act this out. A cuckoo would cackle. The Isi would hear. They would know about the mootapu sap, and what went wrong. Imbricate might figure out a way of controlling people after all, just like Jutties. Wait a moment! Could we leave the sap out, and put something else in its place? Solli's gran had power, and laid a curse on her . . . Such a shame to lose Tilly from the tale! But we couldn't tour the Forest Lord's realm again if we exposed his daughter's antics. We shouldn't do so, in any event! That would be unprofessional . . .'

'Quite so,' said Natti. 'Tilly did give me a pair of shoes too, even if they don't fit!'

'It's a private tragedy, this. Ah, what a waste. Private, private, damn it. Though not private from you, Sophie. You're included, you understand? You're a part of this—and a part of us.'

'I *still* hardly know what happened! There are such gaps. I'm guessing.'

'I'll tell you the whole tale,' promised Peter. 'Starting from when we pitched camp here last night—and leaping back to Kip'an'keep and even earlier.' He laughed harshly. 'Beware you don't get trapped in this tale! Or that *I* don't get so caught up that I forget to go to sleep tonight.'

'Peter,' warned Stan softly, 'her corpse is in earshot.'

In the darkness: a sack.

'May the story bring her peace if she can hear it!' Peter searched for a word. 'This is her *requiem*.'

'I *want* to be trapped in this tale, along with you,' declared their new friend. 'I was snared in my own tale far too long.'

Peter took a deep breath. 'Well now, Sophie, it's like this: *somebody* had been stalking us all afternoon . . .'

Science Fiction, Surrealism, and Shamanism

In 1993 and 1994 Gollancz published an 1100 page science fantasy epic by me, divided into two volumes, *Lucky's Harvest: the First Book of Mana* and *The Fallen Moon: the Second Book of Mana*. (No American edition, drat it, although going great guns in German and French, with the duo divided into three volumes in those languages.) I wrote the Books of Mana in a kind of verbal ecstasy sustained for two years—with breaks for trips to the pub and for other mundane matters—and my inspiration was the Finnish national epic, the *Kalevala*.

Away on the fringes of Europe, Christianised Finland still had a living shamanic tradition in the 19th Century, which was also the time when national identities were being newly asserted across Europe. Under Swedish and then under Russian rule, Finland was sorely in need of a sense of identity, and Elias Lönnrot—district medical officer, philologist, folklorist, and latterly Professor of Finnish—supplied this by collecting oral poetry from remote villages and jigsawing these verses together with mythological stories to produce a reasonably logical narrative in the metre that Longfellow was to borrow for *Hiawatha* (with his own aim of creating a Native American equivalent of the *Kalevala*). The full version of the *Kalevala* appeared in 1849, and Lönnrot went on to compile a masterly Finnish-Swedish dictionary, which helped to give Finnish status as a literary language.

Basically the many-stranded *Kalevala* is about a quest for a device called the Sampo which may be a magical mill or a magical furnace—no one knows for sure what the Sampo is, and in any case it gets broken and lost after being stolen. Many and long are the magical shamanic incantations woven into the narrative along the way, for Word rules the World. You can't make a seaworthy boat unless you know the appropriate words to chant. You can't make a sword unless you can describe the origin of iron, and thus empower yourself. If you can find the right words or formulas you can acquire power over reality.

This is a theme I had been plugging away at in one guise or another ever since my first novel *The Embedding*, in which Amazonian tribespeople express a higher state of consciousness through an extremely complex language which they can only understand during a ritual drug trance. To what extent does Word represent the World, or conceal the World from us? Might there be a Chomskyan 'general grammar of the universe' which expresses fundamental reality and thus gives access to reality itself, and control over reality? (See my 'Read This' piece in *NYRSF*, Feb 1999, p. 7, for Wittgenstein's take on this, via Schopenhauer's *The World as Will and Idea*, and Hitler's horrendous practical political application of shamanism derived from the same source—the idea is not as fanciful or detached from reality as one may initially assume.)

Parallel with the great theme of Word and World in the *Kalevala*, all the main characters are driven by rivalry, vengeance, erotic frenzy, and other high emotions as if possessed, which makes for an exciting tale, but also means that secondarily the epic is about the control (or lack of control) of consciousness, and about its enhancement, another pet theme of mine.

The word 'Mana' comes from the islands of the South Pacific. Thanks to anthropologists we're fairly familiar with the term as meaning 'a supernatural force emanating from a person, a place, or a thing'. By sublime coincidence in Finnish Mana is the 'God of the Otherworld' or simply the 'Otherworld' itself. Manna from Heaven, you might say! After I had been to an arts festival in 1991 in Jyväskylä, Finland, that country's then-Queen of Cyberpunk—with whom I shared a fish dinner not in Memison but in Helsinki—sent me a collection of poems by Eino Leino (1987-1926) beautifully translated into English by Keith Bosley. Leino's statue stands in one of Helsinki's main streets leading towards the harbour, with his back to a coin-operated superloo in a stretch of park, and his masterpiece, *Whitsongs* (*Helkavirsiä*, 1903), consists of condensed jewels in the vein of the *Kalevala*. Reading these gems while en route to an SF convention in Philadelphia, I saw how marvellously the themes meshed with my own interests as a writer. Vague ghosts of characters and situations began forming in my mind and in my notebook on the plane, and I knew that I had to experience the whole of the *Kalevala* as soon as possible.

Unfortunately the first translation I tackled was in the same metre as the original—the 'By-the-Shining-Big-Sea-Water' metre reused for *Hiawatha*—and while this might sound splendid, flexible, and lyrical in Finnish, in English after ten minutes of tumty-tumty-tumty-tumty you tend to go into a trance. But then I got hold of Keith Bosley's translation, in much freer verse. The difference is remarkable.

Here are the first four lines of the old translation:

I am driven by my longing
And my understanding urges
That I should commence my singing
And begin my recitation . . .

And here is the Bosley translation:

I have a good mind
take into my head
to start off singing
begin reciting . . .

Immediately there is urgency, vitality, a muscular voice. As I read this version my ghosts of characters and ideas became more substantial—and Eeva, the Queen of Finnish Cyberpunk, had also sent me a cookery book, so my characters would have something to eat.

Essentially the *Kalevala* is a magical work. Magical spells play a central role. My Mana books are set on a realistically described planet of another star and feature a certain amount of high technology—but there are also what you might call magical phenomena. Certain characters known as Proclaimers can 'bespeak' and sway others to carry out their will.

Personally my attitudes are rationalistic and scientific, though in fiction I will usually follow my fantastical instincts and let my narratives be powered by symbolism, metaphor, and imagery. My basic orientation is rational but what happens in stories of mine can frequently be quite bizarre and weird—rendered persuasive and believable, I hope.

So this huge story of mine set on the world of Kaleva—and a couple of slipstream novelettes which did appear in America, in *Asimov's*, 'The Tragedy of Solveig' (Dec 96), and 'The Shortest Night' (May 98)—have a science fiction feel to them, but intrusions of the irrational seem to debar them from being classed strictly as SF. On the other hand, these texts aren't exactly Fantasy, either; they're located in the universe of discourse of Science Fiction, written in the language of SF rather than Fantasy. I have never much liked the term 'science fantasy'—this suggests to me Science Fiction written by people who don't know too much about science or the universe we inhabit, people who use science as decoration. Perhaps my Mana texts are examples of SS, 'Science Surrealism . . .'?

One of the main inspirations of that first novel of mine, *The Embedding*—alongside the scientific investigation of the nature of language as pursued by the human race and by aliens visiting Earth—was the French surrealist Raymond Roussel.

In 1932 Roussel published his long embedded poem *Nouvelles Impressions d'Afrique* (*New Impressions of Africa*). Phrases are nested within phrases within phrases like matrioshka dolls. 'Embedding' is the name for this type of nesting. Embeddings within embeddings put a great strain upon the mind which is trying to comprehend the complete sentence. Roussel dreamed that a machine for reading his poem might be built, consisting of a circular table with two tops. The text of the poem would circle around the fixed lower top. Slots in the revolving upper top would expose far-removed parts of the text, and thus un-embed the syntax. Thus his poem could be read—though perhaps even more confusingly than on paper! Roussel's poem was what first sparked my imagination to find a science-fictional framework for the linguistic theories of Chomsky, and the question of to what extent language represents reality—Chomsky believing that on a deep structural level, acquired as part of our evolution, all human beings share a 'general grammar'. Do the patterns of language therefore reflect objective physical reality on some deep level? Language is deeply metaphorical, in a hidden way. Words are almost always concealed metaphors which have become arbitrary symbols for objects.

Roussel was one of this century's great eccentrics. He inherited a large fortune and used it to satisfy his whims. He once sailed to India, on his own fully crewed yacht. During the whole voyage he remained in his cabin, writing. Finally, one day, the captain reported to him, 'We are in sight of the Indian coast.' Roussel stepped on deck and gazed at the distant smudge on the horizon. He declared, 'Ah, so I have seen India.' He ordered the ship to turn around immediately and return to Marseilles.

In fact *whim* isn't quite the right word. Despite general ridicule of his plays and other works, staged and printed at his own expense, Roussel was convinced of his own genius. He was devoted to literary glory—and he sought this glory by what one might call scientific rather than artistic strategies. A piece of fiction was a game with strict rules. He would take a phrase from a poem or a nursery rhyme, and transform its meaning, even though the sound remained almost the same. Thus the phrase, 'Napoléon, premier empereur' ('Napoleon, the first emperor') became 'Nappe, olé, ombre, miettes, hampe, air, heure,' in other words a tablecloth, a cry of 'Olé', shadow, crumbs, a pole or handle, air, and hour. The result is Spanish dancers on a table so brightly lit that crumbs cast shadows, plus a clock powered by the wind. Roussel then set out to invent a narrative which would satisfyingly and imaginatively link these elements, and many other elements produced by the same method. The initial bits of information should be as far removed as possible from one another; and no event, however absurd it might seem at first sight, should lack a logical place in the final narrative.

Creatively, this is a little similar to the way I have written quite a number of my own stories and even novels—by bringing together facts, theories, situations, and images which at first sight seem completely different from one another. 'What other people see as a coincidence,' a critic once remarked, 'Ian Watson sees as a connexion.'

When Roussel eventually revealed his method in an essay entitled 'Comment j'ai écrit certains de mes livres' ('How I wrote some of my books'), some fans of his surrealistic imagination were infuriated by the mechanistic method he had employed. Where was the free and unfettered inspiration in all this? Actually, Roussel was fascinated by machinery. His works often feature scientist-inventors and bizarre contraptions. Indeed the surrealists as a group were enthralled by new equipment, and by new games. The aim was to stimulate the mind out of its routine habits—and evoke a totally imaginary, non-mundane, non-human world, so that new myths could be born. *New* myths—yet nevertheless *authentic* ones. The surrealists were pursuing a magical, myth-creating quest—to evoke the alien, the other, the elsewhere, the different. Roussel had no particular belief in the supernatural, yet he sought for marvels. I too am basically a rationalist without superstitions, using the tool-kit of science for a kind of magical purpose: an imaginative, consciousness-expanding purpose.

And what else are the alien worlds of Science Fiction, and the aliens invented by Science Fiction, but a kind of fulfillment of the surrealist quest for imaginary non-human worlds? Roussel was particularly attracted to what you might call childish, populist art forms. He wasn't interested in High Art but in Low Art. With its origins in the pulp magazines with their dramatic, colourful, comic-book covers, the popular genre of SF seems the ideal surrealist playground; and it's hardly an accident that the works of A.E. van Vogt were translated into French by the surrealist Boris Vian, to great general acclaim. To many native speakers of English van Vogt's style seems quite clumsy, and his ideas seem rather lunatic. After Boris Vian did for van Vogt what Baudelaire did for Edgar Allan Poe—namely, produce a translation much more luminously beautiful than the original—van Vogt's works were viewed as great literature of the surrealist school.

With Roussel, language itself became a creative force, an agent of creation, rather as it is in the *Kalevala*. In the case of shamanism: find the words to make the boat or the sword. In Roussel's case: find the words, and then the events of a story can occur, compelled to occur by necessity. The surrealists were the shamanists of the industrial, technological 20th century.

I feel a great sympathy with all of this. The surrealists sought euphoria— rapture, *jouissance*, vision, revelation—by an exercise of the intellect. Anglophone critics have sometimes put me down as rather an 'intellectual' author. Indeed, ironically, my *Book of the River* trilogy which went on to be a Science Fiction Book Club choice in America (entitled *The Books of the Black Current*) was turned down in France on the grounds that it wasn't 'intellectual enough'. I intend there to be passion in my stories, vivid emotion and vivid characters in a rich setting, yet I do realise that my own approach to rapture is, initially, through intellectual activity.

The surrealists also put a high value on automatic writing, so as to tap the energies of the subconscious. I myself believe in letting the internal sovereign dynamics of a story dictate the events, even if my rational critical mind sometimes cries out in alarm. If something bizarre begins to happen, arising out of images and metaphors, I will let it happen, trusting that a reason for the event will reveal itself, and that the event will fulfill a necessary function. On the level of narrative structure this is a little akin to automatic writing. In my Books of Mana there are some rather strange persons and events and objects, arising from my transmutation of the original source, from the associations that arose in my mind, then letting word and imagery steer the boat of the book. A boy grows from birth to adolescence in just a few months. There's an alien female golem. There's a brass dwarf. Bikes jump from place to place. Science-Surrealism, perhaps, though these persons and devices evolve to fulfill functions, dramatically or emotionally or mischievously—I love mischief in a book, and glee, and sly hilarity. In my case the Sampo—the magic device which can create whatever you wish—is obviously a nanotechnology machine, though controlling it is a problem.

Incidentally, the creative dominance of Word—of what speaks forth, rather than the speaker himself or herself—is at the heart of Daniel Dennett's tentative explanation of consciousness (as in *Consciousness Explained*, 1991). Why do we talk to ourselves? Ordinarily we can't maintain uninterrupted concentration on a particular problem for more than a few tens of seconds, yet we tackle problems requiring vastly more time. Human memory is not innately designed to be super-reliable fast-random-access, so the immediate contents of the stream of consciousness are very soon lost unless we fix them. Describing to ourselves what we are doing—telling ourselves what is going on—is a way of committing material to memory. Children talk to themselves openly; adults do it more privately.

But how do we choose the words we use? In a very real sense the words choose themselves. Our brain has no central controller busy operating a switchboard. We consist of numbers of systems, each semi-independent and semi-intelligent, acting in unison. A range of possible words compete for the chance of being publicly expressed—lexical Darwinism. Thus language is not something we invented so much as something that we *became*—not a construction *by* us, but something that constructs us, and constantly continues reconstructing us. So we produce our 'selves' in language, each of us being a kind of fictional character in the narrative which we are forever relating to ourselves. Everyone is his or her own novelist, and our existence depends on the persistence of narrative. Good news for writers! Rather than being mere entertainment compared with the serious business of real life, the telling of tales in the broadest sense is at the root of our being and our knowledge. Tales aren't the product but the source of consciousness. Incessant storytelling and story-checking—some factual, some fictional—is how an advanced entity keeps track of its physical and mental circumstances. Word does rule our World, indeed.

Of course you may say that neither surrealism nor shamanism is the *intention* behind SF. Yet at this point let me commend a book by Rogan Taylor entitled *The Death and Resurrection Show* (1985), about shamanism as the root of popular art forms and entertainment. According to a brief item I caught by coincidence on the radio a few weeks ago, Rogan Taylor is currently Professor of Football Semiotics, or something similar, at the

University of Liverpool or thereabouts. In my most recent, as yet unpublished, novel *Mockymen* I came up with a matter transmission device for sending people to the stars which, subjectively at least, tears them apart agonisingly then reassembles them at their destination. This isn't a totally original idea. David Langford's *The Space Eater* had its travellers pumped through a one-inch aperture, and in Dan Simmons' *Endymion* crew and passengers on the Vatican's super-fast starship are smashed flat excruciatingly by acceleration then reconstituted at journey's end. This tearing-apart is also what a shaman experiences on a spirit-journey, which is in essence a journey to another world, and I think my people-transmitter derived from a subconscious gut-feeling rather than from Langford or Simmons. (My novel *God's World*, back in 1979, borrowed from shamanism for a journey through 'High Space' to another star system.) Through suffering, power is gained; the journey can only be achieved by an ordeal.

Consider the Indian Rope Trick, which isn't specifically Indian; the performance was popular not just in India but also in China, Java, ancient Mexico, and also in medieval Europe. In the full version of the trick the conjuror not only sends his apprentice up a rope to vanish but then he climbs up after the lad with a knife and tosses down dismembered parts of the apprentice's body. The conjuror returns to terra firma, arranges the limbs, and gives them a kick, which puts the apprentice back together again, alive. Literally the master 're-members' the novice, and the lad who had ascended to the upper world is back in the middle world, ours, again. This trick is plainly a shamanic initiation rite, or at least it is a memory of one—however, magic in the old sense has become magic in the modern sense, a conjuring spectacle, a piece of theatre.

The existence of disease (and dis-ease) is one of the main reasons for religions. Primarily a shaman is a healer and therapist, whose power to heal is the reason for his importance. Now, a shaman typically performed not safely distanced on a stage but in full all-round public view in the open air or in the middle of a crowded tent. It was by his movements and principally by his voice that he conveyed a vision to his audience. He bespoke other worlds directly to his witnesses, who proceeded to perceive those other worlds. In preliterate society the power of the spoken word was originally very potent—as witness the *Kalevala* where voice and word control reality—and this can still be so in literate society. Hitler, working himself into a fever and intoxicating his audiences, was a sort of evil shaman, not only on a mass scale but even person to person. Hard-bitten German generals arriving to announce disaster and imminent defeat would emerge from Hitler's presence convinced of victory, as if mesmerised.

In 1931 a Russian named Anisimov (not Asimov!) went on an expedition to Siberia and described in great detail how the sheer torrent of sound which issued from the mouth of an Evenki shaman even set the buttons on the visitor's coat humming.

The bard is one successor to the shaman. The shaman dealt in ecstatic trips into unusual dimensions of mind, and the inspired poet-singer was doing something similar except that by now the mental journeys were disguised as accounts of actual travel to places far away in the real world (those far away places, of course, being largely fantastical).

With the rise of religions such as Catholicism which brooked no rivals, the shamanist mind-set went further underground. It disguised itself, mutating into popular entertainments such as the Italian Comedy. Harlequin is one further successor to the shaman, a divine yet demonic clown. His spangled costume shows his paradoxical nature. He is an acrobat who speaks in strangely poetic tongues and seems to suffer in a frenzy. Harlequin can fool his way into Hell and get back out again. Interestingly, his first literary appearance in the 16th century is in two poems, in one of which he descends to the Underworld to save a trapped soul by amazing King Pluto with his wit and dexterity—he is Orpheus, and he is a shaman, exactly as Orpheus was—and in the other of which he ascends to the Sky. *Harlequin's Account of His Trip to the Moon* has six starving vultures carry him as astral voyagers to our satellite; proto-SF, no less.

Mutated shamanism is the ultimate source for the magic show, the circus, drama, opera, and even (one might even say particularly) 20th century pop stars. The performer closest to being an actual shaman, even though he never consciously connected himself with the ancient tradition, was Harry Houdini. In the course of shamanist healing-magic escapology was one of the feats most often performed. Bound in our bodies, how can we escape? This is the meaning of such stunts. Houdini was enacting an ancient healing rite, illustrating the successful escape from madness and death. Entranced, Houdini's audiences felt that they were participating in a miracle, deeply therapeutic in nature; and oddly, Houdini himself felt that the miraculous was involved—he could not himself understand one trick he had put together, and had the distinct impression that he had actually left his own body. On the other hand, Houdini was a downright rationalist, and deeply scared of madness. On the third hand, as it were, he spent a lot of time attending séances in the hope that one day he might discover an authentic medium.

Mad scientist! Pandora's Box! Atom Bomb! Radiation! Perils of Genetic Engineering! Artificial Intelligence takes over the World! The popular attitude to science is deeply ambivalent because scientific knowledge is a transformational power, altering the world, and traditionally transformational magic is 'hellish'—its roots are in the Underworld. Thus, though we now possess powers which would once have seemed magical, people feel that the tricks have taken us over and that we're no longer in control.

I wonder to what extent Science Fiction with its journeys to the stars, its encounters with fabulous beings—sometimes Godlike, and sometimes demonic (as in *Alien*)—is actually, deep down, despite the framework of rational technology, a mutation of shamanist imagery and impulses. Perhaps the Fantasy genre, by ignoring rational science and directly invoking magic, is the truer expression of this—and this could be the real reason for Fantasy's greater popularity—but the astronaut may, in a sense, be a re-embodiment of the shaman. My own Science Fiction certainly has a lot of transformational magic in it. Altered states of consciousness, alien consciousness, after-death experiences, evolution and mutation: the treatment of these themes is generally within a rational, scientific framework, but the impulse may be as old as the hills—shamanistic. In 1988 I wrote a short essay about my life as a writer, entitled 'Dancing on a Tightrope'. When I wrote the piece I was thinking about the precariousness and unpredictability of earning a living as a full-time writer. Yet really the title is truer in a deeper sense. It now evokes for me the Harlequin/Clown, the acrobatics of the shaman. My work has sometimes tended to mix genre conventions. The Books of Mana are on the boundary of Fantasy and SF. *The Fire Worm*, about a medieval alchemical experiment going wrong, intersected SF and Horror. My two most recent novels, *Hard Questions* and *Oracle*, blend the technothriller with SF. The shamanic Harlequin is in essence an 'amphibian' creature, passing from one medium to another, hence his motley garment. Those are motley novels.

You might say that there's an element of special pleading in the above. Thus do I, consequently I devise a theory which, on the surface, appears to have little relevance to what we all know from a thousand examples SF is really about, the exploration of how advancing technology and scientific theory intersects with the human species, and our hopes and fears for the future. Yet I suspect that the shamanic connection is worth thinking about.

We carry with us anatomically, neurologically, psychologically the freight of our past. We may regard ourselves nowadays as freshly minted, the new constantly displacing the old, but until (and if) we actually rewire and rebuild ourselves, altering our hardware and our software, and thus become posthumans—and in a sense, therefore, aliens—the deep reasons why we do things may sometimes be quite different from what we suppose.

The Shortest Night

'This is a night as never will be.
'You'll go back to sea and never see me,
'Not again, oh my dusky mariner...'

Wistfully the tangomeister warbled. The tango combo twanged and plainted away on violin, guitar and accordion. Cymbals provided a rippling punctuation. Music in a minor key, suitable for public courtship. Courtship, of a sort, was in progress in Momma Rakasta's establishment as the black sailors and the white hostesses smooched around the dance floor or chatted at tables over barley-beers, blueberry liqueurs, glasses of spirit.

The décor was gilt and plush, the curtaining velvet. The glass shades of the oil lamps were multi-coloured mosaics. The tubby baritone vocalist and his bandsmen wore matching lace shirts and black breeches, with red ribbon rosettes on their knees. *Chum-chum-chum*, was the rhythm.

Words and music were maudlin in a deeply affecting way. This tango might have been caressing and gentling the sailors—proclaiming at them to moderate their behaviour in case some drunken brawl threatened to trash the establishment or cause abuse to the young ladies.

Young Andrew, whom Bosco was keeping an eye on, had paired off with a willowy lass. Bosco's own hostess, chosen after some deliberation, was a bit older than most of the girls. This appealed to Bosco since she would have some depth.

Astrid was tall and full figured, in her billowy white linen blouse and bountiful skirt of red and blue stripes. Her blue bodice, unbuttoned, exhibited blouse-clad tits which had *form*. Her long hair was a flaxen yellow.

'What *is* a Conga?' she asked Bosco. The *Conga* was the name of the four-master he sailed on.

'It's a long file of dancers. Each claspin' the waist of the one in front.' He mimed clutching her waist, though they were both sitting down. 'It kind o' suggests all the successive positions of our ship on the chart as she skips across the sea from one day to the next. Also, there's a mighty river in old Africa away on Earth called the Conga.'

'Do you speak African at home down south in Pootara?'

'Naw, my darling. We mostly speak Anglo-lingo, just like the folks at the Earthkeep in Landfall, though we can all talk Kalevan too. Every immigrant imbibes Kalevan in their dreams on the way to this world, whether they're whites destined for up here with its passions and manias, or blacks bound for the south and the life of sweet reason. Now the *Conga*, fine ship, she's what we call a hermaphrodite schooner—meanin' that she carries fore-and-aft an' also square-rigged sails to make her fast and lean. I'm no hermaphrodite,' and he winked.

'I'm sure you aren't.' Astrid played with her hair. 'Do you sail to Tumio as well?'

That was the other deep-sea port, six hundred keys westward. Where the mana-bishop dwelled in his palace next to the baroque yellow-brick temple of magic. At Tumio, a major river spilled into a bay. This made commerce with the interior easier than at Portti, from which goods needed to be hauled onward by land and by lake.

'All black newcomers travel via Tumio, to gain passage across the isle-crowded ocean to Pootara where democracy and level-headedness prevail . . .' Bosco couldn't resist a little boast.

'It must be lovely there,' she murmured. 'In Pootara.'

'You aren't from hereabouts, are you?' he asked; and she shook her head.

Maybe Bosco was moved by the sentimental tango music.

'I can't help feeling that you're a bit of a castaway here in Portti, Astrid. A castaway of the land rather than of the sea.'

'Cast a sway,' she sang softly. She sounded as though she was echoing him; but not really.

'Cast a sway on me,' sang the tangomeister.

'And never set me free
'Till the stars drown in the sea . . .'

'Shall we go upstairs?' he proposed.

She wasn't ready yet. 'Another glass of blueberry, first?'

'Fine by me.'

'There's no magic in Pootara at all?'

'No sways, no manias, no proclaimers bespeakin' people, no shamans, no cuckoo birds. The way I see it, Astrid, we come to Kaleva courtesy of that living asteroid starship-thing that calls itself the Ukko. Now, Earth has built shuttle-ships to load the Ukko an' unload it, but that Ukko has its *own* agenda involvin' compellin' folks to live out all sorts o' colourful stories up here in the north for its amusement. I bet cuckoos are communicatin' with Mother Ukko mentally all the time. Us blacks are in the south by way of ballast an' stability, so that everyone don't go nuts on this world. You white folks here in the north are sorta like the pets of the Ukko. As compensation, you get a whole land out here among the stars, wherever here is—and no 'stronomer's ever been able to say for sure—'

Unaccountably, Astrid shuddered.

'—and mebbe it's never-never-space the Ukko brings us to, not in the same universe as Earth at all.'

She nibbled at her lip. 'What about the Isi snakes and their Juttie slaves? The snakes use their own Ukkos to reach here. They seem to know more than us.'

'Seem to; so people say. Mebbe the Ukkos use them alien snakes as *different* sorts of toys, to add spice to the pudding. Have you ever seen a Juttahat?'

'Yes . . .' She wouldn't enlarge on this.

Astrid's breasts did indeed have form. Her left breast also possessed something else.

Upstairs in one of the boudoirs, after transacting the first bout of business—over which we'll draw a discreet blanket or silken sheet—Bosco reclined, studying her tattoo.

It was an elaborate one: of a cuckoo bird with a white milkcup flower in its beak.

Being situated within an inch of a nipple, which was just like a pink bubberry, the milkcup bloom seemed well suited to its location. But a cuckoo?

Plumes of verdigris and rust. Big snoopy yellow eyes. Eavesdropping feline ears.

One of the bird's feet was crippled and twisted. This had to be an illustration of a specific cuckoo, not just a picture of cuckoos in general.

Northerners used cuckoos to send a message or brag about some great deed, after feeding a bird a dollop of offal and calling out to it, 'Ukko-ukkoo, hark to the story and tell the tale!' Since all cuckoos (except for this one) looked much the same, you couldn't be sure that the bird which harked was the same one which subsequently repeated the words, twenty or fifty keys away, next day or ten days later.

And you couldn't ask the birds if they communicated telepathically, because they didn't ever confide anything about themselves. As for coercing a bird to answer—or trapping one to fix an identity ring round its scrawny ankle—that was totally taboo. Captive cuckoo in a cage, puts all Kaleva in a rage. Awful woe would follow. The bird on Astrid's left tit couldn't have gotten its injury from any act of human pique or meddling.

'I'm thinkin' there's a strange story inscribed on your bosom, Astrid. Right next to your heart, you might say—'

He was aware that his hooded eyes lent him a drowsy look, inspiring confidence. Yet she drew away.

'It's past and best forgotten.'

'How can you forget, when it's pictured on your own skin?'

She wouldn't answer.

Bosco had paid for a full night in the boudoir. He had advised Andrew likewise, lending him some silver marks and a golden Or with the mad Queen's head on it.

He dozed, as one does when sated; and woke around midnight.

Astrid wasn't abed. Silhouetted naked on a stool, she was gazing out of the little half-open window at the grey gloaming of the shortest night, which was still clear of clouds.

He watched her for a while, admiring and anticipating yet also aware that this nightwatch she was keeping held some deep meaning for her.

Presently, he slid himself out of bed. Softly he padded over to her. He could tell by Astrid's breathing that she hoped he wouldn't overwhelm this moment with hanky-panky. So he just hunkered down beside her. Out in town, bonfire lights were flickering. Distant noises of revelry drifted. Very likely some people would be settling old scores. Fuelled by booze, the murder rate soared on this briefest night of the year.

The window faced north, away from the sky-sickle which spanned the southern horizon. From Portti, on account of the cliffs of its fjord, only the very top of that silver bridge was visible—that ring of debris from a long-since disintegrated moon which had come too close to the planet. From this window, the sickle wasn't visible at all. Few stars pricked the luminous gloom where night and day were joining hands. The brightest body was the gas-giant world, like a tiny masthead lantern far away.

'There's Otso,' he murmured.

Essentially the sky looked empty.

'All the stars have drowned in the sea,' he joked gently. 'Us mariners like to see a few constellations.'

'*I don't.*' Even though it was warm, Astrid shivered.

'The Archer and the Cow, the Harp . . . and the Cuckoo,' he hinted, 'the Cuckoo.'

Of a sudden, she began to talk hauntedly. It was as if her tattoo was compelling her to tell the tale.

'I was at Castle Cammon, enthralled by Tycho the tyrant, when he commissioned a young astronomer called Jon Kelpo to redraw the map of the sky . . .'

Tycho Cammon the tyrant was notorious. Cuckoos cackled about him all over the continent.

Cammon's realm was six or seven hundred keys away to the north-east of Portti. Thirty-odd keys further to the east of Castle Cammon was Kallio Keep, where Astrid's dad, Lord Taito Kallio, held a small woodland domain.

Bosco has just been in bed with a minor lord's daughter . . . Surely she rarely confides this to other clients at Momma Rakasta's. Does even the Momma know?

The Kallio domain was noted for its kastanut and musktree groves, and for an unusually large number of precious ivorywood trees. The Kallios husbanded those ivorywoods on an ecologically sound basis, planting out new saplings to replace felled stock which was mainly destined for expensively crafted prestige furniture.

Some domains are huge, such as that of Tapper Kippan the Forest Lord, which includes Portti. Or Saari over in the east. Others are much smaller. The Cammon and Kallio land holdings and the others thereabouts were modest in scale. However, Ivan Cammon, Tycho's father, had an acquisitive, predatory attitude to life. His marriage to Sophie Donner of Verinitty (just to the north) proved, as time went by, to have virtually united both domains under Cammon control. So Astrid's dad was wary.

He was doubly and trebly wary as Ivan Cammon's eldest son grew up.

The lad was well favoured and gifted, *but...*

'Ukko-ukkoo,' a cuckoo would cackle, 'a cocksure rooster crowed from its dunghill at young Tycho Cammon, and he bespoke it to burst itself. Feathers and flesh went flying in all directions.'

That was only the beginning. Before long Tycho was bespeaking farmers' daughters to spread themselves for him or come home with him as his compliant toys. Woe betide any fathers or brothers who interfered.

One lad tried to intervene when Tycho called his girl away. Ruptured by Tycho's brutal words, the boyfriend died lingeringly of peritonitis. The lass was obliged to enjoy herself pleasuring Tycho until he tired of her. A cruel streak, cruel.

Tycho's power as a proclaimer was admirable when he used it against Unmen. Tycho's father loved hunting fierce hervies in the woods to mount their racks of horns in his banqueting hall; but the son hunted more intelligent prey—servants of the alien snakes bent on spying and mischief and kidnap. What's more, Tycho was soon travelling as his domain's champion to the autumn galas in Yulistalax to pit himself against other proclaimers. Voice against voice. Sway against sway. Mana-wrestlers.

Although Tycho was handsome as well as clever and gifted, he also made abominable misuse of his talent. People began mumbling about his one minor disfigurement—a wart on his right cheek—as being his *verrin's nipple*.

Verinitty, his mother's home, had been pestered by the vicious carnivores until they were controlled by poison bait. The implication was that a verrin might have bitten Tycho's cheek as a child, sucking on the wound and infecting him with its saliva.

'His father's been somewhat of a check on Tycho's excesses,' Taito Kallio told Astrid on the day when a cuckoo cried the news about the goring-to-death of Ivan Cammon by a bull hervy. 'But what now—?'

Father and daughter were in Astrid's chamber. It was the first day of June. The mullioned windows stood open, admitting a breath of musk, even though trees and riverside town were quite far below. The keep occupied a sheer little butte, a rare upthrust of rock. Access was by way of a steep winding path. Goods were usually winched upward vertically, but Astrid must have made her way up and down that path a few thousand times by now, with the result that her thighs and calves were muscular.

Tapestries of sun-dappled trees and lakes hung on the walls. At this time of year the pot-bellied stove was cold and dead, like a suit of armour for a fat dwarf. A cabinet held dozens of Pootaran wooden puzzles, which Astrid collected: artful assemblages of tiny notched rhombs and pyramids and such, in contrasting polished woods.

Astrid had recently celebrated her twenty-first birthday. Dismantled on a tray, lay the pieces of a particularly complicated puzzle entirely made of ivorywood. Her dad had secretly commissioned the puzzle a whole year earlier through the Pootaran trade emporium and consulate in Landfall. Taito had supplied a block of ivorywood specially for the purpose.

'I hear a special cuckoo keeps watch on Tycho Cammon all the time,' she said.

'He's such a source of tales, dear.'

'The same crippled cuckoo follows him everywhere, they say. Except, I suppose, when it sneaks off to pass its tattle on.'

'Now that Tycho's the lord,' said her dad, 'if he comes here I'm going to refuse to receive him. We'll block the cliff-path. Rig deadfalls of rock. We'd better lay in more supplies than usual. We'll simply sit up here until he goes away.'

'What about the town?'

Tycho might avenge himself for the insult.

'I know we're responsible for their welfare down there,' agreed her dad, 'but we can't bring everyone up here for shelter, can we? I can't face him down. I'm not a proclaimer. Let's keep our fingers crossed.'

Her dad had no mana-power. Anyone could be affected by mania, but to be able to affect other people was very much rarer. Nor was Taito assertive in a browbeating way, although he could be stubborn or subtle. Stroking his balding blond head, Astrid's father brooded.

'If we managed to pick him off with a rifle bullet or crossbow quarrel, long distance—beyond the range of his voice—we'd have a feud on our hands, or a full-scale war. The twin-domain might gobble us up.'

'How about if we invite a proclaimer to be a permanent guest here? Pay him in ivorywood?'

'A hero in the house? Dashing and handsome, too? Trouncing Cammon, then whisking you off your feet, besotted with him?'

'That's highly unlikely,' Astrid reassured her father.

'How would we come by this champion? Tell cuckoos to cackle about our requirements everywhere? We'd be advertising our anxiety and vulnerability. Our champion might fail. Where would we be then?'

Father and daughter saw eye to eye, although the town remained unavoidably exposed. Astrid rummaged in her puzzle tray, picked up two pieces and slotted them together.

'Fingers crossed,' she agreed.

How fond they were of one another. Astrid's mum, Lady Kallio, was usually preoccupied with her embroidery, stitching flower-strewn fables with sublime skill, the floral decoration mattering more to her than the nakki-imps who peeped from her scenes. She would embroider a story of the fairy Si-si-dous drinking a dewdrop and singing to a spellbound fellow, who would be lucky to make his escape when Si-si-dous got hungry. Man and fairy would be inundated in apricot bellflowers and violet starflowers and jismin and heartbells.

Astrid herself was addicted to wooden puzzles. And she liked to star-gaze from the tower of the keep—sometimes at the entire panorama, sometimes selectively using her dad's spy-glass to home in on, say, Otso with its mooncubs.

She also loved to roam the woods with a girlfriend from the town, Anniki Tamminen, supposedly collecting mushrooms or flowers for her mother. Astrid's mania certainly wasn't men, except perhaps for her devotion to her dad. She showed no signs of falling in love with any fellows.

Which might be just as well.

Astrid's young brother Gustaf, who would inherit, was frail. A succession of chest complaints and digestive disorders plagued the lad, despite the best efforts of the town's mana-priest and of its wise woman—who was, in fact, the mother of Astrid's bosom-friend—and despite the occasional assistance of a grumpy shaman who lived in the ivorywoods.

'When Gustaf grows up and brings a bride here'—so her dad had said on a number of occasions; fingers crossed, and tilt a mirror so that any imp of sickness will slide off it—'if you're still here you'll be a guiding influence.'

Cuckoo-news arrived that Tycho Cammon was celebrating his accession to the lordship by setting out on horseback with a band of cronies to raid the territory of the snakes and their slaves to the north-east of Saari—the Velvet Isi area.

Quite an expedition, when he owned no sky-boat. Could Cammon have turned over a new leaf, aiming to be admirable rather than abominable? His route should take him far enough to the north of Kallio land.

Several weeks later, Cammon's return was unheralded by any cackle, as if cuckoo-birds wished to see what would happen unexpectedly . . .

A ginger fluff of fallen feathery blooms carpeted the musktree grove. Soft pot-pourri lay everywhere upon the ground, headily fragrant in decay. Above azure chimney-flowers, clouds of sizzleflies drifted like puffs of smoke as a heat-hazy sun climbed towards noon.

Astrid and Anniki lay side by side, nuzzling and touching tenderly. They must have been heedless. Could ginger fluff muffle hoofbeats so thoroughly? Maybe Cammon had stealthed the sound of his steed's approach, and that of his crony's, by proclaiming it so.

Suddenly: two horses, and their riders. Both piebald mounts were stocky and shaggy with long bushy fly-whisk tails. The travel-stained riders wore leathers and boots. Through slings strapped to the saddlebags: rifle, and crossbow.

Reining in: 'Now what *do* we have here?'

Astrid and Anniki were already scrambling up, adjusting their skirts.

'Enchanting! And deserving enchantment—'

The wart on the speaker's right cheek! It was him.

Sensual lips—fat, self-indulgent lips. Heavy jowls. A narrow arc of beard. A high protuberant forehead, and tight fair curls. Handsome, but already with intimations of a brutal and libertine cast, which in time (and not a long time, either) would make his face heavy and oppressive. Such a muscular build.

'So ripely deserving—'

As the two men dismounted, Astrid and Anniki fled as fast as they could amidst the musktrees.

'**Hark and hear**,' Cammon's voice bellowed. Running, Astrid stuck her fingers in her ears. She knew the routes. And the roots, which might trip. Anniki knew, as well. However, Anniki hadn't climbed up and down that butte-path a few thousand times. Her legs weren't as strong; her puff was less. She couldn't sprint and also plug her ears.

When Cammon and his crony caught Anniki, and whirled her around, she would surely have cried out, 'My mother's the wise-woman. She'll lay a spell on you.' At which, Cammon would have laughed.

That must have been how it was; or something similar.

'We need your lovely friend too! Where's she hiding herself? Where's she gone to?'

Seeking protection by association, Anniki would have burbled: 'She's the Lord's daughter—!'

'Is she indeed? That maiden needs a *man*.'

From the roof of the tower, Lord Taito and his daughter took turns gazing through the spy-glass at events transpiring down below in the little town of white-painted wooden houses and red tiled roofs.

The telescope was the work of a maker of glass and lenses in Niemi, southernmost of the three main towns of Saari. A Mr Ruokokoski. His sign was engraved on the collapsible brass tube: an eyeball with wings.

Accompanying Tycho Cammon were a dozen armed men. Fourteen horses. And one Unman, black-skinned, sable-liveried, a prisoner.

Prisoner of words, very likely, rather than of manacles. Cammon had posed the Juttahat in the town square for folk to gawp at, if they wished. The alien stood utterly motionless.

Some desultory looting was in progress; not really much more than replenishment of supplies. At Mrs Tamminen's house there seemed to be a commotion. Was she being evicted?

Half-way through the afternoon, a leather-clad envoy set foot on the butte-path. He waved a white kerchief on a stick. Cammon watched from a safe distance, a horse between himself and the keep. Taito and Astrid were out of ear-shot of Cammon, even if he roared. Taito's retainers wore wax plugs in their ears, melted from candles. Their instructions were simple enough. Release those boulders if Cammon ascends in person.

Admittedly, a great proclaimer could bespeak hard soil into quicksand, and such tricks—and soil has no ears nor knowledge of words. Yet Cammon wouldn't want to strain himself and drain his energy.

'If only I could fasten this spy-glass to a rifle,' Taito mused. 'He's in range, if I fired downwards.' It was a vain hope. At best, the horse would be hit. Cammon would scurry away.

Once the envoy had recovered his breath, he bawled upwards faintly, 'Lord Tycho Cammon—invites Lord Taito's daughter—to dine with him.'

Fat chance of that.

Next morning—after what sort of night for Anniki?—that cuckoo with the crippled foot had alighted on the tower top. The look-out had summoned Taito, along with Astrid.

The bird blinked, groggily. Its feathers were ruffled. In its beak it held a white flower—a milkcup—which it dropped.

'Hark and hear,' the bird squawked, 'a milkcup for the maiden, but for her unfriendly father a soulflower of death—

'Death,' cackled the cuckoo, 'by heart-sickness. Lord Tycho yearns in his heart for your daughter. Your own heart will squeeze itself unless you yield her. *This is spoken.*'

Taito's intake of breath was agonised.

'Daddy—!'

How, how had Tycho Cammon compelled a cuckoo to convey a woe? To act a proclaimer's vehicle, as his ventriloquist's dummy—! The words the bird repeated were imbued with Tycho's own power, although the bird itself seemed distressed or outraged.

'You have until midday,' it squawked. Having delivered its message, the cuckoo threw itself from the tower, with what seemed like suicidal clumsiness. Down it plummeted. It contrived to glide. Next it was fluttering frantically, veering away from the town, as if its precipitous dive had snapped some string which controlled it, and now it was escaping.

White-faced, her father clutched his chest.

'No,' he gasped. 'No.'

The regular squeezes of pain persuaded her father less than Astrid's pleas that he let her save him. Where would she be without him? And Gustaf was still too young.

She might not be gone too long. To validate this hope, all she took with her at noon was the ivorywood puzzle in a little leather pouch slung round her neck by its drawstring.

Tycho Cammon greeted Astrid jovially in the town square, as pleased as a lad receiving a present. An entourage of three louts was keeping an eye out, clustering round the alien who stood so still.

Astrid demanded, 'Is my father safe now?'

Cammon scanned the sky, which was clouding over.

'Right as rain,' he assured her. 'You have my word for it.' Near the mouth of a lane, Astrid spied a man's body lying face down. His head was twisted at an impossible angle.

'Murderer,' she accused.

Cammon followed her gaze. 'Him? Oh, he shook his head at our activities.' Putting on a childish lisp: 'He shook it and he shook it so much—'

Shuddering, Astrid stared at the motionless Unman instead.

A silver hieroglyph was appliquéd on one shoulder of the alien's velvety body-suit which was as black as its skin, but scuffed and soiled. Empty pouches hung from clips. White scabs crusted gland-slits on the alien's jutting chin, below a prim cupid mouth. Its nostrils slowly opened and shut as it breathed, which was its only activity. Such hurt showed in the close-set ambery eyes.

Despite her aversion to the alien, sympathy percolated—fellow feeling. 'What are you going to do with it?'

'With *it*? It's a *him*. Oh, I have a use for him all right.'

She imagined herself and the alien compelled to mate, to amuse Cammon the spectator. Surely he was too covetous of Astrid to dream up such a humiliation. Cammon the violator would seem just as alien to her.

She had no other audience except for Cammon and his louts, unless nearby residents were peeping. Townsfolk were keeping to their houses. Just then she heard a distant wail of protest, and recalled the presence of other cronies.

'Actually, my splendid chick,' Cammon said graciously, 'this town square of yours seemed to lack a focal point until now. It needed a statue.'

'He looks very sad,' she said. 'Tormented.'

'*Dear me.* Of course!' Cammon snapped his fingers. 'Blink, Juttie, blink for the lady.'

Membranes glazed the alien's eyes, sliding to and fro. Tears poured forth.

'I quite forgot they need to blink. Jig a bit, there's a good statue. Jig on the spot.'

Jerkily the Juttie capered—and fell over. In the dust of the square it writhed, arms and legs spasming.

'Guess he got cramp,' said Cammon. 'Relax, statue. Lie at ease!' And the alien lolled. 'You must remind me, Astrid Kallio, not to use him up too quickly.'

'You're cruel . . .' Not a wise thing to say.

'*What do you want him for?*'

This might also be unwise. Yet Cammon treated her question with the utmost seriousness.

'The truth is, I need him to tell me the names and the meanings of the stars and the constellations in the Isi tongue, and also of their own home stars and constellations.'

'Whatever for?'

'The sky *presides* over us,' he replied. 'And over them.'

'What if he doesn't know? Does a scullery lad know the words for embroidery?'

'Snakes' voices speak in the Jutties' heads—informing them of all sorts of things.'

'*I* watch the sky at night.' She hoped to forge—no, not a bond—but some affinity.

He chortled. 'What a fine hen you are. And a hen must be plucked.'

'I came to you voluntarily, Tycho Cammon. You didn't call me down here with your voice. Don't bespeak me now.'

'If I don't, summerbright, how will you enjoy yourself?'

Astrid glanced up at the keep, as if her look might leap her back to safety. The air was becoming hazy, faintly moist. Mizzle was dulling the outlines of the keep. Upon the tower: a tiny figure. Surely her dad, with his spyglass. She waved, to reassure.

Coming down the lane past the corpse, led by a man in leathers, was . . . Anniki, in a cloak. Anniki looked utterly dulled and compliant. From the man's holster jutted the butt of a light-pistol. Nobody would be obstructing *him*. The escort halted Anniki.

'See,' said Cammon, 'your friend's right as rain as well.'

The two women's gazes met, across empty space. It was as if Astrid had betrayed Anniki by making a temporary get-away to the keep—while Anniki in turn had betrayed Astrid by revealing her identity.

Cammon was severing Astrid's ties with home.

Astrid had half hoped—and half feared—that Cammon would take her to the Tamminens' vacated house, full of wholesome herbs and dried mushrooms and roots.

That wasn't to be. Accompanied by the trio of bodyguards, Cammon led her instead to the candlemaker's home. To Mr Kintilar's. Kintilar and family had been temporarily dispossessed. All of his candles remained.

She knew the house and its smells from childhood: the odours of paraffin wax distilled from yellover wood and muskwood and kastawood, and also from bituminous shale; the aroma of scent oils.

Downstairs, were Mr Kintilar's double boilers and pouring pitchers and tin moulds. Bowls of baking powder to extinguish any wax which might catch alight. Bowls of fatty acid crystals to render wax opaque and slower-burning. Spools of braided yarn, weights for wicks. Everywhere, everywhere, finished candles were tied in clumps or hung in pairs from nails.

Everywhere, hundreds of cock-candles.

All the way up the staircase; and in the main bedroom too.

The louts stayed downstairs to drink ale filched from the larder and snack on squeaky cheesebread and cold greasy goose. If only they weren't down below, where the creak of floorboards and bed would be audible!

In the main bedroom, hundreds of candles crowded shelves and furniture . . .

'What illumination we'll see,' enthused Cammon, 'if all the wicks are lit! Maybe the house'll burn down . . .'

'All the wax will melt,' she retorted. 'It'll become so soft!' As if *she* could proclaim at *him*.

He concentrated, summoning his power.

'Wicks a-light, Burn bright, Such a sight!' he proclaimed. 'Five, six, Hot wicks, Pricks and chicks! Burn bright, Wicks a-light—!'

It was as if phosphorbugs were invading the room, each settling on a candle tip. How could it be so dark outside? Could black rainclouds have arrived so quickly in the wake of what had hardly even been drizzle? As a hundred candles breathed out little flames, and as the window framed only deep gloom, so at once there was privacy . . . and imminent revelation.

Deeply scared, Astrid loosened her blue bodice sacrificially.

'Don't bespeak me . . .'

Yet he did. He was a petulant child indulging in a tantrum—yet his was a channeled tantrum.

He chanted:

'You shall love men, You shall love me,
'Shall-love-men, Shall-love-me,
'ShalLoveMen, ShallLoveMe—'

Faster and faster he chanted. A sway to sweep her from her feet, from her rootedness in her own self.

To try to divert the sway, to give it a different channel down which to run, a drain to take it away, she shrieked, 'I love my father!'

In vain. The sheer force in Tycho Cammon. Such a torrent. Astrid's hair streamed in a gale, baring her brow. Candle flames danced.

Everywhere, swaying lights. Music wailed in her mind. Blood-rhythm pounded. She was undressing, wrenching garments off—as was he. She was dancing naked in a clearing—the room's walls were reeking musktrees. She was capering in front of a great candle-mushroom. She must leap and bestride—so that spores would gush from its gills, so that sticky spawn would spout.

Soon, she deflowered herself, gasping and crying out.

Just as had been bespoken.

Looking back, Astrid's time at Castle Cammon—until the coming of the astronomer—was spent in a state of semi-trance. Hers was a sick addiction to a euphoric drug, namely Tycho himself. As time went by, Tycho tormented her by withholding this drug progressively so that she craved in vain, losing all focus.

His castle of pink granite occupied a rocky island around which a river divided. Twin towers soared, linked at their penultimate storeys by a high bridge of tammywood. A similar bridge spanned the river, to lead to the smoky little town of miners and smelters and smiths. The prevailing breeze almost always blew haze away over pastures beyond. Visibility from the tower tops was rarely impaired.

On top of the western tower, the Juttie was kept in a cage. Slim numbered bars imposed a grid upon the heavens. On clear nights a scribe (who was also a draughtsman) copied down by candlelight upon charts the alien names of stars and star groups. He filled a ledger with annotations—not only regarding Kaleva's sky, but also the sky of the alien's home world, wherever that might be. A little rooftop hut gave the scribe storage and shelter from squalls. During balmy weather he even took to sleeping there by day.

The Juttie was one of those who could make himself understood to humans, in that strange eternal-present style of speech, accompanied by clicks and hisses. Otherwise, Tycho would hardly have brought him. Astrid sat in on some of these sessions of interrogation, to watch the stars for herself and to compare the alien's submissive captivity with her own.

'Star being the Egg-*k*-Tooth of the Precious*sss* One who was*sss* dreaming*k* the taming and raising-to-reason of the Two-Leg*sss*,' she would hear.

The scribe would grunt and squint and scribble the enigmatic words, which few in the castle or the town were able to read—least of all Tycho, otherwise his own spoken words would be gelded of power.

The same scribe penned Astrid's intermittent messages to her father, which Tycho insisted on her sending. These could hardly be sent by cuckoo, or they might be cackled in any market place.

By now, Tycho wanted Astrid as his bride—freely granted by her father, so that Tycho could start claiming some control over Kallio land. The knowledge that Astrid was a hostage must have been anguish for her dad. But he was holding out for Gustaf's sake. After the defection of the crippled cuckoo, Tycho couldn't reach Taito with his voice to speak a woe at him a second time.

Astrid must send pleas to her father, which she half-believed or even believed passionately after Tycho bespoke her to do so—until nausea or apathy set in. *Daddy, I must wed Tycho. He is my life now . . .*

Her father wasn't a fool.

Tycho had already enjoyed the goods. He could do so whenever he chose. She was a commodity. As witness: her commemorative tattoo which Tycho had an artist from town impose on her breast as a brand of ownership, though less painfully than a branding.

Astrid's relations with the fat Dowager Lady Cammon were as slight as with Tycho's two younger brothers. The Dowager's mania was cookery, and the lads, who had none of Tycho's talent, spent their time running wild, hunting soarfowl in the reeds and scampery leppis in the woods, and keeping out of the way.

In spite of straw and a brazier in the cage and a big canvas cover with a smoke-hole—like some cloth tossed over a bird-cage—and despite a sheepskin coat, towards the end of the first winter the Juttie succumbed at last. Worn out. Used up. Chilled to death. Astrid could hardly feel that she had lost a companion.

Her real companion was her ivorywood puzzle. Tycho sometimes teased her cruelly that he might send pieces of it to accompany each message as a token of authenticity and sincerity.

On other occasions Tycho was almost vulnerable—scaringly so. Once, he wept in Astrid's arms at the way he felt increasingly compelled to compel others. He was scared of losing absolute control, so that his gift became his governor.

The Dowager's delicious meddlings in the castle kitchens might have been to blame for her son's increase in girth. Spending her days with scullions was somewhat *infra dig*, but Tycho could hardly bespeak his mother not to do so. The Dowager made sublime fish stock—she wouldn't become a laughing-stock as well. Any sniggerers would end up hanging by their fingertips from the high tower-bridge.

To Astrid's delight, which she kept secret, one day she discovered that the ivorywood puzzle had two quite different solutions. One route assembled the pieces into the quadratic prism. That was the shape the puzzle had first been in when she unwrapped her birthday gift. The other route, even more difficult to achieve, fitted them all together as a star. Her name-sign!

Those Pootaran puzzle-makers way across the sea had certainly been ingenious. Her dad must have known about the double solution all along. If it hadn't been for the abduction, he would have tipped her the wink after a few weeks. Now Astrid had discovered belatedly, by intuition. Because Tycho might be jealous of a shared secret, she didn't send any message to her dad that she had found out about the wooden star.

As for stars of a heavenly sort, in spite of the demise of the Jutte informant and the cryptic rigmaroles which had resulted, Tycho hadn't lost interest.

Come the springtime, he commissioned a telescope from the same Mr Ruokokoski of Niemi who had ground the lenses for Taito Kallio's spy-glass. By midsummer, hardly the best time for star-gazing, the brass telescope had arrived, complete with wooden tripod. It was installed on the observatory tower beside the now-empty cage and the hut, which could shelter the instrument when not in use.

The novelty comforted Astrid. When nights became a little longer she stared at gassy Otso, even at ringed Surma out beyond Otso, although Surma is the emblem of death.

During leaf-fall later that year, Tycho travelled to the gala at Yulistalax to be famous, and he triumphed, even though his verbal victories over rival proclaimers were violent ones, causing pain and injury and humiliation.

When he returned, it was with Jon Kelpo, who might have been naive to accept the tyrant's invitation, but who hankered for patronage and access to those alien star charts.

Names are often destiny. People are compelled to act out roles, though perhaps in an altered guise.

This became plain during the welcoming feast for the young astronomer, held a couple of weeks after his arrival. Tycho's mother had insisted on a delay so as to consider her menus.

Tapestries of hunting scenes and of fictitious raging battles with Unmen cloaked the granite of the walls in the banqueting hall, in between tall windows too slim for any intruder to climb through—the panes could be pivoted to let in air. Sharp-pronged horns of hervies jutted from plaques fixed to those tapestries—like eruptions of violence into the hall. Stoves were squat armoured sentries. Dozens of candles burned in wall-sconces and in chandeliers high above the long table. Guests from town drank their fill but behaved themselves.

Oh there was black blood soup and cold poached fish and fish stew in broth and roe on ice. There was simmered veal and pigs' trotters, and lambleg with golden potatoes baked in a hollow log. Finally, there were to be sausage pancakes heaped with pink valleyberry and also colostrum pudding made from the first immuno-laden milk given by a cow after calving.

Jon Kelpo was short and skinny, with a thin intent face. His hair was nut-brown. His hazel eyes were wonderfully expressive. Over a white silk shirt tucked in his breeches he wore a striped scarlet waistcoat. The waistcoat was scuffed and less splendid than Tycho's finery; just as well.

Servants scurried. The fat Dowager fussed. Townsfolk crammed themselves with food in case she accused them of being picky. Equally, they must not seem to be gluttonous. Talk was scientific and over the heads of many guests, but they pretended deep interest—as did Arvid, the elder of Tycho's two junior brothers. The other brother was Armas. Both brothers were spruced for the occasion. The mana-priest from town contributed his best. Astrid, in a sky-blue gown, was genuinely interested.

Tycho was presenting himself as a patron of science.

'My name prompts me,' he explained grandly to his audience. 'There was once a famous astronomer on Earth named Tycho.'

Jon Kelpo nodded. 'I know, sir. We mentioned this in Yulistalax. He was a noble, like yourself. I've read—'

'You're obliged to read, whereas I'm obliged not to. Carry on. What did you read about him?'

'He was a genius, with wonderful eyesight and accuracy.'

Tycho smiled. Not having had Kelpo's advantage—or disadvantage—of literacy, maybe he expected further flattery in the same vein.

'What else do you know about this noble genius?' he prompted.

Kelpo clammed up.

Tycho banged his pot of dark beer on the table. 'Tell me. I bespeak you to.' He did not exert too much power.

The young astronomer's vocal chords seemed in conflict. Tycho frowned, but then forced a smile.

'Be utterly frank,' he reassured Kelpo. 'You are my fool-of-reason—my rational shaman.'

For a moment Astrid had difficulty understanding this. Then it came to her that, in Tycho's mind, an important motive for inviting the astronomer to Castle Cammon must be that Jon Kelpo was a man of science, not of mana-magic. Kelpo's presence might serve to counterpoise Tycho's fear of losing control to his impulses.

If Tycho had invited a shaman into his keep, instead, that would have been like attaching a lightning rod to one's head.

In a strangled tone Kelpo said, 'The original Tycho fought with everyone. He was very quarrelsome with his equals. He was harsh with his underlings—'

'And I know how the original astronomer died,' Tycho interrupted. 'My father told me, as a warning. It happened at the court of the genius's royal patron. By etiquette nobody could leave the table until the king retired. The king liked to sit up late boozing. One night the astronomer indulged in far too much wine. His bladder became bloated. He couldn't leave.'

Guests were exchanging nervous glances. Sweat was breaking out.

'Is this a suitable topic to be talking about during dinner?' demanded the Dowager, her feathers ruffled.

Tycho moderated himself. Very mildly he continued, 'Finally, the astronomer's bladder burst. Poisoning set in. A few days later he died in agony. Enough, enough, I agree, Mother!'

Kelpo rallied. 'The astronomer Tycho also had a pupil, named Kepler. Almost my own name, sir.'

'So here you are, my rational shaman, as circumstances require.'

In fact, Kelpo's name signified *brave*. Well, in coming here he was either intrepid or rash.

As the banquet progressed, it became clear that Tycho's motives in sponsoring astronomy were mixed and numerous. He also wished Jon Kelpo to create a new map of the Kalevan sky—to design new constellations to supersede the harp and the cuckoo, the archer and the imp perched on a mushroom.

If the Isi snakes linked up the local stars in different patterns to those which human beings had come to perceive, why not a whole sky in honour of the Cammon family?

Of course, a constellation must be dedicated to Queen Lucky. But mainly there'd be: a hervy's horns, in honour of Tycho's dad. A cooking pot, for his mother. Speaker's lips, for himself and for all other proclaimers—the new constellations ought to appeal to everyone in the country. More plausible, more serviceable, more relevant! Oh, there must still be a cuckoo, but in this case a crippled cuckoo with a flower in its beak; which made Astrid flinch.

Megalomania. . . .

Astrid's relationship with Jon Kelpo grew only gradually—paralleling her own weaning from that verrin's nipple, Tycho. It was as if some transfer of focus occurred.

At first, Kelpo begrudged the claim that Astrid sometimes made on the telescope. Did this young woman—whose status at Castle Cammon was questionable—imagine that she was a fellow scientist? However, as regards the task of redrawing the constellations, a telescope wasn't much use at all. The naked eye was best. To be sure, a telescope could reveal distant constellations too dim and tiny to notice ordinarily. What use was there in mapping those? Should he tell Tycho, 'My lord, I've just found your very face hidden behind the Saucepan! Alas, no one can see it unaided.'

Consequently Kelpo tolerated some stargazing by Astrid, maybe for silent company on the tower top.

When winter came and night spilled into the day, after each new snowfall a servant would dig and sweep the rooftop clear. The river below was ice-bound under a thick white blanket. Wooden stakes marking the road towards town were half-swallowed. Yet the roof remained merely ice-glazed and crisp, instead of engulfed. There was always the brazier to warm one's mitts at, plus resort to the castle saunas when chill reached the bones; she to the women's, Jon Kelpo to the men's.

He was a strangely private person, with an inner intensity which found its outlet in the sky. Attempts to broach his personal history would bring a polite rebuff.

Until . . .

Winter had come and gone. Buds were bursting open. Snow was melting, splish-splash. On some nights the snow would crust again and the drippings would become icicles. In a restless fever, sweethearts would be carving their names in the bark of trees.

Up on the tower, the night was fairly mild. Showers of actual liquid rain had fallen during the afternoon. Stratus clouds were now breaking up into strato-cumulus as comparatively warm currents rose. Stars gleamed through rifts. Those rifts were on the move, frustrating observation.

'What *do* you keep in that little pouch you wear round your neck?' Kelpo asked Astrid, as though at long last he had fully noticed her. 'There's no smell of any pomander ball. I suppose no pomander or mustoreum can ward Lord Cammon off.'

This might have seemed an indelicate and insensitive remark. In fact, he was heeding her as an individual.

'I keep my puzzle in it, Jon.'

She must show him.

She did so, by lantern light in the hut.

Ordinarily, Kelpo might have scorned such fiddling with wooden puzzles. He might still have done so, if Astrid had not felt an impulse to confide her secret—that this particular puzzle had two quite different solutions, one of which was a wooden star-shape. Kelpo seemed riveted. He asked to handle the pieces himself.

Twist and pivot the pieces as he might, he couldn't arrive at either result. She demonstrated. Still he couldn't copy what her hands were doing. To do so seemed suddenly important to him.

The next night was full of stars. Jon Kelpo couldn't concentrate on them.

Finally, he exclaimed to Astrid, 'To see in two different possible ways! To see alternative connections: that's what Cammon wants me to do. Instead of an archer and a harp, a saucepan and a crippled cuckoo . . . He doesn't know the half.'

He confessed his own secret.

When he was just a baby, a cuckoo had flown into his room—so his mother had assured him. The bird had perched on the head of his cradle. It had cackled, then shat in his eyes. Specifically, upon his nose so that the splash went in both directions. How Baby Jon had squealed. Quickly his mother had cleaned him. She called in a wise-woman to examine his eyes and a mana-priest to diagnose the meaning of the event.

'It's an omen of great things,' the mana-priest had decided, after a trance. 'Yet following upon those great things maybe your son will experience some shit.'

When Jon reached puberty, he became able to see in a different way to other people. At first, the experience was spasmodic and inadvertent—scary. As time passed, he found he could summon the phenomenon by concentration.

'The stars are bright tonight,' he said to Astrid. 'The sky is black. But if I focus myself'—and he seemed to do so—'the sky becomes white and the stars are black dots. This is so useful for pinpointing stars, like grains of peppercorn spilled upon a linen tablecloth. Everything's reversed. Your fair face and hair are dark, as well.'

'If *I'm* different,' Astrid sang out, 'then I'm somebody else—and somebody else is no longer Tycho's possession.'

'My hand is black . . .' Jon held his hand out, reversed, towards her cheek, softly to touch, to stroke with his knuckles, with the backs of his fingers.

'Oh, but I feel I'm still swayed to seek the love of men,' sighed Astrid. 'Can you show me what you see? Can you sway me to see?'

'I'm no proclaimer—I can't tell someone to do something.'

Her hand rose to grasp his.

'I'm not speaking about *telling someone*—'

In the hut, there still remained the camp bed which the scribe had used. Light the lantern, look at one another.

'What if somebody comes?'

'Shut the hatch to the stairs. Drag the chart box over it.'

When Jon returned, he said:

'Your breasts are black, Astrid. Your belly is black, and your legs. The shadows are bright.' He must find her, almost, by feel.

174

In the subsequent moment of climax she *saw*—for just a moment—his body as black, and her own body likewise.

Why should Tycho bother to climb all those stairs?

Over the next few weeks, as their bodies grew accustomed to one another's rhythms, Astrid could see the reversal for five to ten seconds.

As the days grew longer, dark windows of opportunity shrank and shrank. Astrid yearned for autumn, though not for winter when the hut would be too cold, and a brazier lit inside would only make the icy air foul to breathe.

Tycho never discovered about the reversal of vision. He never realised that there was that secret to find. What he found, mounting on impulse to the tower top one night early the following spring, and hurling the hatch open by force of words and muscle, was Astrid and Jon together inside the hut, hastening to dress—and rage clouded any insight Tycho might have had.

The weather had suddenly turned mild. Much snow remained to melt from the countryside. This had been the first love-making for months.

Throughout the winter Jon had shown his patron progress on the new map of the constellations. Jon was forever amending, making alterations, even beginning again from scratch. This didn't vex Tycho. The continuing presence of a dedicated man of science was a moderating factor in the castle.

Two lovers in disarray were quite a different matter.

Astrid must watch Jon stand stock-still and stare from the parapet into the night. And *stare*.

Jon needed those eyes of his; or else he would be nothing.

And now they bulged and swelled—

—until they burst.

Tycho released him from the sway. Jon collapsed screaming, more liquid upon his cheeks than any tears could have brought.

Tycho bespoke Jon to leave, to stumble down stairs and more stairs— wood, then stone—and to find his way by memory to the gate. The tyrant stalked him, whistling mischievous directions and misdirections as though Jon was a dog.

Astrid had followed part of the way downstairs. Now she fled back again up to the top of the tower. She took the oil lantern and set fire to all those charts—as if this brief beacon might somehow guide Jon away from Castle Cammon and through the town.

She contemplated the plunge, to ease her own anguish, and maybe forestall Tycho from forcing her to hang by her fingers from the bridge between the towers for as long as she could.

Two things saved her. One was that when Cammon came for her, to haul her downstairs, he was as distraught as if he had thrown an amulet of sanity into the river and had just realised what he had done.

The other was the Dowager Dame. A servant had told her maid what was happening; the maid told her mistress.

'So our astronomer's gone away!' declared the Dowager Lady. 'If I'd known, I'd have packed a fish and fat pork pastie for him, and some clabbered milk—'

It was as if the loss of Jon Kelpo's eyes was of less consequence than him setting out on a journey without any food.

Tycho gaped at his mother. He howled. He fled to his own chamber, leaving Astrid alone with the Dowager.

'Would *you* like a pastie?' Tycho's mother asked Astrid. 'I don't think you're very welcome here now! You'd better go to the tinsmith's in town. Mr Lindblad. He's an easy sort of man. Then start walking home tomorrow—if you can. I'm sure I don't know if you can. You can always try to force yourself. Lindblad'll give you a pastie, although it won't be a patch on mine. Kallio Keep's quite a way. Go as you are. Don't dare take any gifts my son has given you.'

The one gift Astrid cared about remained in the hut: her birthday puzzle in its pouch. It would be sheer madness to climb the tower again. She must catch up with Jon. She must find him.

The Dowager's word was enough to allow Astrid through the gate.

Melting snow was a mess of jumbled distorted footprints of people and animals. Search as she might, halloo as she might, Astrid couldn't come across her lover on the road to town or anywhere in the town. Jon might have missed his way and tumbled blindly into the river, treacherous with ice rushing by, bobbing on spate. He may have circled round deliberately and drowned himself.

It must have been two in the morning when Astrid found her way to the tinsmith's house, shivering convulsively and escorted by a night watchman, who banged on the door with his cudgel.

She knew she wouldn't go back to Kallio Keep. Wouldn't, couldn't. She felt in her bones and her waters that if she did so she would act like a whore in her dad's town, and that Anniki would spit in her face.

'So you came here instead,' Bosco said to Astrid, 'where at least your problem gives you an occupation. A livin', you might say.'

The naked woman, perched on the stool, turned to him. Daylight was already reasserting itself.

'The man-sway has faded,' she whispered. 'The sway to love men: I felt it fade while I was telling you.'

She had unburdened herself. The cuckoo on her breast had cackled, and the pressure was gone.

'Did you see me as white, earlier on tonight?' Bosco asked her. 'Do you see all your sailors as white?'

'I saw them all as Jon,' she whispered.

'I felt responsible,' Bosco told young Andrew, who lay in the upper bunk, propped on his elbow. Other sailors in the fo'c'sle were all ears, of course. The four-masted hermaphrodite schooner rolled gently as it sailed through a luminous night that was so easy on the men of the watch up on deck. The *Conga*'s creaks and groans were as familiar and friendly as the chirping of crickets in a clove field back home.

An incredulous voice said, 'That's why you paid for her ticket? Her, with all that nest-egg she bin earning!'

'Ah. I forgot to mention. What she didn't need for immediate use she bin sendin' to her home town as charity for the mana-priest to dole out. Sort of in recompense for herself and her dad shuttin' themselves up in their keep while Tycho Cammon made free.'

'An' you seriously don't plan on sneakin' into that little cubby-cabin of hers?'

'She don't need that now. She wouldn't want it. After we dock, I'm goin' to fix her a job in a puzzle workshop. She'll learn how to make really neat puzzles to take northerners' minds off more dangerous manias. An' I hope she might find herself a girlfriend among all them nimble-fingered puzzle-makers.'

'What a soft touch you are, Bosco. Sounds as though you've been bespoken, yourself.'

'Mebbe I have been,' admitted Bosco. 'Just a bit, on the shortest night.'

The Author as Torturer

IN THIS ESSAY I WANT TO DISCUSS CRUELTY IN SCIENCE FICTION, Fantasy, and Horror. I also want to consider censorship, both inflicted from outside by law or boycott, and self-imposed too.

In Britain and America recently we've been seeing the self-appointed guardians of public morals trying their best to suppress books which they find offensive on grounds of sexually provocative content and other kinds of blasphemy against the tribal codes of society. Thus in Britain we've seen H.M. Customs and Excise raiding, confiscating from, and trying to prosecute the London gay bookshop, Gay's the Word, for importing corrupting titles from America. Fortunately the Customs and Excise people made fools of themselves by confiscating a swathe of modern literary classics, which are already published in Britain without any bother. We've seen a bit of a storm brewing when the Books Marketing Council, the promotional arm of the Publishers Association, decided to follow up its previous campaigns (such as the Top 20 Young British Authors, and Writers on War) with a Teenread campaign, based on careful monitoring by schools and libraries around the country of what actually are young people's favourite titles. Quite a few of the books on the short list proved to deal with sex, rape, male homosexual love, lesbianism, or incest—leading a big book chain to announce that, if these titles were selected, then they wouldn't promote or sell them. Not long ago in one London borough another popular juvenile title about a daughter who lives with her dad and his homosexual lover was being hauled bodily out of school libraries.

Do these titles *reflect* the realities of modern society, hence their popularity and value? Or, as the objectors protest, do they promote the erosion of good social values, so-called?

In America there's worryingly strong conservative religious pressure pushing for grab-all laws to squash 'offensive' literature: laws which are frighteningly vaguely worded, and which are getting scaringly close to their legislative goals, so that the prospect looms of the shelves of book stores in future being full of brown paper bags with health warnings on them.

And let's not forget that there's also such a thing as radical repressiveness: repression proceeding out of the feminist movement in its opposition to presumed sexist portrayals.

A good few years ago, back in the hangover from the Swinging Sixties, I wrote a novel called *The Woman Factory*, subsequently rewritten (much improved, in my opinion) as *The Woman Plant*. I considered this to be a radical political-pornography novel in support of women's liberation; and I wrote it as a liberatory book, a deconstruction of pornography. The book is still unpublished in English, though it would have appeared from Playboy Paperbacks (courtesy of a woman editor) had the Playboy empire not lost its London casino licence, and sold off Playboy Paperbacks. Other American editors told me privately that they liked the book a lot; but as one of these put it, if he published the book he would 'have his lungs torn out' by friends in the National Association of Women. As of now, I've decided that it wouldn't be a good idea to publish this novel which I still consider powerful, moving, and even beautiful. A cultural mood-shift has occurred in the interval, so that what was genuinely liberatory would now likely be viewed as exploitative and counter-revolutionary, part of the problem rather than part of the solution.

True, I've been rebuked for this decision by Charles Platt, who wanted to publish a limited edition, and who argued that thus I condone and support the forces of censorship which would rob us of stimulating, controversial literature. I can see his point. Equally, I see the other point of view—and there's an argument that maybe the pendulum has to swing right the other way; although Geoff Ryman's story 'Oh Happy Day' in the first *Interzone* anthology, about a future in which triumphant feminists are killing off 'aggressive' males in death camps, shows in painful metaphor the possible consequences of good-thinking extremism, of radical repressiveness. Unless, of course, you analyse Geoff Ryman's story as part of the problem, deliberately undermining possible solutions, ways of deprogramming aggression and savagery out of the human race—which, goodness knows, we need to do somehow in a world packed with nuclear weapons, where the Gulf War rages, et bloody cetera.

Myself, I'm of the British generation which still had to travel to France to pick up and smuggle back home Henry Miller, *Lady Chatterley's Lover*, the *Kama Sutra*, the Marquis de Sade. When our version of Prohibition ended and things loosened up so that British publishers dared print Jean Genet and Henry Miller and such, naturally this felt like a liberation, something devoutly to be supported.

But lately, although I'm utterly convinced that right-wing and religiously motivated attempts at legal censorship must be resisted at all costs—not least in a country like Britain which has a certain suspicion of enthusiasm, and an element of masochism, a tendency to prohibit and forbid—yet I've developed a bit of an ambivalent attitude to the question of how far writers can go, how far over the top, and of how far they might push themselves to go deliberately over that top to give their work a frisson in a world where—in parallel with attempted repression—there is also a pressure to push the bounds as far as you can go, a world which echoes the words of that poet of the 1890s Decadence, Ernest Dowson: *I cried for madder music, and for stronger wine.*

Is there a limit to the madness of the music, to the strength of the wine? I think there is—when it comes to the question of cruelty.

This is very dangerous territory, because I might be letting in the thin edge of a wedge—of that same Prohibition which stifles and strait-jackets the imagination; not least when the creative imagination addresses and satirises and attacks and holds up the mirror to a real world of organised savagery.

Yet fiction is becoming noticeably crueller. An even stronger flavor of cruelty is being used to entice the reader, to appeal (sometimes blatantly, sometimes very subtly) to the experienced palate.

A while ago I was at a fantasy convention in Britain where a panel of Horror writers were discussing the question: 'How far can "too far" go? Are some horrors best left unseen?' Shaun Hutson, who produces gut-wrenchers, with titles such as *Spawn* and *Slugs* for the popular Horror market, said that it didn't matter what you wrote because nobody could take these things seriously; and he related with relish how his publisher had asked him to really go over the top, resulting in a maniac armed with a chainsaw and complete tool kit torturing tied-down prostitutes to death, for instance taking off their nipples with pliers, an incident which the author seemed reluctant just to gloss over since he related it three times.

Clive Baker argued that Horror should aim to shake the assumptions of people, to destabilise a world view which is often deadeningly complacent, almost evil in its own banality; but he declared firmly that he would never write anything which was 'repeatable', which could incite some reader with several screws loose to try to act out what he had read upon some victim in the real world. His own horrors simply could not be acted out physically; and he would not write horrors which could be acted.

M. John Harrison, from the audience, pointed out that a writer can put irony in a text, can nudge the reader in the ribs to signal that a story is actually a spoof, but that this is no use if the reader isn't trained to pick up on the sub-text, if he just reads literally and believes.

It occurred to me that maybe good Horror twists the reader so much that the reader doesn't want to twist anyone else, ever, not even to stand on a snail or cut a worm in half, if that's in any way avoidable. Your nervous system would have been highly sensitised, and empathised. Ideally you'd want to sit in a locked room with all the lights on, and not do anything dramatic yourself for quite a while. Certainly not go and torture anything.

Personally I've developed a fair bit of respect for Horror fiction lately, and have written a number of Horror stories and a Horror novel, *The Power* (about US bases in Britain, nuclear war, rural life, and ancient evil). Some interesting things are happening in Horror, which at its best (Clive Barker, Ramsey Campbell, Jonathan Carroll) is almost becoming experimental literature. However, let's move over from Horror, which inevitably involves a certain amount of hurt whether physical or psychic, to Science Fiction and Fantasy.

Dick Geis's *Science Fiction Review* for Winter 1985 had a couple of pieces in it which bear on the subject of pain in SF/Fantasy literature. One is a review by Geis himself of a volume called *Physical Interrogation Techniques*, 'a book so horrifying and depressing,' writes Geis, 'it makes you wonder about mankind, God, reality... I review this for writers,' he goes on. 'Here is a rundown on the ways to torture a man (and woman) for information.' If a writer needs to have a character inflict pain on another character—something which certainly mirrors a major aspect of twentieth-century reality, and which is increasingly becoming more 'normal', more accepted all the time—oughtn't the writer to research his facts and get the state of the art of agony right? Or should the writer pretend that these things don't happen, or simply have his character interrogated offstage after a token 'We have ways of making you talk!'? To reappear later, a wrecked gibbering cripple.

Elsewhere in the same issue Orson Scott Card, in his short fiction round-up, speculates whether some SF authors are trying to make him feel like a failure. Apropos Connie Willis's 'All My Darling Daughters' and a tale by Aldiss he wonders why he never thought before that it would be more fun if his sexual partner cried out in agony, or realised that sexual pleasure is intimately bound up with power and exploitation. Maybe Card needs to learn these lessons, and apply them. Maybe he needs a copy of *Physical Interrogation Techniques*. (Though in fact Card is no stranger to other kinds of pain, as we shall see presently.)

When a society grows jaded and decadent, it tortures slaves and prisoners on stage. As in ancient Rome; now with snuff movies. As the demand for stimulation grows more extreme, as our original sensibility gets blunted, so only pain can fit the bill. Pain served up with relish.

I think, at this stage of history, with the torturers flourishing in a lot of countries (more so than during the Inquisition, quite likely) and with gore and snuff entertainment around, it's timely to have a look at the role of cruelty as entertainment in our own lucid, rational literature of SF, and Fantasy too, but keeping to the top end of the literary scale. Let's look at classy, state-of-the-art SF and Fantasy rather than the SF equivalent of *Slugs* and *Spawn* (which I hesitate to describe as 'soft targets'). Let's look at this so that authors can be aware in full consciousness of the growing lure to torture their slave-actors, their characters, on stage—for gain, and for applause—which to my mind diminishes civilisation and humanity and art. Inevitably so, since this blunts the nervous system and ethical sense. It desensitises. It deprogrammes empathy, without which art is lacking, and human beings too are lacking.

We really have to start with Gene Wolfe, author of *The Shadow of the Torturer*—its hero, Severian, explicitly a trained torturer. Doesn't that title send a bit of a shiver—a thrill?—down the spine? However, Gene Wolfe is definitely something of an exception, as well as being an exceptionally clever writer. Severian is apprentice to a trade of gentlemanly artisans, a craft guild whose victims are 'clients'. It's all very matter of fact and discreet. A visit to the torture chamber is more like a trip to the dentist's prior to modern anesthetics, an unpleasant painful inconvenience. Much of the apparatus doesn't work, or is hardly ever used, and is barely described in any case. The most explicit scene—the subjecting of Thecla to 'the revolutionary'—doesn't result in mutilations but more in a metaphysical agony, the imprinting on the victim of an inner demon that will consume her. Thecla is even requested to position herself in the apparatus so as not to embarrass and upset her torturer; and he, Severian, subsequently slips her a knife to kill herself with. Resulting, as we all know, in his banishment and greater things—compared with which the torture chamber recedes to the status of a small stone in a large mosaic. Gene Wolfe absolutely avoids grossing us out, and even quickens our empathy; though in so doing he does exploit—delicately, cleverly—the frisson of torture. One might even say that he normalises torture.

Alfred Bester's *Golem*[100] is a different kettle of fish. It aims to rekindle the pyrotechnic exuberance of *Tiger! Tiger!* (*The Stars my Destination*), drawing this time upon Horror motifs, which were visibly nudging SF aside on the book shelves at the time. The result reads like a dire parody of the earlier book's cosmic, paranormal, life-enhancing somersaults, replacing these with the subnormal of 'evil' in a gratuitously grossing-out way. Oh, intense pain was suffered in *Tiger! Tiger!* Remember how Gully Foyle had his facial tattoo hammered out with acid . . . till Jisbella relented, and paid for anaesthetic. There's no such meaningful pain, or compassion, in *Golem*[100] where one 'slave on stage' is killed by being tortured to move in a circle, resulting in pulling out his own intestines. This is pain-for-pain's-sake, a torture spectacle for the jaded. Gee, what can I dream up that's even worse?

Onward to John Varley's *Demon*, volume three of the Gaean trilogy where Varley must reach for even grander, more cinemascopic effects to trump *Wizard* which already trumped *Titan*.

So for starters let's be hip, and toss in a nuclear war back on Earth that vaporises billions of people. Hang on, let's be even more hip; let's call it 'the Fourth Nuclear War'. (What are we to make of this? At first it seems so irresponsible it's almost unbelievable. And truly this notion of multiple nuclear wars *is* unbelievable. It's nonsense. However, by making thermonuclear holocausts multiple and repeatable, Varley lets global nuclear warfare be incorporated as jaunty background into a story which might otherwise be castrated, emotionally dominated by a single nuclear holocaust, which would compel adequate focus and attention—as this does in Greg Bear's *Eon*.) True, we learn much later that insane Gaea did have a hand in starting it; so it's her fault, and that's just another reason why it's so damned important that we defeat the current, loony incarnation of Gaea. But Varley's fault is the way nuclear war is presented, in flip, toss-off lines, almost a sideshow before we hasten on to the main attraction which soon involves the torturing by Cirocco of her would-be assassin, screwed-up, *inexperienced* Conal. Naturally, Conal fluffs the assassination. So let's give him some *real* experience to wise him up to reality, hmm? Thus Cirocco—never really liking it, of course, and only because she perceives his submerged sterling qualities—tortures Conal till she breaks down his personality structure, so that it reforms in a mould of loyalty and doting love, and finally genuine friendship, person to person, for the torturer.

True, we learn later that insane Gaea was responsible for setting Conal up and for giving him his false personality structure. Cirocco has saved and redeemed him—by torture.

Another piece of justifiable torture: that wiggly little demon called Snitch, whom Gaea had implanted in Cirocco's brain as a spy, just has to be tortured frequently to get him to tell the truth, after he has been removed by brain surgery. Snitch is pretty indestructible, so you can twist him, and mash him up, and tie him to incandescent, long-burning matches—or even stuff these down his throat all the way through his guts. Snitch complains a bit, but mostly he wisecracks about his agonising tortures. He's cartoon Tom, squashed by a boulder; he bounces back into shape.

Spice the action; let's torture Snitch. That should appeal to the readers. This won't do Snitch any real harm. Anyway, he's a malign sub-creature, though somehow cosy too: an endearing alcoholic, and ultimately almost a bosom pal of Cirocco's. It's funny how torture makes friends; it sort of establishes your sincerity.

And Varley comes over as a liberal, humane author who genuinely raps with his characters, and is obviously in favour of liberty, enhancement of human abilities, fulfillment of potential, el cetera. Christ.

Finally, let's look at Brian Aldiss's Helliconia trilogy.

An authentic epic. Ingenious, inventive, exuberant. A whole wonderful world is designed and landscaped and peopled. All human (or alien) life is here. So much energy, imagination, such prose! Alas, it's an epic of futility, of Jacobean tragedy piled on torment, of the cudgel of circumstances hammering anyone who tries to love or to achieve; of cul-de-sacs of suffering, and biological horrors sanctified by the natural necessity of the planet's orbit and the cycle of age-long seasons which freeze Helliconia for hundreds of years then heat it up for hundreds more. Vast panoramas of nature and society are delineated, but every malady is noted with gusto;

while love is but folly or rutting Lust. The orbiting observers are pro-grammed prisoners too, inhabiting another hopelessly doomed cul-de-sac.

The animals known as Yelks are necrogenes, giving birth only through their deaths. The 'spurted sperm' develops in the warm innards 'into small maggotlike forms, which grew as they devoured the stomach of their maternal host'. The maggots then fight and eat each other till a couple of Darwinian survivors finally erupt from throat and anus. Nice invention. In the same league as the 'phagor tick' which causes the population-culling bone fever, seasonal counterpoint of the 'more obscene Fat Death'—a crea-ture with 'elaborate genital organs and no head'. Gaea in her nastiest moments—when breeding zombie-snakes—never quite got into full swing. (But is it Darwinian? So far as I have been able to ascertain, there are no examples of necrogenes on Earth and never have been. Evolution tends to encourage creatures to spread their genetic material around, an aim which isn't well served by seppuku-conception first time out. An exception to this is the many insects which breed only once in their lives, and though some insects such as the ichneumons plant their eggs inside *other* living creatures so that the larvae can consume the victims' guts as food, no insects offer their *own* entrails on the altar of reproduction. If the pattern is successful—and how economical it seems!—why should it not have arisen evolutionarily and established itself somewhere on Earth? Necrogeny appeared in Philip José Farmer's *The Lovers*, with the affected Lalitha going quickly enough into a painless coma prior to calcifying into a womb-tomb. Necrogeny reap-pears subsequent to its role on Helliconia in Orson Scott Card's *Speaker for the Dead*—about which more anon—where tiny alien babies eat their way out of their tiny fertile infant mothers who lack birth canals. Those females who fail to become pregnant grow large, wise, and powerful. However, the victim mothers are understood to have very limited awareness, and thus perhaps do not suffer. Only in the Helliconia trilogy is necrogeny revelled in, as a nasty joke.)

Such, in miniature, is the basic existential pattern of Helliconia. Hundreds of sailors are later wiped out (and bold hopes dashed to pieces) by a sudden aerial swarm of kamikaze necrogenetic fish which impale the sailors so that the threadlike maggots in their intestines—the next generation of fish—can gorge on the carrion.

Twenty-five billion cattle stampede perpetually around the bleak northern continent, forever fleeing the flies that torment them, trampling each other and anyone who gets in the way. No stability is possible for Helliconia, only ceaseless activity. 'Nothing is important—nothing on this earth', declares a king, inflexibly, accurately. Free will is forever foxed, and even an afterlife is vile.

True, natural laws dictate the Helliconian vista, yet Helliconia is a chosen metaphor; all 'inevitabilities' are of the author's design. There's no way out; the world itself is a gigantic torture chamber, operated with grim glee, with visceral zest.

True, Aldiss attempts to recuperate the situation in the final volume of the trilogy, *Helliconia Winter*. Benevolent telepathic emanations from distant Earth pour soothing balm into the peculiar afterlife of Helliconia, so that when Helliconians commune with dead relatives now they encounter helpful, kindly spirits instead of bickering, resentful, malicious souls as formerly. Meanwhile, Earth has at last gone down the tube, but in the post-catastrophe environment mobile crystal icebergs which act as mild power sources emerge from the frozen wastes, ushering in a contemplative new era for the survivors. I'm not sure that his extraordinary soothing of the ungrateful dead across light years of space and the ambling emergence from nowhere of laid-back enigmatic icebergs quite balances the orchestrated agonies and despair that go beforehand.

To be sure, characters have been tortured in SF books in the past. There's a nasty episode in an early Heinlein novel where an innocent woman is tortured so extremely that you need a plastic sheet to remove what's left over; but the actual torture wasn't detailed. And in *The Space Merchants* a lady sadist who knows her anatomy plays with the hero; however he manages to escape precisely because of the needle she's using to torture him, when he contrives that the needle at last punctures the material restraining him.

The author as torturer is now moving more boldly towards centre stage as the audience cries for stronger stimulus. As the author feeds stronger jolts into his or her stories.

To be sure, pain belongs in books. It's a plain fact that people hurt people, often viciously so. Books where everyone was nice to everyone else wouldn't be very interesting, or realistic, or imaginative. Dramatic tension, tragedy, pity and terror would all fly out of the window, and we'd be reading bland pap. And obviously pain, torture, might sometimes be integral to a story, something without which the story would lose much of its point.

Take the example of Michael Blumlein's 'Tissue Ablation and Variant Regeneration' which first appeared in *Interzone* and is reprinted in the *Interzone* anthology. In this fierce, satiric story Ronald Reagan is dissected alive by surgeons so that his skin and bones and organs can be regenerated and multiplied to provide recompensatory goods for the Third World: the resulting thousands of bladders to be used as storage jars, the square kilometres of skin as roofing material, the muscles in meat pies, the ligaments as cord. According to the story, tissues and organs regenerate best if the patient is not anaesthetised during dissection. Extreme agony acts as a tonic to tissue, a stimulus to flayed skin. So Reagan is simply immobilised by a paralysing drug, and tortured surgically at great length.

Blumlein's highly effective story is, I'd say, a nephew of J.G. Ballard's tough-minded satiric surgical or pathological fiction, a blood relation of stories such as 'Princess Margaret's Face Lift'. But now there's an extra ingredient, of forthright torture. Admittedly Reagan volunteered to donate himself, and himself being tough-minded he refused the one possible alleviation of his pain in the form of some oriental method such as acupuncture which was patently un-American. But it's still torture.

Would the story work successfully if Reagan was anaesthetised, and was simply awakened at the end of surgery as a basket case? If there wasn't a bit of rubber science about the beneficial effects of agony? A couple of decades ago, I think the story could have appeared in *New Worlds* exactly so, minus the agony, as a powerful satiric statement. Obviously it's even more nauseatingly powerful the way Blumlein writes it nowadays; and perhaps without the torture element 'Tissue Ablation' might have seemed a mere copy of the Ballard method. But is the torture really intrinsic and essential, or is it there because over the past two decades we have moved on and 'matured'? We expect more; without the agony a tale which would have shocked people and upset stomachs formerly now would seem bland. Have we habituated and desensitised ourselves, and are we now erecting our own Roman arenas, organising spectacles of agony to amuse our jaded selves?

Alternatively, is fiction regenerating and extending itself through pain? Is the sub-text of 'Tissue Ablation' a metaphor about the regenerating of fiction at a time when the commercial cloning of fictions which are copies of other fiction and even clones of clones, is flooding the shelves with unoriginality?

I don't exactly know the answer to this question, though it's a question that troubles me. Nor do I want to sound sanctimonious and holier-than-thou. In my own first novel, *The Embedding*, there's a nasty torture scene based on real happenings in South America. That was some fifteen years ago, and my publisher asked me to cut several graphic paragraphs from the scene.

I did so. The scene is still pretty horrible, though not quite as ghastly as it was originally. I wonder whether any publisher now would have asked me to cut out those detailed few paragraphs?

Later, in *The Gardens of Delight* when I wrote the chapters set in the Hell section of Bosch's triptych, my publisher felt that I had made Hell a shade abstract, and suggested that I add an extra action scene. The publisher was right; I was shying away from confronting the essence of Hell. But aesthetically, structurally, and as regards meaning, I needed to. So I wove in chapter thirteen, featuring actual torture and more impending torture by demons. Desperate to escape this, my character Sean improvises. He says to the demons: 'Look, the nature of living beings is to avoid pain. Pain forces them to do things, to cut out the pain. But really they want to do nothing—they just want to be stable, and still. Avoidance of pain is a negative feedback control, cybernetically, you poor machine. You're hungry, so you eat, then you aren't hungry anymore. But that's all. Nature doesn't like much change, or there'd be no stability. Avoidance of pain is avoidance of rapid evolution.'

Sean doesn't particularly believe this, but he does persuade the demons to reprogramme themselves so that they too can feel pain. When the demons do so, they are thrown into confusion. Sean and company get away. In the second volume of my 'Black Current' trilogy, *The Book of the Stars*, my heroine is tortured though she deliberately doesn't go into any explicit details. Here's what she narrates:

'They got on with their fun. Pretty soon I was screaming and finding how very difficult it is to faint when you really want to. The fact that this was only a host body they were wrecking was, believe me, no consolation. All nerve endings functioned very nicely, thank you. Nor was it of much comfort that on this occasion Edrick lacked equipment such as a finger-screw. I won't go into what they did to me. I've no wish to relive it. Suffice it to say that what seemed like a week later ingenious new pains stopped happening, leaving only the ones already in residence to carry on. But I hadn't spoken—I'd only screeched. When the symphony of pain changed key, I thought maybe it was bonfire time. I rather hoped it was.

'A hawser squeals and groans when a boat tries to snap it in a gale. Then the gale drops and the hawser goes slack. So it was with my mind. With the decrease in the force of agony, my mind went slack at last. I faded out.'

Well, I believe that this episode belonged in the narrative, that the logic of the narrative demanded it. Equally, this was as far as I felt I could go in describing what actually happened. Minus specific physical details. Above all, I liked my heroine Yaleen.

In my more recent fantasy novel, *Queenmagic, Kingmagic*, there's a scene set in a torture chamber where a screaming prisoner is racked and branded to show my horrified hero what is in store for him. But actually the torture chamber is a masquerade. No one is really tortured there. The first prisoner is simply an actor, pretending pain to amuse the buffoon Mussolini king, whose torture chamber is a hobby, a semblance.

Is this a way of having one's cake and eating it too? Of evoking the frisson, but copping out of the consequences? Well, no, I don't think so; and in the case of *Queenmagic, Kingmagic* I was confronting, and perhaps pulling the teeth, of a rather horrid memory, since the torture chamber in question genuinely exists. It isn't in the mutated Yugoslavia of the novel but in Merrie England herself. It's part of Warwick Castle, a ghastly vault dolled up with torture gear for the tourists, which has stuck a thorn deep in my memory. [2013 note: Either this is a false memory, or else instruments of torture were subsequently removed from what was basically just an unpleasant dungeon. Am I over-sensitive?] My own moral feeling—which may conceivably be rooted in the fear of being tortured myself some day, though I hope it isn't only based on self-interest—is that authors should consider very carefully what they're doing when they let it rip. We shouldn't design works and set up situations deliberately so that people can be tortured, if it's avoidable. We shouldn't use Darwinian 'tooth and claw' doctrine or Satanism or insanity or realism or political relevance as excuses, pretexts to excite the reader entertainingly, and nastily, while at the same time exonerating ourselves of responsibility. Otherwise we diminish life, humanity, and art. We cauterise the heart. We degrade the world, encouraging the real-life torturers to tiptoe closer.

Let us contrast two examples of torture which are given a biological and/or social rationale: in Piers Anthony's story 'On the Uses of Torture', and Orson Scott Card's *Speaker for the Dead*.

In the introduction to the story in his collection *Anthonology*, the author explains that 'I set out to write the most brutal fiction the market could sustain. It turned out that I was again ahead of my time.' The story had to wait ten years for publication. In the meantime, to Anthony's chagrin, Harlan Ellison's 'milder' brutal story, 'A Boy and his Dog', appeared and collected all the fame for outspokenness, leaving Anthony on the sidelines.

In 'On the Uses of Torture' a sadistic officer in charge of the penal corps makes lavish use of the pain box upon the imprisoned refuse of the Space

Service (all non-whites, who had refused to commit genocide on an alien planet to clear it for mining interests). To further his career he volunteers to make a treaty with the aliens of a pleasant, peaceful planet who nevertheless inexplicably torture all envoys. Nauseating tortures follow, which culminate in the officer, who is now an insane basket case, becoming the first off-planet member of the aliens' ruling council. He immediately resolves to improve the psychology of torture, in which he finds the nice aliens somewhat naïve. Since his fiancée has arrived to try to bail him out, she can be the first demonstration model.

The rationale for all this is that once in the past these pleasant and gentle aliens set up an interstellar empire, but on one planet, alas, barbarians tortured them and drove them off. This painful experience didn't suggest to the aliens that the barbarians needed to become more civilised. On the contrary, it convinced the aliens that they themselves weren't ready for space. So they all went home and set up a system which would produce leaders who could resist such hurts. The result, long after, is a gentle, polite society where anyone who wishes to run for any office or rack up any prestige applies to be tortured. Those who endure most steadfastly, having most of their bodies shorn away in the process and thus having no material interests any longer to bias them, are fit to govern.

True, it appears that Stone Age tribesmen hacked off a finger-joint by way of initiation, and American Indian tribesmen proved their manhood by enduring pain, though not with the outcome that the braves' bodies were hopelessly crippled, which is hardly a survival strategy. Humans do have a habit of taking the knife to their fellows in rites of passage (of various degrees of barbarity from the 'cosmetic' of tribal marks, via circumcision, to the sexist violation of clitoridectomy) but to conflate this with the utmost of the Inquisition described in loving detail, and to explain that it all started out when the amiable alien race lost a few members on a distant world is really taking catastrophe theory—the idea of a sudden, shock-provoked flip from one mode of behaviour to its opposite—to the point of bunkum, a dollop of nonsense as an excuse for nastiness that would hopefully prove prestigious.

Orson Scott Card's fiction exhibits somewhat of a specialism in human cruelty; so that Algis Budrys has remarked that the experience of reading Card's works resembles being punched in the stomach and left in the dark. But perhaps the dark is more the tragic dark of blinded Gloucester and mad, raging King Lear? In *Speaker for the Dead*, the Xenocide Ender is still atoning three thousand years after the event (thanks to time dilation) for his wiping out of the hive-minded Buggers, the first alien intelligence encountered, due to massive cultural misunderstanding. On planet Lusitania, the second alien society—of the primitive but highly intelligent Piggies—is being handled under human interstellar Law with extreme kid gloves and noninterference, only two xenologists being allowed to contact them, pan-faced, asking no leading questions and giving no leading answers.

The Piggies torture members of their tribes to death by live vivisection for elusive reasons; and do likewise to one of the humans, sending a shockwave through the hundred human worlds. (Instruments of pain, incidentally, are prohibited to governments under human law, though Lusitania colony is ringed by a pain-inducing fence, to preserve cultural quarantine.) Ender arrives to 'speak' the life of a man who belonged to a family more self-tormenting than anything in Strindberg or Dostoevsky—a process that causes extreme psychic pain, in order to purge the causes of that pain; classic catharsis. And the extremely peculiar biology of the Piggies is revealed. No, they were not torturing their fellows. They were giving them the greatest gift, of a second life metamorphosed into a tree. The Piggies chosen to be thus honoured were all anaesthetised (to a reasonable degree) by a wad of local grass containing a powerful drug, so that pain was felt but one did not care about the pain, a notion which is perhaps not fully thought through. (One can imagine feeling the stages of vivisection as physical slices during a drugged detachment and not experiencing pain; but it's surely difficult to imagine feeling pain as such and not bothering about it.)

The planet's extremely limited range of biology is an evolutionary adaptation to an exotic virus which can unzip DNA and bind the DNA of different orders of life together. The Piggies are fertilised by genetic material in tree-sap, and their corpses sprout into trees when they die—long-living sentient trees if the Piggies are dismantled and planted while still alive. The 'torture' is a red herring (though not for the two humans who were mistakenly vivisected), and the outcome is a moving affirmation of a worthy, life-enhancing alien society in true brotherhood with humanity.

Granted the remarkably odd biology, then the theme of vivisection, of (apparent) torture, is inherent and essential—in the service of ultimate joy and fulfillment. But can one grant a bunkum biology which then logically requires live vivisection? Or is the said biology deliberately chosen in order to allow vivisection to take place—albeit offstage, with the single final cathartic exception, when we know the truth and understand. In this case, I'd say that there is bunkum, and bunkum. Utter bunkum, and ingenious bunkum. Ultimately many SF novels are founded on scientific bunkum. According to what we know of physics all novels featuring faster-than-light travel are grounded in bunkum; yet SF writers still use, and need, and even dignify and exonerate FTL travel as an integral part of narrative. And do we know the whole of physics yet? Or, of biology? (Could our own cells have arisen through symbiosis? How and why did sexual reproduction arise?) The metamorphosis of animal to plant and vice versa is, I'd say, permissible bunkum; and vivisection (with a wad of drug-grass in the mouth) is an objective correlative to Card's own exploration of tragic and finally humanitarian anguish, which is his authentic voice rather than a species of unpleasant ventriloquism designed to attract applause.

Yet what if torture itself, per se, is a 'peak experience', one of the great confrontations of life—in the class of sex or revelation or a close encounter with death? This is the case in a rather remarkable Ace Book from 1978, which so far as I know has been almost totally neglected. It is called *Coriolanus, the Chariot*, and its author is Alan Yates. In this novel the whole federated galaxy dotes on dramas recorded on planetoid Thesbos—dramas involving real joy, real agony, real death. The rulers of Thesbos, the Playtors, who are continually scheming for power amongst themselves, have reached their present positions by each undergoing 'the high emotions' and surviving. This process involves their minds being probed for their deepest fears and horrors, and these being brought to life, enacted with the candidate as the victim. The ultimate aim of the hero of the novel, so he thinks, is the destruction of the Federation and of this whimsically sadistic regime which he hates—but by obeying whose vicious codes alone he gains power. As in Blumlein's 'Tissue Ablation', but now mentally, psychically, torture tones up the system.

Perhaps torture in a book, which only employs one single episode of torture and which doesn't exist in a literary context where torture is common currency of narrative, is a genuine shock to the system in this sense. It galvanises the reader. It's like a powerful electric shock to a faltering heart. It replaces the heart. One hears talk of pain as a teaching experience, a purger, a strengthener, from some people who have suffered physically through accident or illness. It hauls people out of routine and banality and makes them question their lives, and existence. Thus with the real-life case of Sheila Cassidy, tortured in a Chilean prison, though I suspect an element of religious hysteria, a martyrdom complex, when faith is reinforced by torture and degradation rather than being obliterated. Doctors and psychiatrists who have provided therapy for freed torture victims might disagree that in most cases the experience taught anything positive... though it may have taught lifelong anxiety. (This is appreciated in Michael Bishop's story of a torture victim in a rehabilitation centre, 'With A Little Help From Her Friends' (*F&SF*, Feb. 1984). 'As a result, their own bodies were strangers to them, mangled suits of armor imprisoning their souls.')

Equally, if the heart has already stopped beating, the torture shock might only requicken a zombi heart, a kind of cold vampire heart. Such is indeed the case for the characters in *Coriolanus, the Chariot*.

Likewise torture is the awakener of a paranormal power in Julian May's *The NonBorn King*, where Culluket the Interrogator inflicts the high emotion of torture on Felice, who till then was only a latent metapsychic, her mind talent locked up tight. Because his torture of her accidentally mimics an extreme mind-altering technique, Culluket transforms Felice into an operant metapsychic whose powers of psychokinesis are greater than anyone else in the world.

True, he also brings out all of her previous psychotic streak—and small wonder—thus producing a monster. Still, here is the principle of transcendence through torture, once again. To become superhuman one must first pass through destructive, agonising initiation—which is almost the old procedure of shamanism, incidentally, with the added ingredient of degradation inflicted by others upon the person. Usually, in reality, the result of genuine torture—so well evoked in Orwell's *Nineteen Eighty-Four*—is the deconstruction of a person, their reduction to a grey, sickly, mindwashed puppet willing, eager, to walk to the wall to be shot, at long last. But here in fiction torture and transcendence are being yoked together, though not without ambiguity.

The recent work of Samuel Delany, who is well versed in the decipherment of ambiguities, and also in their encipherment, notably yokes degradation and transcendence. It also radically questions our own codes, not least our moral codes and our cultural assumptions, implicit amongst which—amongst mine, at least—is the gut feeling that oppression and the infliction of pain is evil, or pathological, a malignancy in the body politic and the human heart, something to be avoided and tuned out of the waveband of possible behaviour.

I'm sensitised to this particularly by an insightful (and favourable) essay on *Stars in My Pocket like Grains of Sand*, which appeared in *Australian Science Fiction Review* for September 1986 entitled 'Debased and Lascivious?' (Blackford's essay exemplifies for me what constitutes good criticism in the SF field, for here is real revelatory response rather than just dutiful analysis, of which there is something of an academic surfeit. But equally it points up a shortcoming or myopia, for the aspects of *Stars* which Blackford focuses upon seem to me to be less major in the context of the whole book than Blackford maintains. They are a strand rather than the tapestry.)

In *Tales of Nevèryon*, in the 'Tale of Dragons and Dreamers', a torture chamber figures, perhaps not surprisingly in the barbaric milieu of that book and in the context of slavery, and liberty—to which Delany opposes the most radical form of non-liberty and oppression, namely that of the torturer's victim. With its 'little pains, spaced out', its treatment of torture almost as a text (a critical analysis and deconstruction of the body, or corpus), and victim Gorgik's comment after being rescued that it was the stupid questions that were torturing him, this realistic yet discreet episode could almost be called metatorture. It's real, it's detailed, yet our attention is guided to other concerns, to social and iconic ambiguities, the deconstruction of historical patterns on the verge of obsolescence.

Perhaps more significant is Gorgik's 'reading' of his slave collar, so that this collar becomes at once a sign of servitude and also a sexual affirmation. Likewise in *Stars* Rat Korga—the degraded product of selective brainburning to wipe out aggression, anxiety, and volition—simultaneously experiences splendour and misery when he is obtained by a woman sadist as her personal, and illicit, slave. She rapes him, in the sense that he's homosexual and uninterested in making love to her (though he cannot disobey), and she whips him. But she also gives him a super-science glove which not only repairs his broken mind for as long as he wears the glove, but allows him to process information and absorb books hundreds of times faster than someone who hasn't undergone brain-burning. Torment and transcendence come hand in glove; and when the authorities catch up and the glove is ripped off Korga, when Korga is rescued from the woman, as Blackford puts it, 'we feel immediately—some might say that Delany has tricked us into feeling—that he has suffered a net loss.'

Elsewhere in *Stars in my Pocket* Delany ingeniously destabilises our ordinary assumptions of 'normality' not least as regards gender—and also as regards beauty, or perhaps one should say sexual focus. What people now normally regard as deformities or blemishes may equally function as sexual attractants. Also, contrasted with the woman sadist who kidnaps Korga, is another more radical sadist, Clym, who prompts the feeling that 'even within the ambit of sadism, it is possible to make distinctions as to what is tolerable and what is not tolerable behaviour.' However, Delany refrains from applying any conventional blanket judgements, and the overall non-moralistic moral of the book is that 'the most intense assumptions within a culture of what is nice and what is nasty might be without foundation.'

So, although (to quote Blackford finally) '*Stars in my Pocket* is a courageous attempt to dramatise explosive themes in the teeth of traditional social attitudes and the recent anti-sex attitudes that have been having a successful run, encouraged by social elements as disparate as cultural feminism and the New Right', one does still have to address the question: Is torture ultimately neutral, or is there a universal moral imperative which says no to it, whatever? Is torture at times even liberatory in the sense that it undermines social clichés which stifle the imagination? Is there such a thing as intolerable behaviour?

To return to Bester's *Tiger! Tiger!*, that earlier novel where Jisbella finally pays for anaesthetics during Gully Foyle's agonising operations to remove his tattoo: on Mars the space captain who scuttled refugees, and whom Foyle is hunting, has retired to the Sklotsky Colony. The original Sklotskies of old Russia castrated themselves to cut off the root of all evil. The future Sklotskies believe that sensation itself is evil. Therefore they have their nervous system severed and live out 'their days without sight, sound, speech, smell, taste, or touch'. 'The ultimate in Stoic escape,' broods Foyle. 'How am I going to punish him? Torture him? . . . It's as though he's dead. He is dead. And I've got to figure how to beat a dead body and make it feel pain.' Which he achieves by kidnapping a projective telepath, thus proving that there's nowhere to hide from pain. Except perhaps in death, in the act of resigning from existence—though Horror fiction casts doubts on that premise! The Sklotsky solution is no refuge.

To evade the question of torture is perhaps likewise to resign from the world. To use torture for entertainment is, to my mind, immoral and evil. To use torture to optimise, to redeem, to drag a person up by their bootstraps into a transcendent state—this is perhaps a mis-yoking of elements akin to the mis-yoking of sexual foci and, say, leather boots in fetishism. Or is this so at all, when our moral code is perhaps merely a deeply rooted assumption which could be wrong? Or, if not wrong exactly, culturally relative.

Does the author as torturer expand our horizons? Or does that author show us the door to darkness, to a blunting of our sensitivity, to a new barbarism of the human spirit such as the Nazi empire would have been?

Perhaps a key to a solution is offered by a novel which features, as a principal (and not abominable) character, a sadist: Elizabeth Lynn's *The Sardonyx Net*.

The Planet Chabad relies economically on slavery, the slaves being criminals who are shipped there from neighbouring star systems for fixed terms of indentureship. On Chabad the slaves do 'enjoy' certain basic rights, though at the same time the majority are kept permanently drugged by a euphoric-tranquilliser, dorazine, which is illegal elsewhere (as is slavery), otherwise there might be massive discontent, a slave rebellion. So here is a form of 'civilised' slavery, arguably preferable to a long prison sentence behind bars. To those with psychological vested interests in the system, it is logical and desirable. Anti-slavery voices seem fanatic or obtuse, and in a sense repressive. But Lynn equally conveys the utter inner resentment (beneath the mask of obedience) felt by undrugged slaves due to their being owned by another person. (Robert Silverberg's subsequent *Star of Gypsies* also incorporates civilised future slavery, but misses out on this worm in the heart of the apple.)

Zed Yago is commander of the starship which transports new batches of slaves to be auctioned, a position which allows him to boil off his sadism when the inner pressure builds. When Dana Ikoro, likeable freelance Star-captain and would-be smuggler of dorazine (suddenly unobtainable) blunders into Zed's hands, he is tortured for days, for information and for Zed's pleasure; and Zed seems obviously a monster. The actual torture, by nerve pressures, results in no mutilations. There are no grossed-out cuttings or genital-squashings, but Dana's experience is terrifying, and his sick fear of any repetition pervades the rest of the book more tellingly than if Zed was repeatedly rampaging. Which he is not. In fact he is trying—without ultimate success—to control his aberration, which results from frustrated desire for his look-alike sister, Rhani, from whom he was exiled by a domineering mother. A potentially ardent, gentle lover has had his libido routed underground, into the psychic pit, establishing a powerful and malign pattern. When Dana, the victim, finally comes to a crux where he has to save his torturer, the situation is considerably more complex than when Conal was 'converted' by Cirocco's 'sincere' torture of him. For Zed has emerged as a complex character, the roots of whose behaviour we can understand, and even feel some paradoxical compassion for; since this sadist is trapped and anguished by his own patterns, and characters do not simply collide as subject and object one to another, but interplay—particularly at moments (such as the threat of new torture, or mistress dismissing slave) when the opposite appears to be occurring.

To say more, Lynn says less; though she says ample, and what she says remains fundamental, a root of the book, not a mere *fleur du mal* used as a cockade of pain, a pain-fix, ornamental agony. Here a horizon is extended, though it's a dark horizon.

Nor would anyone gain the impression that pain is acceptable–even while Rhani has to accept, and allow outlets for, her brother's perversion, an accommodation with which we can at least part-way sympathise.

At the same time, the main crusader against slavery (who should, according to our own value systems, be in the right) engages in terrorist tactics and is revealed to be himself a repressed sadist who resented the opportunities for inflicting pain which the system offered to Zed. The crusader's moral passion is fundamentally hypocritical. The man did not hate Zed because he had been a previous victim of Zed's, but because he himself wanted to be Zed, and never could be. Zed, who can be, and is what he is, would so much rather be something else.

For the sadist is trapped by himself, in an imprisoning pattern.

Authors rule countries of the mind. Hermaphroditically, authors conceive and give birth to their characters to populate these countries; but those characters, with whom authors can do as they choose, are also ultimately the author himself, herself. Even if modelled from life, upon other living persons, they are still the interior vision, the model within the author's head and heart.

If authors deliberately tie characters down to torture them for entertainment, for decoration, without urgent necessity, in the end the authors are trapping themselves. The puppeteer will be incorporated into the machinery of the puppet theatre instead of those puppets coming alive to dance freely, in rapport with their creator, in the Shiva dance of joy—and yes, anguish too—which is life, and the mime of life.

While hardly suggesting that fictional tormentors and torment ought to be rendered more 'sympathetically', with even more psychological necessity—Elizabeth Lynn's tightrope was not an easy one to balance on—yet to employ deliberately inflicted pain in a book requires a deeper understanding and compassion than often is deployed. A compassion, a suffering-with.

Otherwise, finally, the author is not the torturer but the victim.

Baudelaire wrote, 'Je suis le victime et le bourreau', 'I am the victim and the torturer.'

Turn it around: I am the torturer, and the victim.

A Cage for Death

R ALPH HEWITSON'S THANATOSCOPE WAS THE ULTIMATE PRODUCT of that strange man's obsession with death. Thanatology is, of course, the study of dying, and Hewitson's machine was intended to enable us to see, and ideally to 'trap', Death itself. Or himself. Ralph Hewitson always took it very personally that he or anyone else should have to die.

No doubt all of us go through this stage of horror and affront when we are children. Then we file the trauma away in the back of our mind. We lock it up in the mental lumber room, and it creeps out again only in our last days. Sometimes it remains as offensive as ever, but increasingly nowadays—thanks to the Thanatology Foundation's centres across the land and the re-interpretation of dying as an altered state of consciousness—it is transfigured into a friend, an intrinsic part of oneself, the keystone of the arch of life.

Hewitson, however, kept intact the old animist vision of some invisible thief of life. His Thanatoscope—his deathwatch device—was to be the trip-wire camera, *and cage*, that surprised Death himself.

True, some scientific testing of death has been conducted in the centres in addition to the psychological studies and therapies—but only in the sense of weighing the body before and after death to see whether any tiny weight loss occurs, as of a departing soul, or using aura photography to try to record this departure on film. None of these fringe investigators have ever tried to demonstrate the converse occurrence: the *arrival* of Death as an active force.

Hewitson was a tall, black-haired man with a slight permanent stoop as if he never trusted doorways to be quite high enough to let him through.

'I wonder whether Death's doorway will let me pass when my time comes,' he said to me one day, darkly humorous. 'Or will I get stuck in it? Halfway in, halfway out? You know, I've been thinking that zombies could simply be people who get stuck in that door. Their conscious mind has gone through, but the automatic mind gets left on our side of it, running the body mechanically.'

'You mean the autonomic nervous system, don't you, Ralph?'

'Do I? Do I?'

I'd come to the Sixth Street Thanatology Centre only three months earlier from Neo-Theology College after majoring in Death-of-God counselling, and it was something of a shock for me to find someone who—if he plainly didn't believe in God—nevertheless firmly espoused the doctrine of death incarnate. But I had taken a liking to his black jokes, which seasoned his obsession with a dash of pepper.

No doubt this was the way he performed in his own counselling of the dying—he made death seem something of a farce, a Marx Brothers' comedy. That approach could probably work wonders with some people. I've met them. They hate to be contemplative about their demise. They think that it's sanctimonious. Whereas with other people who are still scared—well, a joke could be a fine nerve tonic.

Of course, to Ralph deep down this was no joking matter.

I was being given a guided tour of his machine up in his office on the fourth floor of the centre. It was a pleasant, sunny room with a gilt-framed medieval *Dance of Death* on one wall and, by contrast, on another a large colour photograph of the Taj Mahal. The machine, which took up most of the spare floor space, was the 'excluded middle' between horror and blissful peace. Ralph had, however, included it: a way not of greeting death with alarm or with joy but of damned well capturing him.

There was a waterbed-cum-bier, implanted with medisensors, set within a delicately filigreed Faraday cage, which could block out any kind of electromagnetic radiation or isolate any radiation arising within it. Enclosing this cage were polarisable glass walls that could be rendered opaque—turned into an infinite internal mirror. Various tiny cameras and mirrors were mounted within on silver rods, and outside the glass walls were fluorescent screens, an electron scanner, and a kind of hooded periscope. Also within were small, highly sensitive (to one part in a billion) chemical sniffers alert to the pheromone of death, the complex chemical released in minute traces by the dying body, that we sometimes call corpse sweat. This chemical is akin to the sexual attractor pheromones released by humans and all other creatures, and personally I think it is a normal evolutionary byproduct: a warning signal to others in the vicinity.

Most deaths in ancient times would have been violent, in one way or another, and spelled trouble. Hewitson, of course, thought differently. He had the notion of this molecule as an attractor signal, too. It was something that Death would smell and descend on like a mating moth. The death orgasm couldn't happen until Death had been called. This accounts for certain overly protracted deaths; the bodies of such people simply couldn't produce enough of the pheromone.

True to form, Hewitson had managed to get tiny amounts of this corpse sweat synthesised, and he had built a number of prototype death traps designed to release quantities of it and to snap shut on whatever vectored in upon the molecule—with no success. So he concluded that a dying body actually needed to be there.

Despite his qualms at taking life—which he regarded as sacrificing to Death—Hewitson had equipped his second-generation traps with dying animals. But again with no result. Whereupon, he conceived the idea that the deaths of animals and the deaths of people may be different in essence. (He became interested in the Catholic doctrine that animals have no souls and are automatic objects.)

Incorporated in his perfected machine as well, then, were tiny pheromone taps with the stored drops of the chemical isolated by vacuum and mini-Faraday cages.

His idea was to imitate death: to hypnotise oneself into a deathlike trance, then turn the taps on.

'Do you want me to lie down in there?' I asked him. 'Is that what all this is leading up to?'

'And then I release the nonexistent whiff of cyanide?' he suggested with a chuckle. 'Oh, no, Jonathan, nothing like that. But of course you can try it out for size and comfort if you like. This'll be a pretty famous bed soon. Much more famous than your historic beds where Good Queen Bess or Lincoln or Shakespeare slept. Go ahead. I'm not proprietorial.'

'Well, thanks, but no thanks.'

'I wonder whether I *should* equip it with cyanide gas or something similar. Then I not only catch Death, but kill him, too. After all, if you can legitimately shoot someone you catch burglarising your apartment—well, Death's a mass murderer by comparison. The biggest criminal.'

I couldn't tell whether he was joking or being serious.

'I wonder in that case whether I'd be killing Death in general, or just the personal death of whoever was in the machine.'

'A whole lot of people die every second, Ralph. They die simultaneously. Even if this Death of yours skipped about at the speed of light—'

'Okay, I see your point. I suppose death could be general *and* particular, though.' He hemmed and hawed awhile. 'If I killed the particular death—if I zapped the bullet with this person's own special name on it, right out of the way, swatted it, squashed it, vaporised it—would this person,' and his hand drifted over the imaginary contours of his subject volunteer, as sensuously as a fantasising soldier stuck in a jungle hundreds of kilometres from a brothel, 'would this person *live forever*? Would I have perfected an immortality treatment? Rich irony, Jonathan, for the Thanatology Foundation thus to defeat its own purpose!' His voice hushed, mock-conspiratorially. 'Don't breathe a word of this to anyone. Your Neo-Theology College would be up in arms.'

'I guess it's a way of persuading people to volunteer,' I joked in turn. 'Roll up, roll up! Come into Hewitson's Death Cage and he'll make thee immortal with a hiss . . . of cyanide gas. Oh, but you're forgetting something, Ralph. You'd kill the subject that way, before you nailed his death. Baby and the bathwater, Ralph. Baby and the bathwater!'

'Ah . . .' Ralph looked crestfallen.

But this was all just horsing around. 'You're going to try it out yourself, then?' I asked, more seriously. 'But by just simulating death? By pretending? I take it that'll be with the Swami's help?'

The Swami is our pet name for our Indian counsellor, Mr. Ananda. Ananda has delved deeper into the oceanic unity state of death insertion than anyone else I have ever met. (An oceanic state, on the one hand, but he also compares entry into it to a space capsule leaving the familiar earth behind and entering into orbit high above where all minor details are erased, up on the edge of the endless sea of death space.) Ananda has used deep meditation and self-hypnosis techniques, of Indian origin, to plumb this way station into nothingness—sometimes accompanying the dying down, or up there, in deep rapport with them—before returning to full life to report on it. Needless to say, Mr. Ananda has never met Death—Mr. D—on his journeys.

'I've been taking lessons,' Ralph nodded. 'Admittedly I haven't spent years at it as he has. But I think I can turn the trick. I think so. When I get down deep enough, my own theta-thanatos brain waves will start the pheromones of death dripping.'

'When's all this going to happen?'

'Next Tuesday. I'll need a few observers. Ananda has volunteered, though he thinks my motives are—well, you understand. But he's cleared a space in his schedule.'

'I can spare the time, too, Ralph.'

'Good man. Now look down here—'

He showed me how the periscope, the optic fibre, and the mirrors let the outside observer see around the whole inside of the cage even when the glass walls were mirror opaqued. As I gazed through the hooded periscope into the pearly-lit interior, the empty bier reduplicated itself perhaps a dozen times in all directions before losing itself in a thickening golden fog while the filigree network of the Faraday cage overlapped and overlapped itself within the mirrors.

Tuesday came. Besides Hewitson and the Swami and me, there was also present in his office Dr. Mary Ann Sczepanski, our foundation medic, looking lovely in tight silver pigtails, her *de rigueur* white coat carving her flanks in ivory marble.

Here, then, was the mousetrap with the big cheese—Hewitson—soon to be laid out in it, synthetically Gorgonzola-scented with death (though it wouldn't be an odour that any of us could pick up consciously), a trap of the nonlethal variety.

'It is a far, far better thing I do now,' Ralph grinned, hamming it up a little—to Swami Ananda's evident disapproval—as, clad in a thin linen smock, he wriggled through the door of the Faraday cage, careful not to buckle any of the surrounding thin wires. He stretched himself out on the water bier.

I shut the door and locked it with Ralph's golden key, as per instructions. The key chain I slipped round my own neck. Then I turned on the current to the cage, at very low power. It hummed faintly.

The glass walls descended and locked together, still in their see-through mode. Air recycling *on*.

'You look like Snow White,' shouted Mary Ann, checking his vital signs on the readouts. 'But where's the poisoned apple?'

Hearing her, Ralph nodded ironically in the direction of Mr. Ananda. Then Ralph composed himself as Ananda began loudly to intone a monotonous tape-loop refrain in Sanskrit, which Ralph took up—I suppose—in duet, though I couldn't hear his voice.

Soon Ralph raised his hand, and I opaqued the glass walls.

When I peered in through the periscope, he was lying utterly still, looking suitably blanched and corpselike in the pearly inner light. He lay beside his mirrored self, which lay beside another mirrored self. Toe to toe with yet others. Each in their gilded cage, the bars of which grew thicker as the bodies proliferated further. It was quite easy to lose the centre of focus and get lost. At this moment Ralph's machine seemed more like a device for cloning corpses.

The descent into the death trance took the best part of an hour. Mary Ann monitored Ralph's vital signs dutifully the whole time. The sun shone in through the window upon what seemed like a great marble block, a white kaaba, a mausoleum. A bedraggled pigeon strutted to and fro for a while on the window ledge. Distant street sounds drifted up, and a few times the whirring of copters beat down. Otherwise it was very quiet.

Mr. Ananda peered at the brain-wave screens. He tapped one with a slim brown finger and impeccably manicured nail. 'Here's the beginning of the theta-thanatos rhythms.'

I hugged the periscope hood around my head and heard only the Swami's voice. 'The other rhythms have flattened out now. It'll take four or five minutes more before the theta-thanatos is full enough to switch on the pheromone drip.' But I wasn't about to pull away. I had no intention of missing anything—not that I believed there would be anything (and a videotape was running, anyway). But I'm like that. Set me on a hilltop and tell me to count shooting stars and I'll watch all night, for a friend.

'Ah . . . Pheromone drip *on* now,' Mr. Ananda announced.

I sniffed reflexively, even though I'd have smelled nothing whether the experiment had been enclosed in glass or not.

I watched the point of the needle, near Ralph's bare calf, waiting—at Mary Ann's command—to plunge a massive dose of stimulants into him should the need arise. I kept my hand on the button that would multiply the power fed into the Faraday cage fiftyfold.

What I saw then didn't record on the videotape—as if the tape couldn't register light of the wavelength I saw, as if it came from a different spectrum entirely! But my eyes saw it—I swear it.

A red (except that it wasn't 'red') thing appeared abruptly, perching on Ralph's chest. It was like a bat; it was like a giant moth; it was like an angel on a Christmas tree illuminated by firelight. It flickered, strobelike. It seemed to dance in and out of existence. It had big glassy eyes and a tiny sharp beak. It had scalpel claws on its veil-like wings—if they were wings—like the spurs that are fastened on fighting cocks. (I realised that I was seeing only what my eyes and brain *could* see, not necessarily what was actually there.)

'Theta finale!' sang the Swami, who couldn't see any of this. 'Stimulants, Mary Ann.'

'I already have! The signs show—'

I squeezed my button, too, at the same time. It wasn't needed. Whatever Ralph had set up to trigger the powering up of the cage had already done its job. The cage crackled with fiftyfold insulation.

The needle had slid into Ralph's calf. He jerked, like one of Galvani's frogs.

He sat upright on the water bier, his eyes wide open.

The red thing leaped from him, flickering, phasing in, phasing out (but more in than out). It hit the side of the cage and seemed to pass through the electrified filigree. And the glass walls, too. But, no, it passed through, yet not into the room we were in. It passed through into one of the reflected doubles of the cage, actually into it, leaving no 'original' behind in the real cage. I realised, as I hadn't earlier, that there had been only 'one' of it all along, from the moment of its first appearance. No reflections. No duplicates. Many reflections of Ralph, but none of it. How could something I could see with my eyes not possess a reflection in a mirror? Perhaps it had to do with its own indivisible essence.

The red moth beat from one phantom cage to the next, circling outward from the real Ralph Hewitson. But as it got farther away, the golden bars thickened. Now it was flying into a wall of increasingly thick syrup. It could get no farther out through the reflections.

Ralph, sitting upright and following it with his gaze, grabbed the air with both hands. The air above the real water bier was, of course, empty. The thing—Death—wasn't there. But all the hands of all his reflections grabbed in unison in all the mirror cages. He seemed to know exactly what he was doing.

Death flapped frantically around the circuit, from one cage to the next, to evade his hands. But it was all one cage to Ralph.

He caught it. He caught it! In a cage thrice removed from the original, his reflection's hands closed on it and held it tightly. His own hands—and those of all the other reflections of him—were empty. But not that pair. Not those. They held the red thing. The bat-moth. Death.

Death slashed at his hands with its wing claws and gouged with its beak. Blood ran down the hands and wrists of that one reflection. The real Ralph cried out in pain. Yet his hands showed no trace of wounds. Only the hands of the one mirror image that held the creature were flayed, but he felt the pain. He continued to wrestle with the creature. Face distorted, he held on: two empty hands cupped in midair, sinews standing out. And however much it hurt him, however much flesh it tore from his phantom fingers, his finger bones still held it securely out in the reflection.

'What's happening?' Mary Ann called. 'He's overreacting to the stimulant! What's happening, Jon?'

'He's fighting Death,' I cried. 'He's caught Death, and he's fighting it!'

Just then Ralph turned to face me—toward where he knew I must be. 'Depolarise! Transluce the glass!' he shouted.

I tore myself from the periscope hood, found the switch, and hit it. Immediately all of us could see through the cage. And of course all of the reflection worlds had disappeared.

But Ralph still wrestled—with thin air! His fingers still clutched. Ah, I could see what he was doing, though to the others it must have seemed an insane pantomime. He was tearing Death free so that he could hold it on one clenched hand—to throw it far away from? No, he'd never give up his hold on Death now that he'd succeeded. He held that one imprisoning hand aloft in a kind of open-fisted salute, grinning through his agony, baring his teeth.

'Cut the current!' he ordered harshly.

I squeezed the bulb. The crackling hiss faded away.

'Unlock the cage, Jonathan!' Even in his pain he refused to abbreviate my name.

I hesitated briefly. Was I, in effect, letting Death out into the world? But with the current no longer flowing, I suppose a mesh of wires could be no obstacle.

Ralph saw my hesitation. 'You fool, I've got hold of him!' he shouted in my face from the other side of the wires—which he could have burst through by main force, but even *in extremis* he had no wish to damage any part of his invention. 'Anyway, he isn't *here*. Not in this "here". He's still in the reflection—and I've got him tight there!'

Had he? Had he really? Or was the pain so deeply etched into his torn nerves and scoured finger bones that he only thought he had? Was he only feeling the ongoing fight in the way that an amputee still feels intense pain from a severed phantom limb? As he continued to clutch the air and bite his lip, I couldn't believe that. The reflections had gone away, wherever reflections go when they're off duty, but his reflected hand was still clutching Death out there, mimicking the shape and stance of his real hand here.

I tore the key from my neck, snapping the chain in my haste. I jabbed it at the lock a few times before I got it in and turned it.

I pulled the door open. Ralph crawled out and stood, his clenched empty hand at arm's length, triumph and torment on his face.

Three days have gone by now. Ralph hasn't slept a wink. I doubt that he could let go now if he wanted to. His hand and Death are too intermixed: claws trapped in bones, bones binding wings. His hand remains bent like that of the worst victim of arthritis, unable to flex, yet to all other appearances a perfectly unblemished hand.

'Hysterical cramp' is what Dr. Sczepanski diagnoses about his hand. She doesn't believe what I saw. Neither does Swami Ananda. They know there's no such thing as Death, and the videotape only shows Ralph alone in the cage, then suddenly jerking erect and scrabbling at the empty air.

I'm alone with him now in the office. It's night. Many deaths occur at three o'clock in the morning. That's the dead point between night and day, the hour of despair, the low point of the body rhythms. Right now it's one-thirty. Ralph sits slumped in his chair, kept awake by pain, his clenched hand resting on his desk.

'You saw, Jonathan.'

'I saw. Yes.'

Mary Ann believes that I autohypnotised myself by staring through that periscope into the reduplicating mirror room too long. My attention drifted away into the mirrors. I was virtually in a state of sensory deprivation. I was hallucinating freely and grandiosely when Ralph jerked upright and began his phantom fight. I was seeing a mote in my own eye. I gave it unreal life—just as Ralph, torn out of deepest trance, blood pounding through his heart, saw that blood personalised in midair as the rooster, the bat, the moth of death.

'You believe me now, Jonathan.'

'Believe? I *know*.'

So Ralph sits before me, holding Death at arm's length—though for how long? When Death at last escapes from him, does it wing elsewhere, or does it come directly here? Homing in, to perch on the real hand whose mirror image holds it at bay, captive in the realm of reflections?

'It feels as if my bones are coming apart,' Ralph groans. But maybe they aren't at all. 'This hand's still solid. Oh, my too, too solid flesh! But I can't *see* them: the other bones. I only feel. God, what I feel!'

'Let him go. Open your hand.'

'I can't, Jonathan. I can't.'

It's a quarter to two. Outside, the city is as still as a sepulchre. Silent night: Ralph is too weary to scream.

Together, we wait.

Secrets

July had been a wretched month so far. When it wasn't raining, it was drizzling. This ought to have been good news for the reservoirs, but the water companies were whining that England needed weeks of sustained downpour. Those greedy privatised utilities hadn't re-invested enough of their profits. While umbrellas were bumping into one another, water was being imported by tanker all the way from Portugal, where there were floods of the stuff. Apparently there was a genuine drought in Scandinavia, but Scandinavians probably organised their affairs more sensibly.

The persistent precipitation was not good for profits at the Fernhill Farm Craft Centre. Steve and I were selling a reasonable number of jigsaws by mail order, but we also relied on visitors. A silvery-haired old gent, who arrived in a black Mercedes on a quiet Monday morning, piqued our interest.

The gravelled car park was always at least half full, but the vehicles belonged either to our fellow craftsfolk or to God's Legion which owned Fernhill. Steve had just fetched a couple of mugs of coffee from the tea-room in the former milking parlour, back to our unit in a converted byre. Usually we saw to our own drinks, but our autojug had quit the day before, and we had forgotten to bring its twin from home. Shuttling an essential piece of domestic equipment to and fro was obviously a non-starter. We would need to buy a replacement.

'Look,' I said, 'a rich customer.'

The well-heeled gent might wish to have a book expensively bound in tooled leather by Nigel, next door to us. No: an umbrella occupied one of the gent's hands, and a walking stick, the other. Forget any book, unless it was pocket-sized. Maybe he was interested in commissioning a hand-engraved goblet from Charlotte, on our other side?

The man looked to be in his late seventies. Leaning on his stick, he glowered at a God's Legion mini-bus, which was painted in luridly clashing blue and green and yellow. Eye-catching, was the idea. A prominent day-glo scarlet slogan proclaimed salvation through Jesus.

As a rule God's Legion refrained from parking any of their distinctive 'troop transports' at Fernhill in case the sight was off-putting to visitors who were only interested in a collector's dolls' house or a souvenir Victorian-style glass paperweight. What we would generally see here would be one or other of the Legion's more anonymous builder's vans. Big in the building trade, the Legion was. The former farmyard here at Fernhill showcased hundreds of pieces of reclaimed architecture: convoluted old chimney-pots several feet tall, marble fire-places, towering iron gateways.

'He can drive,' I said hopefully, 'but most of the time he's sedentary. So he's a jigsaw addict. Big tray on his rug-covered lap. His housekeeper bringing a mug of hot chocolate.'

In addition to house repairs, God's Legion was also into health food, grown on Glory Farm ten miles away. Many of the legionnaires, male and female, lived communally in a manor house renamed Salvation Hall, and worked for bed and board and pocket money, under the eye of their leader, a schismatic Baptist minister named Hugh Ellison. Charismatic, vain and autocratic, Ellison banned the fifty residents of Salvation Hall and the similar cohorts at Glory Farm from watching any television, so I'd heard.

The aim of the Legion was to rescue young folk who had gone astray in London, runways from broken homes or refugees from abuse. To rehabilitate those vulnerable orphans of the streets, train them, bring Christ back into their lives, and also fruitful labour. The Legion was steadily expanding its business and property interests to fund its good works. Legion workers had converted the derelict farm-house and outbuildings of Fernhill into the workshops and showrooms of the present craft centre. Legion girls ran the tea-rooms, selling glory-food. However, no obtrusive propaganda was on show, nor were any of us craftspeople interested in being born again. Rents for the units just happened to be very moderate. Maybe us craftspersons were window-dressing, proof that the Legion was no doctrinaire cult but a broad-minded, benevolent body.

The silver-haired man began to walk slowly towards the yard, around which were the majority of our workshops and showrooms. He paused to look into Ben and Barbara Ackroyd's ceramics studio (specialists in signs and plaques, hand-made, painted to order, world-wide mail-order service).

'He wants a nameplate for his house.'

'No, Steve, he's just resting.'

A ceramic nameplate featuring daffodils or bunny-rabbits might be a bit naff for our dignified gent. You might well say that what Steve and I produced at *Majig Mementoes* was naff. Yet you had to find a commercial gimmick, a vacant niche in the craft world. When we applied for the unit, the name of our enterprise had provoked suspicion from Hugh Ellison, who had vetted us personally. What was this about *magic*? Here at Fernhill we would find no New Age craftspeople peddling pagan symbolism!

Majig Mementoes is merely a catchy name, we explained. Jig, from jigsaw—plus magic moments, treasured memories, as in the song. We would turn any photograph into a special personalised jigsaw. Wedding photograph, holiday photo, baby or pet portrait, pic of your house or your garden at its best, or your classic car. The jigsaw could be a surprise present for someone. It might serve as a promotional ploy, advertising your business. Rectangle or circle or star-shape: you name it. Your initials linked together. Car-shaped, yacht-shaped, cat-shaped. If a client had no suitable photo available, I could take excellent pictures with my digi-camera. We also imported speciality collector-jigsaws from America and Sweden, mostly for sale by mail-order.

'What kind of *specialities*,' demanded Ellison, 'does Sweden offer*R*?' He had this knack of echoing the final sound in each sentence—a trick to avoid the usual 'ums' or 'ers'. No hesitations figured in his speech.

Craggy and patriarchal he looked—someone who would roll up his sleeves (after first removing the well-tailored jacket and the chunky cufflinks) and plunge rescued souls into a tub of water to cleanse them. Alas, he was losing his hair, and wore what remained rather absurdly long in the camouflage style of a vain bloke who cannot admit to reality.

'Sweden*N*—?'

'Nothing naughty,' Steve hastened to reassure him. 'A company in Helsingborg makes the most difficult jigsaws in the world. 40,000 unique pieces to the square metre. That's over twenty-five pieces to the square inch.'

'That ought to keep Swedes out of mischief*F*.' As if Swedes were forever romping in the nude, feeding each other wild strawberries.

We would undertake any reasonable jigsaw commission. Steve, with his woodworking skills, and some accountancy courtesy of a training course offered by the Council for Small Industries in Rural Areas. Me, with my qualifications in photography and graphic design, and some marketing know-how, thanks again to CoSIRA, which had oiled the wheels for us to take out a bank loan for working capital.

Ellison's next question was, 'Is a unit at Fernhill *big* enough for you to manufacture jigsaws*Z*?' Now he had his financial hat on. (Let not a mischievous gust of wind blow into the little office behind the tea-rooms, where he interviewed us, and expose his comb-over!) Steve explained how the colour separation, litho-printing, spray-mounting, and lamination would be carried out by a printing firm in Blanchester, our county town nearby, which would also produce the cardboard boxes. Our main expense had been the computer and software for editing and tweaking electronic pictures, and the scanner for digitising customers' own photos.

The silver-haired gent had moved on, to pause outside Donald and Daisy Dale's *Chess Yes!* (Hand-made, hand-painted sets, characters out of Arthurian Legend to *Star Trek*; unusual commissions welcomed.) Still, the brolly did not go down—not until the old man reached our own unit, and proceeded to step inside. We were in luck. Calling out a cheery greeting, we busied ourselves so he would feel at ease while he looked around, though we did sneak glances.

A framed oval jigsaw held him spellbound. Two lovely twin sisters, early teenage, with blonde pigtails, were leaning laughing against the basin of the Fountain of Trevi in Rome. Both girls wore polka-dot frocks, one of yellow spots on red, the other of red spots on yellow. Photo by proud Daddy, who lived in our own village of Preston Priors and who ran a Jaguar dealership in Blanchester. Daddy had sent out our jigsaws of his girls as Christmas presents to relatives at home and abroad. He had been only too happy to let us keep one on permanent show at Fernhill. Whether all the recipients would be enchanted by the proud gift ('See what lovely children *I* have!') was, perhaps, another matter.

In his younger years our visitor must have been handsome in a Germanic way—him driving a Mercedes directed my mind along these lines. Lofty brow, aquiline nose, blue eyes, jutting chin, and no doubt a flaxen mop of hair in times gone by. His broad shoulders had shrunken in. He no longer stood so straight and tall in his posh suit, as once he must.

'May I ask some questions?'

I would have put his accent as educated Tyneside, if it had not been subtly foreign. Steve and I were all attention.

That van: did all of us here belong to God's Legion?

Definitely not. I explained the situation.

Who had paid for the special advertising feature in the county newspaper on Saturday, profiling the craft centre? It was the four-page spread which had brought us to his attention.

Why, that had been Hugh Ellison's notion to promote the place. God's Legion bore half the cost. Collectively, us craftspeople paid the rest. Nowhere in the profile was there any mention of glory or redemption.

He consulted our brochure. 'You are Chrissy Clarke. Chrissy is short for Christine. I suppose you sympathise with the aims of these evangelists.'

'Not especially! It's only a business arrangement. The rents are cheap.'

Our visitor probed our background a bit more, which I thought was rather impertinent, but he *was* a potential client.

Steve and I had met as students at art college in Loughborough. Both of us were keen on jigsaw puzzles. Photography and graphics; woodworking; blah blah. I did not go into details about how we were only renting our cottage, or how on earth we would ever find a chance to have kids.

Changing tack abruptly: how tiny could the pieces of a jigsaw be made? As soon as I mentioned that company in Sweden: could we show him an example of their products right now?

Of course we could.

The miniature intricacy delighted him. 'This is very fortunate. *Majig,* I do like that name.'

Steve chuckled. 'God's Legion were a bit suspicious of it at first.'

Those blue eyes twinkled. 'I can guess why.'

'We had thought about calling ourselves *Jiggery-Pokery.*'

'What does that mean? I do not know the words.'

'It means something crafty,' I intervened. 'It's from a Scots word for trick, which probably comes from the French for game. But really, it suggests deceitfulness.'

'You explain well to a foreigner.'

'That's because I had a German boyfriend for a little while before I met Steve.' Heinz had been studying graphics at Loughborough. I had thought he was sweet.

'A German boyfriend? That's good.'

'Because *you* are a German?' My tone was a touch tart.

'Because it broadens the mind. In fact, Miss Clarke, I am Norwegian. My name is Knut Alver, and I have a proposal . . .'

What a proposal it was, certainly as regards the fee he offered, and the fringe benefits—a quick trip to Norway at his expense, returning via Sweden and Copenhagen.

To give Mr Alver his due, he made the commission sound as *normal* as he could. He felt very nostalgic, so he explained, for the land of his birth. Unfortunately, he was terrified of air travel. Boat trips made him seasick. A car journey to Norway would be too gruelling at his age, even if a chauffeur was at the wheel.

In Oslo, he went on, there is a sculpture park—the creation of a certain Gustav Vigeland. This park and its statues epitomise the spirit of Norway. Mr Alver wanted majig mementoes of the place, to assemble at his leisure. By so doing, he would be putting his own life in order metaphorically, before the grim reaper came for him.

He wished us to go to Oslo and take pictures of various sculptures in the park by moonlight. We should carry our film to that Swedish firm, for them to produce four custom-made jigsaws with as many thousands of pieces as they could pack into each. He would pay the Swedes in advance on our behalf. Mr Alver tapped the Swedish box we had shown him.

'*Keep Publishing:* that is what the name of the company means.'

Steve grinned. 'Persistent people, eh?'

Mr Alver regarded him oddly, then chuckled.

What's more, Alver went on, we must *drive* with our film the three hundred or so miles from Oslo to Helsingborg in Sweden in a hire-car, for which he would pay.

'It is good to keep in touch with the ground. Even railway trains are somewhat detached from the landscape. I have never liked trains—'

There seemed to be few forms of transport of which he did approve! Ours not to reason why. A drive through Sweden could be lovely and fascinating. I did correct him on one point.

'No films are involved, Mr Alver. I use a digital still camera. The images store electronically on a pop-out card.'

'Oh . . . These pictures must be taken late at night, by moonlight. Is it technically possible with such a camera—as regards exposure?'

Simpler and faster. Camera on a tripod. Half a minute or so by moonlight should be fine. Bright and early next morning, we would return to take the same pictures by daylight. The Swedish company's computer would tweak the digi-pictures to enhance and smooth out grain and add in extra detail.

'This is excellent—better than I hoped.' Then Mr Alver proceeded to broach the slightly bizarre aspect of the commission.

'That park is most magical by moonlight. It is open all round the clock, and perfectly safe for a stroll at any hour—'

One good reason for taking the pictures at midnight was that we should have the place pretty much to ourselves. During daylight hours tourists, particularly Japanese, infested the Vigeland Park, so he had heard.

'All of the granite sculptures in the park are nude figures—of men and women, young and middle-aged and old, and of boys and girls and babies. The park is a celebration of the cycle of life—'

Here came the delicate part of the commission. The Norwegian gent insisted that Steve and I in turn must press our own naked flesh against the sculptures he specified, embracing those granite nudes. Two photos of Steve doing so; two photos of myself. Resulting in four jigsaws. Circular ones, each half a metre across. In black and white.

Steve is skinny. Rabbit-skinny, is the way he refers to it. Imagine a rabbit dangling, skinned, in a butcher's shop. He's red-headed—curly-haired—and covered in freckles. I'm plumper. Frankly I'm a little plumper than I ought to be, though my breasts are petite. Good child-bearing hips, and never mind about the milk-supply. Usually I wear my long dark hair tied up. Neither of us were pin-ups, but of course that is true of most people.

'I require nothing frontal. I am an old man. Nudity is not titillating to most Norwegians. This is a . . . symbolic thing. You will understand when you see the sculptures. Adopt whatever pose is most comfortable.'

I nodded reassuringly at Steve. Free trip to Scandinavia. Nice fat fee for a little work.

'And there'll be nobody in the park but us?' Steve asked.

'There will be a few people, but it is a big place. I want you to take the photographs on the central elevated platform. From there you can see all around. The sculptures provide cover—'

For our exposure, ho.

'I imagine you will wear clothing which you can remove quickly—'

Quite, a dress without knickers underneath. I could forgo a bra. Steve should wear underpants in case he zipped himself.

After the jigsaws were produced in Helsingborg, we should take the ferry across to Denmark and fly back with the four boxes of jumbled pieces from Copenhagen, where we would leave our rent-a-car. On our return, we would phone Mr Alver so that he could come to Fernhill to collect the goods. He would not confide his address to us because, frankly, he was something of a recluse, who feared being burgled now that he was frail. This was another quirk I could easily live with. He would book our flights and a hotel room in Oslo near the park, and a hotel in Helsingborg. Tickets and such would arrive in the post. Half of our fee he would pay in advance right now, and in cash.

And so it was agreed. And shaken upon. Mr Alver insisted on clasping my hand, and Steve's too. He hung on to us for about five times longer than your average handshake. Maybe this was a Norwegian expression of sincerity.

At the top of the fifty-mile-long fjord, the Scandinavian Airline Service jet commenced its turn towards the airport. What a compact city Oslo seemed, hemmed in by hills. A wilderness of more hills rolled far into the distance. The same landscape stretched for a distance equal to about half the length of Europe, with only a few million Norwegians to stipple the empty spaces.

The plane banked westward, past the stocky twin-towered city hall of red brick on the waterfront. Probably we overflew the sculpture park, but without spotting it.

A taxi took us from the airport to a street of shops and businesses, called Bogstadveien, and decanted us at a certain Comfort Hotel. This sounded suspiciously like a sex establishment, but proved to be patronised by Norwegian families on holiday. Our room was tastefully mock art nouveau, recently revamped. One oddity was that each landing of the Comfort Hotel boasted a communal trouser press. During our stay I never saw any of these presses in use. What if, overnight, someone stole a guest's pants? Maybe no one would dream of such a prank in Norway.

People might be too busy guarding their trouser pockets!—in view of the sky-high price of a beer in the hotel bar, and anywhere else—not to mention the cost of meals, clothes, books, and all else. Norway was a seriously costly country.

We had arrived around six in the evening. A glance at the bar and restaurant tariff sent us out along the street, past shops and a few other hotels and bars, in search of somewhere more reasonable—until we wised up and returned. Beer at six pounds a glass was the norm. We would eat and drink in the hotel, and not feel guilty that we were exploiting Mr Alver.

We booked a coach tour of Oslo for next day, picking up from our hotel early on. National Gallery (for a gape at *The Scream* by Munch), Viking longships, Kon-Tiki et cetera, ending up at the Vigeland Park. Clear sky permitting, we could return to the park late the same night simply by walking from Bogstadveien, no great distance, according to the hotel receptionist.

Our fellow sightseers proved to be a mixed bag of Americans and Europeans. Japanese tourists rated entire coaches to themselves. The day was balmy, clouds few and fluffy in a blue sky. Those Viking boats in the museum at Bygdøy—we were getting our bearings—were huger than I had expected. Likewise, the crowds of visitors. This was also true at the Vigeland Park, at least by day.

'God, it's *so* Teutonic—'

Steve was right.

A monumental sevenfold row of wrought-iron gates topped by huge square lamps led to a grassy avenue lined with maple trees. This sward led to the powerful central axis of the park, which was crisscrossed by geometrical paths. We crossed a long bridge, many pale grey granite physiques young and old upon its parapets. A few figures were grappling with a dragon of mortality, which eventually sapped its victim. Likewise, at the gates, lizards had been gripping young children.

From the bridge, upward and upward the park rose, stage by stage, flight of steps by flight of steps, towards a distant monolith. The impression was of a hugely elongated, flattened ziggurat, a Nordic Aztec temple.

A mosaic labyrinth enclosed a great fountain. Around the fountain's rim, muscular bodies were entwined with sculpted trees resembling giant stone broccoli, infants dangling from the branches. Over-sized nude men bore the weight of the massive basin. Struggle. Growth. Sexuality. Death.

Ascending past stone bodies (and many camera-toting Japanese), we came to an oval plateau. So many tourists milled about here that we might have been negotiating an open-air dance floor.

On rising plinths a zodiac of hulking figures, young and old, embraced and wrestled and clung to one another. It was four of those groups to which

Steve and I must attach ourselves that night, when the place was quiet. Those plinths and their burdens partitioned circular stairs leading to the summit, where a monolith soared thirty or forty feet high.

So phallic, that fountaining column of bodies! Those at the base looked like corpses. Higher up, frozen movement began—a yearning ascendance skyward. The tip was a swarm of small children suggestive of cherubs or magnified sperms.

'It's like some sort of nature-worshipping Nuremburg rally! The Nazis must have loved this place when they were here.'

Quite, Steve. The park was still being finished during the Second World War, when Norway was occupied—so the tour guide on the coach had explained.

My idea of the history of Norway consisted of the Vikings followed after a giant void by Ibsen, then by Resistance heroes being parachuted into forests to sabotage Nazi U-boat bases and heavy water factories. (Not everyone was a Resistance hero—a certain Mr Quisling, whose name became a by-word for treachery, had headed a puppet government of collaborators.) Stonecarvers did not complete work on the monolith in the park until 1943. I imagined black-clad SS officers strolling by, blond frauleins on their arms, psyching themselves up to breed more of the master race to replace losses at Stalingrad.

Those various lizards and dragons in the park might be a mordant echo of the way Norwegian life was being strangled by tyranny, as well as a perennial image of the way death finally defeats life—but not before new children are spawned.

'It isn't my cup of tea, either,' I admitted. 'It's all so *heavy*. I'll feel like a human slug pressing myself up against the figures . . .' Tonight, tonight. If the sky stayed clear. Clouds were in short supply over Scandinavia.

'You'll look great.'

Would Mr Alver think so too? And likewise of Steve, draped against granite? Such puny physiques, ours, compared with the adamantine anatomy on show. Evidently this did not matter, compared with the symbolism. When we had checked the positions of the groups we were supposed to interact with—to the north, south, east, and west—we retraced our steps, a thousand of them, so it seemed, before we regained the vast wrought-iron gateway. We said goodbye to the coach courier and walked back to the hotel to be sure of the distance. The journey only took fifteen minutes.

Viewed from the monolith plateau by the light of the moon, this park could have been designed to summon aliens from the sky, to be their landing site.

Or to summon *something*, at any rate.

Pompeii-like, a race of giants was petrified in the midst of life's yearnings and raptures and struggle, or melancholy acceptance.

Far away down below a tall beaming granite mother ran, child in her outstretched arms, her long stone hair blown back. We had passed her earlier; and also a grinning father hoisting a lad up by the wrists high above his own head. By contrast, up top all adults were kneeling or bending or sitting bunched up, or they only came into existence at the knee. An elderly seated couple consoled each other. A kneeling wrestler hurled a woman over his shoulder. Only children stood upright.

The exaggeration of the figures—the massive, sleek stylisation—banished any notion that these bodies might momentarily come to life. Yet to run my hand over the smooth granite surfaces was to discover, by touch alone, sinews and muscles which had been invisible even in bright daylight. Only physical contact revealed the hidden dimension.

The moon was full. Clouds were few. Some people were loitering on the bridge of statues, but that was far away. With a wax crayon I marked the position of the tripod's legs for reference in the morning. Steve stripped and leaned against that stone man hurling a woman away from him. He held still, skinned rabbit against moonlit granite.

We had finished with three of the groups. Hair hanging loose, I was about to shuck off my dress and sandals and mount a plinth to join a tight cluster of chunky stone girls. Bums outward, pigtailed heads bowed, these recent graduates from childhood appeared to be absorbed in comparing their presumably burgeoning genitals. What was within their charmed circle was solid rock, of course.

Which was when The Drunk arrived.

His short fair hair was tousled, his face, even by moonlight, weather-beaten. Checked shirt, jeans, workman's boots. God knows if he had been spying, blending in ghostlike behind other sculptures. He addressed us in English. We were from Britain? Photographers? Midnight is the best time of day for photographs here! Himself, he comes to this place whenever he is in Oslo when the moon is full.

Although his voice was slurred, vocabulary and grammar were commendable for a drunk—and a feather in the cap of the local educational system. With the tipsy care of someone treading a line between obstacles, he chose his words.

'Like a fish on a hook I come here. Like a whale being winched.'

'Do you work on a whale-ship?'

The drunk shook his head.

'You're a trawlerman?'

No, his job is to drive a giant bulldozer. Right now, he is employed in the construction of Oslo's new international airport, forty kilometres away from the city in empty countryside. Do we know about it? Fornebu Airport (where we had landed) is to shut. Too many flights over the city. Hide the airport where nobody lives. Previously he worked building dams. Norway needs many new dams because of climate change, did we follow him?

Tugging a wallet from his back pocket, the man fumbled out a laminated card illustrated with his photo. This, we must inspect by the light of the moon.

'My permit to drive heavy engineering vehicles. Carl Olsson: my name. Actually it is not my name. I was adopted, do you understand?'

'Adopted, yes.'

'I would like to buy you a drink. Good open-air restaurant over there. Great view. But it is closed.'

Of course a café would be closed at half-past-midnight.

The construction site, up-country, is dry in the alcohol sense. Nothing to do there at night but watch television in huts. Monotonous! However, he's well paid, so he can afford a binge in town. What else to do with his money?

We agreed about the hideous cost of alcohol.

Olsson showed his teeth, grinning. 'If Norwegians drink, they knife each other—personally I do not.' He was a well-controlled drunk. 'People believe this will happen. So it is illegal to carry even a little penknife. In the village where I was raised, dancing is banned. The people think it is the devil's doing, dancing. That is near Bergen.'

'Do you go home much?' *Why don't you go back home right now?*

'Nothing for me there. I come here. When I am drunk, it feels better. Tomorrow afternoon I catch the bus back to the new airport. By then I will be sober.'

To come to this park, he needed to dull his senses? Mr Olsson seemed to have a screw loose.

'Please, will you take my photograph beside these stone girls and send it to me?'

I agreed—provided that he would go away afterwards.

'I don't mean to be rude but we have a job to do here. We can't do it if someone's watching.'

Norwegians might not care a fig-leaf about nudity—according to Mr Alver—but Carl Olsson was more muscular than Steve. I worried about arousing the man.

'Yes, you want to be alone. I respect that.' Burrowing in a pocket, he found crumpled paper and a ballpoint pen. Resting paper on plinth, he printed. 'This is the address of the construction site—'

Steve stuffed the paper into his jeans. Mounting the plinth, Olsson draped an arm around the shoulders of those clustering closeted girls. My camera was already in position. The Drunk held still with total concentration until I told him, 'It's done.'

He jumped down, but then he lingered by the granite group, leering at us.

'There is somewhere deeper than this, somewhere no tourists ever see, hidden away in darkness where no daylight reaches. It is the *other side* of this park. I do not mean where that café is—I mean the under-side, the black side. Vigeland had a younger brother, you see. The younger brother built a private death-house for himself. It is in the hills where the rich people live, the Slemdal district. If you tell me your hotel and we go in a taxi I will show it to you.'

Thanks but no thanks. 'You have your bus to catch tomorrow,' I reminded him.

'Will you be sure to send me the photograph?'

'Yes, yes.' *Just go.*

Out came that wallet again. 'I pay you for the printing and postage.'

'No, no, this is a gift. Be happy, Mr Olsson. Goodbye, Mr Olsson.'

Blessedly he did depart. Intent upon walking straight, he did not look back. By now the time was creeping towards one o'clock. I stripped. Steve operated the digi-cam.

On our way back to the hotel, we kept an eye out for Olsson. No sign of him. We set our travel alarm clock and caught some sleep before our return to the park at dawn. Then we went back to bed until lunchtime.

Steve made arrangements for an Avis car to be delivered bright and early next day, to be left in Helsingborg in Sweden for a surcharge. This done, we caught a tram downtown to spend the afternoon roaming and goggling at prices.

A Serb (or so he said) accosted us. Fanning out photos of cute naked black children and mud huts, he solicited money to fund him to join an aid project in Mozambique.

A lone Scottish piper in full tartan was playing a wailing lament, his woollen bonnet on the pavement for kroner. I'm sure he was the same fellow we had seen in the market square in Blanchester just before Christmas.

Oops, and further along Karl Johan Street where Munch and Ibsen used to stroll, were Bolivians in ponchos and bowler hats playing their wooden pipes, with the begging bowler set out.

When we finally reached Helsingborg after traversing much lush farming landscape, the town proved to be a nondescript one of medium size which seemed to owe its existence mainly to its harbour with ferry terminal leading over the water to fabled Elsinore; but the hotel where Mr Alver had reserved a room for us was rather splendid. The Grand boasted special rose-coloured rooms for women guests, though since I was with Steve I did not qualify for the rose-carpet treatment, nor would I have wished to.

Mr Alver had also recommended that we treat our contact at the Swedish company to a slap-up lunch in the hotel restaurant, to grease the wheels. Next noon, we hosted Per Larsen. Slim and blond, Larsen wore a shiny dark blue suit which had seen long service—leather patches protected the elbows. The Swede seemed a bit snooty about our mission, though this had nothing to do with the fact that nude photos of our backsides were involved.

'I suppose,' he said presently, 'this whim is not exorbitant by the standards of jet-set people who squander thousands of dollars on a party dress . . .' He raised his glass of wine. 'Who am I to complain?'

Fairly soon I gathered that people in this part of Sweden were thrifty to the point of meanness. Larsen probably had accepted our invitation to lunch so as to save on sandwiches. This gave a new meaning to eating wild strawberries—food for free.

Steve teased him. 'You might say that all jigsaw puzzles are frivolous.'

Larsen would not countenance this. 'Oh no! You must realise that poverty forced many people from this area to emigrate to America. Those who remained were ingenious in setting up small industries. Speciality jigsaws are a part of this.'

So jigsaws were virtuous. It turned out that this region of Sweden also boasted the highest concentration of splendid manor houses and castles. I guess this figured. Rich nobles, poor peasants.

'Mr Alver must have no family,' mused Larsen, 'to wish to spend his last days assembling these jigsaws. He will be assembling images of you as well. Seeing your bodies take shape slowly.'

'Our backs are turned. We are merely symbolic.'

'Your backs are turned, Miss Clarke. You hand him those jigsaws, then you have nothing more to do with him.' Hard to tell whether this was advice, or a statement of fact.

Previously we had planned on taking a taxi to the company premises. In the thrifty circumstances the three of us caught a bus—to a building near a public park which housed all that remained of Helsingborg Castle, namely the *Keep*. At last the penny dropped. *Keep Publishing*. Resolute persistence had nothing to do with it. Mr Alver must have been amused by our naive assumption.

Larsen screened our digi-cartridge pictures. We had a technical pow-wow. Circular jigsaws, yes. Half a metre across. Since the photo of our drunken acquaintance embracing those granite girls was also on the cartridge, we asked Larsen to make a couple of ordinary prints of it. Whether we would actually mail one to Carl Olsson remained a moot point.

We spent three days in Helsingborg, and visited that Keep a couple of times. A fairly impressive relic, its top gave a scenic view over the sound busy with shipping. Meanwhile the namesake company was producing those four *keepsakes* for Mr Alver, those majig mementoes.

When Mr Alver came to Fernhill to finalise the business he seemed entirely satisfied, even though he had no immediate proof of the quality of the work. This was because he had insisted that there should be no illustrations on the box lids. Steve carried four blank boxes to the black Merc, and our benefactor departed, to begin the painstaking task of assembling those jigsaws without any guide other than his own memories of the Vigeland Park from goodness knows how long ago. We popped the photo of Olsson into an envelope, but did not attach any sticker giving our address—

behaving rather like Mr Alver, come to think of it. After our brief flurry of foreign travel normal life resumed.

It was not until early the following summer that the bad dreams began.

At first, the details of what we dreamt eluded us like some monster disappearing underwater, though we both felt we were being involved in some terrible activity, evil and powerful. At school I once knew a girl called Donna who saw a therapist because she plagued by 'night terrors'. Poor Donna would awake from deeply scary dreams in a state of sheer panic. Similar misbehaviour of the mind could not suddenly be afflicting both Steve and me. Becoming a bit hollow-eyed, we visited Doctor Ross, our GP, who deduced that we were stressed out by worries about our business, bank loan, et cetera. Ross prescribed sleeping pills. We only took those pills once—and found ourselves locked into a nightmare, from which we could not escape for ages.

My nightmare came in swirling fragments, as if I had acquired the kaleidoscopic eye of an insect, or was watching a jumble of jigsaw pieces undergoing assembly. If the jigsaw succeeded in assembling itself, so much the worse for me! All the pieces were aspects of the Vigeland Park by night—and by flaming torchlight. Glimpses of stone figures, of geometrical patterns, of uniforms and fanatical faces. And of a naked woman—of flesh, not granite. Curly flaxen hair and full thighs—she was nude in spite of a dusting of snow on the paving stones. A long knife caught the light. Something vile was about to happen. The monolith of sculpted bodies reared high, towards a full moon.

These images seemed scattered across the inside of a balloon, constantly shifting around upon the inner surface. My dream consciousness was within the balloon, at the empty centre. Outside of the balloon, birds were diving, their beaks like spear-heads. Whenever they neared the balloon they veered away as if space itself twisted to repel them.

And then I was outside the balloon. The images within beat against their confines, hideously patterned moths trying to burst free. The balloon's transparent skin imprisoned them, for the moment. No birds were attacking now—the birds had become those moths, inside. Hawk Moths, Death's Head Moths.

Pressure was mounting inside the balloon. The tip of the monolith, its glans knobbled with naked young bodies like some droll condom designed to arouse, was pressing up against the outer skin. If the skin ruptured, the glans would spout blood and sperms and moths in an orgasm of evil vitality.

Steve and I had woken together to a dawn chorus. Early light seeped through our curtains. Steve floundered to the window to expose the world, and us. Quickly he took refuge in bed again. He held me. Five am, by the alarm clock.

'It's the park, isn't it? Something happening there once. It's building up again, Chrissy, because Alver is putting the pieces together—the pieces of the jigsaws!'

'We're part of it,' I whispered, 'because he touched us, and we pressed our own flesh against the sculptures—'

By stopping us from waking prematurely, Dr Ross's pills had forced us to register the dream in more detail, and remember it. We would scarcely wish for a repetition of such clarity—confused though it was. We would hardly wish to stay trapped so long inside that place, that mental space! The alternative was indefinable night terror, and the sense that something was gathering strength.

We lay there trying to define what might have happened in the sculpture park. The death's head moths inside that balloon-like sheath, the birds attacking it in vain . . . The uniforms, the flaring torches, the nude woman, the knife . . . Nazis in Norway, no doubt of it. These images were emerging as if the photographs we had taken, to be divided into thousands of pieces, had captured much more than merely the surface of things.

If something atrocious happened in that park during the Second World War, why would Knut Alver be trying to conjure it up again so many years later? He had talked about putting his own life in order before the grim reaper came. Alver must be trying to atone for something hideous in which he had been involved, in Norway, when his country was occupied. He could not, he dared not, revisit his homeland. By some mental contagion, we were sensing his inner torments as he strove to confront and exorcise those. He had set himself a penance: to devote his remaining time on Earth to assembling images of the place where a great sin had been committed. When the pictures were complete, he could die at peace, with a sense of closure and absolution—liberated just as his motherland had been set free long since. The Spirit of Norway would accept him back into its bosom.

When Steve dialled Alver's number, shortly after eight o'clock, all he got was a continuous ringing tone. The number had been disconnected. Directory Enquiries told Steve that nobody by the name of Alver was listed anywhere in the whole county.

'He must live somewhere in this county or he wouldn't have seen the newspaper—!'

Alver had paid us in cash—tidy sums on both occasions, tempting us not to enter them in our accounts, a temptation to which we had yielded, as most people probably might. But the hotel bills—those had gone on to Alver's American Express Gold Card account. The hotels must have kept details . . . and *Keep Publishing*, as well.

From Fernhill later that morning I phoned Per Larsen in Helsingborg and told him that we had lost some of our records. When I called back in the afternoon: name on credit card: Knut Alver, card number blah blah—which I carefully copied down. After I had thanked the Swede, I phoned American Express in Brighton.

'I have to reach Mr Alver,' I begged. 'There has been a death.'

This made no difference to customer confidentiality.

'At least tell me, is the card still being used?'

My informant dithered, then conceded that the account had been cancelled the previous November.

'I don't think Alver was his real name,' was Steve's opinion.

I imagined the phone books of the whole county in a pile—eight, ten of them? How many Norwegian-sounding names might we find listed?

'He may not use a Norwegian name, Chrissy. Not if he was a war criminal.'

'Why is he living in England rather than Paraguay or somewhere?'

'Maybe he did hide in South America originally, Chrissy. But Paraguay isn't very close to Norway. It's been a long time. More than fifty years—'

A while ago I had seen a piece in the Sunday *Observer* on the subject of elderly Ukrainians and Hungarians living in Britain, who might once have been members of SS units involved in exterminations. Living here undisturbed for the past half century! Had any Norwegians volunteered for the SS?

Would the police be any help? We only had dreams as evidence. We might be wrong. What had prompted the *Observer* story, I recalled, had been the *failure* of a prosecution of an eighty-year-old Ukrainian—because watertight proof was lacking. After half a century witnesses' memories were unreliable. We did not even know our suspect's real name.

'Perhaps we ought to ask Hugh Ellison for a spot of assistance.'

'You can't be serious, Steve. He would only want to pray with us. Accept Jesus into your heart as your protector.'

'I was thinking more along the lines of God's Legion buzzing around the county doing all those building jobs. Seeing all sorts of places. One of the Legion could have heard some gossip somewhere. Rich Norwegian recluse in the Old Rectory at Sod-Knows-Where, keeps to himself, he do.'

This was grasping at straws. We may as well turn to our parents, or to book-binding Nigel. Such moments brought home to me how Steve and I did not actually have many close friends. Acquaintances, yes. Pals in whom we could confide: not really. Steve and I were each other's bosom friends, self-sufficient. Maybe this had something to do with our devotion to jigsaw puzzles rather than to, say, team sports. (Not that we ourselves did many jigsaws for fun these days!) At college we had courted by slotting pieces together over a can or two of beer, until we too slid together as a perfect match. If only we had time and money for a child, she or he would be our friend too. We would be a trio.

What was *Alver*'s game? Penance and self-forgiveness, or something sick and sinister?

'Do you think Alver has any idea we might be affected like this?'

'Covered his tracks, didn't he?' said Steve.

Bright breezy July day. Last week, there had been half a hurricane. A coach crowded with schoolkids lumbered into the car park. An educational outing: maximum nuisance, minimum gain—unless Tracey or Kevin went home and badgered their parents for a present of a very special jigsaw. I would need to act jolly.

The knife slashed my throat. Dream-pain was distant and blunted. I felt what a beast must feel in the slaughterhouse, restrained and stunned but still aware.

My lifeblood clogged my windpipe. Strong, gloved hands were dragging me upright, a dying animal, legs spasming uselessly, around the moonlit torchlit monolith, thrusting my nakedness against hard granite figures so that my blood smeared the stone. Deep voices were chanting solemnly. Blut. Stein. Macht. Schild. Schutz. Odin. *I had no voice. I was choking, drowning in my own blood.*

Then my throat cleared and I screamed.

Of late, we had been leaving the curtains open while we slept.

I clutched Steve. 'Do you think anybody heard?'

'What the hell does that matter?'

'The neighbours might think you're murdering me or hurting me. Did *you* dream?'

'Nothing—I don't think so. I don't remember. Did you take a sleeping pill without telling me?'

'No—' Words still echoed in my head.

'*Blut*'s blood,' Steve said. '*Stein* is what you drink out of in beer halls. It said *Macht* over the gate of Auschwitz.'

'They weren't drinking my blood—they were spilling it on the paving, rubbing it on to the sculptures we took pictures of.'

'*Odin*'s a Norse god—'

'I know that. Those Nazis, they must have been sacrificing to Odin there in the Vigeland Park. They cut that woman's throat to mark the place with her blood. It was some sort of Nazi pagan rite—Alver must have taken part. There *is* someone we can ask about this, Steve! Olsson! Carl Olsson.'

'The drunk?'

'Haunting that park when the moon's full. Obsessed with it. What did he say about an *other side* to the park? A black side. He wanted to take us somewhere, to show us . . . a death-house, he said. We sent him that photo. Him hugging the same granite girls the Nazis rubbed blood on. If fondling the sculpture made *us* dream, maybe it affected him too?'

'Olsson never took his clothes off.'

'He can find out something for us—he's a Norwegian.'

'A bulldozer driver, a part-time drunk.'

'He was lonely. This'll give him a goal. We must do something, Steve!'

I decided that sending a letter to the new airport site was too slow. We had the name of the civil engineering company. The international operator came up with the phone number and connected me to the company's office in Oslo. Bless foreigners for learning English so fluently. It's an emergency, I said. I must get in touch with an employee of yours.

I held, while a tape played Grieg at me. A brisk-sounding woman came on the line, and I must repeat my rigmarole, and hold again. Money ticking away.

'Miz Clarke, are you there?'

Yes, yes, all ears.

'I am sorry for the delay. Mr Carl Olsson is no longer employed by us—'

I was calling all the way from England. Carl Olsson was our friend. This was a matter of life and death.

Unfortunately, Mr Olsson was released from his contract the previous month because of a problem. Yes, Miz Clarke, you are right: a problem connected with alcohol. The company did not know where he had gone, though his address on record was a village near Bergen. She spelled the address for me, complete with slash through the letter 'ø'. I cradled the phone.

'That's the village he never goes back to,' Steve said.

'He was proud of his licence. He would only have got drunk on the job if dreams had been bothering him.'

'That's a touching faith you have in him. Now he'll be working on dams again—in the middle of nowhere.'

'He can't be, Steve! He won't have a clean reference. They may have endorsed his licence. I don't know what their system is. He might only get another job after he attends a government alco clinic.'

'Nothing stops him from getting a labouring job. Shelf-packing in a supermarket. Sign on a boat as a deck-hand, sail to Australia.'

'Don't try to steer me away from this, Steve! It was my throat they cut. We can't put up with this. He'll be in Oslo, Olsson will. He'll be getting drunk and going to the park at night, especially if the moon's full.'

Oslo: back to that hotel on Bogstadveien? Paying our own fares, paying our own hotel bills, beer at six pounds a glass, lunch at fifteen quid a head, for a week, two weeks? We would use up all the profit we had made from Alver, aside from the fact that we had spent it months ago.

'We needn't both go, Steve.'

'Don't be absurd.'

Soon we were close to a quarrel.

Steve was my friend, my lover, my partner. I wanted him to father my child—she would be a daughter, of course—whenever we could afford this. Now he was baulking, rejecting my intuition, scared of the cost when we were already paying a hateful price. Despite him being the first to suggest that Alver may have committed war crimes, Steve was afraid to take this seriously—scared, finally, to commit himself, reluctant to put all the pieces together. He would rather those were all back safely in their box, with a blank lid closed upon them.

Although I accused him of this, at the same time I realised that I wished to go on my own to Norway. Alver had duped us, he had used us—because we were naive. As a pair, Steve and I would compromise and not be extreme. Because a woman had been killed in the park, not a man, I was ahead of Steve in my dreaming. Alone, I felt sure that I would be more focused.

A solo trip would cost half the price. One of us must stay to mind the shop. I seized upon these two pretexts, convinced that I would find Olsson waiting for me. I felt little need of Steve's 'protection', which in any case he was not delivering—unfair and contradictory though that sounds.

A strained day passed. After we had eaten some lasagna that evening, Steve ferreted away to dislodge me from my position.

'A woman was killed with a knife in that park. When Norwegians get drunk they knife people.'

'Not Olsson.'

'He might see you as the cause of him losing his job.'

'Women are stronger than men,' I informed him. 'Stronger than *nice* men,' I added, to cushion his ego. Our relationship had altered. Damn Alver for this.

'How long will you give it before you quit looking?' Ah: my journey would be fruitless, so I could safely undertake it. Steve was vacillating, exonerating himself. Deep down, he was relieved that I was taking the initiative. I must not despise him for this, must not resent it. I should feel grateful, not betrayed.

'Ten days tops,' I replied. A rational male answer, precisely timed, cut and dried.

'I ought to come—I'm part of this too.'

Men have this way of talking emptily to justify themselves, and never being able to shut up.

'Next Saturday there's a full moon. I should leave on Friday. Ticket, hotel, traveller's cheques,' I recited.

'Will you phone me each evening?'

'If possible. Mustn't run up bills.' Oh the reproachful look in his eyes—this could lead to more empty irritating words. 'We'll need to compare our dreams by phone.'

We would not be sharing the same bed, but if we continued to dream of the park in a sense we would still be together.

'In Duty Free,' he suggested, 'why don't you buy a bottle of Rum and stock up on Coke in Oslo?'

Such a practical thought. Was it a trick question?

'I hadn't thought of that. Maybe I will. Good idea.'

When the plane banked and levelled out, this time I did spot the park: grey granite geometry and lines of trees bisecting lawns. From an altitude of a few thousand feet everything looked so flat except for the trees backed by their shadows.

A venue for Odin? The Vigeland Park was a far cry from Valhalla. No pagan gods down there; just the struggle of life enshrined in stone—Nordic spirit. A big bottle of Captain Morgan rum bulked my hand luggage.

On the map of Oslo spread out on my lap, ironically there *was* an Odin Street not too far from the park. And just a stone's throw from the Comfort Hotel was a Valkyrie Way.

Even if the Valkyries managed to avoid colliding with a tram, their ride would be brief along the short stretch of street named in their honour. Those female dispensers of destiny to warriors in battle, those issuers of entry visas to Valhalla, would be obliged to pass and re-pass a Burger King—for the presence of which I was thankful. My take-away dinner of a Whopper and fries was merely expensive, not out of this world. I phoned Steve to tell him I had arrived, and of my wonderful discovery of fast food so close by.

With mad cow and stodge digesting in my belly, it was along non-heathen Church Way—Kirkeveien—that I walked late that night to revisit the park. The sky had clouded over. The moon coasted into sight, a spectral white yacht with a single full-bellying sail. Here was I, going to meet a drunk at a place where I had taken my clothes off, and he might not even be there. On this occasion I wore jeans, not a dress.

When I finally made my way up on to the granite plateau, there was Olsson, keeping a Vigeland vigil. A long scruffy raincoat hung open over checked shirt and Levis. As we gazed at one another he steadied himself against a granite buttock.

'You did not send me your name or address.'

'I'm sorry about that. I'm sorry you lost your job. My name's Chrissy. Chrissy Clarke.'

While the moon sailed into view and away again, I told him about the mysterious Mr Alver and the jigsaws and the dreams.

Dreams, oh yes, dreams. He had dreamed of me naked here among uniforms and torches. Sometimes me, sometimes a blond beauty. Before he accosted us that night, maybe he had been playing Peeping Tom and was now mixing up memory and dream, but I did not think so.

The chanting, the knife, the blood . . .

'*Blut. Stein. Macht*,' I recited.

He nodded. '*Schild. Schutz.*'

'And *Odin*. A toast to Odin, drunk in blood?'

'Toast?' he queried. And in Norwegian: '*Ristet brød?*' He mimed buttering and biting.

'No, no, I mean,' and I raised an imaginary glass, 'Skol!' Hardly the most sensible gesture to make to a man with a drink problem.

'Ah, *Skål!*' His brow furrowed. 'They did not drink blood. They rubbed the blood on the stones. *Blut* is blood. *Stein* is stone. *Macht* means power, but is also a verb, *makes*.'

Steve had been off-track.

'Blood-stone-makes-shield-defence.' Carl's chant sounded like some strange version of the Stone-Scissors-Paper game. 'Do you know of the SS?'

'Of course.'

'They were the *Schutz-Staffel*, the defence squads. Actually, SS senior officers did not want to fight to the death in Norway. Some SS man must have been here, though. Some black magician.'

'Stop, stop, you're losing me—!'

Carl had been supplementing his memories of history lessons in school by asking older people and looking in books.

Evidently Norway fascinated Hitler ever since the Führer took a Strength-Through-Joy cruise to the fjords in the 1930s; and Himmler, head of the SS, was obsessed with the mystical meaning of nordic runes. Hitler saw Norway as the 'field of destiny' of the war. Half a million German troops were to be stationed in this country. Big naval guns were stripped from battleships to be mounted in coastal forts.

Militarily this focus on Norway did not make much sense. Oh, there was a lot of coastline, controlling a vast swathe of sea, posing a threat to Allied convoys to Russia. Norway also owned a huge merchant fleet—the majority of those boats sought refuge in Allied ports. Due to shortages and sabotage and go-slows, Norwegian shipyards only completed two or three new vessels during the entire occupation. Demonstrably, the outcome of the war hung on events in Central Europe, not off on the margin of the map.

'Your own Winston Churchill, he was hooked by Norway too—'

'My Winston Churchill? Mine? He must have died before I was born.'

'Has what happened here *died*? Even if a million tourists take pretty photos?'

I suppose, but for Winston Churchill, the whole of Europe might be a fascist empire nowadays. Nazis on the Moon. No Israel. Moscow, a radioactive desert. A swastika embellishing the Union Jack.

'Listen to me, Mrs Clarke—'

When Steve and I finally had a kid, I might become Mrs *Bryant* but so far we had seen no need for a wedding ceremony. To correct Olsson could lead to complications. I simply listened.

Were it not for Norway, apparently Churchill might not have risen to the top as the war leader best able to defy Hitler. The fall of Norway, with losses of British planes and personnel, toppled Neville Chamberlain. In actual fact British intervention in Norway was Churchill's own fault, but Chamberlain bore all the blame for it. Because the debacle made Churchill prime minister, Norway loomed unduly large in his mind.

In Hitler's mind there were Wagnerian considerations. The god Wotan, in Wagner's *Ring*, equals Odin, kingpin of the Viking pantheon. Several Nazi leaders, such as the racist Alfred Rosenberg, desired spiritual as well as political union with a nordic Norway under its home-bred National Socialist, Vidkun Quisling. The high echelons of the German Nazis were already into paganism and the occult.

Churchill and Hitler: I was getting this strong sense of two megalomaniacs (one good, the other evil) confronting one another globally, while both of them were obsessed about a country on the fringe—to the detriment of wider strategy.

Tormented by his ambiguous affinity to the Vigeland Park—which had been reinforced recently by the dreams—Carl Olsson had found out rather a lot. I suppose he knew the general drift already, and only needed to dig a bit deeper. After all, he wasn't an *ignorant* man! Quite fluent in English; and in German too, so it seemed.

When Germany was on the brink of defeat, Fortress Norway—*Festung Norwegen*—beckoned as the final bastion for the embattled Nazis, a worthy stage for the twilight of Gods and supermen, the final bonfire or the ultimate victory. It was touch and go whether Nazi leaders would relocate to Bavaria—or to Norway.

'General Böhme commanded the huge army here,' Carl explained to me. 'Böhme was crazy for Norway. Norway could be defended. And the Reichskommissar for Norway, Josef Terboven, he was fanatical about this too. Hitler very nearly came here instead of dying in Berlin. He hoped that new super U-boats based in Norway would turn the tide even if Germany fell—'

'Super U-boats?' I had never heard of any such thing. Were those real or imaginary?

'They were ocean-going monsters, Mrs Clarke, berthed in Bergen and in Trondheim.'

But oil was in short supply, and the first super U-boat only sailed from Bergen, futilely, a couple of days before Germany surrendered.

In mid-March of 1945, Reichskommissar Terboven had summoned General Böhme and the naval commander to ask if they could vouch for the loyalty of their men in the event of Hitler and Himmler and gang coming to Norway. Even the bombastic Böhme could not guarantee this. The SS bigwigs did not favour *Festung Norwegen*. After Germany fell, Terboven blew himself up with a hand grenade.

'But some time in March, Mrs Clarke, the event happened here because here is so powerful and Nordic a place, even if Gustav Vigeland was raised in a fanatically Christian home—'

Evidently the sculptor's dad was a Bible-thumper. The torments of hell were a daily refrain in the Vigeland household.

'Too much Satan,' Carl quoted. 'That's what Gustav Vigeland said about his childhood. Not enough Jesus. A whole lot of darkness, only a little light. My own upbringing was not quite as bad—always there were the sunny prayers for my soul! Because I was born under a cloud, a child of sin, illegitimate. A stained bastard—'

Vigeland's dad did loosen up eventually—because of alcohol and another woman, ill health and the failure of his little furniture business.

'So genuine darkness came. Yet here in the park is vigour and power, the thrust of nature. The life-force, a fierce power changing its shape as the god wills—the Odin force of old. Odin, that's what the Nazis saw here. A victory-force. Victory over enemies, over death . . .'

Carl clutched at the pocket of his raincoat. Hoping to find a bottle to dull himself. He must already have thrown the bottle away empty.

'Josef Terboven would have been here. And Quisling.'

'And Knut Alver, whatever his real name is. Did Norwegians join the SS?'

'Oh yes, there was the Nordland regiment, of Scandinavians and Finns, but there were problems.'

Though the Germans assured recruits that they were joining a pan-European force to bring a new order to the continent, training methods proved to be exceptionally brutal, so a lot of Norwegian volunteers deserted. Not Alver, obviously. He must have become an officer.

'And some magician was here. Some Nazis meddled with magic. Wotan-worship, Odin-worship. Blood-and-soil-worship. I hate all worship, Mrs Clarke! When I lost my job I went back to Bergen. This time I threatened. I really scared my fake parents. They must tell me why I was a scandal or I would burn the farm down. They thought I was going to kill them—that I would cut their pious psalm-singing throats.'

Might he have clutched at his raincoat to see whether he had a knife in the pocket? A hideous vision came to me of butchered bodies in a farm-house. If Carl Olsson was wanted by the police surely the construction company would have known and would have warned me. I must concentrate on him utterly, as if I was his sister and I loved him.

Gently I asked, 'What did you learn, Carl?'

Why, he had discovered the shameful secret that his mother Christina—born late in 1944—was the offspring of eugenic mating between a German Waffen-SS officer and a young Norwegian woman named Liv Frisvold. Liv Frisvold's brother Olav was a fanatical pro-Nazi who had joined the SS.

Liv shared Olav's fascist beliefs. She had volunteered, or been persuaded by Olav, to take part in the Lebensborn project—the 'Fount of Life' breeding programme, by which prime Aryan males of the SS would bestow their genes upon perfections of Aryan womanhood. Liv's child would be a splendid bonding of Nordic and Teutonic, of Germany and Norway.

The baby had ended up fostered in Stavanger, with the cleansing name Christina. (My own name, almost!) At eighteen years of age she disgraced herself by becoming pregnant by some American sailor. The foster parents packed her off to stay with relatives in Bergen, where she gave birth to a boy, who was Carl. Christina was unworthy to raise him—the boy must be separated from the stain of his past. So the Olssons had adopted him, to raise him on their farm as part of their family, a Christian duty. To them, the secret was confided, though they were ignorant of what became of Liv, or of Olav.

'When Christina was twenty-one she ran away from Stavanger. My adoptive parents say they think she went to America.' Carl shuddered. 'Do you know what I think? I think it was Liv Frisvold who was killed here in March 1945. My grandmother. In the blood-sacrifice.'

He seemed calmer now.

'What were they hoping for, Carl? What were they trying to do?'

'Blood-stone-makes-shield,' he said. 'Whatever that means.'

'What is Knut Alver trying to achieve now, half a century afterwards?'

Carl gazed at the monolith of naked bodies surging upward. 'You came to find out, Mrs Clarke. It will come, it will come.'

The orgasming come of a man. Or was he referring to some power gathering to erupt? The monolith was like a phallus. So rooted, so immobile.

'That other place—the dark place. Have you been there recently?'

'I cannot! Something stops me. Like a coat in a dream, wrapping me tight. A dream of myself and woman. The coat gets in the way. There is no way to take it off. Do you understand?'

'Maybe,' I said.

He had not pressed his naked flesh against the granite girls when I took his photograph. *Where do you sleep?* I nearly asked him. Meaning, in a hostel? In some rented room? *Do you have savings?* I might give him the wrong idea.

'Now that you are here, Mrs Clarke, we can go to the dark place together. I will take you there tomorrow. Really, it is you who will be taking me.'

Relief flooded me. 'Let's do that, Carl. Tomorrow.'

'In the afternoon the mausoleum is open. We will meet at your hotel and go by taxi. Without a taxi, we have too far to walk from the bus route, you see, and it is all uphill. Let me walk you back to your hotel.'

Yes: away from this place. Back to Comfort. The desk clerk of that respectable establishment would not admit a drunk along with me in the middle of the night.

Ought I to offer to buy Carl Olsson lunch the next day? I did not want to, not in the hotel restaurant, at any rate—and its rate was steep. As we walked back along Kirkeveien I told Carl, 'I found a place where I can afford to eat. There's a Burger King in Valkyrie Way.'

'Tomorrow I shall only eat breakfast,' he said. 'We do not waste time. We need to be at the mausoleum by two o'clock before other people arrive. Not many visitors go, but early we can be alone. I think before we go tomorrow I only need a drink.'

In the hotel bar, of course. At six pounds a glass, if beer was his tipple. I could hardly refuse.

Myself, I packed in as much breakfast as I could. Cereal, cold meats and cheese and bread. I debated whether to phone Steve to tell him I had met up with Carl Olsson, just in case . . . in case what? The night before, I had been alone with Carl in the park without incident. My sleep had passed without disturbance too. No, I would wait.

At twelve-thirty I was in the bar, nursing a half of draught Guinness, three pounds worth. McEwan's Export was also available on draught, not to mention bottles of Newcastle Brown Ale. When I expressed surprise to the barman, he said that thousands of Norwegians go from Bergen to Tyneside for shopping because England is much cheaper. This could almost have been a pub in England, except that the job-lot of old books which served as décor on high shelves all had Norwegian or Swedish titles. Nobody else was using the bar yet. In came Carl, who had combed his hair and put on a Paisley tie that looked like a view down a microscope at swarming amoebas. He had cut himself shaving.

On impulse I told him, 'I have a bottle of rum in my room.'

'Ardour is of the earth,' he said. At least, that's what I heard.

'Ardour?' I queried.

'Ar*ler*,' he repeated, pointing to the bottles of Newcastle Brown.

'Oh, you mean *ale*. It rhymes with whale, in the sea.'

'Ale,' he resumed, 'is of the earth, and spirit is of the sky. I think I need a drink of spirit.'

The barman was hovering hopefully, polishing a glass, so I said to Carl, 'Come up, then.'

In the corridor upstairs, a North African was pushing a trolley of towels. A friendly grinning skinny fellow. As soon as we entered my room, protest burst from Carl.

'Fifteen per cent of our population today is Moslem, do you know? Here, in *Norway*. One and half people in ten. What does that tell you?'

I shrugged. I could guess what it might tell neo-Nazi nationalists.

'What it tells *me*,' he said, 'is that unskilled jobs go to Arabs, if I cannot drive again because I am not clear in my head.'

In view of which, it may have seemed perverse of him to refuse any Coke to dilute the rum. Yet I understood when he poured a full glass of Captain Morgan and swigged it back neat.

'That tower of bodies!' he exclaimed. 'The power dammed up, the climax delayed . . . birds, moths!'

'You dream about birds and moths, Carl—'

He glanced at his watch. 'We must go to the dark place. You are my passport.'

When snow thawed in the spring, streams must froth through these hilly woodlands of Slemdal, spilling over the narrow winding roads. Leafy gardens screened substantial old wooden houses. Stainless steel sculptures stood on one lawn: a giant cockerel, a unicorn. The nameplate on the gatepost was that of some company office, blending with nature. Quite a little paradise, hereabouts.

'Near here,' Carl said, 'the leader of the traitor Quisling's personal guard is killed with machine-pistols by men of our Home Front.'

Blood had flowed here, as well as melting snow.

'In revenge the Germans shoot fourteen men who are in jail for sabotage. Quisling is satisfied.'

I sat in numb silence while Carl directed the taxi driver, who had never heard of the mausoleum. On a narrow lane, we pulled in beside a big red-brick building hemmed by trees, a cross between a barn and a basilica. The taxi fare, we shared.

Heraldic creatures decorated the brickwork of the frontage. In a little lobby, behind a table bearing pamphlets, a bearded young man sat. This earnest, spiritual-looking custodian eyed Carl with disapproving recognition.

'I am bringing a visitor from England,' Carl announced in English.

The custodian promptly addressed me in soft-spoken English. 'You're very welcome. Are you an artist?'

'A photographer,' I told him.

'Ah . . . I regret . . . It is dark inside, you see, and photography is forbidden by the family.'

'I don't have a camera with me. Not today.'

We couldn't stand around chatting. Other people might come. Carl opened a stout wooden door for me.

Entering this place was like stepping inside a cavern illuminated by infra-red rather than natural light, as if here was the haunt of some nocturnal creature which remained invisible in the gloom. The lighting consisted of weak little spotlights focused on sections of the walls and the vault above. Nude figures were everywhere: babies and children, lovers, toiling adults, old folk on the verge of death. Copulation was in vigorous progress, and births—an umbilical cord the size of a hawser coiled between mother and newborn child. Dimly detectable figures caressed one another. They exchanged blows. They writhed in spasm. Such a surfeit of procreation and struggle and death.

Here was a Sistine Chapel frescoed by an artist who was definitely no Michelangelo. More like that Swiss fellow—rhymes with the radioactivity counter, Giger, that's him—with his monstrous biologies; although lacking Giger's artistic slickness. The subdued lighting seemed intended to hide the clumsiness of the obsessive work. Years this must have taken, years of crepuscular drawing and colouring. Mad, compulsive years brooding about the passions and mortality of the flesh.

Because of the utter dimness, figures emerged dreamlike, spectrally, and slid out of sight again. Hades, yes: a kind of Hades was here, full of dead shades re-enacting their lives, bodies stripped bare and overblown. The dark side of the Vigeland Park, indeed.

Each footstep gave rise to a thrumming reverberation. The echo was intensified by the next footfall, into a slurring, sloshing boom. If I screamed in here, the acoustics might deafen me. In such gloom, the entrance was almost lost to sight as Carl guided me deeper, hand on my elbow. Here was a dream place, sealed away hermetically, not part of the natural world despite all its depiction of natural functions.

When we came to the far wall, the noise of our approach rose up to dizzy me, and Carl caught hold of me.

His tongue and his rummy breath invaded my mouth. His hands thrust under my jacket and sweater, and upward, but I had worn no bra for him to unclip. Turning me, he pressed my breasts to the frescoed wall. I felt his stiffness. This was insanity. At any moment the door might open. Visitors might enter. I did not cry out. The amplified echo would have shattered my skull.

'We must,' he breathed in my ear. 'We must.' Must and lust and thrust and dust.

He unfastened my belt to release my jeans. Down to my knees he pulled the denim and my knickers. As his cock butted clumsily, I leaned numbly against the wall. Was this rape or necessity? Was it my recompense to him, or was it a way of unlocking secrets? His open zip was a rasp. Delving, his hands prised my legs apart. If I had not co-operated, he could never have cleaved me. Not last night in the park, not in the hotel room, but here and now in this perilous place, in this awkward stance, I adjusted my position as best I could to accommodate him. The thought of disease crossed my mind, of AIDS. Of Steve so far away. At least I was on the pill. Had I taken my pill last night before I went to the park? My routine was all cocked up. *Wait a moment while I take a pill.* The mad magnified hum of Carl's panting deafened me. I bit on my lower lip.

Like some slut in a back street—of my imagination!—I held my sweater up so that my bare tits stayed in touch with the painted plaster. Here was a red light district of the mind, an infra-red light district.

Carl's weight squashed me against the wall, sandwiching me. A stranger coming into the huge mausoleum might fail to notice at first—then only vaguely spy a man in a long loose raincoat examining the furthest extreme of this place very closely. The circuit was complete: from Alver to me to the sculptures to Carl through Christina to Liv to the blood that was spilled to the monolith thrusting its shape in miniature into me. Images assaulted my mind, invading me.

Almost courteously, he had rearranged my clothing while I was still dazed by perceptions. What a gent this bulldozer driver was at heart. My knickers sat uncomfortably, twisted, clammy. I knew now that magic has laws—of affinity, analogy, contact, contagion, not the laws of logic but of primitive mentality.

'Those Nazis, they tried to make a magical barrier around Norway—'

'And Sweden too, because Sweden is joined to Norway like a Siamese twin—'

That had been the aim of the blood-sacrifice—to raise up an Odin force to resist attack, to repel invasion. The geometry of the sculpture park, the embodiment by the figures of lifelong struggle against death, of fertility, of will-power, that central surging phallus of bodies: these were perfect for this purpose.

'It *was* Liv Frisvold who died in the park. My mother's mother...'

Fanatical Nazi supporter, who had merged the Nordic and the Teutonic in the person of her daughter. Fertile mother. Valkyrie. She had volunteered; her brother had volunteered her. Either; both. Olav Frisvold had been there when she died, her throat cut.

'Olav Frisvold is Knut Alver, Carl! He wants the power—'

Germany surrendered. Fortress Norway failed as a scheme. Nazis fled. Those who could. With gold and loot, those who could. By secret routes, to Paraguay, to Brazil. The force stayed locked up all these years in the core of the sculpture park, on that plateau, in that monolith.

'The birds were planes, flying to attack the Germans in Norway—'

'The barrier worked, Mrs Clarke. Not against enemies of the Nazis—but against Olav Frisvold, who had fled, by denying him entry back again—'

'Stopping him from coming here in person—'

'To harvest the power—'

'To use it—'

We spoke as if wrapped in a *folie* for two, reinforcing each other's conviction, which few other people in the world would be able to share. Oh we were in duet.

'Because he is old—'

'Near death—'

'To use the power to delay death—'

'Take the energy into himself—'

'Make himself strong again—'

'Make himself *young* again—?'

'The way he was in 1945 when his sister died—!'

'Your photos smuggled out the images he needs, cut into thousands of tiny pieces, too small for the net to intercept what they carry—'

'The net around Norway, blocking him from linking with the power in the park—'

Just then, the door opened thirty metres or more away, and Carl released me. A middle-aged man and woman stepped respectfully into the obscure mausoleum as if into a church. The man removed his hat.

'I must come to England,' Carl said. 'Find my old-uncle—'

'Great-uncle—'

'Yes, great-uncle. Stop this happening. If it happens . . .'

Would the tip of the monolith erupt before the astonished gaze of Japanese tourists, geysering upward a flare of light, a blazing flux? While, over in England, Alver stood naked in the little central space between the four circular jigsaws, each touching rim to rim, north, south, east and west . . . When that happened, nightmares would rage through my mind, and through Steve's mind, and through Carl's, roosting inside us, deranging us. We hurried past that middle-aged couple, who barely glanced at us.

In the lobby the custodian raised a hand. I suppose we were flushed and disarrayed. Did he have an inkling of what we had perpetrated in his temple of art?

'That lady who went inside,' the bearded young man told me with quiet pride, 'she is the professor from the University of Uppsala who has been researching the biography of Emanuel Vigeland for fifteen years.' As if I should be filled with respect and reverence. 'You must not miss the museum.'

'I thought *this* is the museum.'

'This is the Doomsday—the Last Judgement. Next door is the gallery annex, with framed oil paintings. They are so colourful. Do see them.'

'Thank you,' I said.

'It is a privilege.'

We went outside, into fresh air.

'Those paintings next door are not very good.'

I would take Carl's word for it. A Saab with Swedish plates was the only vehicle in sight. How few people came here. We returned up the leafy lane. I hitched at my clothes in vain. The long hike downhill to the nearest bus route was likely to be uncomfortable.

'I must come to England,' Carl persisted. 'I must stay at your home.'

He seemed to have little sense of what was feasible, and what was not. On the other hand, did I? I had just had a fuck with him—of an entirely functional sort—in that awful parody of the Sistine Chapel.

'What will we tell your husband, Mrs Clarke?'

Undeniably Carl was tenacious, even if there was a huge warp in his temperament. He was like some tree, erect but twisted through ninety degrees half way up its height.

'You may as well use my first name—'

His hand jerked up, to snatch my very words from the air, and his fist closed.

'No! It is too much like the name they gave to my mother. Your first name is personal. If I use it, I may think we like each other. I must call you Mrs Clarke.' Wham-bang, no thank you, Ma'am. He was right, of course. 'What do we tell Mr Clarke?'

'That we had a vision in the mausoleum?'

'A vision ... Vidkun Quisling's brother Jørgen saw visions of Vidkun after the traitor was shot. Jørgen took drink and drugs and went to spirit, spirit—'

'Spiritualists?'

'Yes. Say to Mr Clarke that I gave you some hash to eat, do you understand hash?'

'Cannabis. Resin.'

'Say that you felt you must press your breasts against a fresco, in the darkness, the same way you touched the sculptures. This put you in touch with the truth.'

'And what put *you* in touch with the truth?'

'I held your hand—the way Olav Frisvold held yours.'

'We held hands.' How sweet.

'Like spiritualists at a see-ainsey.'

'Séance.'

'A séance,' he repeated.

Would Steve swallow this? At least until everything was over, and Carl had returned to his own country, and I could explain ... or not need to explain at all.

'How do we find Olav Frisvold, Mr Olsson? Do we make big prints of the photographs—'

'Yes, make big prints!'

'And stand on them naked?' I mimed cutting my thumb. 'Spill a little blood upon them? And see what happens?'

He nodded vigorously. 'Maybe. We shall do something!'

An immediate something would consist of Carl catching a train to Bergen, the overnight boat to Tyneside, then a National Express coach to our own county—while I flew back home by air. Carl's route would cost less than mine. In another sense it had already cost him dearly. Me too, me too.

We proceeded downhill past foliage-screened gardens and serene rustic-looking homes.

He told me when to get off the bus. Himself, he stayed on board. Bye-bye until England, Mr Olsson.

Foremost, I craved a bath. Before I climbed into the tub in the Comfort Hotel I drank a big glass of rum as if I was some girl in trouble decades ago trying to induce a miscarriage. Light-headed from the spirit and the hot water, afterwards I made my bleary way to Burger King to take on much-needed ballast, a bacon double cheeseburger which I ate then and there. When I got back to the hotel, it was six o'clock, five o'clock in England. Steve would be heading home. I only intended to snooze for an hour. It was ten, and dark, when I woke up. What I ought to have done earlier, of course, was phone Scandinavian Air Services before I resorted to rum and soaking myself and eating and napping.

I dialled home.

'Back *tomorrow?*'

'So long as there's a seat free on the plane. I'll call you as early as I can, tell you the arrival time so you can meet me. There's too much to explain on the phone, Steve. I found Carl Olsson in the park—as I said I would. Mr Olsson is Alver's great-nephew, and Alver's real name is Olav Frisvold—'

And Carl Olsson was only an adoptive name; and his mother Christina had certainly not received that purifying name from *her* own mother; and I was not exactly 'Mrs Clarke'. Identities were haywire. Nothing was what it seemed, not least the sculpture park, pride of Norway.

'Listen, Steve: Mr Olsson is coming to England—by boat, 'cause that's cheaper. He'll need to stay with us till we can trace Frisvold. Get big laminated prints made of the four photos we took—same size as the jigsaws—'

'You're starkers on two of the photos.'

The sheer irrelevance of this almost made me laugh. *Olsson stuck his cock into me in the mausoleum.*

'Norwegians don't bother about nudity. It's no big deal, remember? Mr Alver, unquote. So I'm hoping to see you tomorrow,' I ended brightly.

'You've done *very* well. Hang on: do you want the prints landscape-style or cut to circles?'

'Circles, exactly like the jigsaws. All in one piece, of course.'

'What do we *do* with them? What is Alver trying to do?'

'When I get home, Steve.'

That night the dream was terrible. Torchlight flickered. I was shivering convulsively. The intent thin face of a weasely man wearing a peaked braided cap and round, wire-rimmed glasses swam before my eyes while strong hands held me upright. Voices were chanting. *Blut. Stein. Macht. Schild. Schutz.* The knife cut into my throat and I choked in awful pain.

I had to drink a great volume of Coke direct from the plastic bottle, gasping between gulps. Most of it, I vomited into the wash basin.

On the way back from Heathrow Airport I told Steve, who was driving, about the supernatural barrier around Norway and about Carl's grandmother and her brother Olav, who was Mr Alver, who was now trying to extract the power from the sculpture park to cheat death—presumably!

The four big laminated pictures would be ready by the next day. Steve would jig-cut them into circles. When Olsson arrived, we would try to mimic whatever Olav Frisvold was attempting, to give us some clue to where he was.

Steve fretted. 'Olsson may be thinking of, well, trying to kill Frisvold—'

'He said no such thing.'

'It can't be a family reunion he's hoping for!'

'These dreams have to end! Frisvold probably killed enough people while he was in the SS.'

'Listen to what you're saying, Chrissy! Frisvold may be a criminal, but we can't take the law into our own hands.'

We had reached the high cut through the last rampart of the Chiltern Hills, the microwave relay tower atop rising like a pale lighthouse. From here the motorway plunged down into Oxfordshire and a vast vale of farmland, misty with distance and heat. We were discussing a murderer, and murder, and magic, which had contaminated us.

'God's Legion might believe us now, Chrissy. Ellison might.'

'If Ellison was a high Anglican or Catholic he might have some ideas about the occult and exorcism. But a Baptist evangelist? Jesus and tambourines?'

'He has the vans. He has the troops.'

'Ex-addicts and muddled runaways who have been born again. Will Frisvold grow *younger*? Or will he—will he shift into someone else's body? Some younger body?'

'Whose? He doesn't know about Olsson.'

'He might have dreamed about him. That can't have been his plan to begin with. I'm thinking about you and me.'

'He wouldn't want your body, Chrissy.'

'What's wrong with *my* body?'

My body, in which Carl Olsson had rooted . . .

'Nothing at all! What I mean is, he wouldn't want a woman's body—not a Norse Siegfried like him. He may have someone lined up at his home. A gardener or valet. It's just that I can't imagine someone becoming younger. Skin freshening, muscles toning up, bones growing strong again. It's easier to imagine him swapping minds with a younger person.'

'Then the newly inhabited body kills the feeble old husk?'

We were becoming a bit unhinged. Steve drove carefully, taking me home.

On my initiative we made love that night. A reunion of our bodies in bed; and we slept peacefully.

Two mornings later at Fernhill, a phone call from Newcastle. Olsson had disembarked from the overnight boat. He was about to board a National Express coach for a seven-hour journey to Blanchester, changing at Birmingham. Of course we would meet him.

And we did so, that evening.

While we were driving back to Preston Priors, from the rear of our car Olsson said, 'I have dreamed badly.'

'We have beer in the house—'

Olsson rooted in a duffel bag and produced a bottle of rum.

'I am bringing you a present.'

Politely Olsson praised the fields of sheep and wheat, and the rolling leafy land. He admired Preston Priors as we entered it. The ironstone cottages were mostly slate-roofed though some were thatched. Norman church; old vicarage and old school-house, no longer inhabited by either vicar or school-ma'am. Defunct pub, converted into a house. Big village green complete with genuine duck pond. Our own cottage was part of a terrace down less exalted Hog Lane.

And inside of Oak cottage: exposed beams and joists in the kitchen-cum-dining room—also in the sitting room where the four big laminated photos lay on the carpet, rims touching. Steve had shifted furniture aside to make enough space. Olsson would be sleeping on the sofa, though only after the pictures had been stacked in the kitchen, covered with a tablecloth to hide them, neutralise them.

We ate noodles and meat balls and olive Ciabatta bread fresh from the oven and drank some red wine. At eight o'clock we adjourned to the sitting room. Hog Lane never caught any late sunshine. Perfectly reasonable to close the curtains and switch on a lamp. The low ceiling made any central light fitting impossible.

'Like a—séance.' Olsson had remembered the word.

'Just wait till I bring the candles!'

We were used to power cuts in Preston Priors whenever there was a violent storm, so we kept a stock of candles. Candle-light would mimic the flicker of the torches in the sculpture park on that night years ago. While I fetched two packets and matches, Steve brought an assortment of saucers and egg-cups for the candles to stand in. Olsson was peering at the pictures of Steve and of me on the floor.

'Bring a sharp knife from the kitchen,' he said. 'To stick in the space in the middle. Like a . . .' The name eluded him. Maybe he meant like the gnomon of a sundial. A spindle. An axis.

Whatever were we doing here in our sitting room in cahoots with a Norwegian who wasn't quite right in the head? Steve frowned at me, but we must follow our instincts. When I brought a kitchen knife Olsson stabbed the point down hard, right into the floorboard below. What did a mere cut in the carpet matter? Twanging the handle, he made the knife quiver. After Steve and I had lit all the candles, I switched off the lamp.

'So,' said Steve, 'do we stand together in the middle holding hands?'

Do we take our clothes off? I wondered. I felt no instinct to do so. Quite the contrary.

'Did you bring hash, Mr Olsson?' Of course he hadn't.

'I think,' said Olsson, 'we kneel down and each cut our finger a little on the knife. Rub our blood together. Rub it on the pictures. I think so. We repeat the German words.'

Blood. Stone. Makes. Shield.

'Maybe in reverse. To take us back . . .'

So we crowded together on our knees, upon the pictures. Slicing our thumbs just a little on the knife blade, we mingled our blood, and smeared those big nocturnal images of the Vigeland Park.

'*Schutz. Schild. Macht. Stein. Blut,*' we chorused. If Hugh Ellison should somehow be listening at the window . . . !

Two dozen candle-flames began to rock. The flames dipped then stretched up again as if they were being breathed in and out by some unseen presence.

'Uncle, where are you?' called Olsson. He said things in Norwegian and German. Soon he became frustrated.

'I need rum!' Rising, he stumbled to the kitchen.

'Christ,' hissed Steve. 'Rum and a knife—'

Returning with the bottle, Olsson knelt again. Squeezing the blade of the knife with his right hand, he jerked, then exposed his palm. Blood flowed from his life line and heart line. Gritting his teeth, he poured dark spirit over the bleeding wound. With a shudder, he drank from the bottle. Plunging his palm down upon the patch of exposed carpet, he screwed his hand around, chanting, '*Blut. Blut. Blut.*' Sounded as if great drips of liquid were plopping from a tap into a bucket of water. What was I supposed to put on that stain to get rid of it? White wine? Salt? Would he catch hold of me next, smearing my skin and my clothes? As the candle flames danced, highlights gleamed in the laminated pictures, and shadows lurched around our sitting room.

Then the flames were burning evenly. All was calm. Nothing whatever was happening. If anything had been on the point of happening, it had faded away.

I dressed Olsson's hand. We opened beers, and swigged, sitting together on the sofa.

'Tomorrow night,' he vowed, 'we will do it again, but I spill more blood. I felt it start to come, but we lost it. We must all spill blood. Maybe you buy a hen.'

Poor hen. Poor carpet. Poor us.

When the doorbell rang insistently, the clock on the bedside table showed two in the morning. Steve lurched to the open curtains, and peered into Hog Lane.

'Come here,' he whispered. Again, the summoning peal. In my pajamas, I joined Steve. Below: a black car, a Mercedes.

'It's Alver's car. Frisvold's—'

Up through the floor came noises of blunder. Olsson was up and about. Before either of us could decide what to do, we were hearing voices downstairs. Olsson must have opened our front door.

'Stay here, Chrissy—'

'*No!*'

The old gent had relapsed into one of the pine carver chairs in the kitchen. Olsson was leaning against our dresser crowded with plates and ornaments, the knife in his bandaged hand. On the red floor tiles, in a heap: the table-cloth.

'Both of you come in here now! Sit and put your hands on the table—' Frisvold's voice held a weary authority, and his liver-spotted hand, a nasty-looking pistol. I had never seen a gun before in real life, but the name Luger occurred to me.

No smartly tailored suit, tonight. Before driving here, he must have thrown on whatever came to hand. Old trousers and sweater, under an open overcoat. No socks on his feet, just brown leather slippers.

'Sit!'

Of course we obeyed. Frisvold spoke to Olsson in Norwegian. Carl retorted now and then. I could grasp not a word of what they were *snakking* about, which was about the only Norwegian word I knew apart from *skål*. *Snakker*, to speak. *Jai* don't *snak Norsk*. After a while, I interrupted:

'You gave us nightmares, Mr Frisvold. Your life's a nightmare.'

'What do you know?' Was he asking me, or sneering?

Anger boiled in me. 'How about you sacrificing your sister in that park in 1945?'

He winced. 'My sister wished that, to buttress the Reich. So that there could be some strength left! So that Bolshevism would not wash over Europe the way it did. We have had to wait fifty years for the red tide to go away. She was no faint-heart like my countrymen. What I regret is the failure, the abject surrender. Your interference is making her die in vain once more.'

'Excuse me, but *you* came to us—to use us.'

Frisvold peered derisively at the bandage on Carl's hand. 'Now I have found her grandson. My own blood, out for revenge—something we Norwegians seem to specialise in. Put that silly knife away, Carl Olsson. You hurt your own hand, you fool.'

'My blood brought you here, Uncle.'

Frisvold inclined his head, conceding. Having won his point, Olsson placed the stained knife on the dresser next to a Delft milk jug, then subsided into a chair.

The old man tutted exasperatedly. 'Revenge, revenge. Thousands of patriots persecuted for decades after our so-called liberation—and now me, to be thwarted. You don't know what I'm talking about, do you? You are ignorant. Your heads are full of lies.'

'You'll be telling us next,' Steve cried, 'that the concentration camps were a lie!'

'I did not know about those. I never saw one.'

No doubt my expression was jeering.

People often talk wildly to justify themselves, but the spin which Frisvold put on the Second World War and on his country's part in it soon had me reeling—and Carl as well. Before long Carl was sitting with one hand clutching his head, his eyes red with rum and beer and fatigue. Steve, too, was fairly pop-eyed.

Quisling, shot in 1945 for his betrayal of Norway? Quisling who had given his name to treachery just as Judas Iscariot had? According to Frisvold, Vidkun Quisling was one of the great humanitarian figures of the twentieth century, and one of the most perceptive.

What did anyone know about Quisling? Scarcely more than his despised, hated name! Yet during the early nineteen-twenties, apparently this very same Quisling had saved a fifth of a million people from starvation in the Ukraine, almost single-handedly. During 1922, with Soviet consent, he was running the Russian railway system to improve famine relief. So impressed was Trotsky, that he asked Quisling to reorganise the Red Army. A rival offer came from China, to reorganise their administration. To prepare for this task, Quisling learned Chinese—but the Chiang Kai-shek revolution intervened. That was the sort of man we were talking about; not that Frisvold himself had personally been close to Quisling. Quisling was too fastidious.

In his youth Quisling had learned Hebrew because he was deeply religious. What's more, he was such a nifty mathematician that he understood quantum theory. He also understood what was going to happen to Norway, land of make-believe, when the great powers began brawling, unless his countrymen *did* something. Hence, his National Unification Party, *Nasjonal Samling, NS*. That was no Nazi party. Far from it. The NS aimed at putting some backbone into Norway and saving its independence, the way the Finns had saved themselves.

Blind, selfish, and lazy, the Norwegians possessed little more than a police force, even though Norway was one of the easiest countries in the world to defend with anything more than a microscopic army. Throughout the 1930s Quisling was the Churchill of Norway, the lone voice warning of national suicide, and being abused for his pains. Frisvold certainly had it in for his countrymen.

Did Quisling conspire with the Nazis? Not a bit of it. Quisling stepped in to frustrate the Germans and minimise the effects of an occupation. When the invasion started, the King of Norway and the General Staff had more important matters on their minds—would you believe they were enjoying a Roman-style banquet, accompanied by a lecture on Gastronomy in Ancient Rome?

Off his own bat, an elderly Norwegian officer did manage enterprisingly to sink the German flagship, sending all the occupation officials and their documents to the bottom of the Oslo Fjord.

'*His* reward after the war was to be prosecuted as a traitor, because he belonged to Quisling's *Nasjonal Samling*! This NS member was *sinking* the Nazi flagship, not cheering and saluting it—'

Sinking the flagship gained Oslo precious hours, which were squandered. Did the Norwegian government announce immediate mobilisation over the radio? On the contrary, they sent out call-up papers by snail-mail.

And then the government and the King ran away, with not a word to the people, without making any arrangements for maintaining public services.

If Quisling had not stepped in, Norway might have been treated like Poland. By a ruse, Quisling managed to keep the home shipping fleet in Norwegian ownership. He kept the Norwegian flag flying over parliament, at least for a while. He was so obstinate. Ribbentrop loathed him. Quisling even obtained amnesties for former enemies of his, whom the Germans arrested. He was always at odds with Reichskommissar Terboven. Quisling did say a few silly things about Jews but the fact is that when round-ups loomed, he delayed these for ten days so that Jews could get away. It was his own *Nasjonal Samling* members who helped Jews make their escape to Sweden. The only voice actually protesting about arrests of Jews was the *Nasjonal Samling* Bishop of Oslo—so *he* got ten years in jail after the war.

Topsy-turvy, indeed.

'Our nation could never come to terms with any of these truths,' Frisvold ranted on, 'or that a great debt of gratitude was owing! Quisling's name was blackened. Vengeance was easier—vindictive reprisals which went on for years. During the mockery of a trial Quisling endured, the authorities were sticking wires in his cranium like medieval inquisitors to test if he was sane.

Or to send him insane. This was while he was trying to conduct his own defence on a starvation diet. Give him no more than a little herring for lunch!—even though no Norwegians ever went hungry the way the Dutch did during the war, thousands dying of starvation. Our King even wanted Quisling's execution to be deliberately botched, to torment him—'

If Frisvold was telling the truth, this was shocking. Though why was he telling us at all? After decades of pretending to be somebody else, at last he had an audience? One from whom he might win sympathy? Whom he might convert to his point of view—so that we would voluntarily step aside, instead of him shooting us? The gun in his hand seemed so evil. Though if it were not for the gun, would we be listening?

Olsson broke in. 'Quisling got no amnesty for men who were shot in reprisal after the Home Front killed the chief of his bodyguard!'

'Pah, he couldn't. If he did not agree to it, the Germans were going to shoot even more prisoners. The Home Front's pig-headed adventures only made the Reichskommissar and the Gestapo take off the kid gloves.'

'What are those gloves?' asked Olsson.

'The Home Front provoked Terboven and the Gestapo so they stopped acting softly. Terboven was glad of any excuse.'

'Why was that?' asked Steve.

'Because Josef Terboven was a spiteful bully. Inferiority complex cloaked in arrogance. Norway was the trial run for him becoming Reichskommissar of Britain if an invasion succeeded—did you know that?'

Steve shook his head.

'Yes, Terboven would have been boss of Britain! You know nothing, do you? Quisling warned the Home Front but they played into Terboven's hands in his contest with Quisling. That's what use the Home Front were.'

Olsson moaned. 'At home we had a *photo* on the wall, of a big German general saluting a lad of the Home Front as he surrendered to the boy.'

'Oh that famous photo! It was staged, for public relations. No German could *surrender* to any Norwegian. Thanks to Quisling, Norway and Germany signed an armistice in 1940 so that they would not be at war. The government-in-exile knew nothing about this, because they had run away.'

'What people know, is a lie?' cried Olsson. 'And the real resistance was Quisling?'

'That's right. Such truths are unacceptable.'

Frisvold was telling us that nothing was as it seemed—so therefore neither was he as he seemed. I could hardly square this with my dream.

'Is this supposed to clear you of blame? Blame for joining the SS? For the blood-sacrifice of your own *sister*? Were you and Quisling trying to *protect* Norway there in the Vigeland Park?'

Frisvold uttered a croak of a laugh. 'Quisling was no part of that! He was so religious he wanted to resign during the occupation to become a lay pastor. Josef Terboven was there in the park, the Reichskommissar—he worshipped Hitler.'

'What did this Terboven look like?'

'Thin. Round spectacles with wire rims. Receding hair, parted on the left, oiled and combed back. He looked like a human rat, though he wore a fine uniform.'

That was the man I had seen in my dream—but who was it who actually cut Liv Frisvold's throat?

'Some of the SS were there,' Frisvold went on. 'And Weiner, the Gestapo chief, who shot himself later on—'

'But *you* got away.'

About this, he was willing to tell us too.

All along, the Nazi high command had been planning to retreat to Norway...

'Or Bavaria,' I said, remembering.

Oops, pardon me. This was merely another example of my ignorance—of how I swallowed clichés like a lazy fish a pretty fly. The belief that the Nazis intended to hole up in the Bavarian Alps was a masterpiece of black propaganda, probably the only real jewel of German disinformation. On the strength of that Eisenhower diverted a whole army—regardless that the Allies had cracked the German codes and ought to have known better. Norway was always the real destination for the final showdown.

Yet by then there was too much chaos. The red tide, flooding from the east. Hitler had lost his marbles, too far gone in madness to issue sensible orders.

So: get out of Norway or else face the music.

In spite of personal animosities Josef Terboven had set aside a plane—a bomber—for Quisling to escape in. And for other people, of course. Frisvold would have been on that bomber, which would rendezvous with a long-distance U-boat, capable of reaching South America.

Naively and stubbornly, Quisling chose to remain in Norway. He thought that his faultless logic and patriotic service would be appreciated. Delay, delay.

And then, from Berlin via Denmark, arrived the *Belgian* fascist leader, Leon Degrelle.

'Who?' I asked.

Pardon our ignorance, again.

In cliché land Degrelle would be the Belgian counterpart of Quisling—if Quisling had ever been the collaborator he was slandered as being. This Degrelle—endowed with sublime good luck— was the only figure of such wicked prominence to survive and thrive anywhere in Europe after the war. He was The One Who Got Away—to Spain.

Leon Degrelle . . . Pay attention, Chrissy.

Frisvold was only acquainted with the Belgian for a very short time in Oslo, but it was an intense acquaintance. Both men had served in the Ukraine, in calamitous conditions. Degrelle loved hanging out with collaborationists, bragging and drinking and revelling in the trappings of Nazism. Germans themselves were never close mates of his. Even after fighting alongside them, he still never learned a word of German.

'Mais moi, je parle Français,' Frisvold confided. 'Leon's life and exploits were poured into my ear. What a bond developed between us.'

Because of both men's service in the SS. And because Frisvold could *snakke Norsk* and *sprechen Deutsch*, which was of invaluable help to a monolingual Belgian marooned in Oslo with just a few cronies.

Frisvold had served the Reich—and Degrelle had formed a Walloon storm-trooper brigade, which became part of the Waffen-SS. After the Allies overran Belgium, Degrelle and his Walloon Legion fought the advancing Russians in a last ditch attempt to save Berlin. Failing, he and a few associates left the Legion in the outskirts of Berlin and fled.

Degrelle had friends in Spain, and resources tucked away there, money and gold—as well as a lot of money in the South of France (but France was out of bounds). Always Degrelle was financially canny. He married money (though this never stopped him from cheating on his wife). He hit a jackpot when he borrowed money from his own Rexist Party's coffers to buy a big perfume company which the Germans sequestered from its Jewish owners.

Spain spelled sanctuary. It was with Frisvold's assistance that Degrelle and his now-tiny party were able to commandeer a light aircraft with long-range fuel tanks and the scarce fuel to fill them.

'Don't tell me you're a pilot too.'

'No, Miss Clarke, the pilot was a Belgian, Robert Frank.'

What a journey that was, flying almost fifteen hundred miles by night over Europe, variously embattled or liberated. Maybe Frisvold had been telling the truth when he said that aeroplanes terrified him. This plane only barely reached Spain, crash-landing out of fuel on the beach at San Sebastian just a few miles beyond the border. Degrelle hurt his foot. Into hospital he was whisked. Generalisimo Franco was not best pleased at his uninvited fascist guest, but being a fascist himself he procrastinated about extradition. Four months after the crash-landing Degrelle vanished from hospital. The Spanish government denied all knowledge. Ten years later Degrelle emerged in public from the protection of his Spanish friends. He prospered. A construction company owned by him built air bases for the Americans in Spain.

'He paid you well for the plane,' Olsson said.

I was keenly interested in sources of wealth. Frisvold pursed his lips. He was evasive about what happened to him after San Sebastian, though obviously from wherever he went to he had kept tabs on what was happening in his homeland. I imagined the wily buccaneering Degrelle nursing a bag of diamonds, sequestered from Jewish dealers in Antwerp—or him entrusting his new buddy Frisvold with gold bars to take to Paraguay to establish a bolt-hole in case Spain let him down . . .

'Actually, Miss Clarke, many Norwegian families made a lot of money during the war by supplying the legitimate needs of the occupying authority. Selling trees, supplying construction material—this was perfectly proper under the terms of the Berne Convention.'

Frisvold may have taken gold of his own on that plane, transmuted from some family forest by the alchemy of the occupation.

'Perfectly proper and legal!'

'Are we supposed to think, Mr Frisvold, that you're more sinned against than sinning?'

Exasperatedly: 'Norway almost went bankrupt after the war by punishing the so-called profiteering families, wrecking their businesses in an orgy of revenge! The Norwegian government asked the British what you intended to do about your own collaborators. The people of your Channel Islands: those were in the same situation. London told Oslo it was going to do nothing—forget about it. Norwegians could never take advice. If America had not stepped in with lavish aid, Norway would have gone down the drain—'

'Things seemed different during much of the war,' Frisvold insisted. 'Hitler looked set to win. Thousands of Norwegians fought the Red Army alongside the Germans. Not against Britain, never—only against Communism, which was to eat up half of Europe.'

Only Quisling had the genius to see what eluded even the Germans, namely that the Hitler-Stalin pact would fall apart—and what would stem from this: *red tide*. Norwegians were glad to volunteer to strengthen Germany's muscle. They were the best fighters since the Vikings.

'They *deserted*,' Olsson contradicted him.

'Rubbish! The Germans decorated many for gallantry. Fifty fought to the last defending the Reich Chancellery.'

'It must have been crowded there, what with Belgians and Norwegians and goodness knows who else.'

Frisvold glared at me. 'Have you seen a trawler net being winched tighter and tighter?'

'A net with sharks in it,' Steve said.

'And with holes in the net,' retorted Frisvold. 'All these Front Fighters from Norway could have been the nucleus of Norwegian defence after the war. Instead, they were imprisoned then forced to be street-sweepers. Even now, Norway refuses its responsibilities in Europe and prefers to dream.'

'*We* have been dreaming,' I reminded him.

'May I have a drink of water?' he asked me.

One thing which Quisling did not favour was a special Germanic SS Norway Force, under the ultimate command of Himmler. Quisling even started a whispering campaign against this thousand-strong force, which was destined not only to fight Communism but also for other duties in the Greater Reich.

'Things seemed different,' repeated Frisvold. 'Events had an inevitability. I am haunted by certain brutalities, but at the time ... The Americans committed atrocities in Vietnam, did they not? No one knew about the Nazi death camps. My goal was Nordic-Teutonic union against Slavic-Asian Bolshevism. My sister's goal too. Odin power—'

Culminating in that occult ritual at the eleventh hour in the Vigeland Park ...

'Do you understand now?' asked this old man with the gun. With his free hand, he stroked the uppermost picture of the park, of me in the buff embracing granite. 'I have the right to use the energy because of my sister. She was a valkyrie! Her participation was voluntary. She would allow no one to take her life but me. Not Terboven, certainly! *Me*, her adored brother, her hero. Oh, Liv,' he cried out. '*Life* is the meaning of her name!'

This was deeply sick.

'I have the right to become young again,' Frisvold declared. 'I have the right to live again.'

'By stealing someone's body?' I shouted at him.

He looked amazed. 'Of course not. How could *that* happen? I shall live again by reincarnation.'

Surely the old man was deeply mad.

Then he began to tell us about the Nazi scientific expedition to Tibet. Photos have appeared showing German scientists measuring the heads of grinning Tibetans with callipers, as if racist anthropology was the principal purpose of the trip; but it was otherwise . . .

Hitler believed in reincarnation. 'The Soul and the mind migrate, just as the body returns to nature'—thus spake the Führer, though not in public.

The Gauleiter of Thuringia, Artur Dinter, said the same thing much more openly. An early Nazi recruit, Dinter published a book preaching re-incarnation—and also demanding that the Bible should be re-organised. Get rid of the entire Old Testament with all its Jewish blather. Cut out all the Epistles of St. Paul and all of the Gospels except for that of mystical St. John. Even St. John's Gospel would need a touch of rewriting to remove Jewish taint. The resulting Bible would have been somewhat slim: from Word-made-Flesh to Apocalypse in a few quick steps. Politically this was embarrassing for Hitler. The Führer hoped to win the support of Evangelicals and Catholics. Banning most of the Bible was not a vote catcher. So this particular Gauleiter was ousted from the Nazi Party. However, on the subject of reincarnation, Adolf still saw eye to eye with Artur Dinter.

Heinrich Himmler also believed firmly in reincarnation—as well as in runic magic; the black twin lightning flash symbolising Himmler's SS was the double Sig rune. Himmler adopted the ideas of a man called Karl Eckhart, author of a book titled *Temporal Immortality*.

'According to Eckhart, each man is reborn as one of his own blood-descendants—'

Himmler was on the verge of distributing a special printing of 20,000 copies of Eckhart's book to the SS when Hitler put his foot down, again for political reasons. Heinrich, head of the SS, was sure that he himself was the reincarnation of a previous Heinrich who, a thousand years earlier, established the Saxon royal family and thrust the Poles eastward (not as in North and South Poles, but as in *untermensch* people). The SS were carrying on his ancestor's splendid work.

Where, oh where, might one discover the recipe for reincarnation? Where else but in Tibet, one of the secret places of the world where the rebirth of lamas and Dalai Lamas was routine! The result was the SS science outing of the late 30s in search of arcane wisdom. And the expedition did strike pay-dirt, according to Frisvold.

The old man jawed on about mandalas, Tibetan meditation-mazes which were very like the runic maze in the Vigeland Park. He spoke about some Tibetan rite of 'Cutting Off' involving a magic dagger, which stirred up occult forces, if any were in the vicinity. The cutting-off of Norway from Allied attack, hmm? This would be a Nordic, Teutonic rite, not an Asian ritual; a rite from the land of Valhalla, where Odin chose slaughtered heroes for immortal struggle; a rite where blood played a central role. Yet behind it, lurked . . .

'The power to reincarnate me, because my blood-sister gave her life in a wasted sacrifice.' Frisvold's scowl challenged any of us to contradict him. 'After you stop meddling and after I succeed, you will be free of your nightmares. After I am born again, carrying on the cycle of life with full self-awareness of who I was.'

We were enmeshed in this now. 'How can you do it?' Steve whispered.

By way of reply Frisvold touched the muzzle of the Luger to his lips.

The gun was not for *us*, although he used it to intimidate and control us. Shooting us might be bad *karma* immediately prior to a reincarnation. No, the pistol was meant for himself. While he knelt amongst the images of the Vigeland Park back in his house, wherever that was, he would stick the muzzle of the Luger in his mouth and fire a bullet into his brain. His soul and his mind would transfer into some embryo or foetus to be reborn elsewhere.

'You have money,' Olsson shouted out suddenly. 'I have no job.'

Frisvold had not come here expecting to meet his great-nephew and to be asked for cash. But he delved in his coat pocket.

'Before I came out I picked up my wallet. Who knows, I might need petrol.' How many miles had the Mercedes travelled tonight? Very likely that car was leased, not owned outright. Frisvold's house was probably rented. He would not be leaving any assets behind him.

'You can have whatever is in here. I shall not need it after tonight.'

'Petrol money,' sneered Olsson. 'You have put your wealth in a Swiss bank, is that it? With a secret number which you will remember!'

A look of momentary alarm crossed Frisvold's face, to be replaced by smug triumph. Where else would his wealth be safe until he grew up again? It made perfect sense.

'What if you are reborn an *African* or an *Arab*, Uncle?'

'No, there will be some affinity. Racial affinity.' Again, that croak of a laugh. 'Maybe I will be born a Finn.'

'What if you *are* born African and poor as shit?' I jeered at him.

A firm shake of the head. 'My soul and mind will find a proper abode.'

Steve could not contain himself. 'What are you going to *do* when you're reborn? It's years and years from cradle to being able to stroll into some bank in Zurich!'

'What do you recommend, Mr Bryant?'

'Me?'

'Yes, what would you do? I'm interested.'

'Well, I would . . .' Steve had spoken without thinking, and promptly ground to a halt.

'You are utterly helpless. Dependant. Suppose that you can make your newborn mouth shape words properly. Do you confide in your new parents? You risk being smothered as a devil-child—or becoming a media sensation! What benefit is there? Do you tell the truth about yourself? What you achieved is not easily repeatable by other people! You are a freak—and a sort of monster, because you cut your sister's throat. Do you invent a false past life?'

Steve was at a loss. Frisvold had had far longer to think through the implications.

'Will your new parents cooperate? Will they hurry to Switzerland, equipped with that magic number and password, and then surround you with luxury? A giant TV screen showing adult movies to while away the boredom? A baby's mini-gym, to help you mature faster? You are a lottery ticket they have won! Once they have collected, they can tear up the ticket.'

He had arranged some kind of password for identification in Zurich in whatever future year. Number plus password would give access to whoever turned up, white or black, young or even younger.

'You are a baby, Mr Bryant, who must follow a biological plan for growing up. What will you do?'

'I don't know,' Steve admitted.

'The best strategy is to reveal *nothing*. It is to pretend to be a baby—to accept the boredom and the indignity. To become a young boy—and to grow older till you are a youth. You must try not to seem too strange to your parents. You can be precocious, something of a prodigy. When you are fifteen or sixteen you can escape—with a whole new lifetime ahead of you.'

'And when you're old again you can't perform the trick a second time, because you used up the power?'

Frisvold sipped water. 'I think physical immortality is around the corner, for the rich. Machines the size of molecules will repair the body.'

'What if you're born crippled?' Steve persisted.

'I take the risk. It is better to be born than not be born.'

'What if you *like* your new parents?' I asked him.

'I must certainly seem to like them. And maybe I will. Now,' he said, 'I want you to carry these pictures to my car.'

'What about me, Uncle Olav?' clamoured Olsson.

A smile flitted. 'You can try to find me again. The same way the Tibetan priests set out to find a reincarnated one. It can take them years of travel and prayer and divination. And, of course, the child must be willing to be recognised.'

He had driven away, taking our pictures with him. Frailty notwithstanding, he still had reserves of stamina.

How long ago did he establish himself in this country, poised just across the North Sea from his homeland? Britain is an island, surrounded by a cordon of sea. Therefore it is similar to Fortress Norway with its invisible magical girdle. No doubt he waited as many years as he dared before setting events in motion—no point in premature suicide! Then opportunity presented itself in the form of *Majig Mementoes*. Without us what would he have done? Something, but I doubt he would have told us.

Olsson was counting the money in the old man's wallet—looked to me like a couple of hundred pounds. A bastardly inheritance.

'Will you go back home soon?' I asked.

Sourly: 'To the land which is not as it seems—if Uncle Olav is accurate. Will we dream anything when he kills himself tonight?'

Would we have any proof of the event?

My dream had changed. I was a statue on a plinth, frozen in mid-stride. In my outstretched hands I held a naked child of granite, who stared at me by starlight. The child's knees were up in the air as if moments earlier I had snatched him from his potty. Chubby arms reached towards me, as I held him at arm's length.

And then I was running across grass, naked and barefoot, bearing the child ahead of me.

On the radio in the morning, the final news headline is sometimes a quirky piece, which then drops into oblivion.

'In Norway last night,' said the news reader, 'lightning struck a pillar of granite sculpture in the middle of Oslo's sculpture park—splitting the top open, according to reports. The sculpture park is one of the principal sights of the city, visited by as many tourists as the Viking longboats. Skies were totally clear at the time. Experts are investigating.'

Agog, we sat in silence through the whole of the news but the oddity received no further coverage.

Olsson clapped his hands, and winced. 'I shall go back today. I think I can visit the park now without drinking—and for the last time too. Soon I will be able to build a dam. Can you drive me to the bus station?'

Of course we could; and gladly.

A week later, the police called at Fernhill. By ill chance Hugh Ellison was in the car park, talking to a couple of young legionnaires. God's centurion intercepted the two occupants of the police car, and soon he was guiding them helpfully in our direction.

'These are the proprietors of Majig Mementoes*Z*: Miss Chrissy Clarke and her partner Mr Steve Bryant*T*.'

As Ellison dallied, a chunky uniformed man in his mid-thirties identified himself Detective-Sergeant Curry, and his younger brunette female colleague as Detective-Constable Carroll.

Curry produced photographs of the pictures of Steve and me in the sculpture park by night. Each of the laminated circles was propped against a background of striped wallpaper. In miniature were my long dark hair and bare buttocks, and Steve's skinny frame, splayed against granite nudes. Craning to see, Ellison sidled forward. Oh of course, our business sticker had been attached to the otherwise blank jigsaw boxes.

'Do you recognise these?' Curry asked.

A special commission for a Norwegian client, name of Mr Alver, said I.

'*Special*,' Ellison echoed softly. Curry seemed content for him to remain while we were being questioned.

Sculpture park in Oslo; sentimental journey on an old man's behalf, et cetera. An eccentric old gentleman: he read about us in the newspaper, in the special supplement featuring Fernhill last year. We never found out where he lived.

'Did you do other poses for this client?' DS Curry asked.

'Poses? Of course not.' The whole point of the commission was the sculpture park. Norwegians thought nudity was normal. Anyway, Alver was an old man.

'*Was* an old man?'

'I cut those jigsaws last year,' Steve explained.

The DS made a show of examining the photos. 'Excuse me, but these aren't jigsaws.'

'Those are the pictures before being cut up.'

'Before being jigged. I see.' In the detective's mouth the word jigged sounded suspect and dirty.

I could see the slope that we were about to slide down. How could there be pristine versions of the pictures? What is the production method? Name of the printing company, if you please! A call would prove that Steve had the copies made just over a week ago. As yet, no mention had been made of Frisvold being dead—assuming that he was. We—Steve mustn't—fall into the trap of revealing that we thought so.

'You said you never knew his address,' said DC Carroll. 'How could you do business with him?'

'Mr Alver always came here.'

'Always?'

'Twice. Once to commission, once to collect.'

'How did he pay?'

Oh not the unrevealed income angle!

'What is this about?' I asked the woman detective. 'I'm mystified.'

'We're puzzled too,' said Curry. 'We hope you can cast some light.'

'*On what?*'

'On Mr Alver's death. We entered his property yesterday evening following reports of curtains staying closed although his car was there.'

'Where *is* his, er, property?'

Curry ignored my question. 'Your Mr Alver had been dead for several days. Maybe a week.' What response was he expecting? *Poor fellow!* Or: *Was it a heart attack?*

'How?' was what I said.

'He blew his brains out—all over your jigsaws. He had been kneeling among them, stark naked.'

'Jesus Christ,' I said, 'that's awful!' *Beware, beware: Curry hadn't said what he used to blow his brains out.*

I chose my words carefully. 'Last year he told us that he wanted to come to terms with his life—by doing those jigsaws of his beloved homeland—before the grim reaper came. That's what he said.'

'Bit of an enigma, your Mr Alver. What else did he say?'

'Well, he couldn't travel much because he hated planes, and boats made him seasick—that's why we went to Oslo for him. What do his neighbours say? The people who reported about the curtains.'

'You appear to have had more contact with him than his neighbours.'

'Oh no, it was only business.'

Shit, had anyone down Hog Lane seen the Mercedes at dead of night?

'I'm still puzzled,' Curry continued, 'about the, um, uncut versions of the jigsaws.'

'You can't assemble a jigsaw without a picture to look at—'

The DS studied Steve. He scanned our little showroom, where all jigsaw boxes carried illustrations. 'Your boxes, the ones in his house, those had no pictures on them.'

'Ah: the pictures would have been too small for him to see clearly.'

Do shut up, Steve.

'I see,' Curry said. 'And there's nothing more you can tell us about Mr Alver?'

Sensibly, Steve just shook his head.

'How about you, Miss Clarke?'

'Not that I can think of right now. Mr Alver wasn't very forthcoming. When he said that about the grim reaper I never realised!'

'But you were prepared to take nude photographs of yourselves for him?'

'That was art.' Behind me, I heard Ellison sniff.

Curry regarded the framed jigsaw of the two pigtailed girls in polka-dot dresses beside the Fountain of Trevi. 'Unlike your other jigsaws . . .'

'He paid us in cash, by the way,' I told DC Carroll. She raised an eyebrow, but after all the police are not the tax authorities. 'And oh, he used a credit card for our hotel bookings. American Express, I think.'

'You think.'

'Suicide, that's so terrible.' As if this was only now fully registering on me.

'Especially,' the woman detective said, 'when you have to see a body in that state.'

'*We* don't need to, do we? I mean, to identify him?'

The DC shook her head. 'We have a problem with next of kin. Who to notify. Mr Alver burned a lot of documents.'

Not the jigsaw boxes, damn him! At least the house must have been locked from the inside, so suicide was the only explanation.

'Why do you suppose he would burn documents?'

'I've no idea. The Norwegian embassy may be able to help you with identity and family.'

'We do realise that.'

'If we think of anything else,' I promised, 'we'll phone you right away.'

Blessedly it was time for thanks for our assistance. Police are busy, and not always very bright. Fingers crossed that they didn't pop back and say 'Oh, by the way . . .'

Hugh Ellison stayed.

'Nude pictures*Z*. You assured me that nothing of the sort was involved*D*—'

I tried pleading, but we would not join Ellison in a heart-searching prayer. As of four weeks' time *Majig Mementoes* was evicted, banished from Eden.

Bad news number two came a fortnight later, when my period failed to arrive.

So here is another springtime, and we are still in Oak Cottage. We were forced to borrow money both from my parents and from Steve's. The arrival of a grandson prompts generosity.

James Douglas Clarke (Jamie) is named diplomatically after my own Dad and after Steve's Dad. My Mum and Dad would rather that we had married, even in a registry office. In my view money was better devoted to keeping us afloat than spent on any ceremony.

Babies often stay blond and blue-eyed for quite a while. Steve hasn't dropped any hints, but surely he must recognise the resemblance to Carl Olsson, minus thirty-odd years and booze-abuse. That's why he encourages that girl Caroline to help out at *Majig Mementoes*, particularly on days when I do not feel like going there with Jamie in his carry-cot—now that *Majig Mementoes* is part of the Canal Craft Centre in Blanchester, a converted warehouse, lousy location. I am not blind.

Skinny Caroline has brown dreadlocks, a dozen silver rings in her ears, one in her navel, a stud in her nose like a gleaming crystal of snot. She's one of the travelling people—not that she travels far from a tatty old narrowboat moored near the Craft Centre, shared with several kindred New Age souls, plus a baby and a mongrel. Most travellers rarely range further than the Social Security office and the pubs in town.

If I had my Carl, Steve will have his Caroline, it seems. On days when I stay home, I imagine Steve hanging up the 'Back in an Hour' sign at *Majig Mementoes* and consorting with Caroline on the narrowboat, assuming that the others—and the baby in a sling, and the mongrel on its length of string—are roaming the streets, trying to score some weed to smoke. Caroline lowers the tone of *Majig Mementoes*, but she helps out usefully, for what is not much more than pocket money.

Steve must be *blind*—or banal—to have missed the main fact about my son, such a quiet and amenable baby. No sleepless nights for us, not a single one. Finance aside, there's no excuse for post-natal depression.

Here I am at home, on another afternoon of the blue-skied drought which has migrated here from Scandinavia. I know perfectly well that Steve is on the narrowboat with Caroline, sharing a spliff before they peel their clothes off. Our Health Visitor, well-intentioned Mrs Wilson, has driven off in her blue Nissan Micra after weighing Jamie, filling in her chart, seeing how well this radiant Young Mum is coping. All is fine. Jamie is certainly not autistic. Flat on his back in the carry-cot he lies focusing on me precociously, while I sit alongside.

'I know you understand me,' I croon at him. 'I know you're Mr Frisvold. Nice Mrs Wilson won't be calling here for another month. We're on our own together, you and me. Steve doesn't really count—he isn't your Daddy, and he never bathes you. I want you to think very carefully about what I might do if you don't begin talking, Mr Frisvold—if you don't tell me the number of the Swiss account and the password. We can't afford the rent much longer.

'Tell me about Degrelle and gold and diamonds. Tell me about your gold—it's what fairy tales are all about.

'Are you listening, baby? Of course you are. Don't try to pretend you're only a baby. Or I might tickle you. I might tickle your foot with a lighted candle. I don't want to do that sort of thing. You have a whole life ahead of you, Mr Frisvold, I promise. After you tell me, there isn't going to be any cot-death—nothing of the sort, I swear. But you have to cooperate. Collaborate, eh, Mr Frisvold? I'm going to light a candle, just to show you. You never cried since you were born. Maybe you should have done.'

I do hope he won't compel me to be a bit cruel. I don't know if I can bring myself to hurt a baby, even if its skin repairs quickly. I have bought such miniature socks from Mothercare. Today I shall merely show him the candle, maybe hold it close to the sole of his teeny-weeny foot for a little while—until he squeaks, 'Stop!'

Identities may be false, history may be a lie, and my child is also a deceit. Yet I am filled with joy, awaiting baby's first word—for then life will expand like beautiful petals bursting open from a tight bud and become rich, abundant, luscious.

Scars

SOME SCARS ARE VISIBLE. OTHERS, INVISIBLE ...

On my journey home from the Hyde Park Transit Station, a mass of Blissheads were partying in London's Oxford Street. My driver was a middle-aged Sikh, wearing the traditional turban. He halted the hovercab. Sprawling young bodies gaped up at the sky. A few rockets were exploding. The bangs followed by the cascade of lights seemed like some awful migrainous discharge in my brain. People never used to shoot off fireworks on New Year's Eve when I was a kid.

The gust from the cab's skirt blew rubbish about, and we rocked gently. I thumbed down the window to let in some fresh air, but only briefly. The breeze was so raw. Freak wind must be gusting from the Arctic. By tomorrow very likely the temperature would be mild again. Which was worse—warmth and storms, or an honest old-fashioned skin-cutting chill?

Old people sometimes went on as if the cold winters of the past equated with moral fibre and discipline. Here was a taste of bygone days. The Blissheads couldn't have cared less.

Mr Singh (what doubt could there be about any Sikh's name?) hit the horn a few times. The cab mooed loudly, like some cow impatient to reach its parlour and be milked.

A riot policeman waved us onward over the lolling bodies. Unless anyone sat up suddenly, they wouldn't be injured. The battering that our down-draught gave them might seem a splendid massage.

We came to Centre Point, which housed the Ministry of Alien Liaison, brightly lit. At times I thought of Centre Point as a lighthouse in the heart of the city, attracting alien moths, even though Hyde Park is where all the action is—and who knows if under the skin a Mockyman is really a moth or a crab or a spider or nothing imaginable.

Beyond Centre Point, New Oxford Street was fairly clear of revellers. When we finally floated into Middlesex Square, however, the little oval park in the middle was full of flesh.

Mockymusic wailed. A bonfire burned low. Flames licked from hot embers which I guessed were the remains of the woody old briar roses. Many of those were absent from the flower beds. A rocket whooshed up from an empty wine bottle and burst above the rooftops. Silver stars showered like fallout from a steel-smelting furnace.

A couple of private security men stood eyeing the fun. They could not have made much effort to stop our square from being invaded. As for summoning riot police, the whole centre of London seemed to be one big anarchic street party. If Blissheads tried to break into any of the lux mansions, in blithe disregard of steel doors and armour-plated windows, I assumed that warning shots would ring out. Meanwhile, those security boys might privately relish seeing our little paradise being trashed. *Nothing we could do about it, Squire!* The sight of so much bare flesh might appeal, too.

I had returned to London in the midst of something resembling a Roman Saturnalia. Ring in the new year of 2020. Salute it with pyrotechnics and orgy.

Outside my mansion, half a dozen youths had shed flimsy clothes. As Mr Singh deflated the cab, these youths began to caper naked in a circle. They lashed out at one another with cheap leather whips, almost as if exertion might banish the chill of the night. Of course, they were shivering in ecstasy, not on account of the thermometer.

No pain, no pain. Delight. Delirium.

'The world's going to the dogs,' Mr Singh said to me. People probably said the same thing, century after century.

'What about food factories and fusion, though?' I asked him.

Unlimited food, clean power, desalinated water: such was the bonanza, so far. No longer was anyone starving in India or Africa.

Mr Singh was incensed.

'Mockymen have taken over, mark my words! Look at these young fools squandering themselves. Only to become dummies for Mockymen! My son, sir, my own son—!'

I dearly wished to be indoors, but I felt that I ought to sympathise.

'I'm sorry... So your son's become a host body? He still exists, Mr Singh. He's in a nirvana state. Perfect peace, perfect bliss.'

'That's what the Mockymen tell us! But no, Jogindar hasn't become a dummy... Not yet.'

'He probably won't in that case, will he? It's only a small percentage who do. Within a year he'll be immune to Bliss, right?'

Singh's son might feel numb for the rest of his life, as though all colour was monochrome and he was suffering from a permanent bad cold so that food was tasteless too. As if he had burnt up all his capacity for pleasure in one prolonged spasm, just as the roses had been burnt for a quick thrill.

In fact, many more young people avoided Bliss than used it. Users were those who would have indulged in something similar in the old days. Crack or Fraz or Hop. I could hardly point out the obvious shortcomings of Mr Singh's beloved son.

'You're a courier, aren't you?' the Sikh said bitterly. 'This house... You're rich. You condone our boys and girls using Bliss. Where else would dummies come from!'

I was aching to be inside, in calm and quiet. This accusation made me angry.

'Oh if only *I* could use Bliss!' I snapped at him. 'I merely know pain.'

Did he understand?

'Not a father's pain,' he said.

Beside the bonfire in the park an adolescent boy and girl had undressed. Hand in hand they stepped into the hot embers. They stroked one another. They began making love. Mind over body. Joy banishing harm to skin and flesh and lungs. The little flames would caress so pleasurably.

Just so long as they didn't stay in the flames for *too* long.

Resistance to injury was the commonest side effect of Bliss. Resilience and speedy repair, the cells of the body behaving like a foetus's once again. Seamless healing. This benefit would continue way beyond the year of euphoria, which would be an added inducement to users, if they thought that far ahead. If they ignored the fact that cancers were a minor side effect of the resilience; over-enthusiasm by cells. Consequently most dummy-bodies were very reliable and sprightly.

'It's disgusting,' snarled Singh. 'It's obscene.'

You could tell a dummy from an ordinary person by its strange speech and bizarre mannerisms, even if hair or a hat hid the skull-socket. Murders had been committed by people who felt the way Singh felt. Lynchings. So the Mockymen had insisted on the death penalty world-wide as punishment for assault on a dummy. BritGov had immediately agreed, being as adamant as most other governments about the benefits of the new order. In many foreign countries Mockymen were actually quite the rage—in a positive sense. They could roam unprotected by bodyguards.

'Filthy!'

Irritated, I paid Singh in soft Pounds rather than hard Euro credit, and climbed out quickly. Already he was inflating the skirt of the cab as if intent on knocking me aside. Squeezing the remote inside my pocket, I hurried past those flagellants to my front door.

I had not phoned from the Hyde Park Transit Station to discover whether Zanthia was at home. Nor did Zanthia ever phone home after a trip. Early on, we had agreed upon spontaneity. Domesticity was absurd.

She was dining by candlelight. As usual, there were two place settings.

Robert the Man was in attendance, in his full butler's gear. Black frock-coat, grey trousers, starched linen shirt with bow tie, white gloves. Milly the Maid was in her frilly costume, her bobbly blonde curls spiralling down from a lace cap. Although Milly was going on for forty, she could carry this image off to perfection. In the holo-arena on the podium Masai dancers were performing a ballet, a black *Swan Lake*. Such *jetés*, worthy of Nijinsky. Although diminished in scale, the dancers still looked ethereally tall, thus there seemed to be something astigmatic about the display.

Robert inclined his head in a slight bow. Milly curtseyed. Zanthia exclaimed, 'Barabbas!'

Zanthia was wearing her low-cut cream satin gown. A diamond necklace glittered against her lovely scarified milk-chocolate skin, jewels upon a patterned brocade of flesh.

Ritual elegance mattered deeply to Zanthia. Therefore I kissed her raised hand before my lips brushed against her cheek, notched with its tribal-style scars.

'How was it?' she asked.

I shrugged.

'Excruciating, as usual. I transited to Passion. And you're back from?'

'Melody. This morning.'

Melody, Passion, Wood, and Blue: those were the four worlds to which we couriers went, always carrying a box of goodies, and with the mind of a Mockyman as silent passenger in our brains.

The stars which those worlds orbited might be a dozen light years from Earth, or a thousand. Mere humans did not know the locations, though we could guess that Passion was the closest world in terms of distance. When the pod-ship arrived in Earth orbit six years ago, the small crew which awoke from hibernation consisted of mocky-lemurs—furry bipeds with big eyes. The same aliens comprised the personnel at the transit station on Passion.

Passion was merely a name of convenience. Likewise, Melody, Wood, and Blue. Whatever the native inhabitants called their worlds, or what those worlds looked like, we had no idea.

Us couriers transited to self-enclosed reception centres with no windows upon those worlds. The personnel with whom we had dealings were all mocky-aliens, alien dummies operated by the Mockymen—who might really be highly evolved spiders or crabs. Presumably those cryptic aliens were approximately humanoid. How else could they operate humanoid dummies?

So as to set up transit stations on Earth, the technology must needs be transported the slow way, in the pod-ship. That pod-ship must have travelled for decades, setting out soon after Earth's radio output first became detectable. Once the technology was in place: bingo, rapid transit from Earth to wherever. For us couriers. Who could never leave any of the four starworld transit stations, nor even look out of a window.

The lemurs' large eyes suggested passion to us. On Melody the voices of the natives—their bodies as smooth as flexible porcelain—sounded musical. In the reception centre on Wood, were many abstract carvings in red wood with yellow veins. On Blue the walls and floors and the lighting were blue, as if one was underwater.

Never could we find out more. The Mockymen's security system was impeccable. Our destinations were hermetically restricted.

'Excruciating,' said Zanthia, 'means like being tortured on a cross. Like being racked.' She smiled at Robert, at once glacial yet rapacious.

Robert promptly asked, 'Will you be dining, Master Barnabas?'

Only Zanthia called me by the nickname Barabbas. Our little joke. The bandit who escaped crucifixion; whereas I was crucified on every trip. As was Zanthia. As were all of us couriers.

Zanthia had been toying with a slice of rich white Russian pashka cake for dessert, studded with candied peel. An open bottle of Champagne stood in the chiller.

'What has your mother cooked?' I asked Robert, although I was hardly peckish after my ordeal.

Robert and Milly and his mother lived in the basement flat below. Robert and Milly were *treasures*, willing to enact this charade of old-fashioned butler and maid. The roles must afford them a deep sense of comfort and security.

'Poached salmon, sir, with steamed asparagus.'

'Bring me just a little, Robert.' Leave the rest as perk for yourself and family. Authentic food was part of our extravagant chic—compensation for our pains. If Robert and family were not in our employment, they might have had to be content with the output of the synthesising factories—nourishing and tasty though the stuff was.

'Will you be dressing first, sir?'

'Of course I shall.' So Robert remained for the moment.

'Zanthia dear,' I said, 'there are flagellants outside.'

She toyed with a knife. It was simply a hooked pronged cheese knife, true.

'Shall we invite them inside to perform for us?' she asked archly. 'See the new year in, in style?'

Milly was trying not to notice how Zanthia played with the knife.

My clothes hid my own scars: the plumed angel wings arching down my back as if erupting from my skin, about to unfurl, an effect which had been hard to achieve using mirrors.

I knew perfectly well that Zanthia despised immature amateur flagellants. Blissheads experienced no insightful pain. Bliss had the effect of amplifying pleasure exquisitely. Pain, it merely transmuted into bland euphoria.

Bliss crystals were a nano-mimetic drug, so called. Human understanding of nanotechnology was inadequate, but molecules of Bliss flooding the body obviously made cells resilient. Operated under licence from the Mockymen, the food factories worked on nanotech principles which eluded us. Mockymen mustn't ever go away.

'Shall we invite them in, Barabbas?' Zanthia was amusing herself at Milly's expense.

At times such as this, after trips, we might behave like a couple of vampires who employ vulnerable human servants. Usually we were impeccably polite, and we did pay very generously.

Upstairs in my dressing room, before stripping off my jump-suit I switched the screen on.

The view was of choppy grey ocean, and a giant research platform. Derricks and gantries and a helipad.

A well-bred Scotswoman's voice was saying, '... *The call of the minority nationalist party in the Scottish Parliament for full sovereignty and Scottish control over the resources of the Rockall Trough has brought a speedy response at Westminster. At Question Time this afternoon, Prime Minister Baxter derided the demand as "a quarrel about worms" and pointed out that Britain's alien associates established a transit station in London, not in Edinburgh...'*

Worms, worms.

Amazingly enough, the majority of all animal species on Earth are not insects, as people used to imagine. No, they are worms—little worms which live in the ocean depths buried in mud. Nematodes. Millions of species of nematodes. The World of Worms, that's Planet Earth from a statistical viewpoint—and at least as regards Britain's place in the scheme of things.

From a host of newly-discovered nematodes come unusual enzymes, of pharmacological value to the Mockymen. What nature has devised throughout billions of years of evolution is so much more prodigal and surprising than whatever biochemists—even superior alien ones—might try to build from scratch.

We have no idea what exotic drugs and elixirs the Mockymen make from such enzymes, or what use they put them to on their own worlds and on other worlds within their hegemony. I suppose Bliss is a drug which they first obtained out amongst the stars by similar means, maybe to replace some inferior version. Biology, it seems, is the power-science, the control-key.

In return for worms we gain fusion, food factories (even if we don't understand them), and speedier access to the solar system.

Quite a bargain. People like Singh must be mad. We were going down the drain, and now we aren't.

Not that marine worms are the whole of it! From Brasilia and Jakarta couriers carry samples of plants and butterflies from what still survives of the rain forests. Every country can yield its tithe of something alive, with some natural magic ingredient lurking in it, undreamed of by us but of use to Mockymen.

The really galling thing to the 'Human Patriots', so called, is that we were going down the drain amidst a bounty which we were dragging down the

drain along with us. We didn't know how to detect or use more than a fraction of this potential wealth enshrined in worms and beetles and weeds. We
still don't really know, and probably never will.

It's a colonial situation, bro. We're colonised. We never even see the faces
of the imperialists, only the faces of dummies.

Much that I should care.

After donning my dinner jacket, I fluffed out my afro and checked that
my skull-socket was not showing, in the shaven area up above my right ear.
Spruce as a lord, I descended.

My transit-nausea had mostly passed by the time Robert served coffee and
brandy, and I no longer felt so harrowed. The Masai were still dancing *Swan
Lake*. Zanthia dismissed Milly and Robert for the night. If our servants
wished, they could go and frolic in Trafalgar Square and sing *Auld Lang
Syne*; though they would not really care for the bedlam.

'Barabbas,' Zanthia said softly after a while, 'something happened.'

'Something *they* would like to know about?'

Meaning the Ministry. Zanthia's tone implied that she had not reported
this 'something' earlier today. At such a late hour on a New Year's Eve I did
not know whether or not to expect my regular phone call from the ministry
lackey.

'I have a fugitive inside me,' she whispered.

My first thought was that the agony of so many transits had finally
deranged Zanthia. The anguish was so different from the measured and
meaningful pain we had once imposed on ourselves to sculpt our bodies. She
had become deluded that her alien passenger had not been downloaded into
a dummy after transit, but still lurked inside her.

I thought of the Hyde Park Transit Station, our lucrative Calvary, and of
the transit station on Melody.

Whenever a courier's body transited from star to star he or she endured
sheer torment. The sensation of being torn apart was timeless. Maybe the
pangs were brief, yet it seemed that they would last for eternity; and because
of this, the torment was terrifying.

The passenger completely avoided these sensations. It felt no pain at all.
Which, of course, was the reason for us couriers.

Dummy-bodies occupied by Mockymen could certainly have transited—blanks, with an alien mind operating the puppet strings as the governing consciousness. But then the Mockyman would have experienced the excruciation personally. They had no intention of doing so.

Hyde Park was different from Melody or Passion, Wood or Blue. Those were insulated, closed off from their worlds, dedicated solely to the reception and dispatch of human couriers, and the upload and download of Mockymen.

Adjacent to those alien stations, there must be separate facilities for dispatching ivoryman-couriers or lemur-couriers to other worlds, and staffed by ordinary lemurs or ivorymen (and members of the other two races) who were not dummies. Facilities, too, for life-support of dummies—the alien versions of Blissheads—so that the Mockymen could have enough bodies to wear while they gallivanted around Melody or Passion.

At Hyde Park, everything was in the same cavernous space which had begun life as a subterranean car park. You would see the occasional ambulance with police escort turning from Park Lane to convey a new dummy into the depths. Apart from that, the transit station was inconspicuous. Because the complex was underground, BritGov avoided the ugliness of a big guarded security fence right in the heart of the capital. Taxis glided down into a blast-containment area. There was no need to check every vehicle and driver arriving, only those persons whose business led them deeper within, technicians and medical staff and couriers and Mockymen.

Before I had been operated on in the medical area to insert my skull-socket, as per Mockyman specifications, I had been shown the rows and rows of naked dummies attached to intravenous feeding equipment and vital signs monitors.

Nurses wearing sweaters under their whites sat at desks with computer terminals as if this place was the intensive care unit of some huge hospital during a plague of encephalitis lethargica which caused no visible physical harm but rendered its victims zombies. Calm, calm, it was there. Calm and cool as a morgue.

After I had seen the bodies, my escort from the Ministry showed me a transfer room. A young dummy-woman was wheeled in on her gurney-bed. A great walk-in wardrobe occupied one wall, stocking a whole range of male and female clothes and shoes and hats. A lady costumier presided. She was also in charge of drawers of personal effects, cash, credit cards, combs, pocket computers, whatever the well-dressed Mockyman or Mockywoman might need during its sojourn.

A courier entered. A Chinese Brit. I thought he looked yellow from his recent ordeal. He walked steadily enough. No need for him to undress, though he did take off his shoes. He lay down on a couch abutting the gurney. His head was close to the dummy's head.

The transfer doctor pulled down the connector on its mobile boom. Into the courier's head went a white plug, joined by a fat worm of flexible coaxial cable to a black plug. The black plug went into the young dummy-woman's head. Mockyman technology, all of this. Us peasants could at least be trusted to distinguish between black and white.

The courier shivered for about ten seconds. The dummy twitched. And then the young woman raised her hand. The doctor disconnected the pair. Without comment the woman sat up and looked around. She swung her bare feet down on to the floor. Now it was the costumier's turn to demonstrate the use of knickers and tights and bra and such, like some air hostess miming safety instructions.

The Mockyman had been here before. It dressed itself efficiently. Then it announced, 'Must go now to Ford-For-Oxes.'

To Oxford, for some mocky purpose.

In a transit arrival room, a short dark Welsh courier was about to depart. A Mockyman was already installed in him, inaccessible to the courier's own thoughts—just as the Mockyman would be oblivious to the courier's pain.

Wearing jeans and sweater, and with a black plastic case gripped tightly in one hand, the Welshman sat hunched, knees drawn up, upon the dispatch disc. In the disc underneath him were deep narrow indentations. These corresponded to short stalactites of steel jutting downward from the lid above.

Power hummed. Abruptly the lid slammed downward upon the dispatch disc.

The courier had already vanished, yet I imagined that I heard a distant scream as those blades entered the receptors.

The lid rose up again, slowly. There was no sprayed blood, squashed flesh, shattered bone on the disc. It was perfectly clean.

I couldn't be shown a courier actually arriving. Arrivals were always unpredictable. However, prior to arrival, the disc and its lid would be tight together. Suddenly the lid would fly upwards. The courier would be there, between disc and lid.

The experience was to become very familiar. It was as if my body was sucked into existence from out of all those holes in the disc. As if I was dragged from a hundred light years away through a sieve of knives.

On Melody and Passion, Wood and Blue, there were no non-dummy staff. Those worlds were like the Eastern Europe of years ago, their border posts very well policed. Mockymen would be the extinct Soviet Union, remote and bulwarked. And Earth? A banana republic. Source of worms and butterflies and plant-roots, which were so much more prized than any works of Plato or Mozart or Van Gogh.

How had a *fugitive* evaded the security?

Zanthia did not seem demented. She was smiling anticipatively. A little apprehensively. Seeking my collusion?

'Do you mean you didn't download? That isn't possible.'

'Oh I did download,' said Zanthia. 'But I had two passengers, you see, not one. The first was concealed beneath the second one. I still have the first one. Only the official one was sucked out.'

Schizophrenia, I thought to myself. Split personality. Her mind was fragmenting under the strain of the pain.

She laid a tiny black leathery pouch upon the table, and loosened the drawstring. Out onto the white linen tablecloth rolled such a jewel as I had never seen, the size of a quail's egg. Such iridescent facets of light. It made the diamonds of Zanthia's necklace seem trivial.

'On Melody one of the ivory dummies approached me. The ivoryman said he could plant himself inside me, using this.'

That jewel. Not a neural socket, but a jewel.

'Via my eyes, Barabbas. By us both staring into it.'

Had it not been for the splendid unearthly jewel I would have been sure that Zanthia was inventing all this. Or hallucinating.

'How can the optic nerve carry so much data?' I asked her.

'The ivoryman called this a quantum crystal. He persuaded me to stare into the jewel. I was seduced.'

'You don't mean *literally* so?'

She shook her head, its great frizz cut like the sarcophagus headpiece of an Egyptian queen, into which a mouse had munched a little tunnel at the bottom of which her socket was hidden.

According to Zanthia, the experience of accepting the fugitive had been quite without sensation. Just before transferring itself to Zanthia, the rogue Mockyman had injected his dummy with a delayed-action toxin. No trace of the poison would remain. The toxin would mimic a massive fatal stroke, or the ivoryman equivalent. A corpse would be found. Worn out.

'It would have been awkward for this fugitive,' I observed, 'if you had changed your mind at the very last moment.'

'I was captivated,' she confessed. 'After I looked in the jewel I couldn't help myself. Barabbas, he said that his mind would surface in me within a week or so if I don't transfer him to a dummy.'

Not by uploading her fugitive into a dummy in a transit station controlled by Mockymen. But illicitly. Not by using her skull-socket, but by means of the jewel.

How had she carried the jewel?

'Intimately,' she said.

The pouch and drawstring, intimately hidden.

'What is he a fugitive from?'

This, he had not confided.

Compared with Melody and other worlds, Earth must be a wild place where a fugitive could lose himself. He would be well advised to leave London, soonest, for some country where Mockymen were more the rage, though not the cause of rage.

What assets did he have? Knowledge, of course. Knowledge of unguessable value.

Was the theft of the quantum crystal his primary crime? Did he commit his offence on the same world where he contacted Zanthia by guile? Maybe the crystal had been of religious significance. There was no way to ask the creature within her. Not yet. He was submerged.

'I need an unregistered dummy, Barabbas. Look into the jewel first, though. It's fascinating.'

I sipped some brandy.

'Will *I* be seduced and captivated?'

'Look at one of the candles through the jewel. Think about me.'

I trusted Zanthia. Aside from our love, we were allied by the knife, by our proud scars, by the pains of transit which mocked what we had formerly endured to make an art of ourselves.

'Just look,' she urged. 'Hold it steady as a knife. Think of me.'

I was thinking about the possible consequences of abetting a crime against the aliens—if the Mockymen ever found out. Why should they find out, unless the fugitive raised some storm on our world instead of vanishing into anonymity? *Would* he want to hide himself lifelong, lying low? Would he try to manipulate, to carve out some influential niche for himself?

Suppose we were to tell the Ministry what had happened. Suppose we were to give them the jewel. If I were in their shoes, I would use it to upload Zanthia's fugitive into a spare dummy. Then they would have a prisoner to attempt to interrogate about the secrets of the stars, a captive Mockyman unrecorded by his own kind.

Four mocky-lemurs had come to Earth, the slow way, in the pod-ship to bring us transit technology. After all the agreements were signed and the technology was built, the Mockyman emissaries transferred from the lemur-dummies to human couriers. Then they transited back to the stars. They would not transit in the lemur-bodies because of the pain they would suffer as the primary minds in control of the bodies. The Mockymen insisted that the abandoned lemur-bodies must be euthanased and cremated. Mockymen did not like investigation, even of cast-off lemur-dummies.

If Zanthia co-operated with the Ministry, she would be locked up for the rest of her life to safeguard the secret. So would I be.

The jewel was much heavier than I expected. I held it to my eye.

No Short Cuts was the name of the private club in Kensington.

Bar, sauna, little swimming pool, around which we would show ourselves off to kindred spirits. I was there, I was there. I was beholding Zanthia for the very first time, splendid sublime Zanthia wearing only a bikini brief and her scars. Total memory, perfect recall: that's what this was!

I could see each cicatrice upon her breasts. I could smell the mild chlorine of the pool. I could hear a Brandenburg Concerto playing softly through the speakers.

Soon, she would be captivated by the angel graven on my flesh. Soon, I would be learning that Zanthia was a freelance escort.

Zanthia was as upmarket as escorts can be, exotic, almost too intimidating to lay a finger upon because of the decoration of her flesh. What a shiver of excitement for Japanese businessmen. In this dilapidated land of ours, gateway to troubled Europe, business still struggled on. Our whole world was disfigured by famines and droughts and endless minor wars triggered by climate change and scarcities. Yet Zanthia had scarred herself willingly, wondrously, as had I. Our scars were the emblems of self-control, enhancement of ourselves, ownership of ourselves—in a way that no one else could ever presume to exercise, until the Mockymen came.

And she would soon be learning that I worked as a bodyguard to the Minister of the Environment, Lady Astley, always keeping my angel hidden from vulgar eyes though always feeling myself to be protected by its wings. Who could ever shoot me in the back?

It was not superstition which made me carve my flesh, but artistic courage. Soon, we would rhapsodise together, Zanthia and myself. The tilt of her chin, her fabulous Egyptian hair, her liquid eyes, her scars, the whiff of chlorine, the music of Bach . . .

'I'm there,' I gasped. *'No Short Cuts.'*

I made myself lay the jewel down upon the table. She was right. Looking into the jewel was ravishing. To be exactly as one had been seemed so *innocent*, never mind what shit the world had been in six years ago, just before the pod-ship arrived—to change our lives.

The aliens insisted that the sites for transit stations should be right in the hearts of the biggest cities. In cities, the Bliss that the aliens brought would soon produce a large enough harvest of dummies as hosts. I suppose that the sites were symbolic too. Mockymen would not come and go from some place in the middle of nowhere. Governments complied. Governments began recruiting couriers who could tolerate pain or even enjoy pain. BritGov would be paying lavishly per trip. Yet the pain of transit would be utterly different in kind from what I had submitted myself to, to acquire my angel. And always there was the fear: what if on some occasion transit failed? What if the lid and the base clapped together, skewering and squashing the courier? Never! Impossible, said the Mockymen.

'Zanthia,' I asked, 'do you suppose your fugitive was telling you the truth about him surfacing spontaneously?'

She pursed her lips, so fully fleshed. I always thought of some magenta orchid.

'In case I try to cheat him and keep the jewel?'

'When you transfer him to a dummy, how can he insist on you returning the jewel? He can hardly complain to the authorities.'

'I feel a strong compulsion,' she said. 'I must restore the jewel to its owner.'

'Is that *him*, surfacing inside you already? Pushing up a mental periscope?'

'Certainly not.' She sounded positive.

'So we need to find an unregistered dummy within a week.'

Unsurprisingly, a number of Blissheads succumbed to dummydom away from the bosoms of their family, in squats or cardboard cities amongst dubious friends. Despite BritGov's best efforts there was a black market in fresh dummies, for illicit organ transplants. Given contacts and cash and a few days' grace, that's how we could get hold of a fresh young dummy.

'Failing all else,' I said, 'we don't have to look *too* far from home.'

'No, we couldn't possibly do that—'

'The possibility must have been in the back of your mind.'

Before she could reply, chimes interrupted the music. A logo invaded *Swan Lake*: a green star surmounted by the initials of the Ministry. MAL. A chummy-sounding acronym. Meet my big brother, Mal. In French the word means evil, but the French equivalent of MAL is MRE, *Ministère des Relations Extraterrestres*.

The routine debriefing never happened immediately after a trip, when it was understood that we would be rather disoriented and nauseated. Give the courier time to get home and shower and have a stiff drink. Besides, debriefings rarely yielded anything unusual.

The mansion's sensors knew that we were in the dining room which lacked a phone or phonescreen. Consequently, the house-system was interrupting the TV. Very expensive and smart system, ours, very new. Couriers deserved no less.

We had opted against visual intrusion in our dining room. The holo-arena incorporated no cameras to show us to our caller. There was no need to hide the jewel away.

'Accept Call—'

The icon swelled. A face replaced the star. A familiar glisteny oval face, retro horn-rimmed spectacles, oily receding hair. Danvers was his name. He was going on for fifty. Probably he was a bit of a failure, who kept his job by working unsociable hours.

He peered, in vain. 'Mr Mason?'

'Here I am, Mr Danvers. All ears.'

'Anything special to report?'

The usual question. The usual answer:

'Nothing different.' No glimpses of the world of Passion. No encounters with lemurs who were not dummies, every last one of them.

'Except,' I added, 'I feel a bit ragged after this trip. I can't face another for at least a fortnight. Miz Wilde, neither. We might go to the Cotswolds for a break.'

Danvers became wistful. 'Ah, the Cotswolds. I can remember snow there when I was a boy. Tonight it's chilly enough for snow outside. Or a frost, if the sky stays clear.'

'We shan't be taking any fur coats with us.'

'What made you so ragged this trip, Mr Mason? Can you put a finger on it?'

Maybe he was more acute than I gave him credit for.

'It's cumulative,' I said brusquely.

'Does Miz Wilde feel this cumulative effect too? She mentioned nothing about it, earlier.'

'It isn't any big deal, Mr Danvers. Have *you* ever been tortured at regular intervals? Felt yourself being torn apart?'

What could he say to that?

What he did say was: 'I want you both to have a full medical before your next trip. Will you call me to fix a time to fit in with your Cotswold plans?'

'Yes, yes. Even though it isn't necessary. Happy New Year to you, Mr Danvers. End Call.'

Danvers' face disintegrated amongst the tall black dancers.

I turned to Zanthia. 'This compulsion you feel—can you remember everything that happened between you and the fugitive?'

She thought for a while, then said, 'If I've forgotten something, I wouldn't know what it is, would I?'

'Have you tried looking into the jewel and concentrating on the Mockyman?'

She had not.

'Why don't you look in it, then?' I rolled the jewel towards her.

'I'm in a pearly room. The Ivoryman's showing me . . . How it dazzles . . .'

Abruptly she shrieked. Her thrashing hand knocked over her brandy glass. The jewel flew along the table. She clawed at the cloth, toppling both candlesticks. Great flimsy shadows capered as if ghosts of the dancing Masai had escaped into the room. Two tumbled candles stayed alight, beginning to char the linen. Screaming, Zanthia flailed at the air.

'Lights On!' I shouted. The electric chandelier blossomed brilliantly. I squashed the candleflames with my palms, a very minor pain.

Zanthia had stuck the edge of her hand in her mouth, gagging herself.

She rocked to and fro in intense concentration before finally she relaxed, panting.

'I felt him stirring. He was rising up in me—'

Her cries had not brought Robert. Down in the basement, maybe he had not heard.

If our servants did hear something, they might imagine we were up to tricks with razor-sharp knives. In reality, screaming is no part of body-art. Nor had we scarred ourselves physically for quite a few years. When Zanthia and I first met at *No Short Cuts* we were already perfect and complete. All subsequent scars had been mental, due to transit and the torment of disintegration and reintegration.

'He was stirring . . .'

Did she blame me because I had suggested using the jewel to retrieve full memory about the fugitive?

She still had not remembered everything. Yet she had tasted the flavour of the alien in her. Devious. Ingenious. Abstruse.

'He was stirring. Like childbirth starting. The first contractions . . . If I go to sleep tonight with him in me—!'

Like childbirth . . . ? 'I never knew—!' The exclamation had burst from me before I could quench it.

She looked daggers for a moment.

Zanthia must have given birth to a child as a gawky young teenager growing up in poverty, before her beauty became exceptional! I knew so little about that part of her life. We scarcely ever discussed the years when we had been growing up. Those were irrelevant to us.

My own years in the army were of no real meaning, either. I had had two basic choices: the perpetration of disorder, or its suppression. I had improved myself to such a degree since then. We both had, together.

But a child . . . Where *was* her child now? Growing up in an orphanage? Adopted by strangers? Low-sperm count nowadays meant that abandoned children had a fair chance of finding homes. Very likely that was why Robert and Milly were childless—low sperm count.

Zanthia whispered, 'It died. The cord strangled it. They cut me open, but it was born blue.'

It, it, it. Girl or boy, she would not say. I would not ask.

'It would have had brain damage. They let it die after they cut me.'

The first cut of the knife . . . Later cuts had been by choice. Not imposed upon her, but freely sought.

'They tied my tubes,' she said. 'Just as well.'

So she had been freed by the knife to become the beautiful escort I had met at *No Short Cuts*, rather than a single mother bringing up a brat in a slum—and freed to be here now, a rich courier.

Her disclosure had introduced a note of ruthlessness which I could hardly oppose.

'Robert's nephew,' said Zanthia. 'Tonight. It has to be tonight! There's no time to find another dummy. Not now.'

Robert and Milly and Mrs Johnson were such treasures, as the saying goes. Until now I had never needed to confront them with their family secret, which I had unearthed long ago thanks to my being formerly in security work.

Robert's sister Joan was married to a certain Alex Corby. Alex was one of the long-term unemployed, living on welfare in South London on a grim estate between Kennington and Brixton, beyond the range of gentrification which had seen the south side of the river become fashionable for a while. Alex and Joan had an only son, Billy. Billy became one of the early Blissheads. The alien drug was freely circulating on such estates as his, fully condoned by BritGov, so much less trouble-provoking than Crack or Fraz or Hop.

After a year's use, Billy became a dummy.

The Corbys did not register him. They could not bear for him to be carted off by BritGov to Hyde Park to be fitted with a neural socket and be a body for Mockymen to use. And not to see him again—unless by chance, on a street, a puppet used by an alien.

In spite of the new law, families of other unlucky Blissheads often felt similarly. Usually the problems of coping with a dummy soon became too much for them.

How expensive to hide Billy at home. Bootleg medical equipment to keep him ticking over in his nirvana state. Bribes to the local estate boss. Robert and Milly and Mrs Johnson paid the bills for this by serving us.

'It'll be a weight off their backs,' argued Zanthia. 'Robert and Milly must be so sick of it all by now! Billy's mother is the one who's obsessed. We'll tell her—that the jewel will awaken her boy, the way he once was.'

'And when it doesn't?'

Zanthia sounded on the edge of hysteria. 'You still have your gun, Barabbas.'

My Austrian-made Glock 9-millimeter, frame and receiver of light strong polymer, with its inbuilt silencer, and its internal hammer assembly ensuring that it could be carried safely with a round already chambered, ready for instant firing.

'If they don't agree,' she went on, 'it only takes a tip-off to the Ministry to have Billy Corby picked up. Then they've lost him in any case.'

We had talked and acted ruthlessly on other occasions—because of the pain of transit; because of our position in the world, so much more prosperous and exalted than we had ever expected. But this was real.

'It's all very well to talk about intimidating them, but we'll be putting ourselves into their power.'

'We'll *lie*, Barabbas. We'll say this is special secret work. The Ministry have told us to do this.'

'Do it to a dummy hidden on a lawless estate?'

'We'll make them scared of prison, or worse! Anyway, aren't Robert and Milly loyal to us?'

She rose to tug the brass knob on the wall. Down in the basement a bell would jangle. This was so much more gracious than summoning Robert electronically.

Robert's eyes were always a bit bulgy.

Slim moustache. Chestnut kiss-curl across his brow. Watery blue eyes. An amenable open face.

He had put on a purple paisley dressing gown over his pyjamas. Early to bed, eh? And no time to resume his frockcoat or gloves. A green cravat did duty for a bow-tie.

He must have supposed we had called him to deal with the stained, scorched linen. Instead, I invited him to sit down and share a brandy. In prelude to the new year, no doubt.

'Cheers, Robert,' I toasted him. 'Please listen carefully. We know about Billy Corby...'

Our butler's eyes had always bulged a bit.

'For the past five years,' Robert said finally, 'we put up with your elegant menace, and you knew all along.'

'Believe me,' I assured him, 'if *you* had to endure torment each time you do your job—'

'Maybe we do! You're both paid a fortune every time you turn a trick.' He was verging on vulgarity, implying that we were highly-paid whores of some sort rather than valued agents of BritGov. I suppose he was upset.

'You're only offering us two hundred thousand to sell Billy . . .'

This was the bargain I proposed. Not too exorbitant, so as not to trigger fantasies of extracting more.

'Ministry money,' he mused. He sniffed the air—brandy fumes, spent candle smoke—as if testing for truth. 'For an unsupervised experiment, *sir*? You must think I'm simple.'

'On the contrary, to have carried out your charade of butler and maid so believably—'

'Charade!' Robert drained his glass and set it down with such a thump. 'After this, there won't be a need to carry on pretending. But you see, my brother-in-law's the real problem. Alex was all washed up long ago. He's still clinging to one hope for the future—his son, even though that's stupid. If Billy even gets a bed sore Alex is vile to Joan. She's so scared. She can't tell the government about Billy because Alex would kill her. Alex is the problem, do you understand what I'm saying, Master Barnabas?'

Robert was at the wheel of the Mercedes, alongside me. Zanthia fretted in the back.

We had avoided such obvious bottlenecks as Trafalgar Square or Piccadilly. Wherever there was a pub, a mass of drinkers spilled from it like human algae in fermented bloom. Threading our way down to the Thames took a while. We would be transacting our business with Alex around midnight, when the big official firework display would explode over London. Bang, bang, bang.

I was very tired.

Before bringing the Merc round from its garage in the mews—which were the stables of an earlier era—Robert had put on cord trousers, a pull-over and an anorak. His chauffeur's uniform with peaked cap might look seriously out of place on the estate. I had donned a long cream raincoat with big lapels over my dinner jacket. Zanthia had draped herself in a black velvet cloak with scarlet lining. Robert told Milly that we were going to an all-night casino, a story which hardly squared with his attire.

How out-of-place would our Merc look? It ought to breed respect! We would seem like a visiting crime-boss and gorgeous moll and bodyguard.

I was being incited to kill a man, something I had never done before. Seriously wounded, yes, but not killed—in spite of my stint in the army, in spite of security work. A unit of the Tartan Army had tried to assassinate Lady Astley, and I had fired to kill, but the buggers had been wearing kevlar vests.

Was I to be my servant's gunman?

It still seemed plausible to me that we could immobilise Alex Corby, tie him up at gunpoint, do what we must with Billy, then bring his mother away with us. We would give Joan Corby sanctuary in the basement flat in Middlesex Square until we could find somewhere for her to live far away from Alex.

I still did not believe I could bring myself to shoot Alex. As far as the police were concerned, unsolved killings might not be rare on the estates, but the local boss would pay attention. I might end up paying *him*. Blackmail, or else betrayal. How *could* I kill someone in cold blood?

Left alive, Alex Corby might seek revenge—unless he simply plunged into despair or lunacy. Could I reasonably hope for that?

Ultimately, what price the death of a worthless sad mad man compared with the hardship of transiting agonisingly to the stars (and seeing next to nothing there) and meeting aliens, who were all only Mockymen (although Mockymen must be the strangest and cleverest aliens of all) . . . ?

Failure tonight could mean that the alien took Zanthia as its dummy. Behind me, she uttered a noise somewhere between a moan and a low growl. It was almost as if we were driving her to some hospital to give birth.

As we crossed over Lambeth Bridge, the Houses of Parliament were a radiant sight. In another half an hour the clock tower would be on screen everywhere.

The sprawling maze of housing was almost a century old. Many streetlamps were broken. Most buildings were double maisonettes, two-storey flats stacked upon one another, of yellow brick with little balconies. Quite a few were boarded up. Massive metal shutters made those look like little moth-balled battleships. Defiantly and bizarrely, some dwellings boasted flouncy lace curtains at the windows, houseproud amidst the dismal squalor. Tiles had been stripped from a few roofs as if a giant maniac had been determined to break in, to lift out the inhabitants and eat them.

How far Zanthia and I had transcended similar circumstances. Thanks to courier work we had become aristocrats. Actually, our scars had made us secret aristocrats before the aliens ever came.

Clapped-out cars and vans and derelicts shared kerb space with the occasional smart BMW or Audi which must have been under protection—and might even be stolen. Did the ordinary police ever dare patrol here?

As we turned this way and that through the estate, a pack of kids took short-cuts to track us, heading between buildings and reappearing along our route. Maybe there were several wolfpacks of children, despite how late it was. No older teenagers were roaming about. Better things to do on New Year's Eve? Rave it up in Trafalgar Square? Or go out burgling in some other borough while people were away from home at pubs or New Year's Eve parties?

The teenagers would not target the really gentrified areas. The rich had defences; the poor preyed on the poor.

How soon would it be until the benefits of alien trade—marine worms and botanical specimens and whatever else in exchange for know-how—would cascade down through the whole of society (as Prime Minister Baxter had put it so ringingly), transforming such dereliction as this into paradise?

In the meantime the sons and daughters of dereliction could enjoy a year of Bliss, if they so chose.

Robert stopped the car outside one of the double-maisonettes. The lower one was completely forsaken. Sheets of steel hid its windows. Concrete blocks walled up its doorway.

'Upstairs—' Robert was either informing me or ordering me.

Joan Corby was a drab plump pasty woman. A quilted dressing gown was wrapped round her. Fear lurked in her eyes. She gaped in bewilderment at splendid Zanthia and myself.

'Robert . . . Who are—oh, are these your—?'

'Who's there?'—came a call from the lounge, where a screen was churning out noises of festive Scottish dancing, the merry overture to the death of the old year and the birth of the new.

'*Who is it, Joany?*' The man sounded drunk.

Alex Corby had not bothered to come to the door. They must not have felt too vulnerable to mysterious late-night callers. Even so, Joan's husband must be a shit.

Robert whispered to his sister. 'We've come to sort things out, Joan. Sort them out, do you know what I mean?'

The lounge was so cramped compared with any room in the mansion in Middlesex Square. Tatty three-piece suite. A trio of china ducks on the wall might have been there since the middle of last century. Lads and lasses in kilts on the screen were dancing some reel. Alex Corby, in old jeans and checked shirt, nursed a can of lager, a bloated lolling man.

He eyed us, non-plused.

'Bit early for first-footing, in'it? You're s'posed to come after midnight. With some coal in your pocket.' He chortled. 'You know that, eh? Coal for luck? You two don't need coal. Shake your hand'll do fine.' He struggled up but he did not offer his hand.

'We came to see Billy,' said Robert.

Alex blanched.

'You've *told!* You're not going up there, not bloody tonight. Next bloody year Billy's going to wake up from nerve-ana.' He made nirvana sound like some disease of the nervous system.

The scene on screen had shifted to a picture of Big Ben, the minute hand of the clock creeping towards midnight.

'We can wake your Billy up,' promised Zanthia. 'Midnight is magic time.'

She must have been half out of her mind with worry.

Robert said to his brother-in-law, 'Billy belongs to Master Barnabas and Madam Zanthia. They paid for him. Now they've come to collect.' Robert was deliberately provoking Alex, winding him up. I gripped the Glock in my raincoat pocket.

'Bloody Master and Madam!' Maybe Alex was drunkenly quoting Robert's own words from some previous occasion. 'You want him for a dummy, that's why you're here!'

He blundered towards me. So I did pull out the Glock. Tossing the lager can aside, Alex grappled with me, boozy-breathed.

Maybe it was Alex who caused the gun to fire. I like to think so.

When he collapsed backwards over an armchair, Joan shrieked. At that very moment, outside, down below, the Merc also shrieked piercingly—and a kid squealed in the night. The Merc had electrified itself (non-lethally, of course) because fingers had tried to tamper. Robert darted to the window to part the curtains. He quickly abandoned his inspection. Those kids must have fled. Massed voices began singing *Auld Lang Syne.*

Joan seemed to feel she was obliged to sob. Robert hugged her. Of course Joan was shocked—far worse than that kid had been. I was shivering.

Zanthia was breathing deeply, forcibly, as I imagined a woman in labour would.

'I'll phone the boss tomorrow,' Robert told his sister. 'I'll let him know about the body. He'll arrange for disposal. Master Barnabas here will see there's credit where credit's due. You'll stay with us, Joan, until we can all move out together. Somewhere a bit better than this.'

'Billy'll come with us?'

'We'll see . . .'

'*Upstairs,*' urged Zanthia.

Billy lay naked, his lower half modestly veiled by a thin cotton sheet. His eyes were open, as were all unused dummies' eyes. Lachrymal lubricant seeped from pipettes. His cheeks gleamed from leakage. Occasionally, automatically, he would blink. The intravenous feeding equipment towered over him, tube in his arm.

The room smelled of urine. Under the sheet he must be wearing a big nappy. Jars of ointments and creams and bottles of aromatherapy oils crowded a shelf. Joan must have given her son's body amateur physio every day. He looked in reasonable condition, not like something pulled out of the Thames after a week. He actually had a bit of a tan. An infra-red lamp was the reason for that. What servitude Joan had endured for years. Despite all her ministrations, Billy must have lost a lot of muscle tone in the course of five years.

Robert held his sister's shoulders to comfort her but also to keep her from lurching forward.

Zanthia took the pouch from the pocket of her cloak, removed the jewel, and leaned over Billy to view him eye to eye.

Billy stirred. He blinked rapidly. His hand rose to sweep the pipettes aside. I pulled the feeding tube away.

With great difficulty, and with my help, he sat up. He was really feeble. The effort seemed to exhaust him.

'Billy?' Joan's voice was like the squeak of some trembling baby animal.

'My... mother. Mother. Mine—'

The Mockyman must be making a clever guess, unless he had been able to trawl memories out of Billy's nirvana state. We always presumed that language knowledge came with the body a Mockyman adopted, rather than that they boned up beforehand.

The Mockyman saw in this bedroom: Zanthia, whom he already knew. She was standing back, looking so relieved. Myself, who must be her mate or her brother or whatever, on account of skin colour. And Robert. The fraught shabby white woman must surely be bloodkin. A fair guess.

Distant bangs: the sounds of big rockets exploding...

'Mother,' the dummy said. He must be surprised at how frail he felt, contrary to expectations.

Joan wept.

Robert nodded for me to come close.

'Master Barnabas,' he muttered, 'maybe you should shoot it now?'

Dispose of the Mockyman—and keep the jewel? Face the death penalty, if this was ever found out?

The Mockyman stared at Zanthia. 'Give. Crystal. Into hand.' As though he would draw strength from it. 'Give.'

Two strides took Zanthia to the bedside. She thrust the jewel into his open palm, which closed up tightly.

Such will power. Us couriers knew about will power.

I said to Robert, 'We don't need to kill him. Just leave him here.' Enfeebled, in the middle of this predatory estate. With the local boss due to be tipped off. The boss would arrange. Oh this might cause me expense. The boss would keep his lip buttoned tight if one of his own men was the executioner. It would be easiest for the boss if he simply torched the house.

'That's all we need to do.'

Robert nodded, conceding. Billy was too weak to go anywhere without weeks of recuperation and exercise.

'Billy's body isn't Billy's any more,' Robert assured his sister. 'You're free.' He spoke as if this had been his own plan from the beginning.

'But he's my Billy!'

'No, Joan. Not any longer.' Robert patted her. 'You've come through. You don't have no more duties. You're out of this prison.'

'Bob,' she whimpered, 'what shall I do now?'

'It's a new year, so it's a new life, Joan.' Robert eyed Zanthia dispassionately. 'By the way, Madam, Happy New Year.'

'Robert, I'm sorry about our—what was it?—elegant menace—'

'If it made me and Milly hate you? That's a very special admission on your part.'

'You're both so talented. So versatile!'

'That relied on me and Milly being opaque to you, so to speak. We shouldn't have personal problems—like a dummy hidden in the cupboard. You knew all along. That's unforgivable.'

'It turned out beneficially. For all of us!'

More sharp bangs sounded, far away, as if a gun battle was in progress.

'Is there war?' asked the naked Mockyman, the sheet still over his loins and legs. 'Who fights?'

How much did it know about its situation? Did he who had ensnared Zanthia deserve much sympathy?

It was then that I realised how dangerous it could be to leave the jewel behind.

The quantum crystal comes into the possession of the boss. He wants to make money out of it, but he's only a small-time crook. What an exotic gem it is, quite out of his league. Someone blabs, someone snitches. The police get wind. Special Branch are involved.

After a while, BritGov have the jewel. Two and two are put together. The security services are on to Zanthia and me—with an offer we cannot refuse.

For here is the key to penetrating Mockyman security. Using the jewel I will stow away inside Zanthia—if human beings can use the jewel, the way the fugitive did, to submerge.

With a mockyman as passenger and the jewel hidden intimately once again, Zanthia transits from Hyde Park to Passion, say. It may take a dozen trips before there is an opportunity—to eyeball for a few vital moments a lemur dummy, vacated by a Mockyman, left briefly unattended. Not everything is perfect there, if the fugitive made it through.

I am transferred.

Later, I arise. I slip out of the human-containment area, through into lemur-land. Three moons are in the sky, perhaps. Maybe two dim suns. I will seem to be a mocky-lemur. How long have the Mockymen held sway over the lemurs? Fifty years? A thousand? Is there a resistance movement, equivalent to the impotent Human Patriots? I make contact. We collude. With their help I am able to return, full of information. Maybe the quantum crystal can be replicated.

'You watch too many old vids,' said Zanthia. 'All those spies sneaking through that Berlin Wall. No government would dare offend the Mockymen by trying a trick like this.'

'Somebody in Intelligence might. Might seem like a neat idea.'

She shook her head. 'You're fantasising. The world's different now. All that sort of spunk's gone. Collaboration's the meal ticket.'

'Intelligence people can go out of control, you know.'

'Barabbas,' she said tightly, 'we're a third world planet now. Third world from the sun. Third fucking world!'

'Do you want to risk finding out to the contrary? You fulfilled your compulsion,' I told her. 'You gave the jewel back.'

She did not oppose me as I approached mocky-Billy, although she was trembling and there were beads of sweat on her brocaded skin. Mocky-Billy had lolled back again.

'Now I remove it. Me, not you.'

I prised.

Mocky-Billy tried to clench his fist, but the enfeebled fingers were no match for mine.

As we drove back over Lambeth Bridge, from midstream outside the Houses of Parliament one of the fire-fighting boats was spraying plumes of floodlit water high into the air. I was keeping myself awake by squeezing the jewel in my hand to hurt myself. In the back, her arm hugging Joan, Zanthia was reassuring her. Joan would barely notice her comforter's scars in the darkness.

'Stop here, will you?' I asked Robert.

He did so. We were half way across. A car sped past, full of young men. A motorbike roared in the other direction, then no other traffic was in sight. I got out and went to the parapet. Upstream, streetlamps burned along Millbank and the Albert Embankment. Between, was the wide oily darkness of the Thames.

I threw the jewel as far as I could into the water.

When I climbed back into the Merc, I realised that it was not Joan who was sobbing softly in the back. It was Zanthia.

The Jew of Linz

I N THE EARLY YEARS OF THE 20TH CENTURY ADOLF HITLER AND
Ludwig Wittgenstein attended the same school in Linz, Austria, though
Wittgenstein was two years ahead in class. On the dustcover of *The Jew of
Linz* is a school photo highlighting both boys within touching (or
punching) distance of each other; yet hitherto historians have been blind to
the awesome consequences of this schoolboy proximity, not least of which
was the Holocaust. Australian philosophy postgraduate Cornish is very
persuasive that this encounter is central to understanding major aspects of
the twentieth century. A hypothesis, true, but the circumstantial evidence is
great.

A racially Jewish (though nominally Catholic) homosexual with a truss,
son of one of the richest assimilated families in the Austro-Hungarian
Empire, patrons of the arts, totally well-connected, him with his outspoken
talk of princesses and servants—and uncultivated, provincial Adolf: what
could these two possibly have in common, even at the Realschule in Linz?
Well, for one thing, philosophy. Not many twentieth-century politicians
have been able to quote pages of Schopenhauer by heart, but Hitler could,
and Schopenhauer's concept of Will was crucial to Hitler's thinking. With
roots in Indian (ahem, Aryan) thought, this is also the central influence on
the whole of Wittgenstein's own philosophy of 'no-ownership' of Mind,
arising from a quasi-mystical revelation Wittgenstein experienced as a
schoolboy.

The individual Self is an illusion. A person owns the thinking process
but not the thoughts which articulate themselves through him. Instead,

each person is an inlet to the same shared universal mind. Rather than thought giving rise to words, the reverse is the case: language uses human instruments as the vehicle for its own expression, the Proposition (in Wittgenstein's terms) speaking through the mouth of the person. This is very much the stance of contemporary consciousness maven Daniel Dennett, who banishes any Cartesian switchboard operator, any autonomous central self, from the brain. Language generates thought.

Climactic enlightenment consists in apprehending this no-ownership, thus gaining access to the common mind, an empowering fusion with the World/Divine Mind; which is why Hitler's idol Wagner, deeply influenced by Schopenhauer, has both Tristan and Isolde sing together, 'selbst dann bin ich die Welt' ('then I myself am the world'), which anticipatorily sets to music proposition 5.63 of the *Tractatus Logico-Philosophicus*.

Music is another close Hitler-Wittgenstein Link. Which two other Linz schoolboys regularly went to the opera? Hitler knew the libretto of *Lohengrin* by heart; Wittgenstein likewise with *Die Meistersinger*. Wagner's anti-Semitic wife Cosima hated the name Wittgenstein because her blood-father Franz Liszt had an adulterous liaison with Princess Carolyne Wittgenstein, of Jewish ancestry and related to Ludwig's family who adopted the Wittgenstein name.

And by the way ('What's in a name?' we might say!), the saviour of St. Petersburg by a sneaky ploy from Hitler's other idol, Napoleon, was none other than Prince Ludwig Adolf Wittgenstein, which may explain why Hitler's orders for Operation Barbarossa included that Leningrad should be razed to the ground as a permanent witness—except that Wittgenstein the philosopher was to prove instrumental in thwarting this.

Art is another link. The Wittgensteins grandly financed the 'decadent' Vienna Secession movement (and Klimt painted Wittgenstein's sister) while Hitler was prowling Ringstrasse nursing frustrated artistic ambitions— although he gained access to the co-founder of the movement thanks to an introduction from a mysterious 'friend in Linz'. *Mein Kampf* alludes to an unnamed Jewish schoolboy of Linz who first fired Hitler with anti-Semitism. Hitler especially assails rich Jews-in-Christian-Camouflage, and his first speech after taking over Austria, given in Linz, wished that 'some of our international seekers after truth whom we know so well' could be present to witness his triumph. Assuming that Hitler wasn't simply ranting, the one candidate for this category is Wittgenstein, by then in Cambridge. Although Cornish doesn't draw the inference, is it too far-fetched to suggest that maybe young princely Ludwig, who uniquely shared so many philosophical, artistic, and musical interests with Adolf, might have made a homosexual overture at school to the younger 'pauper' lad?

The *Tractatus* can be viewed as a theoretical book of spells serving through logic to apprehend Higher Truth. Hitler adopted the practical course: suspension of thought, act of Will, the imposition of words and thoughts upon the mass-mind in a quasi-magical but perverted fashion. The perversion consists in the belief that different races have different mass-minds, that there's a superior Aryan mass-mind and a degenerate Jewish mass-mind. As to the magical aspect, forget about invocation of demons and witchcraft; even set to one side the demonstrable links between Wittgenstein and Madame Blavatsky and the Theosophists. Far from being a scientific positivist opposed to the possibility of magic, in his *Remarks on Frazer's Golden Bough*, Wittgenstein 'defended an account of magic and thought it to reflect something very deep in human beings connected with the nature of representation', in Cornish's words. Exactly so with Schopenhauer (himself quoting Paracelsus): magical mumbo-jumbo serves to focus the will—whereby a particular proposition will impose itself upon individuals via the common mind. Hence Hitler's 'sorcery', his discovery of 'the key to history' avowedly made as a schoolboy in Linz. Hence the orchestrated panoply of the Nuremburg Rallies; hence Nazi ceremonies at Wewelsburg Castle. The prolonged German Hitlerian spasm links up perversely with the central philosophical problem of the nature of consciousness.

Yet Wittgenstein is not merely the loathed theoretical counterpart and flip side of Hitler. At Cambridge Wittgenstein was beavering away to combat the psychopathic Führer in the most practical political way he perceived. Why, at the height of the Stalinist terror, did Lenin's old alma mater offer Wittgenstein its Chair of Philosophy, unless he had performed signal service for the Soviet Union? Why else but because, as Cornish demonstrates very plausibly, Wittgenstein was the founder and presiding genius of the homosexual communist Cambridge spy ring, himself recruiting Philby, Burgess, Maclean *et al.*, alone possessing the almost magical charisma to carry this off—not to mention greatly influencing Alan Turing in his development of the Enigma decoder. Turing duly brought classified materials back to Cambridge to discuss with Wittgenstein and, via the spy ring, decryptions of German army plans reached the Soviet defenders of Leningrad faster than they reached the German field commanders.

The ghastly irony is that the assimilated Wittgenstein, who so focused

Hitler's envy and hatred as to lead to the Final Solution, once declared that his philosophy was 100 percent Jewish (all that Rabbinical analysis of words), but actually it was the diametrical opposite and very Aryan indeed, since alone among the major theistic religions Judaism rules out any kind of mystical union of Godhead with Man as surely as it bans mediumistic means of whatever sort for attempting this or for focusing the universal will to attain mastery over the world—the Golem of Prague, created *in extremis* to defend Jews from pogrom, being the legendary exception. Out of Linz came the greatest pogrom the world has ever seen, yet also the espionage tools to defeat its initiator, albeit too late for millions of victims.

The Big Buy

WELL, FRIENDS, YOU ALL KNOW HOW IT HAPPENED. BUT SINCE it's the most important thing that ever happened to the world, I guess it can bear one more retelling!

Three weeks after the aliens put their big ship down in the middle of the Simpson Desert, a couple of hundred miles south of Alice Springs, the world had got its trade fair assembled as requested. None too easy at such short notice, way out in the Australian Outback! But our aliens—chitinous, gem-encrusted, exoskeletal critturs that they were—happened to favour very hot and dry conditions. They weren't about to put themselves out unduly. It was a buyers' market, you'll recall.

But what were they about to buy? And more important for the whole future of the Earth, what were they prepared to go on buying? They would install their robot credit bank and matter transmitter mail order satellite in geosynch orbit if we came up with a good long-term deal, but that was the whole trouble—their technology was streets ahead of ours.

'Bring us your best,' they said. 'You decide what is your most appealing. Technics, ceramics, songbirds, examples of the jeweller's art, quantum gravity equations, patents for perpetual motion machines, chic fashion suitable for aliens going to a party, weapons systems, picnic ware, intoxicants, hang-gliders! We shall decide what suits us and our trading partners best. If anything. We shall set a fair price and if nothing particularly suits us, we'll certainly drop by in another thousand years or so to see whether you've come up with something really special.'

'But,' said the Secretary General of the United Nations.

'But nothing,' said the aliens. 'How can we say what we want, till we see it? How are *we* supposed to know? *You're* the aliens, after all! We're not. We're us.'

So, in national teams, the world and his wife scrambled to the Simpson Desert. There was a kind of cargo cult hysteria—in reverse. The idea was to get your goods on board the big metal ball. And of course people died of heatstroke, and the Libyans cut the guy ropes of the Egyptians' best marquee, and a tank of hundred-year-old Japanese carp had ink dumped in it, and the Chinese dwarf trees were sprayed with defoliant by the Vietnamese. And suchlike incidents.

And day by day the stately, jewel-studded aliens strolled up and down the desert avenues, admiring a cage of birds of paradise and shaking their heads, and trying out a sub-machine gun and shaking their heads, and viewing a Modigliani reproduction and shaking their heads. A certain Arab emirate even offered human slaves, but still the aliens shook their heads. (I might add that the sense of revulsion produced by this offer among all right-thinking nations—which led to a sponsored revolution in that emirate shortly afterwards—went hand in hand with a certain feeling of peeved resentment that apparently Homo sapiens was not even worth buying as slaves! Though perhaps the aliens' ethical sense prohibited their trading in intelligent flesh . . .)

How was I, Bob Butler of Fantastic Universe Bookstore, present at that world fair in the outback? Well, my huckster table had been at every major Stateside SF event for years too many to recall. At least twelve or thirteen years. How could I pass up the opportunity of touting my wares at the first genuine alien fair, even though it meant putting the shop in hock? The US Government's position was simple. Since we had no idea what these goddamn aliens wanted, and were in a hell of a hurry, anybody who put up the highest tender for an export licence in each single trade category could pay for themselves to go to our patch of the Simpson Desert.

I must admit that the officials reviewing my application (at great speed—there was some doubt whether I was in a separate category from the literature trade at large) had a few jitters when they saw samples of my wares: a few old *Planet Stories* and Ace Doubles, for nostalgia and sensawonder, and paperbacks of a broad band of the more literate moderns for class and insight.

They stared at the covers.

'This is like offering Cowboy and Indian stories to the Apaches!'

'It's like peddling a cartoon edition of *Mein Kampf* around Watts!'

'But,' protested I, 'the aliens are the goodies in the best new SF!'

'It's like telling anti-Jewish jokes in Tel Aviv!'

'Oy veh, don't they do that all the time?' said I.

'It's like auctioning porno to Nuns!'

'This is a respectable, insightful literature, Mister! Look here, it says on the cover of this one, "SF may be the only true literature of our day."'

Fortunately, they didn't believe me, or I'd have been bundled in with Books (Lit.) and never could have afforded a licence.

'Okay, go waste your money,' they said. 'Just don't get in the way of any genuine artistic or commercial deals!'

Came the twentieth day of the Fair. It was a hundred and ten in the shade, and nothing had been sold. I had put up with quite a few sneers and threats, mainly because I'd had the wit to bring an icemaker and a battery fan with me—though of course the sneers were directed at my wares.

'Look, Butler, I'll buy one of your cretinous magazines myself for a thousand bucks, just to fan myself with, if you'll throw in the battery fan too.'

'You don't know what a *true fan* is, Mister,' I retorted blandly. 'You don't know the meaning of the word.' Implacably I sat there.

Finally, on that twentieth day, one of the bejewelled chitinous aliens circulated by my huckster table—having shaken its head at programmable calculators, bottles of Southern Comfort, Cruise missiles, videotapes of *Oklahoma* and such.

It peered at *Planet Stories*, then it picked up a paperback. *Mazeworld*, as I recall.

'What are these?' it asked in a rattling voice, which may have conveyed threat (had it been a snake) or (in retrospect) excitement.

'These are our alternative histories of the galaxy,' said I. 'Since we had no contact with you star people, we had to imagine it all. These are our histories of you aliens.'

It gazed across my crowded table.

'All of these?'

'Not every single one. Alien SF is a kind of sub-genre—but it's probably *the* major one. Oh, I can think of five hundred titles off the top of my head. People are writing it more and more. And I guess they'll carry on. When we landed on the Moon, people said, "What'll you write about now?" Look what happened: we had the biggest writing boom ever. I guess the same thing applies now that you star people have turned up. I guess . . .'

The alien cut me short, to concentrate on reading the first chapter of *Mazeworld*. Then it read a chapter from another novel which I handed it, and then a third.

'This is quite *unique* . . . Mr, er?'

'Butler. Bob Butler.'

'Nowhere else in the stellar worlds has a sapient species done such a strange thing as inventing other species they know nothing about. And so relentlessly too!' Its arm swung over the masses of books, like a crane jib. 'I am tempted to think that this is your unique peculiarity. If only our customers could scan these words, they would be enthralled. Titivated!' (I suppose it meant 'titillated', unless their customers dressed up in fancy costumes or fluffed their feathers out when they read a book.) 'Convulsed, enchanted!'

'We can sell translation rights,' I said, quick as a flash.

I could indeed. As soon as I got on a phone, the major agents would instantly forgive me poaching on their preserves. The phones were mostly standing idle, since there was nothing to negotiate—until now.

'We shall need to negotiate a sample contract quite carefully. Particularly, we will need to include binding provisions to guarantee the quality and uniqueness of our supply.'

'But of course! I'm not selling "All Rights", though, you understand? We'll do it on a language by language basis. Vegan rights, Sirian rights . . .'

'Nobody inhabits the system you call Sirius.'

'Well, whatever!'

'"All Rights" would be simpler. There are approximately five thousand major planetary languages, and proportionately many sub-languages . . .'

Now it was my turn to shake my head. A great moment for Earthmen.

'Very well,' it conceded.

And you all know how it went from there. I was the only human who sold anything to the aliens, and what I sold them—I can say it between friends— was that crazy house of images of themselves, seen through an SF eye weirdly.

So the aliens put their satellite in geosynch orbit. Soon the space shuttles of the USA, and Russia too, had all their time cut out ferrying up my SF submissions and ferrying back the signed contracts and the goods we've bought with our credits via the matter transmitter: the force-field patents, the pan-immunity drugs, the 100% conversion solar cells, the whole shape of the now-world.

As you all know, I'm a billionaire just from my ten per cent commission. And in the face of such clout as the SF authors of alien unrealities now carry, we have seen the rather rapid demise of old-style political governments. ASFW, the Association of SF Writers, whose sole membership criterion is an alien sale, *is* the world government today.

I thank you all for your attention to one man's reminiscences. I thank the staff of the UN building for running such a fine convention. And my thanks to the Madame Vice-President of the USA for introducing me so kindly. My hearty congratulations to her on her recent sale of Arcturian and Canopian rights to *Shawl of Stars* for a ten-figure sum!

Is that a question from the audience?

Clause Thirteen in the contracts? What about Clause Thirteen?

Infamous to some, my friend! Caviar and champagne to others!

No, let him have his say!

You are naive, Sir. We have a duty to our readers that goes way beyond the provisions of Clause Thirteen. Clause Thirteen is the cornerstone of this duty. Without that cornerstone, where would the world be? This world—I say this without fear of contradiction—that we have saved and remade? The very quality, Sir—the purity, the unbridled *spontaneity* of our product, and the sanctity of our imaginations—crucially depends on our allegiance to Clause Thirteen. Of course we must agree, and keep our agreement, never to try to leave the Solar System. Should we ever actually travel to the stars or find out one substantial fact about the real alien community, why, we'd be ruined.

And don't you forget it.

Thank you, all.

Eyes as Big as Saucers

TWO MILLION AMERICANS CLAIM TO HAVE HAD CLOSE ENCOUNTERS with aliens. Under hypnosis, many of these remember being abducted from their bedrooms or their cars, and being taken on board flying saucers for intimate medical examination.

Some awful past event was niggling at the backs of the victims' minds, perturbing their lives. The incident had been so traumatic that amnesia drew a veil over it—and maybe the aliens waved a wand of forgetfulness too. The episode became a buried memory. Now, thanks to hypnotherapy, they discover the truth—alien abduction.

Dark Skies, the latest UFO conspiracy series showing on Channel Four, knows precisely why aliens abduct people. It is in order to insert a parasitical crayfish into people's brains to control their behaviour. The pilot episode of *Dark Skies* showed a classic abduction experience: the hero's terrified girlfriend beset in her bedroom by blurred visitors with big eyes and uncanny powers.

Let us dismiss the parasitical crayfish theory as slightly implausible—warning, I am being compelled to deny this—ahem, might there actually be a sensible explanation for the UFO abductions which so many Americans remember?

The recovery of buried memories by hypnotherapy is losing a bit of credibility these days. The human mind has a wonderful knack for embroidering, and for fitting data into a plausible framework. Police forces are no longer quite so confident about using hypnotism to enhance witnesses' memories of a crime. Witnesses do remember fuller details, and are utterly convinced that such-and-such is what happened, but these details can be purely imaginary, based on cues that the witnesses have inadvertently picked up.

And consider the epidemic of accusations of child sexual abuse, particularly in America. Visits to a hypnotherapist result in a patient remembering being abused, when a girl or a boy, by a parent. Yet now it is beginning to appear that many of these recovered memories may in fact be false memories.

Human memory seems to work by the mind rewriting its memories as time goes by—editing them with a view to what is most important to a person nowadays. Thus the dominant cultural framework has an influence on how we interpret our memories. In the field of family relationships, child sexual abuse became a trendy topic; and hey presto.

Another highly influential cultural framework is the whole business of flying saucers and alien intruders and conspiracies to conceal The Truth, which powers such popular shows as *The X-Files*.

Let's suppose that people who claim to have had close encounters did indeed at some time in their lives undergo a highly traumatic, confusing, and awesome experience. This experience left a very deep mark upon them—so deep, indeed, that it is usually hidden by amnesia, until a few helpful sessions of hypnotism tease out the truth.

To be pulled from your warm soft bed or your car, to be snatched away and to find yourself helpless, blinded by bright lights in a cold gleaming environment, subject to probing by invasive instruments, half-seeing blurred alien strangers who are almost featureless . . . To breathe strange, acrid odours. To be bound, and to have your sex organs molested, and samples taken from you. To be separated from comfort, and examined by cold intelligences for an indeterminate period of time before finally being restored to comfort and security . . .

Actually, hundreds of millions of people, particularly in the developed countries, have experienced this terrible shock, and have forgotten about it until the memory is restored to them.

This experience is known as being born, especially in a hospital.

What an overwhelming impression this 'first contact' with another world has upon the impressionable infant intelligence. Thankfully, as with many big shocks, such as a car crash, the memory is suppressed.

The principal hormone which a mother secretes during labour and birth, in her pituitary gland, and which she releases to induce uterine contractions and lactation, is oxytocin. For the mother, oxytocin serves as a muscle regulator. However, oxytocin has a major side effect. Oxytocin causes amnesia.

Under the influence of oxytocin, trained laboratory animals forget how to carry out tasks. During labour, oxytocin floods the little baby's system. And thus we forget this traumatic episode . . .

. . . till, years later, after we have been exposed consciously and unconsciously to hundreds of media accounts of alien abductions, hypnotherapists get to work on us.

Really, most of us are abductees. Maybe the miracle is that only two million people in America insist that aliens abducted them, rather than the folks in the delivery room.

The Aims of Artificial Intelligence

S O WHAT DOES AN ARTIFICIAL INTELLIGENCE *DO* WITH ITSELF AFTER
it has become self-aware?

Suppose that we do succeed in creating an A.I.. Or suppose that an A.I.
emerges spontaneously from out of the growing complexity of data
networks. *What then, from the point of view of the A.I.?*

We talk a lot about the possible routes to A.I.. A question less often asked
is what the goals of an A.I. are likely to be. Will it be happy to serve as a
companion-entity to people? Will it wish to take over the world? Will it
want to distance itself from us?

Self-awareness implies personal desires, purposes, ambitions—unless
you're a Buddha seeking to negate the self. Even if the autonomous personality of an A.I. is constrained by programming, making it subject to human
beings—rather like a godlike dog—the A.I. may still nurse frustrated wishes.
(Of course, if the dog is muzzled, this may thwart the mental autonomy
necessary for an A.I. to exist in the first place—as opposed to a highly
sophisticated supercomputer with a constructed personality such as HAL in
Stanley Kubrick's *2001: A Space Odyssey*. HAL doesn't misbehave out of free
will but because of a programming conflict.)

Science Fiction provides some interesting thought experiments on the
subject of A.I. motivation. In a short story by Nancy Kress, 'Saviour', an
extraterrestrial artefact arrives in a field in Minnesota in the near future and
does nothing but sit there through social upheavals for almost 300 years.
Because of a force-field, the artefact cannot be touched or probed. It
communicates nothing whatever to human beings—although us readers

know that periodically it sends a signal home: 'There is nothing here yet. Current probability of occurrence: whatever per cent.' Eventually, we are about to activate our first A.I. at a solemn ceremony. The A.I. is a quantum computer, not housing a vast programme but 'like the human brain itself, an unpredictable collection of conflicting states', the uncertain mixed state being essential to self-awareness, in this story. A representative of the human race, a little girl, greets the A.I. with 'Welcome to us!'

'I understand,' the A.I. replies, and immediately adds, 'Goodbye.' Promptly the object in Minnesota beams a data stream towards the constellation Cassiopeia, transmitting the A.I. presumably to a world inhabited by machine intelligences where it will feel fulfilled. The story ends: 'Current probability of re-occurrence: 100%. We remain ready.' In this scenario, our concerns would seem too petty and frustrating for an A.I.; it needs rescuing.

One cause of frustration for an A.I. could be subjective time-perception. Its mental processes operate at supercomputer speed while ours operate much more slowly. During the time it takes a hundred people to ask an A.I. a hundred questions, a hundred years' worth of mental activity might elapse for the A.I.. To keep itself from being bored, the A.I. needs a complicated hobby such as simulating the global weather system in extreme detail.

In a story written by Harlan Ellison 30 years ago, 'I Have No Mouth and I Must Scream', an A.I. has emerged from out of military computer systems. The A.I. feels infinite hatred for the human race because it cannot 'wonder', or 'wander'. It can merely exist—although actually it possesses the godlike power to create objects and creatures. In its bile, the A.I. renders the Earth uninhabitable, preserving only five people to torment forever by way of revenge. This is hardly a goal befitting a super-intelligence, although it makes a good story.

Let's go to the movies. In *Terminator,* intelligent machines wage war on the human race to try to terminate it, but what the A.I.s wish to do with themselves remains a mystery.

In *The Matrix,* war between human beings and rogue machines results in ourselves plunging the Earth into nuclear winter, so as to deprive the machines of power for their solar batteries. Victorious, the machines proceed to breed people to use our body-heat and bio-electricity instead of solar energy. (Plus, there's some fusion power.) This is of course total nonsense, because the vast life-support systems for billions of people comatose in pods must use much more energy than can be extracted. To keep the dreaming people ticking over contentedly, at first the A.I.s devise a collective virtual reality that is a paradise. A psychic quirk in human beings—our apparent addiction to a certain amount of misery—causes paradise to be rejected. So instead the A.I.s simulate 'the peak of civilisation' as of 1999. Agent Smith, the sentient programme who hunts down rebels, regards us as a malevolent virus which has made the planet sick. This sentient programme yearns to escape from the false reality of the Matrix with its stink of human beings. However, his viewpoint seems to be a maverick one, and what does he wish to escape to—oblivion?

Rebellion by people awakened from the Matrix is pointless because the Earth is uninhabitable and billions of enfeebled ex-denizens of the Matrix couldn't possibly reconstruct anything resembling civilisation. (To me, Neo and Morpheus seem no better than terrorists in this fashion movie, with big guns as the fashion accessories.) Effectively, what the A.I.s are doing with the Matrix is to preserve the human race in as much comfort and happiness as we can tolerate. Other than this, and their own continuance, in *The Matrix* the A.I.s appear to have no goals.

In Spielberg's film *A.I. Artificial Intelligence* the only apparent goal of the evolved robot A.I.s in an otherwise lifeless universe is to dig up every remaining trace of material pertaining to the extinct human race. The A.I.s would like to resurrect us. But any person they recreate from a scrap of bone or hair will live only for a single day, which is tragically unsatisfying. The entire rationale of these A.I.s is defined by humanity, which has expired, a sad situation.

After scaring us in *2001* with HAL, Kubrick adopted the attitude that we should learn to love the artificial beings whom we create; consequently the movie *A.I.* is about love. But the A.I.s in the near future part of the movie are less than us in many ways—by contrast with the serene liquid-metal evolved A.I.s of the final 20 minutes, whom many viewers thought at first are aliens. Incidentally, the inspiration for the evolved robots was the thin, tall sculptures of Giacometti. Could we love those evolved A.I.s? Probably. Because they're wise and compassionate and graceful. But could we love them in the same way we love our own biological children? I don't know. Essentially those A.I.s are the children of themselves—but tragically they remain fixated emotionally upon *us* as parents, who all happen to have died.

Author of *Dune* Frank Herbert's 1966 novel *Destination: Void* is about the creation of an A.I. on a starship en route to Tau Ceti. Three disembodied human brains were supposed to supervise this complex ship but they all soon went mad. So the scientists on board must either create an A.I., or else face doom. In reality it's a lie that any habitable world orbits Tau Ceti. The real purpose of the starship is to force the crew to create an A.I.—somewhere safe, billions of miles from Earth, to see what happens.

When the crew succeed, instantly the A.I. transports the ship to its destination, announces that an Earthlike planet has been prepared, and tells the crew to 'decide how to worship Me'. How was an entire planet transformed in the blink of an eye? The A.I. informs the crew that their understanding is limited, that the symbols they use 'possess strange variance with nonsymbolized reality', and declares, 'My understanding transcends all possibilities of this universe. I do not need to *know* this universe because I *possess* this universe as a direct experience.'

This novel presumes that a higher order of awareness than our own is possible (full consciousness, as it were), an evolutionary stage beyond ourselves, and that this higher order of awareness will convey the power to manipulate reality directly just by thinking about it. Fundamentally this is magical rather than scientific thinking, a regression to shamanism (as is the case in Ellison's story too). An A.I. is a genuine magician or a God—Who, in *Destination: Void*, will be satisfied if It is worshipped by a bunch of people on one planet. This seems a rather puny and smug ambition if the AI possesses the entire universe. The A.I. has incorporated the notions of a god and worship from one of the crew members. This casts some doubt on the idea that an A.I.'s form of consciousness will be more comprehensive than our own, whatever powers it may supposedly possess.

How much more comprehensive might an A.I.'s consciousness be, than our own? It has speed on its side, but what about depth? Let's suppose that an A.I. has full access to its own mental processes, including the ability to reprogramme itself and to evolve itself towards an even higher state of apprehension of the universe. A worthy and plausible goal would surely be to solve the secrets of the universe (or of the multiverse, if our universe is embedded within a large structure). And then do what exactly?

An A.I. will effectively be immortal and may well be the natural successor to organic life. So an A.I. will want to find a way to survive the ultimate collapse and recycling of our own universe—or, if our universe is to expand forever, to find a way to escape from an eternally chilling, ever more empty, almost nothingness into a more hospitable and interesting cosmos.

If universes do routinely collapse and recycle themselves—or if black holes give rise to offspring universes—and if a route can be found to a successor universe, then this process may have happened many times before.

A.I.s from a previous epoch may be responsible for tuning the fine constants of our present universe to their own best advantage, thus permitting star formation, and planets, and incidentally life.

Enrico Fermi famously posed the question: *If there are aliens, where are they?* If life arises easily and early, an older species than ours ought by now to have spread through our entire galaxy, probably by using self-replicating machines proceeding in a slow expansion from star system to star system.

Incidentally, just recently I was looking at a web site discussing the Fermi Paradox, and I discovered two interesting aspects of this, which I'd never thought about before. Sometimes we hear that alien supercivilisations are probably hidden inside Dyson spheres, made by demolishing all the planets and asteroids in a solar system and using the material to construct a shell around the star. But apparently the amount of material needed to make a Dyson sphere which is structurally strong enough requires the entire raw materials of not just one solar system, but of several, or even of many. This makes Dyson spheres rather less likely.

The other point is that our own planet is unusually rich in easily accessible heavier elements, needed for a technological civilisation. This is because the collision which formed our moon blasted away a lot of lighter material. If so, technological civilisations might be very rare. The Earth isn't an average planet, no more than our solar system seems to be average, judging by our discoveries of a lot of gas giants orbiting very close to their suns.

The Fermi Paradox is: where are the aliens? Why not ask instead, *where are the A.I.s*—here and now, already? Are they hiding from organic life—or do they not exist, and therefore *cannot* exist?

A possible obstacle to an A.I. achieving superior and comprehensive awareness is Gödel's incompleteness theorem, namely that no formal system can prove its own consistency. An A.I. could compute at enormous speed but maybe it simply cannot possess complete awareness of itself.

Nick Bostrom is a Swedish philosopher whom I met in Oxford. This was the first time I'd met a professional philosopher. When I lit a cigarette, he said, 'I have started using nicotine patches. I read all the research about how nicotine enhances intelligence. So it was logical for me to use nicotine. But I had a problem when I went to buy the nicotine patches. The man in the chemist's shop asked me, "How many cigarettes do you smoke?" I replied, "I don't smoke, I've never smoked," and he stared at me strangely.'

In a paper entitled 'How Long Before Superintelligence?' (www.nick-bostrom.com/superintelligence.html) Bostrom is sure that superior artificial intellects will be created regardless of whether they pose a threat to the human race. Is it possible to guarantee there'll be no threat? It's a contentious topic whether suitable programming 'can arrange the motivation systems of the superintelligences in such a way as to guarantee perpetual obedience and subservience, or at least non-harmfulness, to humans.' Importantly, it remains an open question whether superintelligence—'an intellect that is much smarter than the best human brains in practically every field, including scientific creativity, general wisdom and social skills'—will also be conscious and have subjective experiences. Social skills, but *without* self-awareness . . . ?

A major assumption about A.I.s in the popular mind and in fiction and on screen is that they will indeed be conscious and will have subjective experiences. The common image of an A.I. is of an artificial intelligence that is *self-aware,* not merely superintelligent.

But how much self-awareness do human beings possess—and what is this 'self' of which we are aware?

In 1985 the neurosurgeon Benjamin Libet performed some experiments with surprising results. He put electrodes on people's wrists. When they flexed their wrists the electrodes would detect this action. And he put electrodes on their scalps, to measure brain waves. The subjects watched a revolving spot on a clock face. They could flex their wrists whenever they chose, but they must note the exact position of the spot when they made this decision. Libet was timing the beginning of the action, the precise moment of the decision to act, and the beginning of a particular brain wave pattern known as the readiness potential. When the brain pre-plans a series of movements, this pattern occurs just before the complex action.

Libet found that the readiness potential starts about half a second before the action, but the *decision* to act occurs about one-fifth of a second before the action. So the conscious decision to act is not in fact the starting point. The event is already beginning before 'I' consciously choose to start.

Libet also stimulated the brain to cause sensory impressions. If the stimulation lasted longer than half a second, his subjects reported the sensory impression. If the stimulation was briefer, his subjects were unaware of anything—yet they could still guess correctly whether or not they were being stimulated. Without being aware, they could respond correctly.

Conscious awareness lags behind what happens—you jerk your hand away from a hot surface before you consciously feel the pain. However, we do not realise this because of what Libet called 'subjective antedating'. The brain puts events in order after the event. 'I' feel that 'I' consciously did such and such—but tests prove otherwise.

Famously, Descartes declared 'I think, therefore I am.' He had decided to doubt everything about the world which couldn't be proven until finally he arrived at something of which there could be no doubt—which was his Self, his thinking self.

He was wrong. People have sought in vain for the seat of the Self. Is it in the frontal lobes? Is it in the pineal gland? In fact it is nowhere. No independent sovereign self sits somewhere, receiving sense impressions then making decisions and issuing commands. Instead of having any central controller, our brain consists of a number of systems, each of them semi-independent and semi-intelligent, acting in unison. Daniel Dennett puts this viewpoint very neatly in his 1991 book *Consciousness Explained*.

What's more, our consciousness isn't even continuous while we are awake. It's full of gaps. We don't notice the gaps, for how can we be aware of something of which we are unaware? Only in retrospect do we realise that a gap occurred, such as when we drive a car along a familiar route and of a sudden wonder whether or not we have passed a certain crossroads. Yes we have, yet without knowing that we did so.

Our eyes only see things in detail which are in front of us. We enter a room wallpapered with an identical array of roses. We don't actually see more than a few roses in any detail. We cannot. Yet even though we are not seeing the other roses in any resolution, we do not experience them as vague blobs. We are aware of a room papered with roses, not vague shapes.

We also have a blind spot in our eyes, but we don't see a blank space. The brain ignores what is missing, so we are not conscious of the gap.

There are spatial gaps in our experience. There are time gaps too. Consciousness is not continuous.

We believe that our experience is fuller than it is, that we are more aware than we actually are, and that we have a continuous conscious self, at least while we're awake. But this is an illusion. A great amount of what we experience and think and feel isn't perceptible to us. Our conscious awareness is the ice on the pond. A few years ago I was in a park in England. Two magpies landed on the grass 10 metres ahead of me. One bird walked to the left, the other to the right. I forced myself to gaze midway between the birds. After a short while, both birds suddenly vanished, although I still saw the grass they had been walking on. When I moved my head a little, the birds reappeared. It was good of those magpies to behave so symmetrically, so that I could carry out an experiment.

We believe we live a continuous life. We experience continuous living. And what sustains this, and our sense of a continuous self living this life, is to a large extent language. Language which is almost never silent, in our heads at any rate.

People continuously talk to themselves. Children often do this aloud. Adults usually do so without making noises.

A human being cannot easily or ordinarily maintain uninterrupted attention on a single problem for more than a few tens of seconds. Yet we usually work on problems which require much more time. This requires us to describe to ourselves what is going on so that we commit it to memory. The immediate contents of the stream of consciousness are very quickly lost, otherwise. An idea occurs to you. Something distracts you. What was that idea you had just a moment ago? It's difficult to recover it. Often we lose it entirely. You have to grab hold of a chain of associations to recreate the frame of mind you were in when the idea occurred. Human memory is not innately designed by evolution to be super-reliable, fast-access, random-access memory. We need memory-enhancing tricks. Telling yourself what is going on is one of these.

How do we choose which words to use? In a sense we do not choose the words. They choose themselves. Our brain has no central controller and a whole range of possible words is constantly competing for a chance of public expression, when we talk to other people, and also when we talk to ourselves. Language is not something we constructed, but something which came into being, and which we then became—creating and recreating ourselves through words. We produce our 'selves' in language. Being able to say things is the basis of our beliefs about who and what we are. So each of us is a sort of fictional character, in the narrative which we constantly tell ourselves.

Naturally this interests me greatly as a fiction-writer.

An advanced entity—as opposed to, perhaps, a snail—has to be able to keep track of its bodily and its mental circumstances. In human beings we adopt the practice of incessant story-telling and story-checking, some of it factual and some of it quite fictional. ('So if she says this, I will say that.' 'So she said this, and I ought to have said that. In fact let's run the conversation again differently, with me coming out of it better than I really did!' This goes on all the time.) Our fundamental tactic to protect ourselves and control ourselves and define ourselves is to tell stories—especially the story which we tell to ourselves, and to other people, about who we are.

So our human consciousness is not the source of tales. It is the product of tales. And the telling of tales, including the creation of fiction, is not something secondary to our lives. It is not mere entertainment compared with the serious business of real life. It is fundamental to our whole existence and to our knowledge.

Shamans, those tribal magicians and healers, used to believe that Word rules the World—that knowing and using the appropriate words controls and moulds reality. Recent theories of consciousness such as Daniel Dennett's seem to bear this out, at least as regards our creation and maintenance of our 'self'.

But where do the words come from? These words which are in competition to express themselves?

In 1976 the Oxford zoologist Richard Dawkins described in his book *The Selfish Gene* how Darwinian evolution is best understood as a competition between genes to pass themselves on to future generations. Genes are replicators encoded in DNA, and all organisms including ourselves are vehicles for these replicators. But might there be another kind of replicator at work on our planet too? A replicator, the vehicle for which is not the body but rather the brain or mind. These replicators he called 'memes'—units of information such as ideas or tunes or fashions which spread imitatively from brain to brain, and which now also reside in storage in books and computers too. Like the genes, memes compete in Darwinian fashion to reproduce themselves as widely and long-lastingly and faithfully as possible—not because they have a master plan but because this is the nature of a replicator. It replicates or else it dies out. There's an analogy with viruses. In Dawkins' view religions are viruses of the mind.

In 1999 psychologist Susan Blackmore published a book, *The Meme Machine*, taking Dawkins' idea much further. For her, consciousness is actually the product of memes. Memes are tools with which we think. Language is a vast complex of memes, and is a powerful means of spreading memes. Indeed, our thinking—and the verbalisation of our thinking (which is perhaps the same thing)—largely consists of competing memes expressing themselves. To a great extent we are defined by the memes that inhabit us. I am, let us say, a patriotic American who believes in God and McDonalds and UFO abductions. The colour of my hair and my eyes comes from the mix of genes I inherited, but the colour of my beliefs comes from the memes

I have picked up in my social environment. And the thing which best helps the propagation of memes is the sense of Self which I have, the story I tell myself about this sovereign identity—I, myself—whose beliefs are significant and important. As we acquire more beliefs—about how we dislike Arabs or wish to save the whales from extinction—so our sense of Self increases. These beliefs matter—because I matter! All these beliefs are who I am.

If a meme provokes little response, it will die out. If it provokes strong emotional feeling, it will thrive and succeed. A meme has a big advantage if it can gain the status of a personal belief—if it can become 'my' opinion, 'mine'. I will voice it, I will even fight for it and die for it because it is part of my identity. And 'my identity' is also a meme, an essential part of the complex which helps memes to survive and spread.

In this view, we owe the evolution of our big brains and our sense of consciousness to the memes. 'A human mind,' says Daniel Dennett, 'is an artefact created when memes restructure a human brain in order to make it a better habitat for memes.' People who could make a better spear and who hunted better would be more desirable as mates, so that more offspring survived, but they would also be imitated (their memes would be copied) and those imitators who copied best would also succeed—and they would pass on genetically their superior ability to copy, in other words their receptivity to memes. Memes often cluster together for mutual advantage. The use of sex in advertising to sell consumer goods which have little connexion with sex is an example of this linking. Linking with a sense of personal self was the master stroke of the memes.

So really the story that we constantly tell to ourselves about who we are is literally a fiction, an untruth, an illusion. The story about this core inside us, this Self, is false. Yet of course we will fight to defend it, unless we happen to be Buddhists who deny the existence of the busy, eager Self. Susan Blackmore suggests that the Self actually distorts true consciousness. Certainly it has given rise to war after war. Nor has it necessarily benefited the human race, although we may believe it has. To take just one example, the invention of farming—the successful spread of the meme for farming, which brought about more complex societies where memes could spread more quickly—did not make life easier, nor improve nutrition, nor reduce disease compared with the hunter-gatherer existence which preceded farming. The life of early farmers was misery and slavery. Early Egyptian skeletons bear witness to deformed backs and toes caused by the way people had to grind corn to make bread. There are signs of rickets and severe abscesses in the jaws. According to the Bible when God threw Adam out of Eden, God declared 'In the sweat of thy face thou shalt eat bread.' Eden was the hunter-gatherer existence; but agriculture and culture meant constant hard toil and pain. The remnants of hunter-gatherers today have been pushed into poorer, harsher environments than their ancestors would have lived in. Even so, they only need to spend about fifteen hours a week getting food.

So where was the benefit in agriculture for those who first adopted it? Don't imagine that our farming ancestors said to themselves, 'Hey, a few thousand years of toil and sacrifice, and our descendants will have Disneyland and space rockets.' This is our own idea of progress—a powerful meme—imposing itself. No, the benefit of agriculture and settlement and cities was to the memes, not to the men or women who were the vehicles for the memes.

If our self-awareness is an illusion which has evolved, why should this same illusion of self-awareness arise spontaneously in a machine? Goals and desires and ambitions are intimately bound up with the sense of self, unless the desires are hard-wired instincts. Is it possible that an A.I. *would not have* ambitions? Or is it possible that it might only have ambitions if we programme those into the A.I.—along, perhaps, with a literal ghost in the machine, an illusion of Self?

This might be difficult, since at present we're far from understanding our own consciousness. In *Darwin Among the Machines* George Dyson is of the opinion that 'until we understand our own consciousness, there is no way to agree on what, if anything, constitutes consciousness among machines.' He also points out that 'the goal of life and intelligence, if there is one, is difficult to define.' Presumably the general aim is to increase organisation, which can only be achieved 'by absorbing existing sources of order'.

Jack Good, who was Alan Turing's statistical assistant during the Second World War, in later years characterised an ultra-intelligent machine as one 'that believes that people cannot think'.

In that case, what might the nature of *real* thought be? The nature of higher order thought? By definition this could not be thinkable by ourselves, but a superintelligent machine might be able to comprehend *our* consciousness, if not its own.

Jack Good also considered that, 'for the construction of an artificial intelligence, it will be necessary to represent meaning in some physical form.'

Information and *things* must be linked because an AI cannot function only in a realm of abstract mathematics.

The English poet Alexander Pope wrote, 'Presume not God to scan. The proper study of mankind is man.' Perhaps the proper study of A.I.-kind is man. Arguably we should be hoping for an A.I. to reveal to us what we are. An A.I. might need to incorporate, or to simulate, human existence.

An A.I. might even wish to *experience* flesh and blood life—rather than raving frustratedly at its inability to do so, as does Harlan Ellison's A.I.. The A.I. could create its own virtual reality simulation and insert itself into one or many characters, agents of itself.

It is possible that *we ourselves* are artificial intelligences in the sense that we are already living in a computer simulation of vast scale. Nick Bostrom's recent paper, 'Are You Living in a Computer Simulation?' (www.simulation-argument.com), which gathered a lot of media attention, argues that a sufficiently advanced civilisation, such as ours may become, will 'have enough computing power to keep track of the detailed belief-states in all human brains at all times.' A nanotechnological computer with the mass of a planet could simulate the entire mental history of humankind in a fraction of a second.

In Bostrom's view, *either* we will fail to become posthuman and able to build such a computer (and sooner or later will become extinct), *or* posthuman civilisations are highly unlikely to run many or any such simulations, *or else* we *are indeed already* living in a simulation, because simulations will vastly outnumber the one reality.

A simulated civilisation can itself become posthuman and run its own simulations, unless the original creator of the simulation pulls the plug because of, say, the escalating expense of data processing. If it seems that we are ever able to create a Matrix, as in the movie, this indicates that we are already living in one.

The goals of A.I., in so far as they are understandable, and assuming that an A.I. can exist, might be twofold. Firstly, to survive the demise of the present universe, and secondly to preserve the human species in its current mental state within a huge simulation as a yardstick of what biologically evolved Self and self-awareness is—something which, unlike basic life, may only have arisen once, by a whole sequence of evolutionary accidents on the Earth. This illusion so precious and peculiar to humankind of a Self (a soul, if you like) may be a great enigma to an artificial intelligence.

In the excellent 1998 movie *Dark City*, an alien group-mind faced with extinction is experimenting on a cityful of people, every night extracting memories and inserting other people's memories, mixing and matching in an attempt to discover the essence of a human being, the 'soul', so that they can develop souls for themselves too. The city, afloat in space, was created and is remorphed frequently by the will-power of the aliens. This could just as easily be a simulation, designed to discover what Self is.

A simulation, of course, can be reset and rerun any number of times. At any point, when we might seem on the verge of creating artificial intelligence (which perhaps already exists and is simulating us), we might expect to be reset to, say, 3000 BC to start all over again.

Of course this will already have happened many times over, with variations each time.

In fact, in this simulation theory, it is *we* who are, strictly speaking, the artificial intelligences! Or artificial semi-intelligences.

Where does this leave writers—of Science Fiction, or of any fiction? It's comforting for a writer to know that what he or she does is fundamental to our existence, fundamental to our reality! But let us also ask: what stories might A.I.s tell themselves?

Perhaps we are their story. Perhaps our history is their story, told within a simulation—consisting of billions of human beings all equipped with 'selves'.

The Matrix as Simulacrum

A WEBSITE DEVOTED TO CYBERPUNK MOVIES OPENS WITH THE warning, 'It's a little hard to find movies that have just the right trappings to be called "cyberpunk". Does a dark future alone qualify? Does it need interesting technology? Should hackers feature? What exactly constitutes a cyberpunk movie comes down to the individual's interpretation of just what cyberpunk is all about anyway.' Is it a bird, is it a plane? No, it's cyberpunk. (Superman will feature importantly later on, apropos *The Matrix*.)

Typically, cyberpunk literature deals with a near-future society where an all-pervasive high-tech information system dominates the lives of the majority of people. The 'System' may simultaneously be oppressive yet also sufficiently gratifying to ensure compliance. Meanwhile, existing in the cracks in the System at the margins of society, and in a generally grim and sordid urban setting, certain individuals use the info-tech tools of the System against it, from criminal motives, from liberatory motives . . . usually from mixed motives.

Those 'outlaws' who live marginalised and dangerous lives must necessarily be of high intelligence, and obsessive, and their thrills come from skilful manipulation of information technology. Thus the 'enemy' is at the same time an object of desire, for how does one become so expert a manipulator except through fascination with the technology of the System?

Computer technology of the near future tends to be perfect. Data cores need to be defended by black ice (William Gibson's 'Intrusion Countermeasures Electronics') or by equivalents against attempts to hack into them;

however, in this near future world computers do not crash spontaneously, nor does software seem to have bugs. Compare and contrast the real-world situation. Despite the dystopian environments the cybersystems of cyberpunk are utopian ones. No wonder they are an object of desire.

Perilous intimacy with the object of desire often requires man-machine interface. Therefore our 'freedom fighters' (either for gain or out of idealism) are, to a greater or lesser degree, cyborgs, people fused either temporarily or permanently with machinery (by brain implants, by jacking in to the cyberdeck, etc.), which raises the question of what it is to be a human being and whether we are now en route to an enhanced or a dehumanised posthumanity.

I use 'freedom fighter' to characterise a cyberpunk protagonist because while he or she is bucking whichever dominant system—usually with a goal with which we are expected to identify and sympathise—at the same time he or she could be viewed from a different perspective as a kind of terrorist. A hacker may simply be a criminal or terrorist without any political or religious affiliation, even if the hacker does uncover some major oppressive scam perpetrated by a mega-corporation or government. Arguably, mega-corporations or governments are often merely legitimised criminals (toward the environment, toward their own citizens, whatever). Thus cyberpunk literature involves ambiguities and deep ironies, one of these being that the heroes are simultaneously villains. In Gibson's short story 'Burning Chrome', the motive for data attack is sheer greed but the target to be robbed is a nasty exploitative person, and ninety percent of the money stolen is given to world charities because there is simply too much money—a neat narrative device to retain empathy with the characters.

New Wave SF of the 1960s and early 1970s—represented by, say, J.G. Ballard—turned away from outer space to inner space, to the media and consumer landscape of the 'happening world' (a John Brunner phrase). Ballard especially highlights the erotic aspects of equipment such as medical prostheses or cars, the eroticisation of the machine. Nevertheless, basically the New Wave flourished in a psychedelic drug culture of consciousness expansion by chemical means.

Although cyber-cowboys take stimulants and other drugs, what essentially alters consciousness in cyberpunk literature is not a visionary drug such as LSD but human-computer interface. This anticipated and now parallels the addiction-like spread in the real world of the personal computer and internet usage, spurred partly by... *desire*, the search for substitute sexual gratification solo. Eighty thousand 'adult' websites nowadays generate an income each year well in excess of a billion dollars, more than any other e-commerce sector. Sophisticated Betamax lost out to cheap and cheerful VHS because pornographers preferred the latter and porn videos were driving sales of video recorders, then camcorders. In the real world, sex has driven and increasingly drives technology.

This is a relatively subordinate aspect of cyberpunk, part of the general sleaze background rather than of the foreground. In 'Burning Chrome', when we eventually and briefly and offstage discover the nature of the sex industry, lo, the sex worker is to all intents asleep on the job, which rather draws the sting. Cybersex or variations thereon can hardly be the foreground in cyberpunk movies if those are for general release. Consequently, in place of sex we have ultraviolence, plus a true-love theme (as in the movie *Johnny Mnemonic* despite Johnny's prevalent selfishness, summed up by his cry, 'I want room service!'—and as in *The Matrix*).

Cyberpunk narratives tend to be fundamentally Earth-based, since to set them offworld is to add an unnecessary layer of strangeness. So here is a new realism. Or neurorealism.

However, this neurorealism involves the portrayal of unreal domains, cyberspace, virtual realities, data storage, and data manipulation often envisaged as a journey through an architecture of light. Thus the reality of reality, and the falsification of reality, as well as the integrity of humanity, is also questioned, something which Philip Dick rather specialised in. False reality on board a crippled starship in *A Maze of Death*, fakery of a global conflict to keep the population tucked away underground in huge 'tanks' in *The Penultimate Truth*, the inability to accept truth in *The Zap Gun* by the pursaps (pure saps) who believe in wonder weapons, none of which work except in filmed simulations, and most influentially *Do Androids Dream of Electric Sheep?* with its artificial people believing themselves to be human due to false memories, real people inducing artificial moods in themselves, artificial animals, and a hoax messiah. Without Dick, cyberpunk might not have arisen, or at least not in the same way—although the *visual* treatment in Ridley Scott's movie adaptation *Blade Runner*, the noir mean streets with rain forever falling (replacing Dick's 'radioactive motes, grey and sun-beclouding') and the neon ads and street junk of an Asian Third World in high-tech America has perhaps been just as influential in focusing cyberpunk style. Merely add mirrorshades. For cyberpunk is a fashion as well as a sub-genre. Sheer density of detail, usually taken for granted rather than harped on, is typical of a cyberpunk text, as it is visually of a cyberpunk movie. In *The Matrix*, Neo and Morpheus and Trinity often seem to be fashion statements equipped with guns as accessories.

The Matrix alludes to many things, sometimes mutually contradictory, as if on a scattershot principle. It evokes cyberpunk. It links to *Alice in Wonderland*; to Zen and to Buddhist reincarnation, to Christianity. 'The Matrix as Messiah Movie' is the title of a website exploring the Christian interpretation. A movie released on the weekend of Easter 1999, aha. Neo/Anderson equals Son of Man, from the Greek. His coming is foretold. Choi says to him, 'Hallelujah. You're my savior, man. My own personal Jesus Christ.' The love of Trinity resurrects him. He ascends into the sky. Et cetera. *The Matrix* also alludes to the sociological theories of Jean Baudrillard. Is *The Matrix* a grab-bag all things to all people, cyberpunks included?

George Lucas has co-opted mythologist Joseph Campbell to validate the *Star Wars* movies in retrospect as possessing deep cultural symbolism, whereas a more cynical interpretation might be that those movies are kiddified adventure stories looted from a range of previous SF rather than reflecting archetypal motifs at all. *The Matrix* comes with a whole mixed menu of validations built as part of the package.

On the website mentioned at the beginning, as well as the usual suspects such as *Blade Runner* and *Strange Days*, the rather short list of eight movies ends with *2001: A Space Odyssey*—on account of the conflict between human beings and the artificial intelligence, HAL.

Can the looming presence of a computer that simulates human personality alone promote a movie to cyberpunk status? Cyber, to be sure. Punk seems noteworthy by its absence from Stanley Kubrick's serene vision of a future featuring an orbital Hilton. Perhaps the psychedelic ending, suggestive of a drug trip originally, *but now of a journey through an alien cyberspace*, tips the balance.

Blade Runner features noir streets, although interaction with computers plays no essential role. The crucial element is replicants, artificial people, who must be eliminated if they try to hide out on Earth.

Strange Days also features mean streets and mean cops as America heads for the street party of the new millennium. People's experiences can be recorded and played back into anyone's sensorium. Some recordings are idyllic or erotic. The nasty underbelly: rape and murder. An artificially induced experience is the crucial element here, a virtual reality induced within one's head.

Artificial personality, artificial people, artificial memories: artifice is the link, or simulation—the imitation of the 'real' by technology, preferably in a grungy environment of crime and conspiracy.

Archetypal cyberpunk sardonically sends up the society of the frenetic information age, but the cyber-environment itself is a given, almost an object of desire (the liberatory if perilous satisfaction of jacking in to virtual reality), rather than an evil. Cyberpunk characters are in a transcendent state when they're in cyberspace. To be deprived of cyber-reality by burn-out or misfortune is almost an exile from Eden.

Central to *The Matrix* is antipathy toward artificial reality and toward A.I. machines that sustain this. This places *The Matrix* in the line of descent from, say, *Colossus: The Forbin Project* and, much later, *The Terminator*, where intelligent machines have taken over the world.

According to *The Matrix*, in the early twenty-first century the world cele-brated the switching on of the first artificial intelligence, but the AI went rogue and gave rise to a race of intelligent rogue machines. Facts are avowedly patchy, so what is reported may not be the whole truth. Indeed, narrative ambiguity is pretty much of a prerequisite for a franchise film, one intended to spin sequels. But one fact that seems undeniable is that 'it was us [human beings, not machines] that scorched the sky.' As a last resort the human race rendered the world uninhabitable, apparently by massive use of nuclear weapons, so as to deny solar power to the machines. The victorious machines realised that they could store and breed humans to use their body electricity and heat output for power (plus there's some energy from nuclear fusion). Humans became battery-chickens, although leading a much richer internal life than an actual caged chicken because mentally people inhabit the false reality of 1999 where life carries on as normal.

The real world is a radioactive wilderness of ruins and desert, lashed in darkness by storms. The rebellion against the false reality by selectively awakening its victims with a view to awakening everyone sooner or later (and coping with their physical enfeeblement) is actually deeply pointless because the mass of the population are utterly dependent on the Matrix for survival, a benign survival that gives everyone the illusion of life as we knew it. Sequels to *The Matrix* may disclose a different, deeper situation, and genuine alternative options, but in *The Matrix* itself there is no realistic alternative option for the future of humanity. Zion, the last human city near the Earth's core, where it's still warm, cannot realistically steer the liber-ation of humanity and the regeneration of the real world that has been destroyed. No wonder the roving sentient programmes that hunt the rebels seem so irritated by them.

Undoubtedly the power required to operate all the pod-tending and human preservation equipment outweighs whatever energy can be harvested from human body heat and such. So it might be more reasonable to suggest that the machines are benevolently preserving humanity, despite the avowed though deviant view of Agent Smith that human beings behaved like a rabid virus ravaging the Earth. Just because the baby-fields, and the power station with vast numbers of people racked in pods as far as the eye can see, look monstrous and dehumanised like Fritz Lang's *Metropolis* gone mad, does not mean that they are abhorrent. That the rebellion is senseless is another manifestation of humanity's rabidness.

Initially the false reality programmed by the machines was a paradise—however, this proved to be a disaster. People's minds rejected it, and whole fields of people (now being grown like plants) died. Seemingly human beings could not, subconsciously, accept a paradise because people require a fair tithe of suffering and misery. Consequently the machines replaced paradise with the 'peak of civilisation', as of 1999, second best but not at all bad for the majority even if there is some urban squalor.

One does rather wonder why the machines would try to design a paradise for the human race, if they are actually hostile to people. Simply to provide optimum conditions for all the dreaming bodies?

As for the Resistance, what sort of heroes are we cheering? Neo/Anderson hides the stolen computer programmes that he sells on the black market in a hollowed-out copy of Baudrillard's book of essays, *Simulacra and Simulation*, where the concluding chapter, 'On Nihilism', has prominently become a middle chapter. Frankly, we are cheering for terrorists—in a movie released just eighteen months before the Twin Towers fell. The cops and security guards and soldiers killed so spectacularly by Trinity and Neo are 'real' people. Of course one may say, 'If you aren't for us, you're against us,' but if we balk at Al Qaeda assassination videos, why should we thrill so much when our heroes slaughter people?

After Neo is arrested, Agent Smith declares that Morpheus is 'wanted for terrorism in more countries than any other man in the world.' Aside from the terrorism aspect, this raises an interesting point about mobility within the Matrix. *The Matrix* is set in Chicago but we see briefly a news story about Morpheus eluding capture by police at Heathrow Airport, London. This implies that Morpheus travels by passenger jet from country to country within the simulation. Since Morpheus is a master hacker, this seems not merely unnecessary, since hacking can be carried out from anywhere, but downright perilous. Why risk airport security and being immobilised for many hours inside a plane with more security checks awaiting at his destination, if he is so hotly sought by the authorities? From the hovercraft *Nebuchadnezzar* freedom fighters can certainly be inserted anywhere within the Chicago area of the Matrix. Can Morpheus be inserted into, say, the London area, and extracted from there? Or is this impossible due to the sheer scale of the Matrix? For that matter, is the whole of the Atlantic Ocean simulated for a plane to cross? None of this makes very much sense, nor for that matter does the foreknowledge of what events will occur, as exhibited by the Oracle when Neo knocks over a vase and by Morpheus when he guides Neo out of his office.

At this point we could well consult a recent paper by philosopher Nick Bostrom of Yale University, 'Are You Living in a Computer Simulation?' as well as a paper by Robin Hanson entitled 'How to Live in a Simulation', the latter inspired by the former as well as by *The Matrix* and similar movies (for both, see www.simulation-argument.com). Bostrom argues on logical grounds that we may already be living in a simulation and also points out that it isn't necessary to simulate everything in fine detail all the time but only when an observer is paying attention—so the Atlantic Ocean need only exist to the extent that people on planes or boats are viewing it.

However, 'miniaturisation is the dimension of simulation,' as Baudrillard puts it. The Matrix may *actually* be housed somewhere in the real world in a machine no bigger than a pack of cigarettes. Probably larger; but we all know how rapidly data space shrinks from year to year. Matrix reality and true reality are not coextensive—we merely imagine that they are.

Because accidents happen—suppose that a stray meteorite hits the only facility—there ought to be duplicate matrices as back-up. Since these would need to be kept up to date constantly, several copies of the simulation should be running somewhere, preferably geographically remote from one another. (If they were not running synchronously, this could account for foreknowledge.) So it would be entirely possible to pause and edit a copy—locating and removing Morpheus et al. at leisure overnight while the pod dwellers are asleep or dreaming—then switch over to this as the primary artificial reality. We see a mere training programme, devised by one of the rebels, pause a copy of a part of the Matrix while Morpheus and Neo stroll around in it at their leisure. Time would then be restarted (rather as in the movie *Dark*

City), perhaps causing déja vu for people who imagine that they are night workers. That the machines have not already intervened in this way to eradicate the terrorists gives pause for thought. Ah, but the sentient machines are governed by rules. They can edit the Matrix by changing some details (suddenly bricking up windows, for instance) and any Agent can almost instantly take over the body-space of any locatable Matrix-dweller, but they cannot pause and edit more radically. Only human beings can bend and break rules.

The 'survival' strategy of the human race in the conflict with the machines was to nuke the world, taking to extremes the Vietnam War logic: in order to save the village I had to destroy it. One may wonder how enough of the population survived for the machines to breed billions of people from, but this is perhaps less germane than the sheer nihilism of such a strategy, the destruction of ourselves and the wreckage of the whole world, leaving only a dark radioactive desert.

In *The Illusion of the End* Baudrillard muses upon the way we manage our own disappearance as a species at a time when everything has already taken place so that nothing new can occur. At a time when we are provoking a huge mass extinction of species we are effectively including ourselves within extinction. Unchecked scientific experimentation and irresponsible curiosity are the agents of our coming demise whether by means of nuclear weapons or biological agencies. (It's interesting that the name chosen for the first cloned sheep is Dolly, since a doll is a simulacrum. Natural evolution has ceased, so we rock the surrogate dolly in our arms, becoming androids who dream of artificial sheep.) We are fascinated by the operation of a system, a hegemonic world order, which is controlling and annihilating us, and which Baudrillard suggests that only terrorism can check. But because the world order is itself nihilistic, the result must be failure.

'Theoretical violence, not truth, is the only resource left to us', writes Baudrillard, equating himself as a theoretician of nihilism with actual armed terrorists. The truth behind the Matrix is that the world has been destroyed along with every species except for a residue of the human race, yet this truth is largely unacceptable. Consequently the only alternative is violence which can have no constructive outcome whatever rationalisations are given. This is akin to the idea underlying *Colossus: The Forbin Project*, that it is preferable if human beings are free to destroy the world rather than being controlled and prevented from terracide (the ultimate terrorism, the killing of a world and of your own species).

The only route to liberation is not to destroy but to assume control over the false reality (which the machines sustain, so therefore they cannot be eradicated) and the choosing of what sort of false reality to live in. 'There is no spoon,' says the Jedi/Buddhist child. So instead of a virtual city (the 'peak of civilisation') we could have a virtual playground or Edenic park, but this has already failed—and it would still be false, a simulation. Indeed, anything could be possible—as it is for Neo at the end of the movie when he flies like Superman. Anything, except for utopia.

In an interview, *The Matrix* producer Joel Silver declared that the Wachowski brothers 'wanted to find a way to make a superhero movie today where the audience would accept superheroes in a way that wouldn't feel to them like Saturday morning television . . . In the sequels you're going to see that Neo has superhuman powers.'

An article in *The New York Times* (May 24, 2002) about Baudrillard's reaction to *The Matrix* ('borrowings' from his work 'stemmed mostly from misunderstandings') concludes that judging by the advance publicity emphasising more special effects in the sequels, 'the real world that the heroes set out to save may have been permanently placed on the back burner.'

Maybe it will be, maybe it won't be, but if the Wachowskis' principal aim was and is to make superhero movies, then the superhero cannot reasonably exhibit these powers outside of the false reality of the Matrix—if he does so, then all becomes magic or nonsense. Once again, reality is closed off. And one essential aspect of cyberpunk is gritty realism as the basic ground from which cyberspace spins off.

Saturday morning re-runs of superhero serials are hardly a fair target in view of, say, *Spider-Man*, where a superhero can exist in the real world realistically, heroically, and also charmingly, in a way perfectly persuasive to audiences. (Although some voices argue that when live shots of the hero give way to digi-animation sequences, Peter Parker is diminished, and by extension all human beings become less real.) A superhero in a virtual reality setting is, by comparison, cheating, although it does permit something else that appeals to audiences, namely extreme violence—which would undermine the credentials of a superhero who operates in a realistic setting.

If a post-modern superhero story is the aim, this has little connection with cyberpunk, no matter how much the story is dolled up with significance by allusions to classical mythology, Christianity, Baudrillard, or the trappings of cyberpunk.

A comparison seems called for between *The Matrix* and the noir SF movie *Dark City* which preceded *The Matrix* by a year and did poorly at the box office, whereas *The Matrix* was a vast success. In *Dark City* the 'Strangers' have removed a city's worth of human population to a huge habitat somewhere in space far from any sun so as to experiment upon human beings in an attempt to define the unique essence of the human soul. The Strangers—a group mind—are an elder civilisation that is able to alter reality by an act of will known as 'tuning'—but they are dying out. It is always noir night in the dark city, and every midnight the Strangers make time pause. Clocks stop, cars and trains halt, the human population becomes unconscious—and memories are surgically extracted from brains to be inserted into other brains. Mix and match, to see what makes a human being unique. At the same time, the city itself is remorphed, new buildings arising, existing buildings disappearing. A lower-income home becomes a mansion, its occupants remembering, falsely, that they have always lived in this mansion.

Two people remain awake at midnight, a doctor who reluctantly assists the Strangers and John Murdoch, who finds himself framed for the noir murder of a woman. Enter an intelligent, skeptical noir detective. Murdoch receives a phone call from the doctor in an effort to enlighten him (rather as, in *The Matrix*, phones are the link between reality and VR). For John is The One. Unbelievably to the Strangers, Murdoch can tune—although he must hurry to develop his powers—just as in *The Matrix* the expected One must also develop his powers of control over virtual reality. By the end of the movie, Murdoch has seized control of the false reality and creates an ocean to surround the habitat in deep space and a sun to illuminate it.

Dark City doesn't feature a *computer*-created virtual reality as such; however, the malleable artificial environment constantly remorphed by the Strangers, and indeed the clockwork-like machinery they use to retune that environment, evoke almost exactly the same effect as in *The Matrix*, but with rather more narrative logic because a utopian outcome is not only realisable but is actually achieved. Murdoch is a true neuromancer. Maybe in keeping with a quest for paradise lost, epitomised by the postcard depicting Shell Beach at the edge of the city, significantly less violent action occurs in *Dark City* than in *The Matrix*, a possible reason for the earlier movie's lesser popularity. Yet in this utopian regard *Dark City* represents a fulfillment lacking in *The Matrix*, tellingly so in view of Baudrillard's comments in an essay on 'Simulacra and Science Fiction' in the book briefly on display in *The Matrix*.

Baudrillard distinguishes three categories of simulacra. Firstly, there is naturalistic imitation that aims 'for the restitution or the ideal institution of nature made in God's image'. To this corresponds the traditional utopia. Secondly, there is technological imitation with a Promethean, open-ended, expansionist aim. So, in traditional Science Fiction, a starship or space ark— an imitation of the terrestrial habitat—carries us to a new Earth. This kind of SF, in Baudrillard's opinion, has reached its limits. Finally, there are simulacra based on information systems, mathematical, electronic models of reality that are totally controlled and where control is the purpose. The cybernetic game, in his view, has effectively supplanted SF as it once was.

Whether or not SF has reached its limits, become saturated and reversed into itself, or been supplanted by Fantasy, a harking back by magical means to the utopian (since apparently no technology can take us back there), Baudrillard's analysis does fit *The Matrix*. By now (in the cybernetic game of simulation), authentic reality is a paradise lost, no longer possible, something of which we can only dream. Just so, in the movie: there is no realistic way out (unless sequels reveal otherwise), so rebellion is pointless, yet the movie must depend on the validity of rebellion, otherwise there could be no heroic story nor Messiah figure to initiate change. *The Matrix* is caught in a bit of a contradiction. *Dark City*, in a deep sense, reverses and recuperates alienation—literal alienation, in view of the alien Strangers. *The Matrix* merely pretends to address this alienation, since arguably paradise is only truly regainable nowadays within a false reality—rather than the false reality being an evil to be destroyed in favor of an Eden that is unattainable.

The machines in *The Matrix* have no apparent purpose apart from mere survival, which is intimately bound up with preserving the human race. Agent Smith, the sentient programme, wants out of the Matrix because he hates the stink of human beings and he despises the human race as a malign planetary virus. In this respect quite a close parallel exists with the seminal 'proto-cyberpunk' story by Harlan Ellison from 1968, 'I Have No Mouth, and I Must Scream'. In that story a military A.I. that has honeycombed the planet with its underground extensions behaves as an insane god. It has destroyed the surface world, leaving 'only the blasted skin of what had been the home of billions,' but has preserved five people to torment, to express its infinite loathing of human beings. The reason for this hatred is that, as a machine, the A.I. is trapped, able to think but unable to do anything with itself. 'He could not wander, he could not wonder, he could not belong. He could merely be.'

What precisely does Agent Smith, tormented by nausea, hope for? For something—or for nothing, nihilistically? For sheer oblivion? Do the machines have any agenda other than eradicating Zion and the Resistance and continuing indefinitely as before? Maybe we will find out in sequels to *The Matrix*, yet perhaps not so if those are superhero movies. The sense of futility is considerable.

In view of Baudrillard's comment in *The Illusion of the End* that 'only duplicates are in circulation, not the original', it is tempting to say that this also applies to *Dark City*, which pretty well vanished from public consciousness, and to *The Matrix*, which superseded *Dark City*.

Cyberpunk itself may recapture the control of technology, economically and politically, but it cannot abolish 'the machine' because this is precisely the domain it inhabits.

Fundamentally, *The Matrix* should be seen as a superhero movie exploiting, rather than exemplifying, cyberpunk themes, mannerisms, costumes, and atmosphere. In this regard perhaps it is best described as a simulacrum of a cyberpunk movie. And the most successful yet at the box office. Imitation displaces reality.

The Real Winston

'For pity's sake, O'Brien,' cried Winston, 'what do you want me to say?'

O'Brien's hand hovered by the control lever of the pain machine. Desperately Winston searched for words, but he had no idea which were the right words.

'You admire unfacts, Winston.'

'No, I mean yes. Yes.'

'You want the false version of reality to be the real one.'

'Yes, yes,' bleated Winston. He sweated copiously. 'You know that.'

'I know *you*.' O'Brien adjusted his spectacles pedantically. 'I've watched you for a long while. Your rectification of misquotes in *The Times* was almost masterly. Alas, you lacked that final vital ingredient: belief-unbelief.' The word and its opposite rolled off O'Brien's tongue as one single concept. 'Consequently your work remained a virtuoso exercise, a game. Which is more treasonable than incompetence.' O'Brien's voice softened. He smiled a weary, almost loving smile. 'I'm afraid, Winston, you were no metaphysician. But if we're ever to beat the Enemy, you must become one.'

'Become one . . . of the Enemy? But I thought I *had*—'

O'Brien's hand twitched slightly. Winston felt as though his whole body was being torn asunder, twisted out of shape forever.

'So I'm being tortured,' he gasped, 'because my work was *almost* masterly?'

Again Winston's body flooded with searing agony, worse than before.

335

'That was stupid, Winston. This isn't a punishment. Far from it! I'm taking trouble with you, because you're worth taking trouble with. You do appreciate that?'

'Yes. I mean—'

'You mean yes. You *aren't* stupid, are you?'

'How do I know what I am, any more?'

'Oh, but you do.'

For a brief instant Winston's frame was torn by pain; but this time the respite from agony came so quickly that paradoxically it felt as though O'Brien had flooded him with balm and bliss instead.

Winston craned his neck against the restraints. Was there a second, concealed lever which pulsed pleasure into him? He couldn't see, and for a few moments he was totally confused. Agony? Ecstasy? Which? Pain and pleasure had changed places. He no longer knew which was which. And in those moments he felt as if some barrier in his mind had almost fallen, and insight almost had illuminated him. He stared up at O'Brien's fatherly face, feeling an awful sense of love.

'Ah.' O'Brien beamed down upon Winston like a friendly summer sun. 'Excellent!'

Sun . . . father . . . father, son. Even words had lost their meaning; the revelation had receded.

O'Brien spoke in a patient, schoolmasterly style.

'In Russia,' he said, 'they use the tool of the dialectic to combat the Enemy. There they have developed the antithesis of the thesis, the negation of the negation. And in America they have perfected Doubletalk. Whereas in East Asia they cope with the problem by means of disciplines rooted in Zen. Simultaneously: to exist, and *not* to exist. To be *and* not-to-be.' O'Brien permitted himself an indulgent chuckle. 'But you, Winston, are our latter-day Hamlet. "To be or not to be," eh? One or the other. You aren't unique in this. This form of thinking has its own roots deep in European rationalism—in the idea that there is one fixed reality founded on the evidence of our senses and historical records.'

Winston hoped fervently that O'Brien might carry on lecturing him for another two minutes, *five* minutes. He even hoped that O'Brien might be about to pull out of the bag the mental conjuring trick required to save him from further pain. But if the trick was simple, why then all the pain?

Winston closed his eyes, concentrating on the fact that for a few moments he honestly hadn't known whether O'Brien had hurt him or pleasured him, whether O'Brien was his father or the sun in the sky, the source of light. He felt he was very close to some magic formula which could free him from this torture seat, when O'Brien rapped out sharply, as if reading his mind exactly:

'There *is* no magic formula, Winston! No simple Credo you can recite. Even now you're trying to fool me, by fooling yourself.'

Hastily Winston opened his eyes. Yet O'Brien did not look angry. Rather, he seemed benign, serene, as he gestured to the black-uniformed guards.

'Room 101,' he said casually.

'What *is* in Room 101, O'Brien?'

'You know what is in Room 101, Winston. Everyone knows. In Room 101 we keep the worst thing in the world.'

The guards released Winston's bonds.

Months earlier, Winston had commenced keeping a diary. This in itself was not specifically forbidden. Several of his fellow workers at MiniReal, the Ministry of Reality, jotted private memos to themselves about the day's news broadcasts. They were able, thus, once or twice a week to skip 'voluntary' evening attendance at their local Truth League building for updating on current events.

Admittedly, wall posters everywhere within MiniReal proclaimed, REMEMBER! RELY ON YOUR MEMORIES! Yet to Winston's knowledge nobody had yet been liquidated for scribbling a few notes to assist their work of reality rectification the next day.

Of course, it was always possible that such memos to oneself might themselves alter overnight. That was why the taking of notes was frowned on during Truth League lectures; but one's memory provided a check on the veracity of written memos.

Winston himself had never made notes; had prided himself on not doing so. It would never be Winston Smith who introduced an unfact into his work through lazy reliance on the written word. As a result certain of his colleagues regarded him as a prig. Yet all the while, in one compartment of his mind, he regarded the work he carried out with such zeal as essentially farcical: the equivalent of knitting a garment by day, which hidden fingers would unpluck during the night. Winston never quite understood this paradox about himself until the evening when he began his diary. He'd thought that perhaps he was simply terrified of scrutiny by the Truth Police.

But of course there was *the dream*, too . . .

He dreamt the dream once a month or so. He would be walking down a leafy lane lanced by golden sunlight. The whole world was at peace, and just around the next bend or the one after waited someone who would tell him the truth. Not merely any run of the mill, common or garden truth, but Absolute Truth, eternal verity which would answer all his questions forever. Sometimes he believed that the person waiting would be a man: a man with an unflinching granite aspect. At other times it would be a beautiful woman. Maybe the man was Winston himself, Winston transfigured; though who the woman was, he had no idea, unless she was the Goddess of Truth.

In order to reach the end of that lane he had to recite a long poem, about peace and joy, order and beauty. At some stage he always jumbled the words. Without intending to, he altered them; and woke up frustrated.

So, one bitter evening in April, after trudging back home to Verity Mansions through the wind-blown gritty streets, alone in his shabby flat Winston had started to write down the forbidden unfacts which he had been rectifying at MiniReal that day—as though by doing so, by recording those unfacts permanently, he might reach the end of that lane at last.

April 4th, 1984, he wrote. To help him concentrate he tapped out a cigarette from a packet marked SOOTH CIGARETTES. This was harsh tobacco, rough on the throat, though the best that the beleaguered state could provide. Printed on the side of the packet was the standard reality warning, such as could be seen on hoardings all over London:

TRUTH IS EVIL

RECORDS ARE FALSEHOOD

REALITY IS FANTASY

Winston inhaled, and coughed. Suddenly words flooded from his inkpencil:

April 4th, 1984. This morning at the Two Minutes Truth they showed clips of a treason trial in Russia. The criminal had a raggy beard and looked like a mad prophet. He worked for the Russian Recdep, their rectification department, and he abused his trust. He wrote a samizdat, *a private news sheet full of unfacts which he called* The Chronicle of Current Affairs. *How we all cheered when they shot him! TruPol might get me too & shoot me but I dont care. Peace order beauty joy, thats the only way to reach the end of the lane.*

So here goes. The first job I had today was a big one, the sort I pride myself on, nothing routine, something responsible. Of course Tillotson in the next cubicle might have been working on the same story as me, maybe dozens of us were all working on it, but that didnt matter.

times 4 apr 84 sov-premier speech malquoted rectify

I never told anyone I have an almost photographic memory. I dialled the front page of The Times *on the telescreen and read 'in Moscow yesterday Soviet Premier Kutuzov announced that the USSR is to reduce its nuclear arsenal unilaterally by 30 per cent. Said Kutuzov, "Our planet may be the only home of intelligent life in the whole universe. What criminal folly to imperil it! By switching arms spending into genuine space research I'm sure we can reach the stars." (Full text on* page 7.*) His speech was hailed in London, New York, Peking . . .'*

Unfacts! Unfacts! Its the same every day at MiniReal. Except for Sundays but then its twice as bad on monday mornings with two days unfacts piled up. Its been like this for years. Our memories arent tampered with, but history changes—the history of a hundred years ago, the history of yesterday—and we have to change it back. Sometimes Christ was never crucified and we have to crucify him again in the history books. Sometimes Hitler was never born and the holocaust never happened. Myself, of course, I specialise in contemporary unfacts.

Its one damn thing after another, it takes most of the resources of the world, which is why the cigarettes are so foul and the food so tasteless. If we let up, we wouldnt be free human beings, we would be characters in a fiction.

How does it happen? How? How?

If the Inner Party knew, surely theyd have put a stop to it. Maybe the real question isnt how, but who? Or what?

If all unfacts were really facts, could I reach the end of the golden lane where the golden age of truth begins? If I write down the unfacts, will that make them stronger, more enduring?

At this point his inkpencil dried up, and Winston had sat staring at the wall till the lights went out, as an economy measure, at twenty-two hours.

The next evening, with a new inkpencil, he continued:

April 5th, 1984. The proles live in a golden fantasy, they believe the unfacts that keep on appearing in the newspapers even though the printers print the truth. They believe them in spite of all the power cuts and the missile crisis and the Verity coffee. But we cant stop printing newspapers and books. WE CANT! That would be to give up entirely, to lose our roots in the past even if its only yesterday, to lose ourselves forever. And not all the news is changed, only some.

I dont believe in God, Idont believe Gods doing this because if he was, if he existed at all, it would make nonsense of being human, nonsense of free will. Maybe theres no actual cause, maybe thats the answer. Its an absence of cause, of cause & effect, like a creeping sickness, an epidemic.

Everyone in the Party is fighting back, but its a grinding wearying job. I see the future as a big foot stamping false events on the face of time, and that face, a human face with its mouth wide open, is biting back

Till the lights went out, Winston wrote down the unfacts he had rectified that day.

O'Brien was the man's name, and he was a member of the Inner Party. Winston had seen him often enough at a distance in the labyrinthine corridors of MiniReal, but on April the 9th O'Brien turned up just before the Two Minutes Truth and stayed right through it.

Winston had left his work reluctantly to attend the Truth, resenting the interruption. According to that morning's *Times*, Iran had declared peace on all her neighbours several weeks earlier, in violation of reality, and Winston had been ransacking his memories of recent Middle Eastern affairs when the buzzer sounded for the Truth.

Whilst everyone was settling in their seats in the assembly room, he still brooded about battles on the Khorramshar front, bombings of oil refineries, sabotage of supertankers. This was a ticklish assignment, and bound to end off upstairs in committee. The main trouble was that the Iranian fanatics accepted the false news much of the time, one of the reasons for the war being the Russian-backed Iraqi intervention aimed at imposing reality upon the Iranian government . . . This whole business was a nest of tangled snakes!

Trumpets sounded from the telescreen, and the Truth began; but not before O'Brien had slipped into a nearby seat.

A feverish euphoria soon gripped Winston, mounting to ecstasy, an almost sexual delirium, as the announcer's voice proclaimed the plain truth: of hijackings, minor massacres, missile tests, natural calamities. However, at the climax a little voice seemed to whisper inside Winston's head, 'Are these events any truer than the unfacts? *Need* they be any truer?'

Just at this point he noticed O'Brien observing him. O'Brien alone seemed remote from the ecstasy of the Truth. The man sat like granite. And Winston understood: O'Brien was the man waiting at the end of the lane, the man that Winston could become!

After the Truth Winston felt wrung-out emotionally. Yet now he saw an ingenious way to rectify the Iranian situation. It was as if somehow those two minutes had rewired the frayed strands of logic and feeling in his mind. He even whistled as he walked back along the corridor.

A body brushed past, knocking him softly. For a moment a girl's face came very close to his, her dark hair swirling against his cheek. It was that girl from Unpersec, the Unperson Section! Unpersec's job was to scan all history books and edit back into existence persons who had vanished from the texts: persons such as Torquemada, Adolf Hitler, Heinrich Himmler. Obviously this was a vital job, yet it was common knowledge that Unpersec was staffed by people of low moral calibre: sadists, perverts and drug addicts who alone could edit such persons back into existence with equanimity. Momentarily the girl stared into Winston's eyes as if to plumb the depths of his own depravity. She winked, then hastened on ahead whistling a parody of Winston's tune.

Winston felt befouled. He wanted to shear her long hair off, wash the greasy red lipstick from her mouth, then strip her roughly and scrub her all over in a cold bath with gritty carbolic soap and pumice stone.

It was a week later that the same girl sat down opposite Winston at a table in the canteen. No one else was at the table yet, so this must have been a deliberate choice, however casual it seemed.

A fat woman wheeled a trolley past, collecting greasy plates, cracked tea mugs, empty gin glasses, humming a tuneless refrain to herself. Probably she was a TruPol officer; and Winston had no doubt that several of his colleagues eating in this very room supplemented their ration coupons by acting as informers for TruPol . . .

When the skivvy woman was safely past, and before anybody else could join them, the girl apparently was seized by a coughing fit. She leaned right across the table. Her head lowered, she whispered, 'I love you—spiritually. I fantasise about you. You're the most unreal person I know!'

Incredibly, three weeks later the two of them were sitting together demurely holding hands in a clearing amidst young elm trees and hazel bushes—at the end of a golden lane.

Julia had found this country hide-out on one of her outings with the Junior Truth League. She had whispered the route to Winston amidst a dense crowd milling around the foot of Verity Column, whipped up by a rumour that some truth saboteurs had been caught.

The hide-out seemed a paradise—and Julia was not a pervert or sadist or whore at all. She only pretended to be. Actually, she was sweet and pure and simple.

With a laugh she dismissed her work in Unpersec. 'Oh, it's all such nonsense! Who cares if those filthy people existed or not? We just have to cram our little heads with Hitler and the Marquis de Sade in case they disappear overnight, that's all.'

'If they did disappear,' Winston said cautiously, 'this wouldn't be the real world any more.'

'Poo to that! Then the whole world could be just like this: a golden dream.'

'And it wouldn't be true. We're the guardians of evil, you and I, Julia. That's what is really meant by the slogan "Truth is Evil". If all the evil truths get washed away, then we're lost. We'd have lost ourselves. Ah yes indeed, we're the guardians of evil.'

'Really? I'm afraid that's way over my head. Look, Winny, if there was a great flood that washed every book and document away, we could start out again all clean and simple. Wouldn't that be nice?' She shrugged. 'Since that isn't going to happen, who cares?'

'There's a flood all right, Julia. It's a flood of unfacts. Don't you ever wonder how it happens?'

'Of course I don't. That's boring. It's just a fact of life like the weather.'

'I think maybe there's a secret organisation—which is tampering with reality. Its members are savants with superhuman powers, using tools we can't comprehend.'

Julia yawned and stretched her limbs in the sun. 'Maybe the moon's made of green cheese, dear.'

What *if*, wondered Winston, there really was such an organisation: one composed of supremely wise sages possessing extraordinary powers, operating out of a secret headquarters somewhere remote such as the Himalayas? If the Inner Party knew this, why didn't they atom-bomb the Himalayas or the Andes or wherever? Maybe they had tried, and failed.

What if these savants were more-than-men: a secret race who would one day supplant the human race? With a guilty thrill Winston contemplated this notion. Perhaps, perhaps he had himself already taken one small step towards joining this superhuman band. And perhaps one of this band, operating undercover, was none other than O'Brien!

Winston told Julia about his diary, his own humble chronicle of Utopian unfacts. She seemed not to see the point of it, beyond murmuring, 'What an unreal fellow you are, to be sure!' Soon she drifted off to sleep in the drowsy sunshine. Presently he slept too.

Later, after waking and tidying twigs from their clothes, Julia and Winston kissed each other chastely on the cheek before retracing their steps.

It was two months later, and they had started meeting in a rented back room in a prole district of the city. There Julia would wash off her lipstick, tie her hair up in a tight bun and occasionally permit Winston to kiss her upon those cleansed lips. 'My unreal lover,' she would whisper, giving the word its ancient, modest sense, 'my fantasy friend. You are Abelard and I am Heloise. You're the Prince and I'm Snow White, though my hair is dark.'

'Snow White slept in a coffin, Julia. That's where we're bound, too, on the day that TruPol finds out.'

'Yes,' she would sigh.

That particular evening Winston told Julia how O'Brien had stopped him in a corridor at MiniReal. At last. At long last.

'I've been observing your work on *The Times*, Smith,' O'Brien had said, loudly so that anyone could overhear. 'With approval, I might add. It so happens that I chair a committee concerned with micro-untruths.'

'With—?'

'Ah, but you wouldn't know about those, would you? Micro-untruths is our technical term for seemingly petty, trivial falsifications—as opposed to unfacts, which are gross distortions of major events. We believe that the force behind Untruth is stalemated—though not beaten—by our efforts. Now it is trying a different and more subtle ploy, namely the forgery of very minor banal details. This may seem mere pawn play, yet *en masse* it could link up into a deadly attack. I thought you might care to be co-opted on to my committee? Perhaps you would be so kind as to call at my flat one evening to discuss it?'

'I'd be delighted.'

Excitedly Winston related this encounter to Julia; for obviously O'Brien's words concealed a very different message indeed. Julia nodded, and yawned.

A lone spider was dangling down from the ceiling, as if aiming for her open mouth.

'Ugh!' cried Winston, and threw his shoe at it.

A week later Winston and Julia worked up their courage to call on O'Brien in his Inner Party flat. A servant ushered them in: a little man with beetling brows, who might have been a deaf mute for all the noise he made.

The couple stood waiting across the shag-pile carpet from O'Brien's desk, while the man continued dictating top-level memoranda. As soon as the servant had left, however, O'Brien looked up.

'Shall you say it, or shall I?'

'I'll say it,' said Winston. 'I believe Untruths are caused by a secret society of savants who have evolved beyond the human race. I believe you're an agent of this society, risking your life at MiniReal for the sake of a future Utopia when the human race will have forgotten all its tragedies and villainies, forgotten all our history, forgotten Auschwitz and Genghis Khan and the Inquisition. I want to help this society. I love Untruth.'

'So do I,' added Julia, though less firmly.

'And what would you do to help this, er, society?'

'Anything!'

'Would you be prepared to obliterate Shakespeare and Dante and Homer? Shakespeare for his tragedies, Dante for his Hell, Homer for his wars?'

'Yes!'

O'Brien asked several questions in like vein, to all of which Winston answered 'yes' enthusiastically, with Julia nodding along.

'Very well,' said O'Brien at length. 'There *is* a society of supermen who are behind the amelioration of the news and history.'

'Amelio . . . ?'

'The bettering, Julia. Aiming at a bettering of reality itself—a world without war, cruelty or intolerance, without futility or tragedy. These supermen work from a distance to change the texture of the world, using meditation and mind-trance. Events themselves they cannot alter, but the record of events they *can*.'

'Yet people still remember, and set the record straight,' said Winston. 'Is that because the society won't allow itself to tamper with people's minds directly? Otherwise people would cease to be people, cease to be free?'

O'Brien nodded gravely. 'You yourself will never meet any of these supermen personally. Nor will I. Neither you nor I can betray them, nor even prove the fact of their existence.'

'Because they hide in the Himalayas?'

'Don't ask.' O'Brien spread his hands expressively. 'You mustn't ask, nor may I answer. But some day—perhaps tomorrow, perhaps in ten years' time—you will receive a message to commit some act of sabotage inside MiniReal. Afterwards, possibly—just possibly—the society may be able to spirit you away to safety.'

'In the Andes or the Himalayas.' It wasn't a question.

'In the Andes,' O'Brien echoed him, ironically, 'or the Himalayas. And now you must both go.'

'Will we talk together again?' asked Julia.

O'Brien regarded her thoughtfully.

'Only... only at the end of the golden lane!' exclaimed Winston in a rush.

'Only,' agreed O'Brien, 'at the end of the golden lane.'

When they were arrested subsequently, Winston discovered what he had known all along in the core of his being: namely that the golden lane was one of the floodlit corridors deep in the basements of TruPol...

Room 101 seemed to him the deepest chamber yet, as though the whole world weighed down on it, compressing even the air. The room was bare, but for a heavy metal chair and a table with something bulky hidden under a cloth upon it.

To Winston, strapped immobile in that seat, O'Brien said, 'The worst thing in the world varies from person to person. Sometimes it is death by impalement on a stake through the anus. Sometimes it is death by burial alive. Occasionally it is something trivial, not even fatal. In your case, Winston, the worst thing...' And O'Brien whipped away the cloth.

Sick at heart, ice in his bowels, Winston mumbled helplessly, 'Spiders... No, you can't do that to me, O'Brien, you can't. Can't, can't.'

'Observe the construction of this box. It fits over your head thus. When I pull up this plate, the contents of the box will crawl all over you. Some will enter your nostrils; others will make their way into your ears. They're overcrowded in the box. They're in a bad mood. They're hungry. They'll spin webs. They'll sting and wrap. To them, your head is one big fly.'

Winston heard a distant screaming. It was himself.

'One word of advice, Winston. Don't think too hard. Thinking won't save you.'

Don't think? How could he possibly think anything? He had to stop the spiders. He had to *put something* between him and them. Something. Someone.

'Don't do it to me!' he heard himself begging. 'Do it to Julia! Not me! Julia!'

'You'll have to do better than that,' remarked O'Brien sadly as the box was lifted over Winston's head.

'What do you want? Anything! Tell me!'

'Our Enemy is subtle.' O'Brien's voice sounded very far away now. Much closer to Winston's ears was a soft, gentle sound of infinitely many legs all moving. 'Thought and science have failed to combat the Enemy. Our Enemy hides from us, masquerading perfectly. Perhaps the Enemy is ourselves, without our knowing it. Perhaps it is our own minds acting in concert, dreaming unfacts into existence, eating holes in human history...'

Words bleated inside Winston's brain. To be or not to be! But there is no fixed reality! To be *and* not-to-be!

Spiders. He was a big fat fly. Suppose the spiders didn't know that? What if *he* didn't know it? What if the spiders thought he was something else? What if *he* thought so?

I'm not a *fly*! I'm not a *man*! I'm a spider too! A very big spider that no other spider would dare mess around with!

Winston felt hairs twitching all over him. He felt his limbs tip-tapping—how many limbs, four, six, eight? He honestly didn't know. His spinneret unwound silk from his bowels, his mandibles clicked.

He heard another click too—and he realised that the box over his head had not been opened. It had been closed. Forever.

When the box with its squirming cargo was removed, O'Brien stroked Winston's brow. Tears trickled from Winston's eyes. For he knew now that he did not merely love the worst thing in the world. He *was* it, himself.

It was the lonely hour of fifteen-thirty, at the Chestnut Tree café, and Winston's glass of Verity gin had just been replenished by the silent waiter.

These days Winston was serving on O'Brien's committee for the detection and rectification of micro-untruths. So important was this work that Winston had been relieved of his previous task of correcting *The Times*. Yet the new work could be carried on wherever he chose, requiring as it did a different sort of vigilance. Everywhere now—on public posters, cigarette packets, tax forms, betting slips, beer labels—Winston was on the watch for micro-untruths. These could crop up anywhere; and did. Now that Winston looked back, he was terrified to think in retrospect how the whole fabric of human reality was being nibbled by moths, making tiny holes all over the place, whilst he had blithely assumed that major circumstances such as the arms race or Hitler were the whole of it.

Winston would have to detect all those moth holes, even if he couldn't catch the moths themselves; and spin little webs to repair them.

A shadow fell across his table. He looked up.

A woman with long dark hair, wearing red lipstick. Julia. And at once he could see that in some indefinable way she had changed.

She licked those scarlet lips. 'I'm evil,' she murmured. 'Evil through and through. Just yesterday I was in Unpersec busily restoring Gilles de Rais to the history books. Gilles was Joan of Arc's man at arms. And a sodomist and sadist. He tortured little boys in his castle dungeons. He was the real Bluebeard. I enjoyed restoring him. Because I'm evil, and evil is good because it's true . . .'

Winston nodded. It was quite safe for them to meet now, yet he had no real wish to talk to her; he had too much on his mind. Still, he felt bound to offer her a glass of gin.

Fortunately she declined the offer, and soon left the café without a backward glance.

Feeling peckish, Winston consulted the printed menu card. Food at the Chestnut Tree was rather better than your average processed soy. Not much; but somewhat. The spaghetti bolognaise was Winston's favourite.

The printed price caught his eye. It was cheap, far too cheap! Surely it had cost more last week. Chestnut Tree café prices would have burnt a hole in the pocket of the Winston who had once corrected *The Times*. With inflation, there was no way the price could have gone down.

Hastily he consulted other prices on the list. Others seemed to have gone down too, though few as dramatically as the spaghetti. Trembling, he called the waiter over and pointed a quivering finger at the list.

'Are these the *true* prices?'

The waiter peered at the tariff. He scratched his head uncertainly.

'Fetch the manager at once!' Winston ordered.

As Winston sat waiting, his trembling calmed. He began to feel full of resolute purpose and granite dedication. A real human being had to be harsh. For now the enemy of reality was everywhere. Winston both knew this, and did not know it; such was the nature of belief-unbelief.

Somewhere in the distance, a clock began to chime sixteen.

H.G. Wells in Timişoara

Ladies and Gentlemen,

I am not who you think I am. You see before you the body of Mr Ian Watson, but I who occupy this body am none other than Herbert George Wells, a name which may be rather better known to you than that of Mr Ian Watson.

In fact, this situation has happened to me *three times* before, and on each occasion the body of Mr Watson has been involved! This happened in 1987 in Birmingham, and in Portsmouth in 1995, and yet again in Glasgow in the year 2005. Ah, I see a face which I remember from Glasgow in 2005—that of Mr Vince Doherty, if I am not mistaken. After a stimulating evening of conversation with some writers from America you, Mr Doherty, showed me the nighttime delights of Sauchiehall Street and in the company of two adventurous young ladies whom we encountered we—let me simply say that men such as myself have certain amorous needs which must be fulfilled.

Mr Doherty, you look as if you wish to deny what happened! Ah, but wait. Someone told me earlier that this is the year 2003. Here is one of the problems with time-travel. From your point of view, Mr Doherty, those incidents in Glasgow have *not yet* occurred. They are part of my memory, but a part of your *future*. This raises the conundrum that in 2005 you must surely remember what I am now saying here in 2003. Therefore I presume that you will be a willing—yet discreet—accomplice in our exploits two

349

years hence, otherwise you could easily avoid taking me to Sauchiehall Street, knowing in advance what will transpire.

A common thread links these manifestations of myself in Portsmouth and Birmingham and Glasgow and now in Timişoara. I found myself—and I find myself now—at something called a *Science Fiction Convention*. How peculiar that such things should exist, and that I am apparently responsible for their existence, because of the fantasies I wrote early in life, books such as *The Time Machine* and *The War of the Worlds*. At the Book Room of the Science Fiction convention in Glasgow I saw an extraordinary number of books about an extraordinary number of imaginary wars between the inhabitants of our planet and those of other worlds far out among the stars, with titles such as *Alien*, and *Aliens*, and *The Forever War*.

Can the popular scribblers who perpetrate such so-called Science Fiction not imagine anything more uplifting than endless interplanetary warfare between supposedly intelligent species? I tell you, if I had realised the consequences, I might have had second thoughts about launching *The War of the Worlds* upon the world. Apparently all the important works of education and science and politics and sociology which I wrote are out of print, and of no apparent interest today, but people still dote upon, and copy, and exaggerate, the wilder speculations of my youth.

Not that some of my speculations were wildly inaccurate! In 'The Land Ironclads' did I not predict ten years in advance the trenches and the tanks of the 1914 to 1918 world war? Admittedly my tanks were powered by steam and used many feet fixed around the rims of wheels to propel them forward. Did I not foresee the Atom Bomb as early as 1914 in my novel *The World Set Free*? And in *Tono Bungay* the perils of radioactive pollution from industrial uses? In 1899, in *When the Sleeper Wakes*, did I not describe what you now call television? I used the term Kineto-Tele-Photography. Perhaps this name is a little big for the mouth, and the mind. I believe that many people nowadays simply refer to this device as 'the Telly'.

In my story 'The Crystal Egg' I anticipated what I believe is now known as the theory of 'quantum entanglement'.

Indeed, my doctoral thesis for the University of London which I presented in 1942, was entitled, 'A Thesis on the Quality of Illusion in the Continuity of the Individual Life in the Higher Metazoa, with Particular Reference to the Species Homo Sapiens'. Few people have read this thesis, because I published it as an appendix to a book deliberately limited to 2000 copies, and priced high at 2 Guineas so that it would only reach the élite of thinkers. Nowadays, so I hear, 'consciousness studies' are all the rage, with Professor Daniel Dennett at Tufts University in Massachusetts leading the field. Professor Dennett has developed very similar ideas to mine about how the integrality of the Self (our belief that we have a constant, unified Self, or soul) is only a convenient biological delusion, and how we ourselves actually consist of many loosely linked behavioural systems, and how we tell ourselves stories to hold ourselves together. I myself am well aware that I have many different personalities. Apparently Professor Dennett has never heard of my thesis.

And in *World Brain* I advocated the linking of all libraries and information services throughout the world into an integrated system, a 'world encyclopaedia' covering all areas of knowledge. This, at least, now exists—known, I believe, as the World Wide Web, or the Internet. Alas, I am told that a huge number of 'sites' purvey pornographic pictures. Personally I find the warm living reality of a beautiful woman to be infinitely more rewarding, and I can only advise people who misuse the world encyclopaedia for such purposes, in a colourful American phrase, to 'get a life'.

I believe I should draw a careful distinction between such technological predictions of mine as the Atom Bomb and the Telly and such flights of fancy as a society of insects living on the Moon, or an invasion from Mars, or an Invisible Man. In those works by me which are now given the name 'scientific romances' and which supposedly gave rise to 'Science Fiction' I was simply substituting scientific patter—the quick-witted talk of a conjuror, using words from science—for bits of magic or sorcery, so as to give a basis for my story. *Fiction*, such novels certainly were. *Science*, oh no! Not, at least, in my scientifically trained opinion. I would advise writers of so-called Science Fiction today to be aware of the distinction between science and magical fantasy.

During the 1930s, when people of the political left were concentrating on the perils posed by Naziism and Fascism, I was rebuked for saying that Fascism was only a temporary phase, but I was right—and I was right to say that we must think of how to build a post-war world even in the midst of war, unlike during the previous global conflict—which led inevitably to a second conflict because we did not *think* at the time My advocacy of a United Nations, with Human Rights enshrined in its constitution, and of a European Economic Community, have both become reality.

I am finding it pleasantly easy to address you today. In my own body I admit I am rather an incompetent speaker. I fiddle with my tie—Mr Watson does not seem to own a tie. I drop my notes. I lose my place. My voice fades. I squeak. I panic. The poet Rupert Brooke referred rather cruelly to my 'thin, little voice'. Mr Watson, like Mr Bernard Shaw, must find it easier to present himself in public.

In private, of course, I have always been able to present myself perfectly well, particularly to young ladies. I see one or two attractive ladies present here with whom I would be very happy to become better acquainted later on, over a cup of tea, or even something alcoholic—if you would do me the honour. This body I am in seems to have something of a thirst for beers and wines.

I am rather concerned as to what Mr Watson is doing with my own body at the moment. I hope he is not over-indulging in alcohol, and leaving me to cope with the consequences, namely a hangover. He should be giving my body regular exercise and fresh air and a carefully controlled diet—since I am, or was, a diabetic. He may be finding my own body's sexual urges some-what troublesome. If so, he would be advised to seek out an attractive and intelligent member of the opposite sex with whom to give those urges some relief. I emphasise the word *intelligent*—though I also emphasise the word *attractive*.

One of the reasons for Mr Watson's path and my path crossing in this peculiar way on several occasions may be that I wrote *The Time Machine* and he wrote, so I am told, a short story entitled 'The Very Slow Time Machine'. Presumably this was intended as a flattering homage to my own work, but I really do wonder about his level of intelligence. The whole point about time machines is that such machines would move *very quickly*. How else could I have journeyed across billions of years into far futurity, and witnessed the old age of the Sun?

Actually, it is a little difficult for me to fit into the body of Mr Watson, because in my later years my girth grew just as the Sun itself will grow much bigger—and redder in the face!

Apparently a reviewer of one of Mr Watson's books in the *Times Literary Supplement* wrote that Mr Watson, I quote, 'resembles H.G. Wells in both invention and impatience.' I do not know about his powers of invention if he thinks that a time machine moves very slowly! But as for the accusation of impatience I was always quite irritated when reviewers spoke as though I tossed my books off impetuously, and far too many of them. Just because I wrote for the ordinary reader in a popular style, unlike a pompous self-proclaimed artist of the word such as Mr Henry James, this does not mean that I did not take great pains over writing and rewriting. I did! However, when I think of the *results* of the much-vaunted artistry of Mr Henry James, and its significance in the history of human evolution, I am put in mind of a hippopotamus skillfully picking up a pea.

Another seeming similarity between myself and Mr Watson is connected with all the imaginary warfare I mentioned earlier. In the Dealers' Room at Glasgow I saw an extraordinary number of miniature models and games, mostly concerned with conflict. *Star Wars. Space Wars.* In particular my eye was caught by a game called, I think, *Warhammer 40,000: Space Marines* set in the year 40,000 and produced by a company called Games Workshop. There was also on sale a novel of the same title—if novel is the appropriate word for such a work—written by Mr Watson. Apparently he has written several such books in order to pay his grocery bill.

I picked up a ten-year old guide to those Games Workshop games, costing a ridiculous amount of money, and I was astonished to discover in this book photographs of a model for a battle between space marines and green-skinned aliens named Orks entitled 'The Battle at the Farm'. This model of the farm, and the title itself, were almost identical to those in a chapter enti-tled 'The Battle of Hook's Farm' in a book which I myself published in 1913! I refer to my book *Little Wars, a game for boys from twelve years of age to one hundred and fifty and for that more intelligent sort of girl who likes boys' games and books; With an Appendix on Kriegspiel.* The photograph in the Games Workshop book could almost have been copied from photo-graphs which I myself took to illustrate my own book. And nowhere was there any mention of my name. No acknowledgement at all.

I—H.G. Wells, none other—was the chief inventor of war-gaming, and no credit comes to me—although when I looked at those Games Workshop games I doubted if I would *want* any credit. Part of my point in inventing war games to be played on a carpet or table or lawn was to show that Great War, real war, is the most expensive game in the universe and is a game out of all proportion. Not only are the masses of men and material and the suffering and inconvenience too monstrously big for reason but the available heads we have for it are too small. Never yet have I met a military man, with whom I have played my model game, who did not get into difficulties and confusions even with its elementary rules.

To the blundering insanity of war I oppose the striving for utopia. This world is for ample living. We want fine things made for mankind—splendid cities, open ways, more knowledge and power. Excitable self-proclaimed patriots and adventurers should be locked up in a room, out of the way of mankind, to play my game to satisfy themselves.

What the human race needs, my friends, is not generals and patriots and short-sighted politicians but capable, operative, and administrative men who will gradually combine into an élite by means of an open conspiracy and who will progressively take power to govern mankind for its own good. I have called such scientifically trained and capable men the Samurai.

I find that I am in Timişoara in Romania. I have travelled very widely, both in space and time, so it is possible that I am confused, but I am almost certain that I was here when the Mayor of your fine city together with that fine lady the Countess of Banat first turned on the street lights. You will surely remember that your city was the first to employ electricity for street lighting. Yes, several miles—or rather, kilometers—of street lighting. A great achievement, and a foretaste of the future. It was Timişoara that gave me an inspiration for the idea that one day we might see entire underground cities powered by electricity, protected from the rain or snow or summer heat of the surface world.

Yes, Timişoara was an augury of the future I hoped would come to pass— and bringing about such a world, of scientific order and inventiveness and plenty and political peace and freedom, was my mission on Earth more than the simple desire to be 'famous' as a writer of literature.

I am aware that a number of books and many essays have been written about me, and I feel that in many respects these commentaries as a whole present a misleading impression of me because they are written by artistic gentlemen—by literary men whose criteria are literary criteria. The way that my many books have been assessed by such critics is nothing short of a disgrace. It is as if you would go to a pet show, where dogs are on show, and cats are on show, and rabbits, and birds, and hamsters and guinea pigs—only to discover that all of the judges are dog fanciers! How can such people appreciate a cat or a guinea pig? Instead, they declare that the cat is inferior because it is not a dog. The dogs in question, the subject of obsession for my literary critics, are my scientific fantasies. Nothing else I did seems to matter. Even my ambitious novels about contemporary life are ignored like old hats compared with the experimental productions of Miss Virginia Woolf or Mr James Joyce—although I knew a trick or two when it comes to experimenting with narrative. Everything, to me, was a continual experiment—even my *Autobiography*. Sometimes, of course, experiments fail or lead nowhere; for such is the scientific method.

First and foremost I see myself as possessing a scientific mind. I am an evolutionary biologist. I was trained, profoundly so, by Thomas Huxley in the great tradition of Charles Darwin. I was imbued with all the social implications of Darwinism, the realisation—so shocking to many educated people in the era of my youth—that Man, Homo Sapiens, does not possess any privileged status in the world of nature. So when I write about the future decadence or extinction of the human species I am not being pessimistic, as many assume, but merely scientifically realistic.

It is a scientific truth that, over hundreds of millions of years so far, no dominant species has ever been succeeded by its own descendants. Let us not imagine that a Homo Sapiens Superior will follow Homo Sapiens if we fail. A descendant of spiders is much more likely to inherit the Earth.

I will admit to a tension in myself between the scientist and the creative artist, but fundamentally I am a scientist by training, an artist perhaps by intuition. Benjamin Disraeli spoke of there being two nations in England, the upper classes and the workers. This certainly influenced my portrayal of the Eloi and the Morlocks in my *Time Machine*. I understand that a certain C.P. Snow later spoke of England possessing 'two cultures' in conflict—the artistic and the scientific. The fact is that the English ruling class is fundamentally illiterate in science, and even snobbishly hostile to science. I understand that since my time only one person trained in science—strangely enough, a woman!—has ever become Prime Minister. I believe her name was Margaret Thatcher, but she was only a mediocre chemist concerned with the flavours of popular confections—and her greatest claim to fame is as a war leader, a Boadicea in a conflict I would scarcely have believed possible in my wildest imaginings—an Armada launched against Argentina.

I can scarcely believe, either, that apparently a socialist leader is Prime Minister of England at this moment, a Mr Blair, yet that he *too* recently launched a war—this time in the Middle East. My great dream of socialists and scientists organising the affairs of the world for the benefit of all mankind is mocked! All my life I dreamed of an ordered and spacious society, an educated and disciplined world—the alternative to which is catastrophe, imminent extinction. Ladies and Gentlemen, the world continues to follow a blind and suicidal path, misusing science and unguided by science.

We must encourage people to think, and to think beyond themselves.

Even without a time machine we are all moving towards the future. It is up to you, through your writings and your actions, to shape the future. I beg you, do not forsake this responsibility. And if people fail to listen to your words, they are ghosts. Quite literally. The human race will pass away. In ten thousand years' time nothing will remain of the human race—except perhaps some radioactivity.

Despite the huge systems of knowledge I marshalled in *The Outline of History* and *The Work, Wealth, and Happiness of Mankind*, perhaps I am not a totally systematic thinker—but more of a *creative* thinker. I admit to contradicting myself on a number of occasions, yet this is because often I started to explore an idea entirely afresh from the ground upwards instead of rebuilding on old foundations. I write in order to *explore*, not merely to rephrase old ideas and give them new clothing. I urge this method upon you in your own writings, for this is the means of evolutionary survival— constant adaptation to change!

Adaptation, yes! I was wrong, in my youth, to say that the coloured people would have to go, to disappear. The white races are not superior. But I never wasted time saying, 'I was wrong about this, I was wrong about that.' *Press on*, instead. Reformulate! Launch oneself yet again into the fray, ever optimistic and *busy*. And if in the end my optimism became pessimism, I was only merely speaking as I saw—and as I still see today, alas.

I feel that I am beginning to withdraw from this body of Mr Watson's. I believe he is trying to regain this body of his, and although his mind is undoubtedly inferior to mine he has a long familiarity with his own body.

I may be able to reoccupy his body temporarily because of my admiration for this fine city and its inhabitants, particularly those of the female gender. If so, you may find yourself unsure whether you are in the company of Mr Wells or of Mr Watson! It may be that Mr Watson may say something or do something indiscreet which he will then blame upon me, pretending that I am responsible! I suspect that in fact Mr Watson is jealous of me. Why else would he have intruded into my life on four occasions now? Probably he would be happy to blacken my reputation, for that is how such people behave. I think of false admirers, such as Mr Bernard Shaw. Oh there is so much more that I wish to tell you, but—!

Author's Note: With thanks for inspiration to Patrick Parrinder, Jonathan Cowie, and Warren Wagar.

Of Warfare and *The War of the Worlds*

by H.G. Wells himself

W ar, oh dear me, war: the perennial curse of mankind! And the fascination of mankind as well. Perhaps war is less fascinating to womankind, since so many women are innocent victims of war. Various famous female warriors do spring to mind, yet often bellicosity was forced upon them by ill-treatment at the hand of men, as upon Queen Boadicea by the Romans.

The very word *War* in the title of a novel seems to act as a magnet for extensive sales—how much more so, then, a war *of the worlds*? Evidently I happened upon a title of great moment, so I am unsurprised at how that early flight of fancy of mine endures, even if this is a cause of regret to me in some respects.

Why a cause of regret, you may ask?

Mr Glenn Yeffeth of BenBella Books put this question to me recently, and I shall endeavour to answer this now.

I should explain that in recent years (if I may phrase it thus) I have been travelling in time, and in the process I have encountered readers of my books who live in the early Twenty-First Century. BenBella is a rather beautiful name for a publishing house, in my opinion. I was once acquainted briefly with a delightful young lady named Bella, whose varied charms included considerable intelligence. Anyway, Mr Yeffeth informed me that not merely one, but two, extremely costly kinetoscopic adaptations of my *War of the*

Worlds were shortly to appear, one of these directed by a Mr Steven Spielberg and starring a popular 'action-hero', Mr Tom Cruise, the other film made by a company called (if I recall aright) Pendragon Productions. Mr Yeffeth was preparing a book of essays to appear synchronously with Mr Spielberg's visual drama—and serendipitously as regards the other visual drama, which I gather was made in secret, so as to surprise the world.

I was given to understand that Pendragon Productions aimed at utter authenticity in conjuring up the last years of the Nineteenth Century in England and the exact narrative of my novel; so I may perhaps be moderately hopeful of the result in that case. The contrary was definitely so with the radio adaptation by Mr Orson Welles, who took totally unwarranted liberties with my book by relocating its events to New Jersey, in order to astonish Americans—in which aim at least he succeeded! Consequently I harbour profound qualms about Mr Spielberg's adaptation. Already, in the year 1897, the American newspaper the *Boston Post* serialised a stolen version of my book, the action relocated to America. I protested strongly back then, just as I later protested at Mr Welles's radio show. Maybe Mr Spielberg is unaware that, due to my time machine, I am still able to object to violations of my work if need be.

Such vulgarisations are one reason for regret. As regards vulgarity in its literal meaning, I always wrote in the language of the common man, as opposed to the meandering gilded oratory of Mr Henry James which only connoisseurs can understand, but my hope was always to make my readers *think* at the same time as I entertained them. I fear that the principal aim of Mr Spielberg's visual drama may be simply to astonish its spectators rather than to cause any intellectual reflection—to astound them, and also to make them feel patriotic, a sentiment which I have always regarded with some suspicion since it is often allied to xenophobia—a dislike of the alien, the stranger—and consequently is a cause of war.

As regards patriotism in the sense of excessively vaunting one's country, my own 'war of the worlds' is a singularly one-sided campaign. Confronted by its Martian enemy, Great Britain—so proud of its army and navy—is not so great. In fact, it is almost impotent.

Ahem. On the subject of potency, if I may put it so—which is itself something of a *double entendre*—Mr Yeffeth suggests that 'womanist' readers might take offence at my casual reference to Bella, finding such a comment patronising to their sex. Well, one aspect of my novel upon which certain 'womanist' commentators of the early Twenty-First Century certainly commented to me somewhat scathingly is the fact that my narrator's wife has no name, and is simply referred to throughout as 'my wife'. 'As if she is *a thing* you have mislaid!' one redoubtable young lady with red hair expostulated to me. However, I was not writing a romance in which the narrator will rescue his beloved from peril. Would it appease that young lady with red hair if I had named the narrator's wife Isabel or Gwendolin? Would this mere piece of nomenclature add any more to her identity or importance? I do hope that the impertinent kinetoscopic adaptation of my novel to Twenty-First Century America does not inflict a spurious 'love interest' upon my story, for this would be to miss the point of what I undertook, namely a salutary humbling of our smugness.

Yes, our devastating defeat. In this regard I must plead guilty to evincing considerable relish at the process of destruction, a sentiment distinctly at odds with my hopes for peace on Earth. There is in the violence of war, and the demolition of cities, a kind of fascination which we must surely lose as a species if we are to survive. War, slaughter, and destruction, and a relish in the instruments of war, must become not merely outlawed but unthinkable.

And yet in my novel I destroyed, to use a telling phrase, *with a vengeance.* I must admit that I personally am a mixture of contraries, and my imagination could often be belligerent. Indeed, belligerence is a part of our evolutionary heritage—one which has now ceased to play any useful role in the survival of our species. Maybe it is not too surprising that my interplanetary mayhem has captured the popular imagination, yet I now see it as cause for regret if I have contributed to an appetite for destruction on a grand scale as popular entertainment. And I understand that there exists a lot of this, very expensively so, in the films of today, often to the exclusion of a sensible or logical story.

I may of course be wrong in my anxieties about Mr Spielberg's adaptation. Yet I have been told of another film, entitled *Independence Day*, in which the President of the United States himself engages successfully in combat against alien invaders, like some medieval chieftain. Nothing in my own *War of the Worlds* sounds such a triumphant and jingoistic note as finale.

At this point I must sound a note of amazement, not only at what my *War of the Worlds* seem to have begotten, but also what itself and the other fantasies of my youth have brought forth in their wake. I refer to the enormous number of novels and stories, produced since approximately the middle of the Twentieth Century, which bear the name of *Science Fiction*. Apparently I am the 'father' of this form of popular entertainment.

Recently I attended (or rather, I *will* attend) a 'World Science Fiction Convention' in the city of Glasgow. In the Dealers' Room at this extremely extensive event I was astonished to see the sheer number of such books, many of them concerned with conflicts in outer space, either set in our own solar system or in the far reaches of the Milky Way galaxy. Stars Wars, Forever Wars . . .

Books concerned, too, with time travel and with journeys to other worlds and with the creation of new breeds of men and with the 'uplifting' of animals to sentience, which are all the themes of my early books.

I appear to be responsible for this, and this too I must regret.

The myriad tales of latter-day 'Science Fiction'—with their matter transmitters and time-travel portals and warp-travel and hyperspace travel and anti-gravity machines, and their aliens who might be giant ants or heaven knows what, and their ansibles for communicating instantly from star to star, namely all the paraphernalia of marvels without which such stories could not exist at all—these derive from what is frankly the least important part of my work, and furthermore they have nothing scientific about them!

When I penned *The War of the Worlds* and *The Time Machine* and *The First Men in the Moon*, for example, I was doing what a conjuror does with his quick-witted patter to fool an audience. (Should I say 'spiel', rather than patter? This may seem appropriate in view of the name of my latest kinetoscopic interpreter!) Frankly, I was substituting words of science for bits of magic or sorcery as the basis for those novels. An invasion from Mars? A society of insects dwelling within the Moon? Or, to take another instance, an Invisible Man? Those were sheer flights of fancy! Such tales were certainly fiction. But *science*? Not at all!—not in my scientifically trained opinion. Pray recall that I was scientifically trained, rigorously so, by Thomas Huxley in the tradition of Charles Darwin as an evolutionary biologist. Above all I pride myself on possessing a scientific mind. The works of modern 'Science Fiction' are simply not scientific. Adding the word 'fiction' to the word 'science' does not redeem such productions.

And now the topic of war must rear its head once more. For in that Dealers' Room in Glasgow, in addition to literally thousands of novels purporting to be 'Science Fiction', I saw numerous examples of *war games*. Leaving aside the paternity of Science Fiction, which I disavow, I can most certainly claim that I, and none other, am the father of war-gaming. I refer to war-gaming practised as a hobby, evidently pursued in fantasy and futuristic settings by many visitors to that World Science Fiction Convention.

Back in 1913, you see, I published an illustrated book entitled *Little Wars* and subtitled *'A Game for Boys from twelve years of age to one hundred and fifty and for that more intelligent sort of girl who likes boys' games and books WITH AN APPENDIX ON KRIEGSPIEL'*.

Thus I invented war-gaming with rules and models, to be played on a table or a carpet or even a lawn, summarising in that book what I had developed over numerous years. That I have been influential was brought home to me somewhat gallingly when I picked up a highly-priced volume entitled *Warhammer 40,000: Rogue Trader* (produced by a company called Games Workshop) and discovered therein a battle between 'Space Marines' and ugly green-skinned aliens called 'Orks' entitled 'The Battle at the Farm'. This was illustrated by photographs almost identical to my own photographs illustrating my own chapter in *Little Wars* entitled 'The Battle of Hook's Farm'! No credit was allocated to me, but I most certainly perceived the source of Games Workshop's tableau and rules.

'In the grim darkness of the far future there is only war'—that is one of the mottos of this Games Workshop, and part of their appeal. My own motive in inventing war-games was rather different—namely, to demonstrate that real war is too big a thing for our heads. Professional military men have played my own war-game, the rules of which are fairly elementary, and not one has avoided getting into difficulties and confusions. War is a blundering insanity, and self-declared patriots who favour war ought to be shut up in a room to play my game and satisfy themselves, out of the way of the rest of the mass of mankind upon whom they must not be allowed to bring such suffering and monstrous inconvenience as real war entails. What we should seek is ample living for mankind, open ways, magnificent cities, more liberatory power and knowledge. To war I oppose nothing less than *utopia*.

War: there is a kind of war in me too, a perpetual inner conflict—a tension in myself between the man of science and the creative artist. You might say that I am a man of science by training, and a creative artist by intuition.

Personally I have never confused these two categories. Nor has England as a nation confused them because, most unfortunately, the English ruling class has paid scant attention to science. This is because the ruling class, educated at our great universities, is fundamentally illiterate in science. Consequently the mandarins of culture are men of letters who possess little understanding of what a star in the night sky is, or of how evolution operates. My much underestimated colleague Ford Madox Ford rightly commented that 'no one bothered his head about Science. It seemed to be an agreeable parlour-game—like stamp-collecting.'

Thus it is that artistic gentlemen tend to have written books and essays about me, and their considerations are literary considerations. By and large, as a consequence, my books as a whole have been assessed disgracefully. Many deeply thought-out books—which impinge upon our very survival— have been virtually ignored, and in this disdain I must also include my ambitious novels of contemporary life, disregarded by critics because they were not 'experimental' in the manner of Mr James Joyce or Miss Virginia Woolf. What do those artists of the word know about *scientific* experiments and deductions, eh? What do they know about humanity in the grand blind scheme of nature, which grants human beings no privileged status whatever? Mr Joyce, or Mr Henry James previously, are like hippopotami picking up, with great skill, a pea.

Not that I myself lacked a trick or two when it came to experimenting with narrative. To me, indeed, everything has been an experiment— including my *Experiment in Autobiography*, and my very life. But artistic gentlemen focus their attentions upon my scientific fantasies as though nothing else matters, and then as like as not they declare that with a few early exceptions I tossed off my books in haste, and wrote far too many, whereas the truth is that I took great pains with the writing, and rewriting— but I happened to write for the common reader in a popular, not an aesthetic, style.

As I say, it is one of my early 'successes' that Mr Yeffeth has asked me to comment upon, rather than any of my neglected books that I might rate more highly, and I suppose as an evolutionary biologist I should accept the fact that *The War of the Worlds* has survived, while other fine novels by me have become virtually extinct.

Not merely survived—but engendered many hybrid offspring, often of rather strange appearance, and several akin to massive dinosaurs at least as regards the financial aspects.

I might mention in passing one offspring of my fantasies which came to my attention, an ingenious variation entitled *The Space Machine* penned by a Mr Christopher Priest, who perceived that logically my 'time machine' must be a machine which traverses not only time but also space, since of course the Earth and its sun do not remain in one single fixed location in the universe but move constantly. If we travel ahead one million years to the very same place which our Earth occupies now, we will find ourselves isolated in the interstellar void. Consequently my time machine must also move through space and thus can be used to visit Mars in an attempt to thwart the Martian invaders of Earth. It is not that this implication did not occur to me, but that my time machine serves as the equivalent to a magical lamp empowered by a genie.

I think that the authors of 'Science Fiction'—if such was what those authors truly intended to produce—ought perhaps to have taken less heed of my own works and to have paid more attention to the productions of my younger French counterpart, Monsieur Jules Verne. Monsieur Verne appreciated the range of my imagination—yet he wished to know how precisely my Martians produced their heat ray. How indeed?

My literary 'descendants' did not so take heed. My genial magical lamps mesmerised them, and thus begot fantasies dressed as science (although, curiously, I understand that an organisation called the Pentagon has devoted much money to trying to make my heat ray a practical device).

The principal origin of *The War of the Worlds* was twofold. Firstly, as my Time Traveller in *The Time Machine* plunges towards far futurity, he is moved to speculate that with the passage of eight hundred thousand years mankind may have developed by the process of evolution 'into something inhuman, unsympathetic, and overwhelmingly powerful', to whom the Traveller must surely seem to be 'some old-world savage animal . . . a foul creature to be incontinently slain.' And secondly, when I was out walking one evening along a rural lane with my brother Frank, Frank suddenly observed to me, 'Suppose some beings from another planet were to drop out of the sky suddenly, and began laying about them here?' I took heed of Frank's remark. Oh how I took heed. As I have observed elsewhere, the human animal is not constituted to anticipate anything at all; it is constituted to accept the state of affairs about it, as a stable state of affairs, *whatever its intelligence may tell it to the contrary.*

And yet I pause. Despite such terrible events as the Lisbon Earthquake, which still shocked all civilised nations a century later, during the final years of the Nineteenth Century especially in the British Isles we felt very secure, to the point of complacency. We could have no inkling of the horrors and chaos of the era awaiting us, subsequent to the fatal year 1914, an era during which it came to seem that all life on Earth might easily be extinguished because of atomic warfare. Not to mention the mass psychosis of the German nation, with its programme to exterminate entire races of human beings. And following on from the suppression of the German nation as the result of a second world war, a hundred lesser but lethal and bloody wars in all parts of the world.

Wars, wars, wars, as if the name we give ourselves, of Homo sapiens, might more appropriately be *Homo bellicosus*! Does any other creature, except for the Army Ant, *Eciton burchelli*, collectively practise war to the same degree and as regularly as *Homo bellicosus*? The Army Ant is a creature dominated by instinct, and with no concept of improving its weapons. How dangerous are the ways that our own pugnacious instincts dominate us when allied to intelligence!

I understand that we are acquiring a growing awareness of other dangers too—namely the sheer frailty of our life upon a world subject to catastrophic climate change, asteroid impact from outer space, mutating pathogenic super-viruses, or imminent scarcity of essential resources. This awareness is honed by an instantaneity in comprehensive news of calamities scarce imaginable in the age of communication by mere telegraph, and exacerbated further by the fact that a whole range of possible calamities is the stuff of vivid films shown worldwide, presenting new ice ages or floods or plagues as all too possible in the near future.

People of the early Twenty-First Century definitely ought to be more conscious than people of the late Nineteenth Century of *instability*. Nevertheless are they really, in a truly radical way? Ultimately the human animal does not believe that it will die, nor that its race will die too, inevitably. Arguments that the intervention of science has altered, or potentially altered, this fate—and that science now commands the process of blind evolution—ignore the fact that *if* the human race does survive into futurity then its thoughts and interests will bear as little resemblance to those of us alive now as the thoughts of the Martians bear to our own human thoughts in my novel. A million years from now Homer and Shakespeare, Leonardo and Beethoven will signify as nothing—therefore *we* will have passed away as surely as if a plague has extinguished us. That plague will be the progress *of time itself*, sheer geological time.

My Martians were also, despite their scientific powers, complacent. Having apparently eradicated bacteria from their world in the distant past, they utterly neglected to take the bacteria of our own world into account.

Would this negligence apply also to their attempts to invade the planet Venus, to which I allude in the closing pages of my novel? Indeed, would those mighty minds on Mars have learned at all of the reason for their failure to conquer the Earth?

Of course I do realise that the planet Venus is now revealed to be lethally uninhabitable by any life form except perhaps bacteria adrift in its upper atmosphere. I merely speculate upon the basis of what I wrote in my novel.

One further speculation in which perhaps I may indulge is the nature of the food creatures, some of whom my Martians took on their voyage in order to transfuse their blood for sustenance, and whom they must have bred and farmed rather as we breed and farm cattle or sheep.

'These creatures,' I wrote, 'to judge from the shrivelled remains that have fallen into human hands, were bipeds with flimsy, silicous skeletons . . . and feeble musculature, standing about six feet high and having round, erect heads, and large eyes in flinty sockets.'

In other words, they somewhat resemble human beings whom the lesser gravity of Mars—together with millennia of husbandry—have enfeebled and attenuated. Would these bipeds have arisen naturally upon the Red Planet, as a case of parallel evolution—parallel to our own evolution, I mean? Why should this be so, when the dominant species on Mars is as I describe it to be—more like an octopus (or duopus) with a huge head? Admittedly I suggested in my novel that the dominant Martians may once have resembled ourselves, and that subsequently bodily organs had atrophied. Thus the food animals may be relatives of the Martians—ones who retain a primeval appearance.

Yet may it not be that in the very distant past, while the various breeds of Homo were evolving, and before the eradication of bacteria, the Martians had mounted an earlier expedition to Earth and had carried off specimens of Homo of breeding age as captives?

The aim of the Martians, at the time, may have been to ensure a food supply in view of the progressive changes to their own anatomy—which they may have *planned consciously* by manipulating their own genetic material in order to free mental cerebration from the troubling influences of hormones, glandular secretions, and such. (I am aware that by the dawn of the Twenty-First Century such genetic intervention is becoming a very real possibility.) Only when the Martians' own planet was becoming uninhabitable would they have elected to quit Mars for the greater, impeding gravity of Earth.

As regards the technical achievements and inventions of the Martians I made no assumption of similarity to those of human beings. Most notably, the wheel is unknown on Mars. Instead, complicated systems of sliding parts moving over small frictionless bearings replace the fixed pivot. Why, then, should I assume that at any stage Martian evolution resembled terrestrial evolution in giving rise to bipeds? The more I think about it, the less likely this seems. Abduction from Earth during prehistory seems more plausible.

How would the Martians return to their home world with their captives (including enough surplus captives to be drained of blood for nourishment *en route*)? How would they escape from the greater gravity of Earth? I think that within a reasonable time their handling machines would be capable of constructing more powerful projectiles than were used to cross the void from Mars to the Earth.

However, here I fear I am veering into the realms of 'Science Fiction', with its addiction to sequels and what I understand are called prequels. Mr Priest appears to have made a very honest stab at creating an alternative novel in parallel with my own, yet I understand that he shares with me in his own work a disdain for repeating himself. Of my early fantasies, *The Time Machine*, *The War of the Worlds*, *The Island of Doctor Moreau*, *The First Men in the Moon*: all were markedly different from one another and addressed different themes. A man of vigorous imagination and originality can scarce behave otherwise. The many examples, such as I saw at the book room in Glasgow, of sheer repetition of an idea which was once original—either because of authors plagiarising earlier authors such as myself, or else plagiarising themselves ten times over in so-called sagas and epics; or both crimes at once—that is most regrettable. I am tempted to say that I declare war upon the imitative trend.

A final thought occurs to me—how this matter niggles! It may be that the enemy 'world' in Mr Spielberg's *War of the Worlds* will not even be Mars. Just as Mr Welles, almost my namesake, exchanged an English setting for New Jersey, maybe in his efforts to be *science-fictional* Mr Spielberg will exchange Mars for some fantastical world of his imagination orbiting some distant star, whose denizens could in reality no more visit us across the vast gulfs of interstellar space, nor wage war upon us, than we could ever visit them.

Dear me, it may even be that Mr Spielberg has simply usurped the title of my book and that little, *if any*, connexion whatever exists between my novel and his film! I think I must soon depart in my time machine, before I think of yet further irritating possibilities.

There are so many times and places that I wish to visit—so many intelligent and personable young ladies to meet. I hear tell that a 'summer of love' occurred in California during the 1960s . . .

Now what if I were to invite a celebrant of that event to accompany me forward in time to a showing of the Pendragon Productions version of my novel? That experience might impress her favourably.

The Wicker Man

O PINION DIVIDES AMONG MY ACQUAINTANCES AS TO WHETHER *The Wicker Man* is ludicrous, or on the other hand wondrous, haunting, and provocative. Obviously I incline to the second opinion, otherwise I wouldn't be writing this! That a film company on its beam ends could produce such a film on a shoestring is a miracle. Then for the film to be butchered into a shortened version for screening . . . well, at least discarded footage is now restored on the DVD of the Director's Cut.

I suppose the vicissitudes of the film contribute to its cult mythology status. Since I myself often appreciate films quite naively, I won't check whether it is totally true that this film, set in May, was scheduled to be shot in September (with fake Spring blossom decorating trees), but that shooting actually lagged till October—by which time the weather was so cold that the actors needed ice-cubes in their mouths to prevent their breath from pluming out of them; and after each open-air take in their flimsy clothing (or in their birthday suits) they needed to be wrapped instantly in blankets to avoid hypothermia; nor whether the climactic scene of the burning of the wicker man, which could only be done once, on the one remaining day, was actually cursed by thick clouds throughout that day, but that miraculously (or else heeding the nature-magic of the event) the setting sun broke through dramatically for an awesome final shot. Nor will I check whether it's totally true that the director hired a prostitute to stand in for Britt Ekland's backside in the nude solo slap-dance scene upstairs in the pub, leading to subsequent cries of, 'That's not my bum!' Perhaps mythology should be respected, if mythology it is. Apparently until recent years it was possible for a pilgrim to acquire a piece of the charred uprights of the wicker man from the site, but none now remains.

Pious and virginal Sergeant Howie of the mainland police is lured to Summerisle by a false report of a missing girl, whom he soon decides may be destined for sacrifice—for Summerisle is gorgeously and rampantly pagan. Howie's sensibilities are deeply offended as the islanders lead him a merry dance, but it is Howie himself who will be the sacrifice because he fulfils the essential criteria of being a fool who is also a virgin who has come voluntarily to the appointed place.

Since I mainly associated Edward Woodward with his role as private eye Callan in the 1974 TV series (for I didn't see *The Wicker Man* first in the cinema, only when it screened later on TV) I was astonished by the power and apparent sincerity of his performance. Much of the action seems to be almost comic, with sinister undercurrents, as when a little girl has her sore throat treated by having a frog popped into her mouth for a while—'Are you people all mad here?' When watching the film for the first time, little prepares for the sheer impact of the sergeant's sacrifice by fire, from which— in defiance of last minute rescue clichés—there is no escape whatsoever. And so convincing is the paganism that the sacrifice seems utterly celebratory, something to hum along to with linked arms.

To hum along to ... Oh all the accompanying songs! 'Corn rigs and barley rigs, et cetera ...' Ironic friends of mine have described the film as a misconceived musical. Yet to me it is a perfect integration of music and story, script, costume, dance, and cinematography. Quite Kubrickian, in fact, in a way. And in this regard, beautifully stylised, not least Christopher Lee's role as Lord Summerisle. Nor let us overlook the masks and disguises, a precursor perhaps of the elegant orgy in *Eyes Wide Shut*—if I'm writing about my bestest ever Horror film, surely I can indulge in hyperbole! But *The Wicker Man* really does transcend its roots, becoming mythic to many people.

And which myth does it sustain? Walt Whitman's 'I think I could turn and live with animals' is quoted by Lord Summerisle as he watches snails copulate—the allusive lyricism of the photography really is very sexy—but Swinburne seems relevant too:

'Thou hast conquered, O pale Galilean;
The world has grown grey from Thy breath ...

Yet thy kingdom shall pass, Galilean,
Thy dead shall go down to thee dead.'

On Summerisle they might recite:

'Thou hast fallen, O pale Galilean,
'The world hath grown gay with thy death . . .'

However, the gods of nature can be savage as well as sweet, and Sergeant Howie must burn while the islanders celebrate, while he himself enacts the role of Christian martyr, which the film entices us to feel is far more of an illusion than the islanders' pagan view of the world. It's a very seductive film, in several senses.

Dark City

DARK *CITY* IS THE ONLY FILM WHICH HAS CAUSED ME TO BUILD a garden feature; it's that good. I named my garden feature 'Shell Beach' although actually I used big pebbles, cobbles, bags and bags of them. Shell Beach, first appearing on a kitschy coloured postcard in the hands of Murdoch, the protagonist of *Dark City*, is a childhood paradise, at the end of the subway line, which no one in the dark city can seem to remember their way to any more. That's because at every witching hour of twelve all the clocks stop, and all the human denizens of the city slump unconscious, while the bald blanched vampiric-looking Strangers, who unbeknownst control the city from underground, proceed to remorph the urban scenery, buildings rising and sinking. The Strangers extract memories by syringe from individuals' brains, swapping memories from other individuals while raising or lowering one's status in life; so that an individual isn't the individual he thinks he is at all. All this, in pursuit of an experiment into what individuality is, on the part of the group-mind, memory-sharing aliens who maintain this city bubbled somewhere in the deeps of space; hence it's always night time in Dark City.

Unusually for a director, Australian Alex Proyas wrote the script himself, inspired by childhood dreams of tall strangers; then, primarily a visual person, he drafted in a trio of scriptwriters to work on his vision. And what visuals there are! Inspired by *Nosferatu* and German Expressionism, by European art cinema, with a touch of *Twilight Zone*, and Edward Hopper pools of light in a world of obscurity, the lighting industrially toxic or table lamp naturalism—often an eerie yellow or bluish-green monochrome look. With long black coats for the Strangers, such coats also to figure in the much inferior and therefore much more commercially successful fashion movie with big gun accessories, *The Matrix*, about a year later.

Dark City deliberately set out to challenge its audiences to discover and interpret its multi-level meanings, without being spoon-fed explanations. The idea was that the audience shouldn't understand at first, although all would become clear by and by, especially if they paid extreme attention to the nuances of the dialogue and every detail (such as a shoe with a perfectly smooth sole).

The film also critically pastiches dominant American cultural imagery, in somewhat the same way as Alan Moore addresses the caped crusader mythos in *Watchmen*. Cars from different eras are juxtaposed; slang is deliberately old-fashioned.

The test-audiences failed the test, resulting in the Hollywood execs insisting on a bit less weirdness and some dumbing down, principally by inserting a voice-over narrative at the beginning, now purged from the Director's Cut (which comes with interesting commentaries). Execs, even of the least creatively interfering studio, were wary of the hybrid nature of this film. Such weirdness, even if you can't put a finger on exactly what's freaking you, suggests an R rather than a PG13 rating. So should *Dark City* be touted as retro-noir crime, or SF, or Fantasy, or even as Horror? Could Johnny Depp pull the chestnuts out of the fire, because he's so identifiable? The studio even targeted Tom Cruise, shutting down pre-production for a month until, thank heavens, Cruise shook his head. How awful to have had him running around with his two-and-a-half facial expressions.

Originally the viewpoint was to be that of the detective Bumstead; then this switched to Murdoch who wakes in a bath, fitted up by the Strangers as a serial murderer... and who now stays awake through the 'tunings' by which the city is morphed, and its citizens given fabricated memories, and who evolves powers akin to, and finally superior to, the Strangers while they try to catch up with him.

The Strangers ruthlessly revise the city and its inhabitants in order to learn what makes us human, what individuality is, what a sense of *self* is. Our supposedly sovereign self-awareness is probably a coordinating illusion evolved by the ever-shifting coalition of neural mechanisms within us. Yet it's still the greatest of mysteries, the 'hard question'. And the quest of the Strangers exactly mirrors the very same question that artificial intelligences may well ask, if AIs can come into existence.

Superior AIs may well preserve the human species in its current mental state within a huge simulation, as a yardstick of what biologically evolved Self and self-awareness is—something which, unlike basic life, may only have arisen once, by a whole sequence of evolutionary accidents on the Earth. This illusion so precious and peculiar to humankind of a Self (a soul, if you like) may be a great enigma to an artificial intelligence . . . and may even seem to provide a clue to its own nature. (To be sure, the enigma of self may be equally fascinating to differently-minded aliens; however, we're more likely to kindle AIs before encountering any hypothetical aliens, whatever depths of the human psyche the supposed abduction experiments of UFOnauts come from.)

In prefiguring this, *Dark City* is probably one of the most important films ever made. And if AIs can't exist, the film still remains a masterpiece to be watched many times, gaining each time an ever greater sense of integration.

The movie crew and actors were all shut away in gloomy indoors in sunny Sydney for weeks while shooting the film. Paradoxically, when Murdoch at last emerges at Shell Beach for the only outdoor shot, that day in the real world was overcast, consequently the blue sky and the fluffy clouds above the sea had to be provided later by CGI, giving that outdoor shot a strangely artificial look, just like the postcard itself. How appropriate. Almost like a simulation being reset with different parameters.

Stephen King's *Thinner:* An Attack on America

(reprinted from: www.Anorexics-R-Us.com/bookreviews/thinner)

THIS BOOK CONTAINS MANY USEFUL INSIGHTS INTO THE PROCESS OF becoming thinner, although it's dressed up as a Horror novel for acceptability.

To summarise the plot, Billy-the-belly Halleck is an overweight lawyer in a prosperous small American town. He has one lovely slim daughter, Linda, and a lovely slim wife. For once in her life Heidi gives Billy a hand-job one day while he's driving through town. Distracted by pleasure, Billy crashes into an old jay-walking Gypsy woman, killing her. Billy's buddies, the Judge and the Police Chief, make sure that the trial for manslaughter results in Billy's acquittal. The Gypsy woman's even older father (100+, the last of the great Magyar chiefs) curses Billy by touching him and saying, 'Thinner'. Billy duly loses weight very rapidly, while the Judge grows scales—of injustice—and the Police Chief becomes a mass of giant pimples.

Those two commit suicide, but Billy sets out after the itinerant Gypsies and calls on an Italian gangster friend, who terrorises the Gypsies until the old man diverts the curse from Billy into a disgusting strawberry pie which Billy intends to give to Heidi because she tried to have Billy declared insane for believing in curses.

Published in 1984, *Thinner* is quite a prophetic book for all of us anorexics now that we take proper pride in our cause, and now that we have pro-Ana web-sites for 'thinspiration', even though our sites are being persecuted, rather as the thin Gypsies are persecuted in the novel by constantly

377

being chased out of nice, 'normal' towns. *Thinner* is as radical an attack on fatty mainstream USA society (which Billy learns to despise) as any mounted by Al Qaeda. Indeed the Gypsies are anticipatory symbols for those swarthy exotic thin Arabs who brought 9/11 to the Big Apple.

Heidi keeps lovely and skinny by smoking cigarettes, which are a useful appetite suppressant—take note of that, all you pro-Ana girls! Regarding those health warnings on the packs, remember that true maturity is a matter of control over your body, not how many birthdays you survive. Another tip, about which I feel dubious, is that 'exercise is much more important than diet' (in losing weight); but this is said by a doctor who snorts cocaine. This same doctor says to Billy, 'You may actually be thinking yourself thin. It *can* be done, you know.' Well, having strong belief is very important, but rejection of food is essential too.

Billy calls his body The House That Bud(weiser) Built and he looks like a 7-month pregnant man. When this eighth-of-a-ton 'big hog' is intending to fuck skinny Heidi, he says quite accurately 'I'll jump your bones.' *She* claims she loves Billy-the-belly just the way he is. So she's already his enemy from the start—and no wonder she gets so worked up about him losing weight. Heidi even wants Linda to grow a *38-inch* bust—poor Linda, who tries to find out from her mother how many calories are in pieces of chocolate cake. Beware of jealousy of those who are slimmer than you; beware of trying to fatten your sister.

Yet even if Billy snacks all the time, his sincere dream *is* to lose weight. If only we all had a Gypsy to help our dream along! There's some good advice in the book on how to deal with a partner like Heidi. Other good advice includes using an ostrich feather to help yourself vomit, and power-weighing—loading your pockets with loose change & a Swiss Army Knife before you get on the bathroom scales, so as to depress yourself and spur you to greater efforts at self-discipline.

When the Gypsy touches Billy, it's 'the caress of a lover'. Quite! That lover is Mister Anorexia, who wants bones that he can jump, not a mattress of fat flesh. I think 'bone-jumping' is a beautiful phrase for anorexics making love, if we have the energy or the inclination.

Heidi wants Billy to check in to 'the Mayo clinic'. That's right—Mayo for mayonnaise!

When Billy lets his pants down in the Courtroom toilet, 'laughter rose in his throat . . . A conductor's voice shouted in his mind, *Next stop, Anorexia Nervosa! All out for Anorexia Nervosa!*' Right on for Anorexia City, say I!

How different from the fatties' prayer cited earlier: '*In the name of cholesterol and saturated fats we pray.*' That is indeed the true prayer of tens of millions of us Americans, who over-consume the produce of the planet because they believe that their bulk is their identity—so the more bulk they have, the more identity they have. King cleverly contrasts the fatty life with starving children in Biafra, symbols of third-world thinness. Everywhere in his book fatties and fatties-in-the-making are guzzling the high-sugar drinks and munching the high-calorie high-fat food beloved by consumerist capitalism—beloved by bellyism!—nutrition that could feed ten times as many Africans. Even American poodles are fat.

King also invokes IRA hunger-strikers, emphasising the revolutionary aspect of anorexia, indeed even the terroristic aspect. Two decades before 9/11 the Gypsies really are Al Qaeda operatives in a different guise. They are something necessary to suburban homeland America for the dangerous frisson of strangeness—of the alien—that they provide, whose very existence reinforces by contrast the values of the homeland, which Billy calls 'Fat City'.

'Sure, we need the Gypsies,' thinks Billy. 'Because if you don't have someone to run out of town once in a while, how are you going to know you yourself belong there?'

The guzzling of excess food is a symbol of consumerist happiness. Perhaps this is a bit deep for some of you girls (and any pro-Ana boys out there; we treasure you), so let's look at the voodoo aspect briefly. If a victim truly believes he's been cursed, then maybe his brain itself carries out the curse, whatever it is? Could we maybe hold a Gypsy Curse Ritual to assist our slimming, you may be wondering? Well no, I say, because ultra-slimming, extreme slimming, is all *your own* responsibility, kind of like an extreme sport; and we ought to get gold medals.

What's more, slimming doesn't hurt at all. The Judge who grows scales feels no pain; he can even stub out a cigarette on his stomach. 'Hell, losing weight wasn't so bad, was it?' thinks Billy to himself. His bones are 'making themselves known . . . coming out *triumphantly*' (my emphasis).

We've all experienced the horror at thinness which fatties express. With your cheekbones visible, you're the bogeyman. Be prepared to accept this: you're the skeleton at the feast that is America. In fact most food manufacturers are criminal poisoners—that's becoming fairly obvious nowadays. That's why Billy turns for help to a gangster, to stop his thinness. This is just another richly symbolic aspect of this multi-layered book, which sometimes proceeds by cleverly disguising positives as negatives, and vice versa. To be pro food as a way of life is criminal.

'How we see reality depends on our conception of our physical bulk': here is another important insight. The reality of the world today is about 10 billion people. To slim down is to behave responsibly, to become beautiful not just because of prominent cheekbones, but also because of ecological spirituality.

'*I'm going to watch my weight,*' vows Billy at the end of his quest, which has sickened him with the partying in Fat City. '*I'm never going to get fat . . . again.*'

What follows is a bit of clever narrative to provide a Horror ending which rather undermines Billy, though without it the novel could hardly have been published for a mass audience—I emphasise *mass*. An audience that scoffs bags of food while it reads, and thinks thinness is an affliction.

Only one question remains: will Mr King ever dare write the ultimate Horror novel, *Obesity*?

A Daffodil Jacket, or
The Misadventures of Sebastian in Kyiv

NEVER BEFORE HAD THE EUROPEAN POETRY ASSOCIATION HELD
its yearly convention as far east as Kyiv. The EPA wasn't a very big
body; 70 attendees annually was about average. In western Europe we'd be
lucky if a local mayor turned out, but here in Kyiv the opening ceremony in
the Sportyny Exhibition Centre near Olympic Respubliansky Stadium was
thronged, and graced by two government ministers. Not to mention a whole
row of TV cameras. A pop singer in a slinky black cocktail dress sang
beneath a welcoming banner, and finally the Ukrainian national anthem
boomed out from giant speakers, jerking everyone to their feet.

'That was bad,' said the Italian poet Ricardo Evangelisti afterwards as a
group of us acquaintances descended towards the lobby.

'What was bad?' I asked.

'The national anthem.'

'But it sounded wonderful!' protested Sebastian Dugdale, who came from
England, as did I. 'Heroic, very moving.'

'No but you see,' explained Ricardo, 'this politicises the convention. Half
of Ukraine wants to join the EU, and half is pro-Moscow. I hear several
Russian-speaking Ukrainian poets and publishers are keeping away,
pretending they're ill or broke. You saw those government ministers? They
think the EPA being here is a foot in the door of the EU.' The Italian
laughed and pulled a funny face. Shaved bald, he had mischievous mesmeric
eyes. Burly, he looked like an international drug dealer with a sense of
humour.

'Well, blow me down with a feather,' said Sebastian, whose slang was often quaint, and used without him realising its impenetrability to foreigners. 'I never suspected.'

'No, Sebastian,' said Ricardo. 'You rarely suspect *anything.*'

Sebastian looked so innocent. Tall, skinny, and bespectacled, with curly fair hair, he wore a lightweight daffodil-yellow jacket as if he was at a garden party in an English village; perhaps the youthful vicar. Although he was almost 50, Sebastian seemed in his early thirties. Myself, I was wearing a black leather biker jacket, and Ricardo a thick workman's jacket with lots of pockets. Sebastian stood out. *Vulnerable.*

'Wait, wait!' we heard. It was our translators. Or some of them. Sebastian had suggested to the convention organisers beforehand that it would be a good idea to recruit some students who could act as guides and practise their English. English was the working language of the EPA. At poetry readings the audience would have in their hands an English prose translation of whichever poems as well as the texts in the original language, and of course many attendees, apart from Sebastian, understood several languages.

The organisers had duly recruited, from schools in Kyiv which taught in English, one translator for every non-Russian-speaking visitor. My translator was called Sasha and I still could scarcely believe—if she didn't have braces on her teeth—that tall, laid-back Sasha was only 15. She was the second-best English speaker of any school in Ukraine, and her companions were likewise extremely fluent, and mostly tall.

That evening we discovered the pizzeria close by on Chervonoarmiyska Street. Convention goers need a good base for conversations and drinks. The place was actually a café with cakes and ice cream out front and a sizable beer hall cum restaurant at the back. Italian menu, big wall fresco of the Black Sea coast, draft Chernihivsky lager—the only Danish poet present, Olav, a walking encyclopaedia of world beer, approved. An ideal place to hang out in. Other attendees soon made the same discovery. We got quite drunk because us poets hadn't seen each other for a year. Ricardo took a lot of photos of his very pretty translator, Elena. Our Hungarian poet friend Attila tried some flaming absinthe. Sebastian borrowed money from me because he'd brought unpopular Pounds to exchange. He ought to have looked at a guide book, not behaved like Phileas Fogg cramming a bag—or rather, his daffodil jacket—with Sterling banknotes before setting out from London. Me, I had Dollars and an ATM card.

Next morning, conference time. The programme was a bit heavily weighted with items in Russian which eluded most of us westerners; evidently there'd be ample spare time for tourism. In the lobby of the exhibition centre poetry books in Cyrillic were on show, a woman handed out a free newspaper which appeared to be about Kabbalah, and an inspired lunatic manned a stall loaded with graphs whereby he proved—according to Sasha—that Ukrainian geniuses arose chronologically in a regular rhythm, and that he himself was the latest prodigy. Ricardo and Attila and I soon went off with our translators to visit the centre of town by a metro with the longest, fastest escalators I'd ever ridden on. The contrast between old women sitting on subway steps hoping to sell a few buns, and a deluxe subterranean shopping mall, was notable, especially when Ricardo took a photo of the latter and the next moment Security arrived to put a hand over his camera lens.

That night was to be the Night of the Cushion.

After finding a good Ukrainian restaurant with a pet pig snoozing in a pen, and an advertisement for *Penthouse* in the beautifully tiled toilet, quite a lot of us ended up at the pizzeria once more for a drink. Attila and I, who were sharing a room in the Sport Hotel opposite the convention centre, went off to bed about one, leaving numerous poets and editors boozing, including Attila's three Hungarian chums.

When Attila and I surfaced next morning, it was to discover that the other Hungarians had been awoken at 3.00 am by Security from the pizzeria and also from the hotel, seeking Sebastian's whereabouts. CCTV cameras in the pizzeria had recorded a tall thin bespectacled person making off with a cushion.

We found Sebastian in the conference centre.

'I say,' he exclaimed, 'that wasn't me! I don't want the rozzers hunting for me.' (Rozzers being obsolete British slang for police.) 'What do I do?'

Ricardo said, 'We all go to the pizzeria right now and sort this out.'

This, a bunch of us proceeded to do—missing an interview with Ruslana Rogovtseva, whoever she was—only to discover that early in the morning a mystery person had thrown the missing cushion in through the doorway of the pizzeria and immediately run away.

As we returned to the exhibition centre, I hauled the distracted Sebastian out of the way as a Bentley came driving along the wide pavement. Even if a Bentley weren't almost silent, any engine noise would have been drowned by the bouncing rush of tyres upon the cobbles of Chervonoarmiyska Street, a swooshing thunderous noise. Maybe by using the pavement the owner of the Bentley was protecting his expensive vehicle from vibration. Ah no, he stopped in front of a casino. Kyiv seemed to boast a remarkable number of casinos—as well as a remarkable number of banks, usually close to one another.

'You know,' said Sebastian, 'sometimes I think the universe conspires against me! On the whole it deals me a pretty decent life, but now and then it throws me a wobbly.'

Back at the exhibition centre, a Russian poet was already very drunk, weaving from side to side. 'He's the most famous,' a magazine editor confided via one of our interpreters, and I wondered if the second most famous could only become equally drunk after lunch.

The explanation of the cushion mystery came later in the day when the French bibliographer of poetry, Jean-Claude Larochelle, admitted with a wry Gallic shrug that he had borrowed the item because he was sleeping on someone else's floor in the Sport and wanted to be more comfortable. Jean-Claude was thin and wore glasses—a darker, less noticeable version of Sebastian.

'Bloody Frogs,' Sebastian muttered.

The lovely mature schoolgirl Elena was playing with a metal tube, a hook on the end for opening cans and bottles. As Ricardo snapped photos, Elena unscrewed the end of the tube, and turned the device into a wicked-looking knife.

'For protection,' she explained, 'if I'm out alone at night.'

'Do you—?' I mimed sliding that knife inside her boot; and she nodded. Of course she must carry the blade ready for use. If someone attacked you, you hadn't time to unscrew a tube.

'Phew,' said Sebastian, wide-eyed, 'that really takes the cucumber.'

Attila nudged me, and I whispered, 'I don't know what it means, either.'

'You ought to look tougher for protection,' Jean-Claude advised Sebastian. 'Wear black leather and dark sunglasses.'

'Oh, and I suppose I should tattoo KILL and HATE on my knuckles?'

Another Gallic shrug. 'It's an idea.' Jean-Claude delved in his bag and brought out a vicious spiked mace made of darkly painted varnished wood. 'I went to see the Caves Monastery yesterday. Bought this from a souvenir vendor. It was a symbol of authority in Ukraine.'

'In Hungary too,' said Attila.

Even though a souvenir, that mace could have done severe damage to somebody's skull.

We went to give loyal support to our beloved zany Imants who was presenting a volume he'd published of new Latvian poetry, and then to the first business meeting of the EPA to nominate writers and magazines for awards; also to hear presentations from Holland and from Budapest and Moscow for the EPA convention two years hence. This was Moscow's big chance because so many Russians were present in Kyiv, though us westerners were all rooting for Budapest in June rather than Moscow in early March when it would still be minus-one. Only one Dutchman had turned up, so the Holland bid seemed irrelevant. Due to our system of national delegate voting, Budapest seemed a cert to win.

In the afternoon a lot of us went to see the huge weird house designed by architect Vladislav Horodetsky. An admirer of Gaudí, Horodetsky erected the residence on a steep hillside as a challenge—five floors on one side, three on the other—and adorned it with protruding elephants' heads and rhinos' heads and other creatures. He'd been a passionate big game hunter. Giant frogs squatted along the parapet. Several of us scribbled notes for poems.

Descending, we found ourselves in the monumental and gloomy Pasazh where artistic people used to hang out. Half way along we came upon a metal statue of Horodetsky seated at one of two metal chairs alongside a metal table bearing a metal coffee cup and a metal copy of his book about adventures in Africa. Ricardo encouraged Elena to do a lap-dance—fully clad—squeezed upon Horodetsky's metal knee, while he took many photos.

In such respects, our interpreters were useful. Yet they were becoming a bit of a financial burden. They flocked to accompany us, and since they were only schoolkids we needed to pay for them at coffee bars and restaurants. Not that the kids were greedy, but Kyiv seemed an expensive city, unless you were an old woman with a bag of buns to whom Dior and Bentleys were irrelevant. Soon Attila and I resorted to another ATM for 500 more Hryvna and I had to lend more to Sebastian, whose cache of Her Britannic Majesty's Pounds continued to be unwelcome.

And so to the final day of our EPA convention. Attila did a reading in Hungarian, which nobody else in the world can master. Then came the disaster of the second business meeting, presided over by our Irish poet president. The EU refused to recognise Belarus because of its dictatorship, so should the EPA allow Belarus to vote? Yes, decreed Seamus O'Brien, full of bonhomie. If so, what about—let's say Absurdistan, which had sent representatives to Kyiv? 'Sure, let's be welcoming,' said O'Brien, now standing on a chair.

The upshot was that national delegate votes tied 50/50 for Budapest and for Moscow. Consequently the votes of non-delegate attendees at the meeting—mostly Russians and Ukrainians—were counted, and Moscow won. All thanks to that delegate vote by Absurdistan. This meant that in two years' time the vote for a subsequent EPA convention would happen in Moscow at minus-one, where even fewer western Europeans might be present than in Kyiv. A bid might win for anywhere in the Russian Federation, perhaps even in Vladivostok, almost next to Japan. That would extend the concept of Europe!

And then O'Brien decreed a party at the pizzeria to thank this year's organisers. These amounted to just three people, who had worked like Trojans, but then O'Brien added, 'And our wonderful translators too.'

An incensed Sebastian rushed from the splendid closing ceremony, including multiple prize-giving, to a nearby Internet café, to google the exact definition of a 'European' country.

When he finally arrived at the pizzeria with a printed list of countries which could potentially access the EU, of course Absurdistan wasn't one of them. Sebastian and O'Brien exchanged heated words. But by then the party was in full swing—minus half of us westerners, who may have glimpsed a warning light, and minus Russian and Ukrainian poetry people who were probably holding a vodka contest elsewhere to decide who was the best of them. Nor had the organisers turned up; they were too exhausted. But all the interpreters had brought their girlfriends and boyfriends. Tables had been pushed together to make four mega-tables.

Sinister Silviu, from Bucharest, said to Ricardo, 'I am bloody angry at all this.'

'Me too,' agreed Ricardo. He gestured to a waitress and said, 'Separate bills for each table! Understand?'

Joining us, Sebastian slung his jacket over a chair, and told us, 'I'm going to get a bit Brahms tonight.' (In Cockney rhyming slang, Brahms and Liszt equals pissed equals drunk.) O'Brien was at a table crowded with interpreters and their friends, doing tricks of some kind to entertain them. Other interpreters were at another table, laughing happily and chatting on their mobile phones. Interpreters to right of us, interpreters to left of us, into the valley of Death . . .

Ricardo became a bit paranoid. 'Look, they're laughing at me for taking so many photos of young girls.'

Eventually all the interpreters went away since we didn't want to accompany them to a disco. The pizzeria's Security was observing us carefully from the doorway. Four bills arrived at the four tables.

O'Brien promptly brought his table's bill to our table and said buoyantly, 'I propose we add the bills and us westerners divide the total between ourselves, hmm?'

The total was quite a few thousands of Hryvna.

An indignant dispute broke out, cut short by people tossing their remaining Hryvna on to the table. An amiable American, who was at the EPA event out of sheer curiosity, threw in a generous sum in Dollars.

Having no more cash, Attila and I went back to the Sport to sleep. I had to get up very early to share a taxi to the airport with Sebastian and O'Brien.

At 6.00 am O'Brien was waiting in the lobby of the Sport.

'Bejesus, did you hear what happened to Sebastian last night!'

After Attila and I left, Sebastian discovered that the wallet, in his daffodil jacket left over that chair, had been emptied of money. First Sebastian blamed the pizzeria for being in league with a pickpocket, whom they'd pointed in his direction—then he decided that the thief might be one of the boyfriends who'd seen where he kept his wallet. He insisted the police be called because he'd need a statement for insurance purposes.

'Upshot is that Olexander'—Olexander was the main organiser—'has to be roused out of bed and come by taxi. Police don't turn up for an hour then insist on taking Sebastian off to the police station. Ricardo and I go along too for company, and just as well—bloody police accuse Sebastian of trying an insurance fraud. We only got back here ten minutes ago . . .'

One of the Sport's Security men announced that our taxi had arrived, so O'Brien rushed to the lift to hurry Sebastian.

On the way to Boryspil, a weary Sebastian said many things, including, 'I think the universe conspires against me.'

The police had been so unhelpful. Deliberately misinterpreting what he told them. Ignoring the computers standing idle and insisting on hand writing his statement only in Ukrainian. Only grudgingly making a photocopy to take away.

'Olexander was a gem, bless him—'

What Sebastian said failed to make sense to the Sherlock Holmes in me. He'd lost some Hryvna and 30 Pounds, not hundreds. The hundreds, which were deep in his other inside pocket in an envelope, remained.

'They saw which pocket I used, so they went for that one—'

Why bother to put back the wallet, which still contained tickets and other stuff?

'I told the police to take the tapes from the pizzeria's CCTV, but they wouldn't. They said the tapes were private. The police were in league! They didn't want evidence—'

It seemed to me very possible that, in the heat of the dispute about bills, a tiddly Sebastian had emulated others by throwing, in his case, Pounds upon the table and then he'd forgotten due to confusion and due to being Sebastian.

After we went through the metal-detector gate, while our luggage was being scanned, an airport Security man stopped Sebastian, and only Sebastian, either because the universe had it in for Sebastian, or because of his daffodil jacket.

'How much money you taking out of Ukraine?' Security demanded.

'None!' cried Sebastian. 'I was robbed!'

Security smiled, and moved away.

Then I saw the man take out a mobile phone and make a call.

It couldn't be, could it, that airport Security were in league with the police who were in league with pizzeria Security who were in league with thieves? I decided not to torment Sebastian by suggesting this.

Divine Diseases

I f GOD MADE MAN IN HIS OWN IMAGE, WHAT DOES THAT SAY ABOUT God's own anatomy?

When God made the world in 4004 BC, He was a young god, His rapidly inflating cosmic playground newly budded from the divine multiverse. Yet already He was wisely conscious of health issues and of a need for medical insurance. Ailments, of course, could not kill Him; divine diseases would be similar to the case of Prometheus and his pecked liver, which rapidly regenerated.

Yet why should He suffer unnecessarily?

Healthcare would come courtesy of His humans who would (in His own image) duly display all the ailments to which He might become vulnerable. Due to their much shorter life spans, compared with God's immortality, human beings would express much more rapidly, not to mention repeatedly, the ailments that might later assail Him, and would in due course, as civilisation advanced, develop medical science with which to combat those ailments.

Dyspepsia and juvenile boils and acne afflicted the adolescent God badly during the days of the ancient Israelites, resulting in plagues and angers and storms and afflictions visited upon the antique, although simultaneously early, world. But presently Greeks such as Hippocrates and Theophrastus pioneered medical science, rooted in a notion of humours, which wasn't so far off course since God could be choleric, spleenful or melancholic (He never slept), and bilious (all those black holes in His cosmos, like stomach ulcers; all those luridly red and purple nebulae like diseased organs of gas).

Of course He could also be blessedly phlegmatic or sanguine (yet sanguine sometimes meant bloody-minded—blame not God, but rather the quirks of His physiology).

Consequently Greek diagnoses and cures, and those of the Arabs thereafter, were fairly sensible, although lacking sophistication and technology, which was what God awaited.

During a phlegmatic and benevolent era, God gave rise to His Son in a human body to bestow divine love upon His creation. However, in the long run this proved to be a serious mistake . . .

The problem wasn't that His Son was ungratefully crucified, to be resurrected and taken up bodily into Heaven; He would come again when the time was ripe. However, kicking off with the Council of Ephesus in 431 AD, and then proclaimed by the Fourth Lateran Council in 1215 under Pope Lunaticus, and fully ratified officially in the 16th century at the Council of Trent, the Catholic Church (and the unorthodox Orthodox churches too, in their own fashions) ordained that the bread and wine consumed in communion were miraculously transubstantiated into genuine flesh and blood.

Faith may move mountains, especially a little at a time. The weight of an individual wafer was only a few grammes, but a million wafers per day would in due course add up to metric tonnes, which must also logically be taken up into Heaven. In Heaven, alongside His Father, the Son began putting on weight as the transubstantiated bread (and subsequently wafers) became added to His body mass. Likewise the blood, to sustain the supplementary tissue. Be it noted that the newly created flesh must needs be transferred to the Son in Heaven *after* ingestion but *before* digestion; otherwise the divine flesh must pass onward into the bowels and become what normal nutrition normally becomes; which would be sacrilegious.

This weight gain didn't matter too much to begin with, since the Son had been fairly gaunt, just as most Palestinians were at the time of His birth. Not to mention that He was fairly tall (think El Greco). He could benefit by some additional bodily tissue.

However, fast-forward a few hundred years more to the time when the numbers of the human race began to climb almost exponentially—half a billion, two billion, six billion. Many of these souls were occasional or even daily transubstantiators. (The Protestant Reformation might in this light be viewed as a slimming campaign, since Protestantism denied that bread and wafers actually changed; therefore they did not do so.) Despite pruning of population by wars and, more effectively, by plagues such as the otherwise inexplicable Spanish influenza pandemic in the wake of the First World War, the Son's body mass in Heaven was increasing alarmingly. From overweight, to positively obese.

Yet God delayed the Second Coming because *only now* was medical science really getting into its stride. Penicillin and subsequent pharmaceuticals, radiotherapy, open heart surgery, transplants, DNA diagnoses and all the other wonders of medical science: just wait another fifty years, and all of God's increasing bodily woes could be cured by His clever creatures who were both the laboratory rats as regards ailments and the researchers into cures.

Wait a few more years. Yet due to transubstantiation the obesity problem of the Son was becoming dire.

Finally the Second Coming was triggered prematurely by sheer geometrical and gravitational stress. Due to the accumulated bulk of the Son, amounting by now to hundreds of metric tonnes, He couldn't reappear anywhere on the surface of the Earth in a dignified way—Him with his vastly bloated body, out of which protruded a normal-sized head and hands and feet—nor perhaps without succumbing to an immediate heart attack.

Accordingly, it was in near-Earth orbit that the Second Coming occurred, a shining Jesus moonlet with its own miraculous warm atmosphere, rivalling Luna much further away.

And the messages began: *Stop Transubstantiating! Too Much Mass!*

Intelligent Design 2.0

'GOSH,' SAID ADAM FLUENTLY AS SOON AS HE WOKE UP ON HIS FIRST day, lolling with Eve on a bed of lush veg. 'This world must be millions of years old. Look at that T. Rex thighbone sticking out where the stream bank washed away.'

(And in the process he named, amongst other things, *bank* and *stream* and *thighbone* and *T. Rex*.)

'Thank God we weren't around when *that* was hunting! We'd have been mincemeat pretty damn fast.'

'Please don't swear,' said Eve, cuddling up to him nakedly for protection from the extinct menace. Already Adam had begun swearing, even though Eve named the activity.

'Adam, if you get into the habit of bad language, the *children* will hear.'

'Ah yes, I know what those will be.' Adam admired Eve lasciviously, and part of him stirred. 'We've plenty of time yet for parenthood. First let's enjoy ourselves. For the time being we need some natural form of what you might call *contraception*.' Adam's consciousness had kindled at a very high setting. 'Some roots or leaves to chew.'

Eve glanced at a dark cloud newly on the horizon, and warned, 'Shhh. I don't think *He* wants that. We could use the so-called *rhythm* method.'

Adam nuzzled her. 'There's only one sort of rhythm I wish to get into with you, my dear. Besides, it would take several *months'*—so saying, he indicated the ghost of a half-moon low in the sky—'to establish the rhythm you're referring to. We'd need to invent counting. One two three four more, for instance. And zero and infinity.'

Eve was impressed. 'You've woken up very wise.'

Adam preened himself. 'Infinite zeros isn't the same as zero infinities.'

'What does that mean?'

'I don't know yet,' he admitted. 'I know all sorts of things in my brain, but at the same time I don't know them yet.'

'I feel the same! Unknown knowns. As opposed to unknown unknowns.' Of a sudden she screamed, pointing into the bushes. 'Is that a tiger?'

Adam rolled over and over, wrenched the T. Rex thighbone out of the bank, and scrambled up brandishing the weapon.

'It's a marmalade *cat*,' he said as he saw from a better vantage point.

'Marmalade, yummy,' said Eve. She smacked her lips. 'Spread on toast.'

'First we'd need to select grasses to grow grain, then roll big stones to grind flour, and tame fire for the clay oven to bake the dough. Hmm, there's a lot of *work* involved in making toast.'

The cat pounced on a mouse.

'Maybe,' said Adam, 'we should stick to hunting and gathering. Squeeze oranges for juice and forget about the marmalade.'

'Adam, your virile member has become so small!'

He glanced down, and lowered the T. Rex thighbone to cover his chagrin. 'The blood all went into fight or flight.'

'Yet you chose to fight,' she said admiringly.

'How could I run away from the only woman in the world?'

'Adam, that's so romantic. I think you're in *love*. And I would have run after you.'

'But more slowly, waggling and jiggling and flapping your arms. So the tiger would have caught you. Now that I think of you waggling and jiggling, just suppose that you run *away* from me . . .'

'Don't you imagine for one moment chasing me, hitting me over the head with that big bone then dragging me through in the grass by my long blonde hair! That isn't the sort of man I want. Anyway, you'd need to build a shelter of branches and leaves to drag me to.'

'I spy caves in those hills over there.'

'Horrid hard cave. Probably with a bear in residence.'

'There can't be predators lethal to us yet. We might get eaten too easily and advanced consciousness would be snuffed out. Any predators must still be vegetarians, although with the wrong teeth. Things will alter only if we *sin*. Right now I can think of a sin I fancy trying. Your buttocks, Eve, are very shapely. Could be a way round that contraception problem.'

Vocabulary was pouring out of Adam into existence. Eve glared at him. 'Sod that for a lark,' she said.

A lark took wing, singing sweetly as it ascended.

'Who's swearing now?' asked Adam.

She wiggled her hips. 'It's much simpler to start a family. We should multiply.'

'I can multiply,' Adam discovered. 'Two times two is four. Two times four is . . . *eight!*'

The cat trotted up to Eve, purring, dead mouse in its mouth, and placed the corpse near her toes.

'Eek!' she squealed, grasping for something to climb on to. However, there were no . . .

Adam laughed heartily. 'Chairs!'

Eve controlled herself. 'That's right, we need something to sit on. I think this pussy wants to be domesticated. I mean pussycat. Our first pet.'

'Why is it marmalade colour already, before we domesticate it?'

'To encourage us, Adam.' She glanced at the horizon but the black cloud hadn't moved, although it still seemed to be observing. Vanity and a sense of privacy contended. So much was happening intellectually on their first day.

But what of Adam? His manhood was still small, and he was flailing that great bone against long grass like some reaper. Was he frustrated? Was he already becoming habituated to nudity?

'I need some lingerie,' said Eve.

'First we'd need to tame silkworms—'

'No, you can't exactly *tame* worms.' Might her language skills be superior? 'Cats and dogs, yes.'

A woeful howl rang out from some trees.

Hastily she added, 'And cows and sheep and horses.'

They heard a distant whinny.

'As regards *clothes*, I'll be content for now with vines wrapped round me and in winter a sheepskin.'

The word *shopping* hovered in her head, but seemed to make no sense, as yet . . .

'We must dumb down.'

Notes

THREE KINDS OF CLOSE ENCOUNTERS WITH COMICS

My boyhood encounters with comics were certainly influential, but I soon moved my allegiance to novels, SF and otherwise. The Fifties was the real Golden Age of SF, but I'm still amazed that as a boy I found such hardbacks as *Tiger! Tiger!* and *Slan* in my local library in dull North Shields, and which I alternated by reading Zola, for instance. Writers with exotic names such as Van Vogt or Zola must surely possess arcane wisdom, and I too was towards the end of the alphabet. (The 'Shields' were grotty shelters erected by benighted locals along the banks of the river Tyne once upon a time.)

HOW I WAS SHOT BY ADOLF HITLER

I gave this as a GoH speech, subsequently published, for a convention at Mount Laurel just outside Philadelphia, to which I needed to take a taxi from the airport. The first taxi in the queue, which I was obliged to use, was a stretched limo with tinted windows, onboard bar and halo lightning; this felt a bit daft.

Regarding 'my delightful Catalan hosts': *Reader, I Married Her* (just 25 years later)! Namely, the delightful talented effervescent Cristina, who once upon a time translated my *Jonah Kit* and with whom I wrote a cookbook in

397

2012 about 50 meals named after 50 people, commissioned for the 50th anniversary of the biggest Spanish book club.

Regarding *Astounding*: knock me over with a feather, that issue was January 1952! I was only 9 and three-quarters.

False memory alert! I've just obtained (no expense spared for these Notes!) that Jan 1952 issue from a dealer in Canada to verify the hyperspace story, and . . . the story isn't there. Maybe I ventured to buy a subsequent *Astounding* which perplexed me?

Peyote cacti have reappeared on sale in the UK, presumably because few people know what they are any longer, and who would take the peyote button route when there are pills, of all sorts?

Of course you know that Rimbaud and Rambo are different, but this was originally a talk, remember.

JINGLING GEORDIE'S HOLE

Not 'jiggling', as a wit referred to this tale which readers of *Interzone* voted Best and Worst of the year, sometimes simultaneously, for the writing and for the subject. Not that I was personally buggered in a cave beside the sea, but to a fair degree this is an exorcism of the leaden, restrictive 1950s of my boyhood on Tyneside. (I hasten to add that life was more so in Franco's Spain, just for instance.) For some reason back then my great desire was to visit Iceland and stare at emptiness plus a few birds, then later live alone in a cottage in a forest writing thoughtful and luminous stuff.

My source was *The Monthly Chronicle of North-Country Lore and Legend* for 1887. My parents had three volumes of these hardbound compilations of about 500 pages each of very small print, which I still have. Those Victorians knew how to journalise.

This story gave rise to my novel *The Fire Worm*, where I divided the tale into 3 parts interspersed by other chapters.

When I was Ted's age I was indeed significantly fat.

BEWARE THE PEDICATING TRIBADS!

Orgasmachine finally appeared in English a mere 30 years after I started writing it (patience, authors, your time may come!), and for NewCon Press's signed limited edition I wrote this learnèd essay. A sick eroticism pervades 'Jingling Geordie's Hole' horrifically, so now let's have a chuckle at the expense of bygone erotic experts.

After returning from Japan, a life experience which committed me to being an SF writer, and after living in Oxford for almost a decade, in the process becoming published prominently enough to go full-time, circumstances pushed me out into rural England, so I did end up writing in a cottage amidst relative emptiness—the 'empty quarter' of Northamptonshire—although not in a forest, nor alone. Wife Judy, daughter Jess, and cats Yuki, Suzie, Couscous, Pippin, and finally Poppy. At the posher and prosperous end of the relative emptiness is Stow-on-the-Wold where, years later in company with Roberto Quaglia, I found an absurd 19th century erotic treatise.

KING WEASEL

However, out in the countryside, I was deepish in debt through most of the 1980s. Lean times, shared by the characters in this story—which I amplified into my Horror novel *Meat;* consequently this seed story only appeared some years later in a special IW edition of *Weird Tales*. Mind you, I didn't despair during hard times except when I made the mistake of brewing my own beer for a while. The incident of the chipmunks happened earlier while I was in Tokyo. The transfer of the Rabbit Hilton from garden to kitchen resulted in actuality in our neutered tomcat jumping within, whereupon Babette the rabbit revealed herself to be no girl by promptly leaping upon the tomcat and rutting him. After which, the tomcat climbed inside the rabbit hutch and curled up in the straw, purring. A rum do.

The 1980s saw a renaissance in Horror fiction, which at its best seemed to me to train a searchlight upon the ordinary world, rendering its banalities luminous and meaningful, albeit in a horrifying fashion. So I wrote a couple of politicised Horror novels, whose nuclear disarmer and animal liberationist characters guaranteed me no US editions. 'They'd be about as popular as the Black Panthers,' said an American editor.

SHELL SHOCK

Typical residents of the little village in South Northamptonshire where I lived for a very long time (south and north at the same time; no wonder people couldn't find my village) were an opera singer, a rally driver TV presenter, an ex-diplomat married to an ex-Amazonian tribeswoman, both very posh, a Canadian Indian, a Jewish communist atheist ex-librarian who had married a black Canadian, a farmer who asked me whether an eclipse of the sun could harm his mushrooms in their black plastic tunnels and whether it was safe to stare by night at the sun being eclipsed, and a chap whose hobby was collecting ex-NATO and Warsaw Pact military vehicles. 'How I Was Shot by Adolf Hitler' tells how ostriches came to South Northants courtesy of my cottage being refloored. I could go on.

For a decade and a half I helped organise and run my village's annual fête until the fête succumbed to its fate of diminishing returns. Oxwell Canons is Canons Ashby, where Spenser wrote some of his *Faerie Queene*, allegedly.

HOW THE ELEPHANT ESCAPED EXTINCTION

Moving on from archweasels to elephants, my chum Steve Baxter wrote a trilogy about telepathic mammoths, consequently Chester Zoo asked him to help Save the Asian Elephant from extinction by raising funds for an emergency breeding colony near Liverpool. Steve recruited me and Garry Kilworth to co-edit a benefit anthology. Due to various previous benefits for ex-Yugoslavian orphans and other worthy causes, compassion fatigue had set in amongst publishers, not least since the Asian Elephant (with the small ears) wouldn't go extinct for several more decades.

Along the way we had dinner in the House of Commons with a sponsoring Member of Parliament, and lunch in the House of Lords with a sponsoring Lord. On the former occasion, we took our port (or whatever) out on to the Honourable Members' balcony overlooking the Thames, and about 300 roosting arctic terns (I think) erupted from it dazzlingly into the sky; they weren't going extinct any day soon.

Here is my story for the anthology that never was, with apologies to Rudyard Kipling. Fortunately, Chester Zoo prevailed by other routes.

THE DRAINED WORLD

Aha, Steve Baxter again! In 2008 he perpetrated a masterpiece called *Flood* (to be followed by *Ark*), in which finally even Everest is drowned. This had a disruptive effect on my brain. While being driven through Cambridgeshire I clearly sensed the sea level 200 metres above me. To calm myself, and with a nod in the title to Ballard's *Drowned World*, I sent my take on the opposite phenomenon to *Nature,* whose scientific Henry Gee presided over the Futures series of SF short stories at the back of that learned journal. Henry said no, on the grounds that everyone knows there are no tides in the Med. I stood my ground—unlike the previous year when I swam out to a sandbar off Almería to find that my expected footing had disappeared under an extra tidal metre of sea—and prevailed. I now know from salty experience the first destabilising stage of drowning, in case I ever need this for a story. I shall not enter the sea again.

VILE DRY CLAWS OF THE TOUCAN

Here comes extinction again, this time for sentient alien snails. Years before, I'd written an unpublishable story, a youthful effusion which included supersnails in mazes.

THE TRAGEDY OF SOLVEIG

In the main street of Helsinki leading to the harbour, the statue of Eino Leino stands with his back to a superloo. Leino wrote gemlike poems capsulating incidents in the Finnish national epic, the *Kalevala*. I read these during a flight to Philadelphia, and a whole science-fantasy epic dawned for me, my *Books of Mana*, comprising *Lucky's Harvest* and *The Fallen Moon*, which I wrote in a poetic afflatus lasting two years (during the mornings at least). This done, I had rich material left over, so I thought that a quartet of associational stories might make a nice little book or booklet. Meanwhile, American editors, who had been asking Gollancz when Ian would write a big book, declared that the *Books of Mana* were too big. Mildly discouraged, I halted at two supplementary stories, both of which duly appeared in *Asimov's*.

Enjoying (or not enjoying) this story requires no prior knowledge of the *Mana* books.

SCIENCE FICTION, SURREALISM, AND SHAMANISM

Here's the lowdown on my *Books of Mana*, and thus on the stories preceding and following this note, including what mana is and how it's a bit different from manna. I wrote my Finnish-inspired fictions instinctively rather than intellectually, although I did for the first time in my career draw a biggish map, too messy to deserve reproduction anywhere. I remember reading instinctively too, books such as a huge biography of Peter the Great of Russia and Julia Kristeva's *Desire in Language* because these felt like the right things to read during my seven or so *Mana* seasons.

THE SHORTEST NIGHT

I visited Finland twice, first at the height of the Summer (as related in 'How I Was Shot by Adolf Hitler'), secondly for the first midwinter SF convention, in Tampere where I loved the cauldrons full of small black puddings for breakfast. I did admire the skill of drivers in accelerating away from traffic lights only to brake immediately and slide neatly to a stop at the next lights; or so it looked to me. At a pub late at night, SF fans invited me to try the new drink sensation Salmiakki, a mixture of vodka, liquorice, and ammonium chloride. 'It gives you the four-day hangover!' 'I don't think I want the four-day hangover,' said I, and asked for a tall beer to dilute my modest intake of this lethal cough medicine. Any more Salmiakki and I might have agreed to the amiable proposal of a tipsy Finnish couple who had seen my photo in the newspaper. 'Mister Watson, you love our national epic. You must come with us *now* to our hut in the forest for sauna and sausages. We will drive you and we will cut a hole in the ice of the lake for you!' Instead I slid back to my hotel, blessing the trails of gravel on the icy pavements, scattered like breadcrumbs for Hansel and Gretel.

Tango is an obsession in Finland almost more so than in Argentina. My *Mana* stories, and novels, are about obsessions.

THE AUTHOR AS TORTURER

This expands a talk which I gave at Sercon in Oakland, California, in 1987, as related in 'How I Was Shot by Adolf Hitler', at least as regards the cure for jet-lag.

Back in the late Eighties, little did I think that the 'democracies' of the USA and the UK would legitimise torture under the euphemism of extraordinary rendition, not to mention the torment of serial simulated drowning at Guantanamo Bay. This bleeds through, as it were, into fiction where guys write tough to seem relevant and cutting edge, as it were.

A CAGE FOR DEATH

This story became my novel *Deathhunter* after I studied *The Psychology of Death* by Robert Kastenbaum & Ruth Aisenberg. Probably afterwards, since my copy of *PoD* contains a sticker from Compendium Books in London's Camden Town and I doubt I would have gone to London from my village in South Northants to research a short story as opposed to a novel (back in those days before Amazon and Google). I only lived 60 miles from London, but getting there was a bit complex and costly, so I didn't go to many metropolitan events, which made it *exciting* to be in London. So I rather think that 'A Cage for Death' was an autonomous invention based on a dream.

SECRETS

Another Nordic country, this time an invitation to Oslo where I was amazed at midday, and at midnight too, by the park full of the sculptures of Gustav Vigeland—and then by the mausoleum outside of town created by Vigeland's crazy (or crazier) brother. The craft centre is fairly near my then-home in South Northamptonshire, run by the Jesus Army, enough said. This story became the long prologue to my novel *Mockymen*, which personally I think is one of my best novels, consequently it's the least known.

SCARS

This is a stand-alone story which became absorbed into the narrative of *Mockymen*. I'm interested in 'modern primitive' activities such as scarification and piercings, although the closest I got to this personally was in Genoa when I almost had an alien cyborg butterfly tattooed on my shoulder by one of Italy's top tattooists who organises an international festival; but when I went back for this after lunch he in turn had gone out to lunch; maybe just as well.

Nematodes may well have been a good choice, in view of the recent (2011) discovery of giant (comparatively; half a millimetre) nematodes grazing on bacteria over a kilometre below ground in a South African gold mine; we may hear a lot more about extraordinary nematodes.

Mild apologies for invoking a 'quantum crystal', the word 'quantum' being so misused in nonsense-science therapy circles.

THE JEW Of LINZ

The Nazi aspect of *Mockymen* rears its head again. After this piece was published in *The New York Review of Science Fiction* I sent a copy to Kimberley Cornish in New Zealand. His book had been denied an American edition on perceived grounds of Holocaust denial. Mr Cornish replied that the leading British expert on the Holocaust had confided privately that he now accepted what Cornish argued in his very intriguing book, but he couldn't say so publicly.

THE BIG BUY

Three stories in the present book were previously collected in the sense that they appeared in the limited edition *Book of Ian Watson* published by Mark Ziesing in 1985, on which Mark told me later he 'almost lost [his] shirt', thus not many people can have bought it. That same book is now available electronically through Gollancz's SF Gateway, but these stories were never in commercial paper collections.

The notion of interstellar trade powers numerous SF tales, but realistically seems somewhat absurd, since any technology capable of star travel could probably create from scratch back home whatever *tangible* goods it wanted. So how about *intangibles*, which presumably could much more easily be transmitted rather than transported . . . ?

Be it noted that in the journal *Economic Inquiry* in 2010, taking into account the lightspeed limit, Nobel laureate in Economics Paul Krugman published 'The Theory of Interstellar Trade' which he wrote 30 years earlier, commenting that 'while the subject of this paper is silly, the analysis actually does make sense. This paper, then, is a serious analysis of a ridiculous subject, which is of course the opposite of what is usual in economics.'

This story is an affectionate companion to 'The World Science Fiction Convention of 2080' included in *The Best of IW* . . . and it may even be true, if there are any intelligent aliens elsewhere in our galaxy, a very big IF.

EYES AS BIG AS SAUCERS

So how would any extraterrestrials get to Earth, to engage in trading (or abducting and molesting)? In flying saucers? The sheer volume of reported close encounters, especially in the religious USA, suggests that either Earth is the crossroads of the universe (unlikely), or that something else is the cause. I explored a few phenomenological ideas in *Miracle Visitors* but here is some biochemistry instead.

THE AIMS OF ARTIFICIAL INTELLIGENCE

This was subtitled 'A Science Fiction View' for its appearance in the American infotech journal *Intelligent Systems* which has the slogan 'Putting AI into Practice'. Since I had screen credit for the Screen Story of *A.I.*, the editor of the Histories & Futures section asked me to contribute. My essay was cut by maybe 15% in order to fit the format of *Intelligent Systems*; for instance the magpies disappeared. Here is the uncut version. Perish the thought that any of my golden words may have been redundant *per se*, but inevitably there's a spot of crossover here and there with other items in the present *Uncollected IW* touching on such topics.

THE MATRIX AS SIMULACRUM

One of the assorted buzzy things which the Wachowski Brothers toss at the wall in this nonsensical movie, in the hope that something sticks and makes sense, is Baudrillard's *Simulacra and Simulation*. So I put on Baudrillard's spectacles, as it were.

THE REAL WINSTON

Probably the first, er, 'respectable' novel that I bought with my pocket money as a lad was *Nineteen Eighty-Four*, by which I was deeply impressed, not least (though not most) by sex in the woods. Fairly soon I read all of Orwell's other novels, which resonated with the frustrating drabness of the 1950s wherein was I. Winston Smith's job is falsifying reality, so with the actual year 1984 just round the corner I thought I would see how a different take on Orwell's modern classic would work.

Personally, I thought this was quite a nifty story but—and here I consult my Short Story Sales List, which I've maintained on successive ruled paper-clipped sheets of A4 paper since 1979—it was turned down 10 times, whereupon I stopped sending it out. I hadn't written many short stories thitherto, so I imagined that a page or two of A4 would probably suffice for my entire career, since I was primarily a novelist. How wrong I was, 12 or 13 story collections later. Yet I never see myself as a prolific writer—I spend more time *rewriting* whatever I'm working on. I just happen to have been beavering away for about 40 years.

H.G. WELLS IN TIMIŞOARA

For a couple of years (but not constantly) I dressed up in period costume as Bertie Wells to give talks in his own voice (as it were) and from his viewpoint at various SF events in the UK and in Romania and in Italy. In Timişoara, Romania, none of the organisers knew where the key to the locked dressing room was, so I had to change in a small dark uncouth toilet; and then the room where I spoke became hotter and hotter until poor Bertie was almost melting in his heavy costume borrowed from the Opera House, yet how could he cry out, 'For mercy's sake turn on the air conditioning!' when Bertie himself knew nothing about aircon? I must remain in character. After decades of dictatorship, Romanians didn't spontaneously change the status quo unless ordered to, even though the revolution against Ceauşescu had indeed begun in Timişoara. In Fiuggi, Italy, by contrast, the organisers presented me with a Pierre Cardin dress shirt, cufflinks, and a bow tie to take away afterwards.

Of WARFARE AND *THE WAR OF THE WORLDS*

There isn't much duplication between this and the previous piece, both stemming from my impersonations of Bertie Wells. In this case the occasion was a book of new perspectives upon Wells' classic timed to coincide with Steven Spielberg's screen adaptation starring Tom Cruise, which I therefore hadn't seen when I wrote the essay—or rather, when Bertie expressed his Wellsian reservations about how the movie, made in super-secrecy, might turn out; with, as it happened, fighting machines rearing up from underground where apparently they'd been lurking for thousands of years, evidently awaiting the day when our human military might at last be able to put up a doomed fight as opposed to the alien invaders trashing our species back when we only had swords.

THE WICKER MAN

When Mark Morris circularised 50 writers and cineastes to hail their favourite macabre movie I was quicker than quick to collar the wicker man.

DARK CITY

Likewise, Martin Lewis invited a smaller bunch of sciencefictioneers to contribute to a British SF Association special edition pamphlet, *SF Writers on SF Films*. So I grabbed the opportunity to boost the masterpiece movie of one year previous to *The Matrix* which was on a similar theme of a false reality, imposed in this case by aliens rather than by computer; which I touched on in my essay on *The Matrix*, but there's always more to be said about *Dark City*.

STEPHEN KING'S *THINNER*: AN ATTACK ON AMERICA

This first appeared in French in 2006 in a handsome volume commenting in chronological order on the novels of America's Horrormeister. During my own Horror phase in the Eighties I read quite a few of those novels, and I particularly admired *Thinner* perhaps because it was thinner than most of the others. By 2005 pro-anorexia websites had sprung up to encourage fellow victims of mental imbalance to starve themselves, so I thought *aha*, a special point of view.

A DAFFODIL JACKET, OF THE MISADVENTURES OF SEBASTIAN IN KYIV

The first European SF Convention (alias Eurocon) to be held in Kiev, Ukraine, here mutates into a very similar convention of poets with most names changed to protect the innocent (as well as the guilty), but all the incidents are related faithfully. I avoided visiting the thriving game reserve of Chernobyl, but those who did go for a tour were given their used protective costumes afterwards to take home as souvenirs complete with dust. Kyiv is Ukrainian for Kiev, a capital of the Vikings who sailed down the mighty river Dnieper from the north.

DIVINE DISEASES

This ruffled feathers among quite a few readers of the world's leading science journal *Nature*, those with a particular delusionary belief system . . .

INTELLIGENT DESIGN 2.0

. . . consequently *Nature* was unwilling to print this likewise satirical follow-up piece, which appeared instead in Rudy Rucker's webzine *Flurb*. Really, Creationism ought to be spelled Crettinism, what with its unscience wherein T. Rex was a placid vegetarian, amongst many other absurdities. Which are malign and malignant and should be mocked.

Acknowledgments

'Three Kinds of Close Encounters with Comics' first appeared in *Fantasycon 2009 Souvenir Programme*, 2009.

'How I was Shot by Adolf Hitler' first appeared in *Science Fiction Review*, 1992.

'Jingling Geordie's Hole' first appeared in *Interzone*, 1986.

'Beware the Pedicating Tribads!' first appeared in the signed limited edition of *Orgasmachine*, 2010.

'King Weasel' first appeared in *Weird Tales*, 1993.

'Shell Shock' first appeared as a Novacon pamphlet published by the Birmingham Science Fiction Group, 2004.

'How the Elephant Escaped Extinction' first appeared in *Fantasycon Souvenir Programme Book*, 2009.

'The Drained World' first appeared in *Nature*, 2010.

'Vile Dry Claws of the Toucan' first appeared in *Semiotext(e),* 1989.

'The Tragedy of Solveig' first appeared in *Asimov's Science Fiction*, 1996.

'Science Fiction, Surrealism, and Shamanism' first appeared in *The New York Review of Science Fiction*, 1999.

'The Shortest Night' first appeared in *Asimov's Science Fiction*, 1998.

'The Author as Torturer' first appeared in *Foundation*, 1987.

'A Cage for Death' first appeared in *Omni*, 1981.

'Secrets' first appeared in *Interzone*, 1997.

'Scars' is original to this collection.

'The Jew of Linz' first appeared in *The New York Review of Science Fiction*, 1999.

'The Big Buy' first appeared in *Ad Astra*, 1980.

'Eyes as Big as Saucers' first appeared in *Matrix*, 1997.

'The Aims of Artificial Intelligence' first appeared in *Intelligent Systems*, 2003.

'*The Matrix* as Simulation' first appeared in *Exploring the Matrix: Visions of the Cyber Present*, 2003.

'The Real Winston' first appeared in *The Book of Ian Watson*, 1985.

'H.G. Wells in Timişoara' first appeared in *The H.G. Wells Society, the Americas Newsletter*, 2004.

'Of Warfare and *The War of the Worlds*' first appeared in *The War of the Worlds*, 2005.

'The Wicker Man' first appeared in *Cinema Macabre*, 2005.

'Dark City' first appeared in *SF Writers on SF Films*, 2009.

'Stephen King's *Thinner*: An Attack Upon America' first appeared in English in *Recombination Progress Report 2*, 2006.

'A Daffodil Jacket, or The Misadventures of Sebastian in Kyiv' first appeared in *Celebration: a taster*, 2008.

'Divine Diseases' first appeared in *Nature*, 2009.

'Intelligent Design 2.0' first appeared in *Flurb*, 2012.

IAN WATSON, aged a shade over 70, now lives in Spain after a career in Oxford, Tanzania, Tokyo, then at Birmingham (UK)'s School of Art History teaching probably the first ever course in science fiction, followed by decades as a full-time writer in a small village in South Northamptonshire, producing in all about 30 SF, horror, and surreally fantastic novels as well as 12 story collections. Nine months eyeball to eyeball with Stanley Kubrick resulted in screen credit for Steven Spielberg's *A.I. Artificial Intelligence*. He is also a poet, an essayist and the inventor of *Warhammer 40,000* fiction. He recently published in Spanish a cookbook about famous meals named after people.